THE
GAME

Martin Kemp is a founding member of the iconic 1980s band Spandau Ballet. His subsequent award-winning acting career has encompassed stage, screen, TV and radio.

Martin is married to Shirlie Kemp and they have two children, Harleymoon and Roman. Martin lives in Hertfordshire with his family and pets. *The Game* is his first novel.

📷 @martinjkemp
🐦 @realmartinkemp
f /martinkempofficial

Also by Martin Kemp

Ticket to the World: My 80s Story

THE
GAME
MARTIN
KEMP

HarperCollins*Publishers*

HarperCollins*Publishers* Ltd
1 London Bridge Street,
London SE1 9GF
www.harpercollins.co.uk

Harper*Publishers*
Macken House, 39/40 Mayor Street Upper
Dublin 1, D01 C9W8
Ireland

First published by HarperCollins*Publishers* 2023
1

A catalogue record for this book is available from the British Library

ISBN: 978-0-00-862679-2 (HB)
ISBN: 978-0-00-862680-8 (TPB)

Set in Sabon LT Std by Palimpsest Book Production Ltd, Falkirk, Stirlingshire

Printed and bound in the UK using 100% Renewable Electricity
by CPI Group (UK) Ltd

To my family, Shirlie, Harleymoon and Roman
who make life just perfect.

WHO IS JOHNNY KLEIN?

Is Johnny Klein you? everyone always asked. *Are you writing about a character, or is it yourself?* Well, there's a big part of me in Johnny, but there's also a big part of lots of rock stars I have met over the years, from Townshend to Bowie, from Jagger to Iggy, the boys from Quo or the guys from Queen, it's all of them, squashed together in a fictional enigma. I didn't invent Johnny Klein to write this book; he has been with me for years, an imaginary friend, someone to keep me company when I was out on the road for years on end with my band. I would use it as my alias, checking into hotels under his name, booking restaurants, even ordering my deliveries, the two of us becoming one. Johnny Klein's name was on everything I had, it was even on my laminated bag tags that followed me several times around the world as we played in hundreds of cities around the globe. He has literally been my companion, my confidant, my best mate for decades.

It was in 1990 when I first wrote the character down, starting as a television show idea that I passed on to the producers of *The Krays*; it was an idea I *knew* I had to do something with. My biggest fear back then was what would I do if it all went wrong, if the success and all that came with it was suddenly taken away. Would I spend my life being pointed at? 'That used to be him, the famous one, the pop star.' Night after night I'd wake up in cold pools of sweat after dreaming I was back at school or back in my printing apprenticeship; not because I was afraid of work – I've always worked hard, no matter what I've done – but because, in my dream, I was still famous, the failed pop star who once had everything most people dream of, but had it all taken away, and everyone else enjoying every second of it.

Johnny Klein isn't the rags-to-riches story of just another pop star, the overconfident narcissist looking down on his adoring subjects, soaking up the fame, money and adulation. It's more of a riches-to-rags story of one of the biggest stars in Britain, a phenomenon in the Eighties, one of the most recognised faces of the era, on everything from magazine front covers to television chat shows, until it seemed that face was literally burned into everyone's psyche. Only now, for Johnny Klein, it really has gone wrong and he's forced to sell up, lock, stock and barrel – his worst nightmare coming true. This is really the story of Johnny Klein surviving, making his way in an ordinary world, and finding out in the process who he really is.

Fame is a hard thing to live with at the best of times. It has its payoffs and its upsides, but constant recognition is difficult, and the hardest thing of all is to be famous and broke. Imagine having to come out from behind those electric gates and high walls and be forced to take the bus again instead of the limo, obliged to work your way back into real life, where you're more ashamed than proud of the name you were given, where you would prefer people to whisper it rather than to shout it as they once did.

Famous and broke are two words that shouldn't go together, shouldn't be mentioned in the same sentence, but Johnny Klein, the one-time rock star who lived his life in an orgy of success and glory, finds himself with no choice. His cards have been dealt, and this is the hand he has to play with . . .

Sometimes you win, sometimes you lose. It's all a spin of the wheel. The only way you can be sure not to lose in this life is not to play the game at all. Don't put your chips down, just stand back and watch others take the chances and reap the losses . . . or the glory.

Johnny Klein, *Smash Hits,* **1987**

1
END OF THE BEGINNING

Monday

The supersized TV threw kaleidoscopic light around the unlit cavern of a room. Eerie figures leapt across the walls like the shadows of Japanese bunraku puppets. The high ceilings and wooden floor made a perfect echo chamber for the rhythmic thunder exploding from the two stacks of Marshall speakers balanced precariously to either side of the ageing back projection screen.

'And now, it's the band you've been waiting for . . . here with their latest smash, it's Klein, with "Don't Go There".'

It was a decades-old rerun of *Top of the Pops*. The bespectacled figure of Mike Read, everyone's favourite DJ at the time, stood centre-screen in Studio Two of BBC Television Centre in White City. He'd perched on that flimsy metal bridge, flickering with multicoloured lights as it hung over what was possibly the most famous stage in Britain, the raised platform on which hundreds of major league pop and rock stars from the UK and beyond had performed alongside equal numbers of wannabes, whose dreams and ambitions would ultimately never survive the dog-eat-dog cruelty of the music business, Eighties payola and the hunting packs of managers and agents always so keen to pull you apart and fit you back together, Frankenstein like, in their own frustrated pop-star image.

Guitar chords boomed and a sequencer kicked in, creating that perfect synth sound of the Eighties, a classy combo of Trevor Horn's ABC and the jangly guitar cool of Lenny Kravitz.

The mesmerising figure of Johnny Klein sauntered to the mic, the cameras closing in, manoeuvring sensually around him as he struck pure magic from his Gibson Gold Top, the sea of girls moving to the front rhythmically, like a shockwave from a tsunami.

He was an instantly eye-catching figure, clad in a pristine white Katharine Hamnett parachute shirt, a bullet belt from Camden Market slung low on his narrow waist, and a pair of shiny leather jeans, which fell perfectly onto his black studded Seditionaries boots, an ensemble that harked straight back to teenage days spent hanging out on the King's Road outside Malcolm and Vivienne's uber-famous punk landmark shop, SEX, with its giant, backwards-spinning clock. All of that energy and rebellion was written deep into his trim, well-muscled form and pale, insolent features, not to mention those piercing blue eyes under that sharp, jet-black fringe.

His looks were 'angelic', someone in the music press had written, 'but not quite, because there's something devilish there too'.

The teenage girls of the nation would be swooning already, even though Johnny hadn't sung a word yet. With a flamboyant flourish he launched himself into a song familiar throughout the land. It wasn't just a hit with every radio station; you couldn't stand in a queue without hearing the person next to you humming it, couldn't walk through a supermarket or stand in a lift, or even wander the streets of your town without Johnny's voice caressing you from some open car window; a voice that wasn't great (by his own admission!) but which was easily good enough for rock and roll.

'Christ,' the man in front of the giant-sized screen grunted to himself.

He was slumped in a bulging, black leather La-Z-Boy, his bleary eyes locked on these visions of the distant past, as he took another long, tired drag on his Marlboro.

It had never just been about his voice. The Johnny Klein of the Eighties was the complete package, his look, his sound, his musical ability, his natural charisma, his knack for seizing the moment – all combining in a made-to-measure pop star. Even then, it was a rare alignment. So it was little wonder that his wolfish smile adorned teenagers' bedroom walls from London to Aberdeen, that he regularly featured on the front of *Smash Hits*, *Record Mirror* and even *The Face*. He was an establishment-friendly blend of Elvis, Marlon Brando and David Bowie, a record company's dream, a man who men wanted to be, and who women wanted to be with, and a regular, not just on *Top of the Pops*, but on weekend music shows like *Saturday Superstore*. He even hit the prime time, and made the absolute most of it, when he used his interview on *Parkinson* to tell the world that he was seeing Laura Hall, the glamorous TV presenter, whom every red-blooded male in the country wanted as their girlfriend, and that they were engaged to be married. Naturally it sent his record company into a spin, fearing that married life, and maybe fatherhood to follow, would dull some of that lustre, but like everything else Johnny touched at that time, it turned to gold, winning him even more reams of frenzied tabloid discussion.

And now it was over.

The man in the La-Z-Boy stared unseeing at the TV, the smoke from his Marlboro curling up his arm, up through his shaggy salt-and-pepper grey hair. He took another drag, scratching at his stubbled chin. With a sniff, he raised the whisky glass to lips cracked by dehydration, draining the dregs. The phantasmagoric images reflected in a pair of eyes, once ice-blue, but now dulled, their whites tinged red. He was a shadow of what he'd been, a Jacob Marley's ghost of rock and roll yet to come.

While the fairy-tale froth on the screen played to itself, the viewer's blurry gaze focused instead on the clunky old VHS located beneath it, specifically on the word PLAYING, as it winked on and off in fluorescent green.

God, I was fucking good, he thought.

Then a shrill, protracted buzz pierced his consciousness, an electronic calling card demanding immediate attention, breaking him from his reverie. He didn't move, not straight away. It was too much trouble. Instead, he slouched there, insulated in this last enclosed bubble of a former existence, the heavy black blinds on the windows repelling even the midday sunlight. The front doorbell buzzed again. For longer this time, more aggressive, the finger pressing the button refusing to budge. It sounded more like a drill as it bored into senses he'd successfully numbed over the years.

Johnny had no urge to respond to it. And he'd never been one to give up. In a battle of wills, he could always hold his own, keep an argument going for days, weeks, months, indefinitely, even if he knew he was completely in the wrong. It was a mule-like stubborn streak that had served him often. But this was different. Cornered in this fucking rat-hole, slouching inert like a lump of useless jelly, was hardly going to help.

He hit the remote switch and his earlier incarnation, that mesmeric figure, that angel who was also a demon, surrounded by a forest of upthrust hands, winked into blackness.

Just for a moment it was beautiful, that blackness, the blissful silence.

Turning his head to one side, Johnny stretched the tendons in his neck which audibly cracked.

He fingered another button, and motors commenced whirring, daylight shafting in as the electric blinds folded upwards, glimmering through the billions of dust particles floating over the empty bottles of Jack Daniels, the over-flowing ashtrays and odorous scatter of pizza boxes and chop suey cartons. Wearier than words could describe, his very bones creaking, Johnny ran nicotine-brown fingers through his greying mop before slowly and heavily levering himself upright. He tottered for a second, then trudged to the panoramic window with its stunning view of the extensive front garden and winding gravel drive.

The lawns had seen better days, and the Venus de Milo

fountain on the right stood dry. Her waters had ceased to flow years ago, thanks to blocked and corroded pipes, leaving her shapely form cracked and clotted with moss.

At the end of the drive, a pair of tall, black wrought-iron gates, intimidating enough to keep the fans at bay when they'd flocked here from all over the country, were cluttered with the rain-wet rags of hundreds of handwritten notes declaring their everlasting adoration for Johnny Klein.

However, more relevant today was the white van sitting on the other side, not to mention the large chubby guy in the thick sheepskin coat and tweed flat cap who stood by the intercom. Even as Johnny watched, the caller pressed the buzzer again insistently.

Johnny moved to the intercom monitor and saw a face distorted to near-comical girth by the fisheye lens. He hit the talk button. 'Yeah?'

'That you, Johnny?' asked a gruff northern voice. 'We're here. It's twelve . . . well, it's after twelve, actually. But we agreed midday with the estate agent, d'you remember?'

Johnny glanced through the window again. A thick-set bottle-blonde had emerged from the van as well, wearing a large puffer jacket on top of a shiny pink tracksuit. Her hair hung in a ponytail that looked more like a chunk of rope.

'You there, Johnny?' the man asked, starting to sound frustrated.

Johnny blew out a long stale breath. 'Bollocks.'

He hit the entry button. Outside, the gates clanked and clattered as they swung inward. He didn't bother looking out again, his tired eyes roving across the last few things he owned: his command centre, which had never looked so dusty and dented, and a few raggedy boxes, badly duct-taped together, a couple of gold records poking out of them.

Even now it was hard to believe that this spacious and yet depressingly empty room had once been the cockpit of his fast-moving life, the beating heart of his and Laura's happiness. How many birthdays, Christmases and Number One records had they celebrated in here? It was large enough to host their wedding reception, and indeed it had done, not to mention the riotous party it had descended into, 'space cookies' being dished out alongside rivers of champagne, even his own parents, conservatives with a small 'c', finishing up in the fountain, swearing that it was one of the best days of their lives.

Thank God his mum and dad weren't around to see him now, though deep down, he so desperately wished they were. But all that aside, it struck him again how much he'd taken his success for granted. The folly and fearlessness of youth had prevented him even considering that it might all come crashing down eventually. Why would he have? It was never his job to check royalty statements, to keep a beady eye on outgoings, incomings, office bills, staff bills, mortgages or even the multimillion-pound insurance policy his press team had taken out on his hands as a hugely expensive PR stunt. He'd had *people* for all that.

He'd had *people* for everything.

That was one of the things that had driven Laura out.

Well, that and the other stuff.

A hefty thudding sounded from the front door.

As Johnny slowly made his way out there, his elbow

caught a white glass vase displayed on a clear Perspex plinth. He didn't react even as it toppled from side to side, watching instead, interested to see if his luck could get any worse. Which it did. As the vase fell to the parquet floor, slowly turning in the air like a prima ballerina pirouetting in perfect motion, before disintegrating into thousands of glittering shards, a key was inserted into the front door, and a craggy hangdog face edged around it, breaking into a nervous grin on seeing the former occupant.

'Ah, Johnny . . . I mean Mr Klein.' That northern accent again. A pudgy hand appeared, a shiny new key swinging from it. 'Sorry, but, erm . . . the estate agent gave me the keys. Sorry, she wasn't sure whether you'd still be here or not.'

Johnny studied him for a long moment, then, a showman to the end, spread his arms wide. 'Sure, no problem. It's all yours, man. Lock, stock and two smoking barrels!'

The man's smile broadened. 'Call me Dave, please.'

He opened the door properly, shuffling inside, his large physique rendered bulkier still by his sheepskin coat. Rather awkwardly, he adjusted his Peaky Blinders-style cap. Bling jewellery glinted on his fingers and wrists. He glanced down, observing the heap of newly shattered glass, bit his lip but didn't comment. Instead, he slid the remains aside with his brown suede loafer.

'Have you got everything you need?' he asked, presumably puzzled as to why Johnny was still here. 'It's nearly one o'clock, you know?'

The situation felt surreal. There was a time was when Johnny Klein had been wanted everywhere, sometimes earning a tidy sum just to show up at a premiere or to endorse some brand he had absolutely no interest in with a smile, a handshake, a 'thank you very much and goodbye'. Now he was being kicked out of his own gaff.

'Sure,' he said again. 'I'll grab my stuff and leave you to it.'

Johnny trekked down the hall, then up the flight of stairs to the first landing and through the double doors leading to his bedroom. Inside, mirrored side tables framed a giant unmade bed, its sheets of white Egyptian cotton so rumpled and stained you'd have thought Tracey Emin had spent days, maybe weeks, assembling them. A small canvas holdall sat on the end of the white chaise longue. Johnny paused in the stillness of the moment.

There were often good memories attached to bedrooms; however the one that was seared into his brain was anything but and he could have done without it invading his mind. He relived it again nonetheless, picturing the moment he'd walked in and found Laura packing the last of her things into a designer carpet bag. She'd had enough. Enough of the booze, the drugs, the hangovers, the suspicions and rumours, the half-truths, the out-and-out lies.

She was sick to the back teeth, she said, of reading about his exploits in the Sunday papers. She wasn't just some rock and roll doormat.

He made no attempt to deny it. At home, he was a boy, a literal man-child, mothered by Laura, who would kiss his cheek at night when he moaned in his sleep, or stroke his head when he laid it on her lap and told her he'd always love her, that he never wanted to lose her. But when he climbed aboard the tour bus, sometimes only minutes after leaving the motorway pick-up point where she'd dropped him, he was a rock god all over again, a dark and reckless force, a beast of varied, voracious appetites, ready and eager to take it to the extreme, just as so many of his rock idols had done before him.

He turned his eyes to the bedroom window. At the far end of the drive, instead of the white rental van and the big guy called Dave and his peroxide-blonde missus, he remembered Laura and Chelsea hand in hand, his daughter wiping her eyes as they climbed into the waiting taxi.

'Johnny?' a soft voice intruded into his thoughts.

Mona stood in the bedroom doorway. As always, she looked far younger than her thirty-five years. Something to do with her miniskirt, knee-high leather boots and tasselled leather biker jacket, but also her slight, girlish build and natural beauty. She had perfect skin, huge dark eyes, long black lashes, her jet-black hair currently styled in a short pixie bob.

'The guy downstairs?' she ventured.

Johnny was still distracted. 'Downstairs? Oh yeah, Dave.'

'Dave?'

'Big fella. Silly hat, sheepie.'

'Yeah, that's him.' She regarded him worriedly. 'Think he wants you out. This is his place now.'

'Yeah.'

Mona worked for *Classic Rock*, which made her a journalist on one of the last few music mags still in existence since the internet ran its great scythe through most of them. Being around Mona made Johnny feel a bit better about himself; her energy, her vitality, her intelligence, all gave him a shot of adrenaline that he didn't get from anything else. It had taken him a while to get his head

16

around it, but Mona was something he hadn't had for a while – a friend.

Though at the moment, even Mona's presence was failing to work its usual spell.

He grabbed the canvas bag. It was dishearteningly light, containing only a couple of pairs of socks and underpants, an Alice Cooper T-shirt and a pair of black Levi's once reserved for weddings, funerals and the odd Goth gig.

'Seriously, Johnny,' she asked. 'Are you all right?'

'I've had better days.'

She looked him over, visibly affected by the sight of his old 501s hanging tattered at the knees and his black silk shirt, now crumpled and sour with sweat. 'Johnny, I'm so sorry about all this.'

She'd obviously wanted to come here in a spirit of moral support, but he could tell the sight of his meagre belongings thrown into a few bags and boxes was challenging her positivity. He shrugged again, but his once-handsome face was a mask of pain. 'Good things never last, Mona. Got to enjoy them while you can.'

'What about your gold discs?'

Johnny thought about Dave, the new resident, already making himself at home downstairs in his command chair. 'Let him have them, he's bought this place as a job lot. That means *everything* in here, so, there's no point whining about it. Time to move on.'

'It's not over, you know. I'm sure it's not.'

'Can you look at me and keep a straight face while you say that?'

She barely missed a beat. 'Hey, people's luck can change, but talent doesn't. You'll get back on the right track somehow.'

He took his khaki army jacket from a peg. 'What *is* the right track, Mona?'

'Well, to start with, you're not finishing up in some craphole flophouse with roaches in the walls and rats under the bed.' She folded her arms, giving him a no-arguments look.

He glanced at her, puzzled. 'I've spoken to my uncle,' she said. 'He wants you to stay with us in Brick Lane, above the restaurant. Till you get yourself sorted. He was a massive fan of yours, you know.'

'Mona . . .' The offer felt more like a kick in the nuts. 'That just makes it worse.'

'It's only temporary,' she added quickly. 'Consider it a new start. Don't think about what you're losing, think about the possibilities. You've been stuck inside this mausoleum for too long.'

'Yeah, well . . .' He yanked open the top bedside drawer and scraped out the handful of cash left in there – a couple of hundred quid, tops – and shoved it into his back pocket.

'At least it was *my* mausoleum.'

2
GRACELAND

Monday

Mona had been sent from Bangladesh as a young child to live with her uncle in the UK. The reasons for this had never been fully explained to her, just that her parents felt that it would be a better life for her in Britain. Her Uncle Rishi, who was already over here, was a legend in his own right. He and his wife, Aahana, opened the first Indian restaurant on Wilmslow Road in Manchester, which later became the world-famous Curry Mile. When Rishi was widowed at an unexpectedly young age he found the associations of that place too painful to stay there, and so moved his business to London, specifically Brick Lane in the East End, the beautiful cultural melting pot where the shadows of Dickensian London met the empire's mid-twentieth-century diaspora. By the time Mona arrived, it was the heart of the Tower Hamlets Bangladeshi community, famous for its long parade of restaurants, most of which had sprung up to cater for the global influx of workers. And it was in this vibrant, colourful world that she'd grown up.

She drove Johnny there in her uncle's small blue delivery van, the name of his restaurant, Graceland, emblazoned down its flanks in flowing golden letters.

From Mill Hill to Brick Lane was only a ten-mile journey, but the two locations might have been worlds apart. The broad leafy avenues of Hampstead and Islington gave way to narrower and noisier streets, the open sky becoming a latticework of thin overhead strips as they hit the East End and penetrated deeper into a maze of warehouses, most now gentrified into trendy bars and hipster apartment blocks, far from the teetering rookeries they had been when Jack the Ripper roamed the streets of Spitalfields. From Hackney, the blue van weaved its way through the logjammed traffic on Bethnal Green Road, throwing a right at the Truman's brewery, and heading into Brick Lane itself.

As usual, it was thronging both with visitors and residents. Brick Lane never slept, as Johnny recalled. Not from mid-morning, when the first maître d' adjusted his bowtie and stepped outside to commence enticing passers-by to lunch, right through to the wee small hours, when the dustcarts trundled through. Now, at lunchtime on a Friday, he was assailed by an atmosphere hazy with rich aromas: herbs and spices, bhajis sizzling in fryers, chickens roasting in tandoori clay ovens.

Mona chattered away merrily, occasionally honking her horn and shouting in broad cockney at some vehicle or cyclist who was getting in her way.

Johnny had first met her a decade ago, when she'd come to his Mill Hill mansion to interview him, and they'd got on like a house on fire. Mona had been delighted that he'd consented to the interview, especially as he'd been going through one of his reclusive periods at the time. For his part, Johnny found her honesty and wide-eyed innocence refreshing. They'd discovered that they shared a sense of irreverent humour, not to mention a fascination for those earlier days of rock and pop music. Of course, from Johnny's perspective, it hadn't hurt that Mona was a bombshell, and he was under no illusions that, when she'd first got to know him, there'd been more than a little bit of fan-girl in her fascination for him and his glamorous lifestyle that he could easily have exploited. Despite prior form in that regard, he'd found her youth endearing rather than tempting at that point in his life. In the years that followed, and especially once he'd become estranged from Laura, they'd settled into an uneven friendship, Mona always seemingly on hand whenever he was in a hole. Thinking about it now, Johnny still wasn't sure what was in it for her.

'You know one of my uncle's favourite sayings?' Mona said cheerfully. 'The future is only a heartbeat away. You should think about that, Johnny. You've got loads of time to turn things round.'

He glanced at her as she drove. 'The future's only a . . . isn't that in a song too?'

'Probably.' She nodded brightly. 'I told you, he's obsessed with contemporary music. Listen, you'll love him.'

'Leo Sayer, yeah? It's from "When I Need You".' Mona nodded again. 'Your uncle brought you up on the Bible according to Leo?'

'Leo came into the restaurant for dinner about ten years ago. My uncle never forgets stuff like that . . . getting a visit from a Seventies icon. Anyway, we're here. Guess which building's his?'

Johnny peered out. A colossal billboard, located above the nearest restaurant door, towered almost to the skyline. It was at least forty feet high and clad most of the upper section of the building's front. The image on it, which, somewhat ingeniously, appeared to have been constructed from thousands of miniature plastic discs, all rotating in the wind, depicted Elvis Presley. It was not Elvis in his lean and youthful prime, but an older, tubbier version, the 'Vegas Elvis'. His double chins wobbled as the October breeze set the discs spinning.

Over the top of the mural, the restaurant's name, Graceland, had been painted in gigantic gold script. It dazzled, caught in the midday sun.

'Fucking hell!' Johnny exclaimed.

'I knew you'd be impressed.'

'Er . . . yeah.'

Mona pulled into a vacant staff-only bay in front of the entrance.

'You sure he's got room for me here?' Johnny asked.

'Course he's got room.' She applied the handbrake and turned the engine off.

She jumped out and bustled round to the back, opening the rear doors to get his bag.

Trying his best not to look too unhappy about this, Johnny climbed out of the van, gazing up again at the dramatic, technicolour hoarding.

All the reservations he'd harboured about the optics of a one-time rock and roll legend reduced to the status of attic lodger in an East End curry house – especially

22

one like this, which it wouldn't take the paparazzi long to find – were briefly forgotten as it struck him just how much of a music fan Mona's uncle had to be. He ought to have realised sooner. Clearly, he had steered his niece along the same path.

'We going in, then?' Mona asked, clinging on to Johnny's bag. When he reached out for it, she retreated a step. 'No. You're our guest, remember?'

'Mona . . . look, you know I can't do this.'

Her face fell. 'Why not?'

'It's just . . . I've haven't got two coppers to rub together. Does your uncle realise that?'

She smiled again. 'That won't matter, I promise you.' She grabbed his arm. 'Johnny, you've entertained us all for years. We're just giving a bit back. Look . . . Leo Sayer accepted his free curry. Why can't you accept a free bed?'

He had no answer to that, and sighed as she opened the restaurant door and ushered him in ahead of her.

'Don't be embarrassed,' she said. 'I've told you, it's just till you get back on your feet.'

The moment they entered, they were greeted by the sound of live singing. At the far end of the dining area, Johnny was amazed to see a small stage, about a foot high, framed by two curtains made from crimson velvet. In the middle of it, a man gyrated about as he presented his very own version of 'Blue Suede Shoes'. He was murdering it, every note way off, while his dancing verged on the ludicrous, but under the UV lights his white Lycra rhinestone-studded jumpsuit crackled with static electricity. The diners occupying about eight of the twenty or so tables seemed to be enjoying it, clapping and cheering him on.

'Our house superstar,' Mona explained, returning a wave that the performer gave her. 'Ravi Sharma, though, perhaps for obvious reasons, he prefers to be called Elvis.'

The restaurant itself was sumptuous, filled with red velour and with handsome blue glass chandeliers dangling overhead. On one side an ornate frieze portrayed a rural village, the river running through it lit by myriad tiny LEDs, which created the illusion of liquid motion. There was also a massive aquarium in which four sizeable lobsters sat with their claws taped together.

'Quick warning,' Mona said quietly, nodding at the tank. 'My uncle's pride and joy is his lobster balti. It's delish, but it's also the most expensive thing on the menu, so though you'll be eating here for free, it's probably best not to ask for that.'

Johnny bridled at the mere suggestion there was any dish, no matter how exquisite, that he couldn't afford to eat three times a day, month after month if he wanted to, and all washed down with however many bottles of Bollinger he fancied. Then reality crashed in again, and he felt a rush of blood to his head, swaying on his feet. It was a frequent occurrence of late – it was literally like dying.

'It's Johnny Klein!' someone shouted. 'Can I get a selfie?'

A couple of guys had just paid their bill and were about to leave the restaurant, but one of them, the older of the two, had suddenly laid eyes on the new arrivals, and without being invited, had come blundering over, digging out his phone.

'My ex-missus used to love you!' he guffawed.

He was a hefty, middle-aged bloke with a plaid shirt stretched to bursting over his big shoulders and thick bullneck. Before he knew it, the guy had one arm around him and was lining up his selfie.

'She won't fucking believe this!' he chuckled, hitting the button three or four times.

Clearly, it was all about getting one over on his ex. That probably explained why it didn't matter too much to the guy that Johnny was now a stone or so heavier than he'd been in his pomp, that his hair was greying and messy, his face unshaved. He gave that well-practised smile all the same. There was no sparkle in it, but any kind of recognition today was an improvement on nothing.

'Cheers, old son,' the guy said, stepping away. He was already focused on the pictures rather than their subject. 'Can't wait to WhatsApp her with these.'

He nodded to his sidekick, grunting something unintelligible, and the pair of them left the premises, his mate smiling an embarrassed thanks.

Johnny spotted Mona looking on sympathetically. He wasn't the only rock star in her life. She'd interviewed dozens, past and present, and some were now her mates too. Nearly all the old ones had told painful stories about how difficult it was to move on, to get to grips with the notion that time had finally caught up with them. But she probably had no idea how deeply and secretly shaming it was when you could still cause a stir with the public, who, while they might not fall over you in droves anymore, were still eager to get some of that rock-star glitter on themselves, blissfully unaware that you were now an imposter, a beggar at the banquet.

'Johnny Klein, Johnny Klein!' an excited voice cried out.

Mona broke into a smile. 'My uncle,' she mouthed.

Johnny turned as Graceland's proprietor hurried from the direction of the bar.

'Oh my goodness, what a delight, what a pleasure!'

At least Mona's uncle didn't seem to care about any of that.

He was a small man with a round, friendly face and a bald head, only a few white curls visible behind his ears. He wore an open waistcoat over his smart shirt and tie, but his sleeves were rolled up and his glasses rested on his shiny pate.

'I still can't believe it!' he said, his face beaming with delight.

'Didn't you get my message, Uncle?' Mona said, giving him a hug.

'Of course,' he said. 'But I wasn't sure if you were serious.' He grabbed Johnny's hand as though greeting a long-lost son and pumped it energetically. 'Johnny Klein, the greatest pop star of the Eighties, staying as my guest! Can I get you some food, a drink from the bar maybe?'

Mona jumped in. 'Johnny, this is my uncle, Rishi Mistry.' She gave an expansive shrug and another of her irresistible smiles.

'I, erm . . .' For a second, Johnny was lost for words. This was the friendliest reception he'd received in he didn't know how long.

'Don't bother with that Rishi business,' Mona's uncle said. 'Call me the Major. Everybody round here does.'

Wasn't Elvis's manager called the Colonel?

'You know, Johnny,' the Major said. 'I've seen you on TV so many times. I have all your music. Your albums, your singles, your twelve-inch remixes, all of them. I'm your biggest fan. I'm sure I can say that. Once, I even bought

Mona a full-size cardboard cut-out of you – when she was a small girl, obviously – so we could take you on holiday with us. I will never forget. Everywhere we went with you, we took a photograph. I'm sure Mona can find them and show you.'

'Probably best if we park that idea, yeah?' Mona interjected quickly, frowning at her uncle.

In the background, Elvis was going into his big karate-kicking crescendo, which seemed to be the Major's cue to get up on stage himself. Once the applause had died down, he snatched the mic from Elvis, who stood by proudly, his petit features shining with sweat under his sideways-tilted turban.

'Ladies and gentlemen,' the Major shouted, 'please show your appreciation for Elvis Sharma!'

There was renewed uproar from the diners.

'Everyone round here loves Elvis . . . our Elvis, I mean,' Mona confided in Johnny. 'He's a phenomenon. He's the sweetest of men, but it's mainly for his performances. He's out of tune, he gets the words mixed up, but they seem to love him more because of it. Uncle Rishi's a massive fan, but they're also second cousins, so Ravi gets a lot of leeway.'

The Major was still addressing his captive audience.

'And this afternoon we have a treat for you . . . we are joined here at Graceland by a very special guest, a true superstar. Ladies and gentlemen, I give you . . . *JOHNNY KLEIN!*'

The response was muted. A few heads turned his way. There were one or two nods of recognition, but other expressions remained excruciatingly blank. Johnny wanted the carpet tiles to open up and swallow him. As he'd reminded himself on coming down here, the East End was populated these days by a twenty-something hipster crowd. For every middle-aged cockney builder, there'd be dozens of young, well-heeled urbanites, including the majority of diners in the restaurant. He doubted their collective memory stretched much further back than the *X Factor* era. To be fair, someone whooped as the penny dropped, and there were a couple of claps, but how much of that was due to politeness he couldn't say.

The Major, oblivious to this, leaned over to Elvis and whispered something in his ear, causing him to stiffen, as though he was on the parade ground. Johnny threw Mona a haunted look, but didn't get a chance to speak before the Major came lithely down from the stage, bringing the singer with him.

'Johnny . . . please meet Ravi "Elvis" Sharma, Brick Lane's greatest undiscovered talent. He's going to be huge one day, just like you.'

Johnny nodded awkwardly. 'Great show.'

Elvis gave a nervous but grateful nod.

The Major now slipped something out of his pocket and, rather surreptitiously, pushed it into Johnny's right hand. He looked down at the item he'd been passed and saw that it was an ancient C90 cassette tape, its paper insert scribbled all over in blotchy biro.

'It's a demo I funded for Ravi here,' the Major said quietly. 'He recorded it a few years back, but I always said I would try to get it into the hands of someone who can help him. When I heard you might be joining us today, I told him that this could be a chance . . . you know, with your contacts in the record business.'

Johnny turned the tape over, bewildered by the stone-aged technology.

'He's so versatile,' his host added. 'He doesn't just do Elvis. Oh no. You wait till you see his Sinatra, or his Mick Jagger. Now, I might be biased, but I think he's better than the real thing.'

Johnny forced himself to nod. 'I'll see what I can do.'

The Major beamed. 'Thank you. It will mean so much to both of us.'

'Uncle Rishi,' Mona cut in. 'Can I show Johnny up to his room now? We need to get him settled.'

'Of course, of course. Johnny . . . you're welcome to stay here as long as you wish. And eat as much as you like, whenever you like . . . all on the house. Just, erm . . .' He turned thoughtful. 'The lobster balti is our speciality . . . but, I, well . . .'

'It's OK, I don't do lobster,' Johnny said.

The Major looked relieved. 'Ah, well, each to his own, I always say . . .'

'Come on, Johnny,' Mona said, winking and sticking a thumb in the direction of the restaurant's bar.

The Major beamed again, before turning and making the rounds of his guests, eager to confirm that their lunch was the best to be had on Brick Lane.

Mona took Johnny's hand and, still carrying his bag, led him behind the bar, then through a back storeroom, where she opened a door on a steep flight of wooden stairs.

'Hope you haven't got a dicky heart,' she said. 'You're right at the top.'

He said nothing as he followed her up, guessing they were directly above the kitchen because the aroma of cooking was now so rich it was almost intoxicating. It had only diminished a little when they reached what had to be the attic. Mona pushed at a small white door. There wasn't much of a room on the other side. Just a bed on bare, white-painted floorboards, a side table, a battered old leather armchair in the corner and a single small circular window, almost like a porthole.

'Come in.' Mona threw his bag onto the chair. 'I know it's not much, but—'

'The future's only a heartbeat away,' Johnny said, beating her to the punchline.

Mona smiled and indicated another door. 'Shower and loo.'

Johnny glanced around, checking everything out. He suspected his body language was enough on its own to indicate his feelings about his new pad.

'Mona, look, thank you. Fuck, this is awkward. I mean, I really appreciate what you and your uncle are doing, but—'

'But what?' she enquired, apparently relaxed about what she clearly suspected was coming next. 'Johnny . . . I wouldn't say this unless I considered us really good friends, but what other options do you have? You're broke and you have nowhere to go. It's that simple. And it's now October, winter's coming.'

Johnny was silent, struggling with the inescapable logic.

'You can live here rent-free,' she said. 'For as long as you need to. You can eat and drink too. All on the house. And trust me, it's some of the best nosh on Brick Lane, and that's saying something. Even then it's only a stopgap. Soon as you're able to, you can move on. No one will be offended.'

'Mona . . .'

'Are you going to get a better deal somewhere else?'

Johnny cracked a jaded half-smile. 'Mona, as long as I live, I'll never receive a better deal than this. And I'm going to pay you guys back, I absolutely promise that. But what will I say to Laura and Chelsea? I can hardly have Chelsea over to stay here at weekends, can I? Laura would think I'd lost my mind, even if Chelsea didn't.'

Mona pondered that. She knew all about Johnny and Laura's shattered relationship.

It had seemed at first like a match made in heaven. The handsome, happy-go-lucky Jack the lad, notorious for his talent and charisma, not to mention for his wild, untamed ways and the legions of girls who swooned around him, bewitched by TV's beautiful It-girl, a strong and independent woman who suffered no fools, brooked no nonsense and spoke out expertly on a range of controversial issues. Talk about fire and water, talk about opposites attracting. But perhaps in the end it had all seemed too much like a fairy tale, because that's exactly what it was. Laura Hall had been twenty-five years old when she'd married Johnny Klein in 1999, only eight years younger than he was. But even then, it had soon started to feel as if she was cramping his style. It wasn't that Johnny didn't love Laura – Mona had no doubt that he did – or that he didn't appreciate a stable home life, but when he was out on the road, touring, the married-man thing didn't fit his image. Determined to maintain the illusion that he was still free and easy, always available, he'd preferred to keep Laura in the background. It wasn't that he wanted to play the field (though he did), but because as the twenty-first century progressed he feared that his hordes of screaming fans might drift away in search of someone closer to their own age. The only surprise to Mona was that Laura had hung on as long as she did. Add to that, the drugs, the booze, the groupies, the lurid tabloid tell-all stories, the trouble with the tax man. She and Johnny had separated only a year ago and weren't officially divorced yet, which meant they'd now been married for twenty-four years.

'How old is Chelsea?' she asked.

'Fifteen.'

'Well, there you go. Fifteen . . . she's not a baby anymore. She'll understand. People split up, Johnny. We're all allowed to be happy.'

Johnny wondered who Mona thought was happy right now. 'It's just . . . well, she's only ever lived in Mill Hill.'

'She's not there now, is she?'

'Suppose not.' He thought about that as he wandered around the room. 'Ever since they left, she's been living at her nan's.' Thinking about it, his daughter's current experience of life was probably no great improvement on his. She too was stuck with a guest bedroom in someone else's house, even if it was her grannie's. 'I'll go and see them as soon as. Tell them where I am.'

He was suddenly struck by the room's window and the wooden hoarding on the outside of it, which blocked out most of the daylight except for the perfectly round hole cut in the middle. Even then the light was poor, because a dark gauze appeared to have been stretched over the hole on the outside.

'What's with this?' he asked.

'Ah . . .' Mona adopted an estate agent's patter. 'That's one of this prize apartment's most unique features.'

'Yeah?' He lifted the window panel and leaned out. He couldn't quite stick his head through the hole, thanks to the gauze on the other side, which presumably was to create one of the giant billboard figure's tinted lenses, but he got close enough to be able to look down through it onto Brick Lane. Looking out through the window, was like you were looking at the world through Elvis Presley's eyes. Well, one of them.

He drew back again. 'A King's-eye view.'

Mona's smile faltered. 'How about cash, Johnny? That pile of crumpled notes in your pocket won't go very far.'

'I'll manage.'

'I doubt that. Look . . . I know it's probably painful thinking about this, but if you need a regular income, I'm sure Uncle Rishi can fix you up with a job. Part-time, if you'd prefer. He always needs delivery drivers.'

Johnny had to swallow back a response so sharp that even Mona would have been offended. His ego, never far from the surface, flinched at the mere suggestion.

One-time rock god, available now on Deliveroo.

He knew he had no right to feel outrage, but that headline alone would kill him. Surely some beggars had at least earned the right to try and be choosers.

'I'm fine,' he replied. 'Honest. One of my old mates, Pete James, asked me to call around this week. He says he's got a project he needs some help with.'

'Pete . . . ?' She gazed at him long and hard. 'Pete James? *The* Pete James? The guy from The Whack?'

'Who else?'

She still seemed lost for words. 'That's great. I mean that's *really* great. What is it, session work or something?' Mona did a little dance of excitement.

He emptied his bag on the bed. 'Let's not get ahead of ourselves. I don't even know what he's offering yet.'

The Whack were a four-piece outfit who'd come onto the music scene about a decade prior to Klein, as part of that first, original wave of British punk. Lead guitar and vocalist Pete James had been a founder member and a key figure in keeping the band relevant as they'd diversified through a range of styles over the years: from punk to New Wave to synth pop to goth rock and finally now into hard rock. They were still going and still headlining.

'You're a sly one, you are,' Mona said. 'I didn't know you knew Pete James. He's music biz royalty. If I'd known that, I could've bagged some inside info off you for when I was doing that article on him the other week.'

Johnny shrugged. 'If I'd offered you that, he wouldn't be offering me a job now, would he?'

'Well, you've obviously got nothing to worry about.' She opened the bedroom door. 'He's probably got a spare penthouse you can use.'

He nodded and tried to smile. She still didn't get it. The fewer people who knew that he'd been reduced to beggary the better, especially when it came to his former peers. No, he'd go and see Pete James about a job – that would be embarrassing enough – but that was the limit of it. He certainly wasn't mentioning that he no longer had a roof over his head.

She edged out onto the landing. 'I'll let you get settled. Things are coming up roses already.'

He had to admit that her optimism was infectious. Maybe he *could* look forward to hooking up with Pete and seeing what was what. If he went round first thing in the morning, he might be earning good money by this time tomorrow. He wouldn't be back in the game yet, of course. Not at the level where he wanted and needed to be. Technically, he might still be ruined, but at least he could still play a guitar.

'See you later, Johnny. By the way, you might need this.' She flicked a blue plastic card on the bed. Johnny picked it up; it was an Oyster card.

'Very funny.' He popped it in his back pocket all the same.

Mona flashed him another one of her thousand-watt smiles, and Johnny went over to close the door as she headed downstairs. As he did, the discordant wailing of Elvis floated up from below. It was 'Hound Dog', and Graceland's Elvis was *definitely* killing it.

3

OLD TIES

Tuesday

Johnny hadn't ridden a London bus for over three decades. He wasn't even sure how regularly they were supposed to turn up. He waited at the stop anyway. It was just around the corner from Graceland, next to a double-fronted second-hand furniture store signposted 'Vintage', though behind its dusty front window stood a pile of heavy brown Fifties dining tables and chairs that had probably been bought as a job lot from some South London warehouse. If it hadn't been for the kebab shop next door, the whole side street would reek of mothballs.

It was a mild day for October, the sky clear and eggshell blue. At least that was an improvement on the broken grey cloud cover of the previous day when he'd walked out of Mill Hill, so it made him feel slightly better and seemed to kindle a spark of hope. All the same, he huddled into his khaki jacket and tugged down the peak of the Graceland baseball cap he'd borrowed before setting out from the restaurant that morning, ensuring that most of his face was concealed.

Only one other person waited at the bus stop with him: a middle-aged woman in a raincoat and scarf, who spent most of the time fiddling with her phone. But she was the perfect age to have been a fan of his during his heyday, so he stood with his back partly turned away.

Did it really matter if anyone recognised him, he wondered. They might want a selfie, but would that be such a disaster? And if he was getting on a bus rather than into a limousine, well, it might serve to make him seem a little more human. Johnny also wondered if he was letting his ego run away with him, considering his experience with the twenty-somethings in the restaurant.

All the same, he avoided eye contact with the woman. First off, how was he ever going to repay the Major?

Johnny now deeply regretted the distaste he'd thinly disguised on first arriving at Graceland. It wasn't that the place was scruffy or dingy – no more than he was, anyway – but it was such a comedown from what he was used to. It had been a real shock to his system, thinking that it could be his new home. All that did was make Rishi's heartfelt generosity even more overwhelming. If the Major had noticed that Johnny Klein was a reluctant guest in his establishment, it didn't seem to matter; he'd been nothing but smiles and hugs.

Ravi Sharma's demo tape still sat in Johnny's pocket. Ravi 'Elvis' Sharma might be a great Brick Lane character, he was no singer. He wasn't even novelty-circuit standard. Not that Johnny had any pull, even at that level. What little goodwill he had left in the industry he needed to keep for himself right now.

Anyway, Mona was more likely to know someone who could make things happen for Elvis than he was. On which subject . . . what to do about Mona?

She was still the bright-eyed kid, the eager cub reporter with whom he'd gradually become friendly over a series of in-depth interviews and stories. She *wasn't* a kid anymore, not at thirty-five. She was a friend. A hot, good-looking friend, admittedly.

From Mona's perspective, though, things were very different, even if she did a good job of suppressing this. Was she in love with him? He suspected she was a bit. Why else would she be so eager to please such a washed-up loser? Please God it wasn't pity.

He shook his head in frustration.

It was hard to imagine the alpha male that was Johnny Klein of the Eighties, that 'demonic angel', ever being reduced to a state where members of the music press pitied him. And then there was Laura.

Laura . . . he felt his heart creak at the thought of his wife.

Not yet his ex, but well on the way . . . his lifelong soul-mate, or she *had* been.

What were they now?

Decree Absolute pending, that's what.

These agonising thoughts were interrupted as a huge angular shadow blotted out the autumn sun. The bus had arrived, halting noisily alongside them.

The doors wheezed open and Johnny stepped back, letting the woman climb aboard first. For half a second, just after he'd nodded and smiled at her, he was gripped with terror that she might recognise him after all, ask for a pic, wonder why he was travelling the streets of London on public transport. But she did none of those things, smiling back with gratitude, then showing her pass to the driver and waddling off along the bus's otherwise empty lower deck.

Johnny nervously tapped the Oyster card on the reader, almost afraid that it might bite him, scrambling upstairs quickly after it gave a reassuring *ping*. That deck was empty too, and he gratefully made his way to the back seats, the bus swaying as it jolted away from the kerb. Before he could sit, he swept several items of garbage to the floor: an open KFC box filled with scrunched tissues and gnawed-on chicken bones, and a dog-eared copy of the previous day's *Metro*.

On the back of the seat in front someone had used a sharp point to scratch a jagged-lettered slogan. It read:

> Spending time reading this?
> You're an even sadder bastard
> than everyone thinks.

The fucking thing could have been written for him specifically, he mused. Glancing further around, there was plenty of other graffiti, most of it obscenities scribbled on the ceiling in marker pen.

He couldn't be further from the million-quid tour bus that he'd once used almost as a birthright, its private upstairs lounge complete with a gleaming range of spirits, plush armchairs, sofa beds, tinted windows, video games and porn movies on demand. He wondered if he'd been a little premature in assuming rock bottom had arrived yesterday when he'd been forced to leave his home. The only way wasn't up – not yet, at least.

Johnny patted his jacket, feeling the lump of his ancient Motorola in the inside pocket. Like the rest of the planet, he'd had a smartphone until recently, but it had confounded him most of the time, and before his contract had been cancelled for non-payment, he'd spent most of his time blocking numbers from credit agencies chasing more enormous outstanding bills and fines.

At least the sale of Mill Hill had finally paid them off. But he and Laura had been left with virtually nothing, and any royalty payments he might get would go to Laura and Chelsea to keep them afloat.

Yeah, the flip-top Motorola suited him just fine – the cockroach of the technology world. No news was good news these days and Chelsea and Laura could get hold of him if they needed to and that was enough.

He watched the world go by as the bus headed west. Everywhere he looked, it was a dismal scene. Men and women trudged the pavements, weighed down by bags that were too heavy for them, looking wearied and worn by the weight of their troubles. Drug addicts and the homeless panhandled on streetcorners, no one stopping even to spare a word, never mind some change. Cars sat jammed alongside each other in bottled-up traffic, red-faced drivers arguing through open windows. Ordinary, everyday life . . . and how very, very ordinary it seemed. And yet, even this felt as though it was out of Johnny's reach.

Struggling to fight off a new wave of despondency, he looked down at his feet, his eyes falling again on the issue of the *Metro*. Purely by accident, his gaze fell on a front-page headline.

Jones laughs at police 'incompetence'

The cogs in Johnny's mind turned sluggishly these days, but he felt them spark into life. He reached down and grabbed the paper, checking the headline again.

It was that name, 'Jones', that had caught his attention, and the picture accompanying depicted a guy in early middle age with a lean face, a trim moustache and a shaven head. It had the look of a police mugshot, but the subject of it seemed relaxed about his predicament, almost amused.

Johnny read the opening para.

Alleged London gangster, Karl Jones, who was acquitted of attempted murder at the Old Bailey last December, has spoken out for the first time about the 'ridiculous lack of evidence' that police brought against him . . .

Karl Jones. An 'alleged London gangster'.
That settled it. It was the same guy.

Jones, 59, of St Katharine Docks, Tower Hamlets, who walked free from court three days before last Christmas, described it as: 'Funny, and not at all unexpected' that several 'supposedly key witnesses' including his 'so-called victim' failed to offer any useful evidence against him . . .

St Katharine Docks? Karl Jones had finished up in that flash neck of the woods?

He reappraised the picture, and now that he knew what he was looking for, it came swiftly into focus. A face he hadn't seen for so long, though in truth, it hadn't changed all that much. The curly fair hair had gone, the deceptively smooth, handsome features had narrowed onto the lean bone structure beneath, but without doubt it was the same Karl Jones he'd run around with back in his youth, a pair of tearaways together.

Even in grainy black and white, the steel of Jones's cold grey eyes was now unmistakable, his confident smile more like a cocky sneer.

He was a couple of years older than Johnny but had been the terror of Finsbury Park even in his early teens. OK, it hadn't been a high bar. By the Seventies, most of Haringey had been in a state of neglect and disrepair, like the rest of the country. But there'd been no doubt that Karl Jones was a born troublemaker and a nasty piece of work. The Old Bill had picked him up regularly, whenever there was an incident of any sort (usually because he was involved).

Not that their juvenile gang days had been the last time Johnny Klein and Karl Jones had had contact. There'd been that business in the late Eighties too. Johnny had put that one out of his mind in recent times, mainly because he'd had too many other things to worry about. Now though, the mere mention of that name, Jones, brought a flood of ugly memories back.

The Eighties was an age ago, a lifetime even. The slippery bastard would almost certainly have been up to some form of villainy or other since then, and when Johnny read on, all those suspicions were confirmed.

According to this news story, it had been rumoured for some time that he was at the heart of a drugs distribution network that covered much of North and East London. His firm were believed to be only a small part of a much larger worldwide operation, but it clearly paid well.

More recently, it seemed that Jones had been on his way home one evening, after attending a well-publicised charity event, when a young journalist, intent on exposing him, had accosted him near his front door and questioned him about the drugs allegations. Jones, normally careful to keep his own hands clean, had beaten him so viciously he was arrested and charged with attempted murder. And yet, when it got to trial, several key witnesses were mysteriously unable to remember exactly what had happened. Even the young journo had told the police that his extensive facial injuries had been as a result of another incident the same night when he'd tripped and tumbled down a flight of stone steps, while the fact they'd retrieved Jones's DNA from him might be explained because he'd been the one who'd found him and tried to assist.

'He was in a right old state when I came across him,' Jones told the court. 'He was very confused and didn't know what day it was.'

Johnny sat back, pondering how Jones had managed to get away with something so shocking. Where was God at times like this? Yeah, he'd pissed it up and done his share of drugs, and he'd slept with a whole raft of girls even while he was married, but he'd never really *hurt* anyone. He'd never stolen anything, or used violence . . . So, why was *he* being punished while some toerag like Karl Jones, a bloke with no discernible talents at all, none that were legal anyway, went steadily from rags to riches?

He glanced from the window and saw that they were already in Chelsea, the bus making its way along Eaton Square, which was lined with palatial houses, all glimmering white, like rows of giant wedding cakes.

As the bus swung across Sloane Square, Johnny swayed to his feet, worked his way along the top deck and descended the staircase, but no sooner had he reached the lower deck than he realised that the woman from the bus stop was still on board, and was cautiously approaching him with a shy smile.

'You're Johnny Klein, aren't you?' she ventured.

His blood pressure rose a little; there were still several seconds before they reached the next stop, time enough for her to wonder why the fuck he wasn't being ferried around by a uniformed chauffeur.

'Knew it was you,' she said. 'Mind if I get a piccie?'

As the bus slowed towards the next stop, Johnny was poised to apologise and say that he had to get off, when he glanced past her and saw several other passengers were watching with interest, most of them smiling kindly with fond recognition, which stole the words from his mouth.

Yeah, he might be in a mess and was worried sick that people would mock him for it, but so far people just seemed happy to see him.

'Sure,' he said, with a smile. 'No problem, love.'

He shuffled next to her as she extended her phone arm, grinning broadly, and meaning it this time. No sooner had the shutter clicked than the doors hissed open; Johnny's timing was perfect, the bus rolled to a stop and he jumped from the open door and onto the pavement outside.

Pete James's house was a short walk on foot. It sat parallel to Chelsea Embankment on Cheyne Walk, where a small, neat park faced a row of beautifully preserved Georgian townhouses. It was smart for sure, but also very quiet and sedate, certainly a world away from the jazz and jangle of Brick Lane.

Pete's house was notable for the black baroque metalwork around its windows and the Victorian-era glass lantern over its elaborately carved front door. Johnny hesitated outside. He'd been here many years ago, at the end of the Eighties, to celebrate the release of Pete's solo album, *A Kick in the Dark*. His memory of those days might be foggy, but his recollection of this place remained vivid. Inside, it was sumptuously furnished and decorated, a shrine to Regency grandeur. And it wasn't just that; it had a history for being an entertainer's retreat. Dusty Springfield had rented it in 1965, Hendrix for several months in '67, while Mick Jagggger had lived here in the early Seventies. It was the perfect rock-star abode, and he remembered swearing to himself back then that one day he would own a place like it. He'd never dreamed that, instead, he'd be coming to its door with a begging bowl.

Bracing himself, Johnny felt more than a little self-conscious as he tested the seven-foot-tall front gate, only to find it locked, and so hit the buzzer on an electric panel attached to the right-hand post. Doubtless, he'd be checked out on camera before anyone decided to open it. He took a deep breath.

A crackle of energy sounded, and a tinny voice followed. '*Yep?*'

Johnny leaned against the intercom. 'Erm, is Pete at home? I'm expected.'

'*Who are you, mate?*' the voice said, sounding suspicious. It also sounded as though its owner had come straight from the backstreets of Glasgow.

Johnny steeled himself, determined to maintain his old swagger and self-belief. 'I'm Johnny Klein.'

There was a brief pause, then: '*Hey pal, why don't you go and fuck yourself?*'

'No, wait . . . I really am Johnny Klein! Christ's sake! Where are you?' He swivelled around, searching for the tell-tale lens of a concealed camera. 'Tell Pete I'm outside. He'll vouch for me.'

'*You think we've got time for shite like this? Get the fuck off our porch!*'

'Wait a minute . . . what the fuck!' Johnny was too startled to think coherently. 'Just listen . . . Pete told me to come. It's really me. It's Johnny.'

'*And I'm Gerry Rafferty.*'

'No you're not,' Johnny retorted, now realising who he was dealing with. 'You're fucking Don Slater.'

Another lengthy silence followed, and then a rasping chuckle crackled from the speaker.

'*Seriously, mate,*' Slater said. '*You think I wouldn't have recognised you?*'

'Fucking hell, Don . . .' Johnny scowled. He felt more than a little riled by the snidey trick but needed to keep a lid on his anger. 'You gonna let me in or what?'

With a *clunk*, the gate opened. Johnny sidled through

and ascended the steps feeling more like a whipped dog than a former rock god. Before he'd reached the top, the front door to the house had opened and Don Slater stood there. He was a solid block of a guy in his early sixties, not tall, probably a couple of inches shorter than Johnny's six feet, but all his years of good living hadn't softened him in the least. His belly was larger and his one-time granite features had rounded a little. A single flap of his paisley shirt hung out over the top of a pair of brightly coloured Bermuda shorts, while his hair, which was silver-grey, as befitted his age, was shaved down the sides and slashed into a flat wedge on top, giving him a barnet Kirk Brandon would have been proud of.

'Fuck me,' he said. 'It really *is* you.'

Johnny shrugged. 'How you doing, Don?'

'Better than you, I think.'

Johnny shrugged nonchalantly. 'Maybe, mate. We'll see, eh?'

Slater didn't step aside, eyeing the new arrival. His smile remained in place, but somehow the cordiality didn't quite reach his eyes. It struck Johnny that the guy didn't trust him. He was making allowances for one of Pete James's old muckers, but he himself would stay wary until the guest proved there was no need for that.

The Scot, who wasn't a musician himself, had first hooked up with Pete while The Whack were playing working men's clubs in the late Seventies. Johnny had no real idea what role Slater played now, though most likely he was whatever Pete James needed him to be any time of the day or night. 'Fixer' was the word most observers would use.

'If that's who I think it is,' came a shouty transatlantic

voice from somewhere deep in the house, 'stop tormenting the poor bastard and let him in!'

Slater backed into the interior. 'Don't worry, mate. You're always welcome here.'

Yeah, Johnny thought. *Said the spider to the fly.*

4

FACE

Johnny followed Slater down an entrance hall decorated in dark silk Oriental wallpaper and decked its entire length with what looked like original oil paintings. Off the passage to the right was Pete's music room. Slater went straight in, Johnny tagging behind.

It was spacious and airy, but crammed with trophies. Priceless Fenders, Rickenbackers and Gibsons sat glinting on their silver stands. Rows of gold records covered three of its walls, while the fourth comprised a single colossal bay window looking down into a private garden. The daylight streaming through it bathed an old Steinway grand piano, providing the room's centrepiece.

Pete James sat behind it, tinkling on the worn ivories.

He didn't get up to greet Johnny, just threw him a disinterested look as he played a morose but affecting pattern of minor chords. He might have been The Whack's lead

49

guitarist officially, but he'd always been multi-talented when it came to music. At first glance, he was in better shape than either Johnny or Slater, looking trim in loose-fitting denims and fluffy slippers, but his hair, which he wore down to his shoulders in messy straggles, was dyed a garish shade of bright chestnut.

'You thirsty, man? Tea, coffee, sumfink stronger?' Pete still had a touch of his cockney accent, but some of it seemed to have got lost somewhere above the mid-Atlantic.

'I'm fine, thanks.'

Johnny *was* thirsty actually, but he was eager for his host to get to the point. The atmosphere in this place was stilted, not quite as warm as he'd been hoping for.

'So, how are you, Johnny?' Pete asked.

'Well, you know . . . ducking and diving.'

'More diving from what I can see.'

Johnny frowned, unsure how his old mate could see anything, considering he hadn't really looked up from his Steinway yet.

'Word gets around in this biz,' Slater said by way of explanation. He'd seated himself in a corner, on one of the window seats. 'Everyone's favourite phrase is "it's all over for them".'

'You off the gear?' Pete asked. 'The booze?'

'I'm too old for all that now,' Johnny replied, looking out at the manicured lawn and landscaped garden.

That wasn't strictly true where the booze was concerned, but he wasn't downing a bottle of Jack a day anymore. Slater appraised him closely. 'You go detox?'

'Sure.'

'Anyone we know? The Passage? The Sanctuary?'

'My bank.'

'One good thing about being skint . . . you can't afford the old charlie anymore.'

He turned back to Pete. 'I'm well and truly off the gear, mate.' At least he could be honest about that; every so often, some of his darkest memories would resurface like pockets of foul gas, and they were all related to drugs. 'That's somewhere no one needs to go.'

Pete nodded thoughtfully. 'Listen, Don . . . think we need to give this man some respect. Takes a lot of courage to do what he's done. So . . . what are you up to, man?'

'I've got things to do . . .' he bluffed. 'Things that'll keep me busy. Not *too* busy though.'

Pete pondered this for a moment, a dramatic pause that lasted a bit too long. 'Because . . . as one musician to another, and because we're old muckers, I might have something for you.'

Johnny's shoulders sagged a little. 'Cool . . . thanks, man. If you're looking for an extra guitarist, I'm the guy, as you know.'

'Relax, bro—'

'I'd need to borrow one of these bad boys.' Johnny indicated the stunning array of six-strings. 'Assuming that's OK—'

'Johnny—'

'Or I could pick up an Epiphone . . . if you could front me a few quid.'

Pete raised his voice. 'Hey man, relax! I've already got a second guitar. JJ Stevens. He's a genius, cross between Robert Fripp and Eddie Van Halen, God rest the poor sod.'

'Put me on rhythm then. Keyboards even. I'm like you, I can fill in anywhere.'

51

'Every slot's taken for the time being, man.'

Johnny frowned, confused. The Whack had disbanded, reformed, broken up and reconfigured repeatedly since their formation in 1976, the line-up always changing. Pete, as band leader and chief songwriter, had been the only mainstay. All these years on, whenever he was recording or touring, he'd mostly call in favours or hire session guys. It didn't seem unreasonable that Johnny had assumed he'd be offered something like that.

'Those slots filled by people who are better than me?' he asked.

'Sad truth is, Johnny,' Slater cut in, 'your best days are past. Reputations alone count for nothing in this business. You know that.'

'I can show you otherwise.'

'I hope you do,' Pete said, apparently sincerely. 'If you can get the old band back together, go out on a nostalgia tour or something . . . fuck, they pay decent money. The Saudis love that shit.'

Johnny felt as though his stomach had hit the floor, along with his ego. Their big idea was that he reform Klein?

'But in the meantime,' Pete added, 'I'm more interested in *this*.'

He took something off the Steinway's music rack, a book of some sort, and tossed it over. Johnny caught it and found himself staring down at a coloured snapshot of his younger face, or rather half of it, complete with slicked-back hair and heavy black eyeliner, as he peered around the upright fretboard of his Les Paul. It was the cover to *Road Warriors*, his own hardback photo collection from 1989, which had originally been conceived of as a way to chronicle Klein's world tour of the previous two years, but which, when it became clear that some of the images it contained were a cut above average, and had got him a book deal that was worth a hundred-thousand advance.

'Fuck me, Pete,' he said, bewildered. 'You've still got one of these?' He hadn't owned a copy of the book himself for over a decade and it was long out of print.

'Why the hell not?' Pete asked. 'That's good stuff.'

Johnny flicked through, casting a quick, critical eye over the succession of alternating black-and-white and full-colour plates. Drummer Mike Penfold, eyes all but dead, hair a mussed nest, a cig hanging from his lipstick-smeared mouth as he sat propped upright in a messy Parisian hotel bed; bassist Tim Carson, sweat-soaked and offering a fist-pump salute to so huge a crowd in the Rotterdam Ahoy that it looked more like an invading army; 1987-89, Russell Withers, rhythm guitar and keyboardist, Lee Giles in the foyer at Tokyo airport, grinning from ear to ear amid a scrum of beautiful girls.

Johnny shook his head. 'I was an amateur.'

'It sold a quarter of a million copies plus.'

Johnny slammed the book closed, his mind reeling at the thought of all the royalty payments he'd snorted up his nose. 'Only because of who I was.'

'If it had been crap, they wouldn't have published it,' Slater said.

'OK . . .' Johnny turned it over in his hands, plucking at the protective cover, which was creased and tattered along its edges. Personally, he'd never considered *Road Warriors* anything more than a coffee table book, a nice little earner on the side, but even the notoriously opinionated *Rolling Stone* had said good things about it. 'Well, I've always been a dab-hand with a camera. Ever since some groupie left her Olympus Trip on the back of a tour bus in '85 and I nicked it.'

'Yeah.' Pete arched a flame-red eyebrow. 'But what about now?'

'Look, Pete, I'm here because I'm skint. I haven't picked up a camera in years. I don't even own one anymore. I gave the last one to my daughter.'

'Doesn't matter,' Slater said, 'we'll get you some up-to-date kit.'

Johnny glanced from one to the other. 'What the hell is this?'

'I want you to do some snooping,' Pete said. 'On my behalf. And my dollar.'

'Snooping?' Johnny was incredulous. 'That's the job you're offering me, seriously?' He didn't know whether to feel disappointment or downright despair.

'Could be worth a lot to you,' Slater said.

Johnny shook his head. 'Snooping? Why me?'

'It's a bit sensitive,' Slater said.

'Which is why I want a mate doing it, someone who knows the score,' Pete explained, 'not some money-grabbing flatfoot who'll do the work but might be tempted to spill his guts for a second payday from the tabloids.'

What could be that serious?

'OK, Pete,' he ventured, 'so you know I won't try to do the dirty on you. And I can take a decent shot. Good, cool, fucking awesome. But, mate, none of that, on its own, qualifies me for work like this.'

'There's something else too.'

'You're a face,' Slater added.

Johnny gave him a sidelong look. 'Thought you just said that counted for nothing?'

'For the guy you'll be snooping around, it will.'

'Hopefully, enough for him to take you into his confidence,' Pete said.

Johnny frowned. 'I'm not doing anything illegal. I came here to see if you needed a guitarist, not 007. My life's a bag of shit as it is.'

'What if we told you this guy's scum?' Slater said. 'That he'd serve his own mother to the hangman if he saw some dough in it?'

Despite himself, Johnny was intrigued. 'Who we talking about?'

'First, are you in or out?' Pete asked.

Johnny shook his head. 'No. Don't you think I should know who he is before I decide?'

The other two exchanged glances.

'The alternative is I walk,' Johnny said. 'I'm a musician, not a secret agent.'

'OK . . .' Pete sat back on his piano stool. 'There's a reporter that's been sniffing around, trying to dig up dirt on me.'

Johnny's stomach lurched again; he hoped they weren't talking about Mona.

'You heard of Jerry Fox?'

Not Mona then. But who was Jerry Fox? He scraped around in the corners of his cranium, and a memory came to him. 'Fleet Street heavyweight?'

'The same,' Slater said. 'Been around for decades, showbiz a speciality.'

'Though these days, showbiz *exposés* are more his line,' Pete said.

Slater added clarity: 'He sells scandals to the highest bidder. And he does nicely out of it.'

Johnny almost laughed. 'And you want *me* to get to know this guy? You mean just in case he isn't already planning to reveal my tragic story to the whole world?'

Slater sighed. 'Get over yourself, Johnny. We told you: the world already knows everything about you.'

'Plus it doesn't fucking care,' Pete said. 'Washed-up performers are not news, seeing as they're ten a penny. But he'll want to know you all the same. Mainly on the basis you might have some stories for him.'

Johnny thought for a moment, and it made a twisted kind of sense. He was well-connected but also skint. Would he tell some tales for dosh? Probably.

'Be a doddle,' Slater added. 'Someone like you. You won't need to work your way in. Fox'll open the door himself. He'll never suspect you're doing us a favour.'

'And what do you want to know once I'm in there?'

Pete shrugged. 'Whatever shit he's into.'

'Why would anyone care what someone like Jerry Fox has been doing?'

'That journalistic rarity, integrity,' Slater said. 'After all that phone-hacking shit, those guttersnipes have had to clean their act up.'

'And once I've found this shit and photographed it, what're you going to do with it? Is this blackmail, Pete? Because I've told you I'm not breaking the law.'

'No, no, that's too strong a word,' Slater said. 'More a lesson that should've been taught a long time ago. It'll make a change to show Jerry Fox how it feels when someone muckrakes your past.'

'You know the new single launches in two weeks?' Pete said, his face briefly flushing with annoyance.

Pete seemed to take it for granted that Johnny *would* know. Johnny, who of course *didn't* know, having spent far too long recently stumbling around in self-absorbed stupor, literally a zombie lost in his own funereal world, could only wave a hand as if to indicate that surely everyone knew.

'I'm lined up on every TV sofa, it's gonna be massive,' Pete said.

'Congratulations.' Johnny tried not to sound bitter.

'This is when we think Fox is going to strike. He really wants to spoil the fucking party.'

'Why, just out of interest?'

Pete waved that aside. 'The usual. I'm only one of a number of A-listers who he's got in his sights. You know what Britain is today, mate? We love pulling people down. Especially those who scumbags like Fox decide have had their time in the sun.'

Johnny *did* know that. Better than Pete James could imagine. But he still wanted to know more. '*Has* he found some dirt?'

Slater cut in. 'That info's none of yours, Johnny.'

Pete shook his head. 'Let's just say a little bird's warned us he's getting very excited about a story that's going to break in about two weeks' time.'

Johnny nodded. 'Just when the single's coming out?'

'Not if you get something on Fox first,' Slater said.

Johnny pondered. It *was* still blackmail, but warning a

predator off rather than trying to crank some green out of them made it more palatable.

'How much?' he asked.

'You get something good,' Pete said. 'Something we can use . . . five grand. Cash. In your hand.'

'What if I get nothing?'

Slater snorted. 'That's unlikely.'

'Unlikely but not impossible.'

Pete turned serious. 'You don't deliver, mate, I don't pay.'

Johnny sighed. 'You see, that only works for me if we back-end the deal.'

'I don't get you.'

'The five grand will come in useful, but this whole thing's still a big risk, and to persuade me to take it, I want something else on top.'

Pete's eyebrow arched again. Even Slater looked surprised. Presumably neither of them had expected this bedraggled remnant of their old comrades to try and haggle. If Johnny was honest, he wouldn't have expected it from himself, but suddenly he knew that he couldn't leave here without progressing at least a little way back to where he needed to be.

'OK,' Pete said, 'shoot.'

'I want in.' Johnny gave a quick, tired laugh. 'It's as simple as that. You've got a good thing going here, Pete. But you're not The Whack anymore. Not The Whack everyone remembers. You bring hired guns in and out as it suits. All that matters is you know they can do a job. And, well . . . *I* can do a job better than most. You *know* that.'

There was a long, pregnant pause, Johnny's old mate never once breaking eye contact with him. 'Look, I'll tell you what,'

Pete eventually said. 'I can make a few phone calls, maybe get you a special guest gig on someone's tour. That'd be good dough, and even better exposure . . . put you back in the shop window, so to speak. But I can't *promise* anything.'

'You'll try, though? I've got your word on that?' Johnny slid his hand into his pocket and felt Elvis's tape. At that moment there was little difference between the two men, both waiting on someone else to open a door for them.

'Sure.'

It amazed Johnny that he *was* OK with that. Anyway, he reckoned this was about as good an offer as he was going to get.

'I also need some of that money up front,' he said. 'I've got two weeks to do this thing for you, but that's still two weeks. How am I going to live?'

Pete gave him a long, level stare. 'You're really that short?'

'Why do you think I've said yes? This is hardly my line, is it?'

His host considered. 'I'll give you five hundred up front. Now, do we have a deal?'

Johnny nodded, a sense of relief sinking through him. It wasn't much, but the fact he'd got something was an improvement on when he'd arrived here.

Pete turned to Slater. 'Go get the camera. By the way, Johnny, this thing goes tits up, we're denying any interest. Got it?'

'Yep, this never happened, I get it.'

Slater returned and handed Johnny a camera bag. 'Most people use their phones these days, but this one is small, and the best in low light, even at night. There's some info inside.'

Johnny raised a questioning eyebrow.

'Bit of background, where he'll be and all that. You'll need to get cracking on it too. Time isn't our friend, mate.'

'Right, Johnny-boy, we have work to do.' Pete was businesslike. 'And so do you, so if you don't mind.'

He swivelled back to the Steinway, his fingers returning to the keys.

'Sure . . . I'll be in touch.'

Johnny allowed Slater to show him from the room, but not without tapping a lazy two-fingered salute to the side of his head. Which Pete didn't even notice.

Feeling vaguely dazed, he made his way to the Chelsea Embankment and took a seat on an ornately scrolled iron bench facing the river. Thirty minutes earlier, he'd been looking for a gig in Pete's band, envisioning a return to form as an axe-swinging rock star who could tour the globe once again. And now *this*.

Anxiety hit his lungs and he breathed out hard. *Bollocks*.

The varnished leather camera bag, complete with shoulder strap, sat alongside him. He took out the camera they wanted him to use. It was a brand-new Sony and, according to Don Slater, one of the best bits of kit on the market. Unfortunately, Johnny hadn't handled a camera of any sort for at least a decade. He wasn't what you'd call a technophobe, but he'd fallen a long way behind the rest of society in recent years. Even the sheet of instructions read like a set of hieroglyphics.

He strode to the balustrade, his gaze fixed on the churning waters.

He wasn't sure whether to chuck the camera in, or himself.

Am I up to this?

In a way, it was funny. The camera was like a metaphor for this whole thing. The entire situation had hit him like a ton of flying horseshit.

And he didn't have a clue how to make the fucking thing work.

5

HOME FIRES

Wednesday

'Home is where the heart is,' Johnny told himself as he stepped down from the bus in Muswell Hill, though he couldn't help wondering, when your heart had been ripped out, did that make you homeless or completely lost forever?

He hoped it was only the former.

It was a beautiful autumn day, the sky blue, large golden leaves falling from the chestnut trees that lined the streets of this quietly affluent North London suburb. It struck him that this district had always been one of the capital's best-kept secrets. It was only a stone's throw from the hub of activity that was Highgate and Hampstead, and yet much quieter and had a warmer, more neighbourly vibe.

After he and Laura had finally parted ways – just remembering that moment, that very last argument, cut him to the bone – she had moved herself and Chelsea into her mum Susanna's pad in Muswell Hill, a smallish but elegant

Victorian-era townhouse, very smart and respectable, and located in the middle of a handsome redbrick terrace, which sloped seamlessly away down a lengthy incline. In the conversations they'd had since, Laura had assured him that walking away from her home of so many years, not to mention Johnny and the life of luxury she'd become accustomed to, had been the hardest thing she'd ever done.

'But what choice did you leave me?' she'd asked him. 'Seriously, Johnny, how could I go on living there? It was no life at all, really, was it? Not for me. And not even for you.'

He hesitated before knocking on the front door. It was true that he wanted to see them. Well, he wanted to see Laura and Chelsea (Susanna, less so), but he had an ulterior motive for calling round. The trick was not to make it look too obvious.

The house wasn't large inside, but big enough for Laura and Chelsea to stay there. It was a sad reality of the Kleins' marriage that, even before they'd officially split up, this had become Laura and Chelsea's place of refuge whenever an argument at home got out of hand. That had usually happened when he'd come home from tour, when the liggers and yes men had stopped collecting their *per diems* and the screaming that reverberated inside Johnny's head had come to a stop. Even from his earliest days, he'd struggled to return to earth after he'd been on the road. He'd found it hard to adjust to family life; shopping and school runs. He'd always excused himself by believing that he was hard-wired to live in the darkness, which now felt like an overly romantic euphemism for lying in his pit all day loafing, until the time came to drag himself out and make another ten thousand adoring souls wobbly at the knees.

Little wonder Chelsea had found her own private patch of sanity at her nan's, where she could escape their weird 'rock-star family' existence and live like the rest of her school friends.

Susanna answered the door.

She was quite trendy for a granny; a handsome cross between Joanna Lumley and Jane Fonda. For seventy-five, she kept in shape at the gym, while her white chin-length hair was coloured a dark blonde once every two weeks at Giovanni's on the high street. Her skin was still remarkably smooth, so much so that Johnny used to sit back after every Sunday lunch and play his own private game of 'hunt the scars', though whether she'd ever had any work done, he never knew, as her lush locks were always far too coiffed and tightly sprayed to see past her ears.

Looks aside, she wasn't always the best company, despite his efforts to win her over. Her self-filter seemed to be permanently switched off. That was if she had one at all where *he* was concerned. Needless to say, today she was even less impressed to see him than usual.

'Oh, it's you.' Her eyebrows knitted together in a frown. *Voldemort.*

'Erm . . . hiya, Susanna? Any chance I can speak to Laura?'

For a split second, he thought she was going to say 'no'. She seemed to be contemplating it as she stood there, regarding him with barely suppressed disdain. When she finally relented, she did so without a word, turning her back on him and heading inside, leaving him to close the door behind him. It was the second time in two days where he sensed that he was allowed in only on sufferance.

He followed her through into the kitchen, where she resumed whatever conversation she'd been having with Laura, who was seated at the table, eating toast and finishing off a cup of tea while listening to the radio news.

'I thought I might go over and see Margaret this morning,' Susanna said, as if Johnny's arrival was barely worth commenting on. 'She's not doing too well at the moment. You know, after her Tony passed?'

Johnny hovered on the threshold of the kitchen, taking in his wife, Laura, who hadn't noticed that he was here yet, and seemed to be miles away. So often in the past he'd seen Laura and her mother engage in conversations where neither of them actually seemed to be listening to the other. 'I've got the washing machine man booked in for eleven,' she replied. 'Then I'm going to see Doctor Healey. I can't have another night like that. Honestly, I haven't felt like this for years.'

'You've got a visitor, by the way.' Her mother threw her head in his direction without bothering to look at him.

Laura glanced up. Sheepishly, he waved from the doorway.

She put her mug down, her green eyes flashing in surprise and with what Johnny hoped was a touch of warmth. 'To what do we owe this pleasure?'

'I, erm, well . . .' He could hardly tell them the real reason. 'I can pop round and see you and Chelsea now and then, can't I?'

'Not at this time on a school morning, no. You remember that, surely? You know, school . . . Monday to Friday and all the days in between?' He allowed her comment to sail over his head while a car horn honked outside. She stood up. 'That'll be Sharon.'

Johnny had some vague memory that Chelsea's best friend at school was called Julie, and that her mum's name was Sharon.

'It's her turn for the school run this morning,' Laura explained as she bustled out. 'Mum, take some of those cakes you made over to Margaret . . . Chelsea won't eat them.' She called up the stairs: 'Chelsea! You've pushed it to the limit again! Come on, Sharon's here!'

Chelsea came pelting downstairs, in her uniform, school bag slung over her shoulder. Each day she resembled her mother more closely: green eyes, perfect smile, her brown hair inclined to fly all over the place when she was in a rush. She also had that perfect peaches-and-cream teenage complexion.

She stopped at the bottom of the stairs. 'Dad! What're you doing here?'

He shrugged, grinned. 'No reason particularly. I just, you know . . . thought I'd drop by.'

'Sorry, gotta rush. Bye!' Chelsea grabbed the lapels of his jacket and pulled herself up on tiptoes to kiss his stubbled cheek.

She hurtled out. He followed her, stopping in the front doorway, seeing a silver-grey Volvo estate idling at the kerb. Chelsea waved again to him as she scurried across the pavement and leapt in.

'See you,' he said quietly as the car pulled away.

Laura appeared alongside him. 'You'd better come back inside. We don't want the neighbours talking, do we?'

Fuck the neighbours. But he kept the thought to himself as he followed her in.

Susanna seemed to be on her way out as well, neatly folding herself into a coat as she stood in the hall. Though she'd mentioned visiting someone called Margaret, he doubted she'd been planning to go this early in the day.

'Hope your friend's OK, Susanna,' he said as she strode past.

She nodded curtly but made no response. She was well-practised at being cold as ice.

As the front door slammed behind her, he wandered into the kitchen again.

Laura stood with back turned, engaged in the washing-up. Capital Radio was on in the background. Susanna always had the radio on first thing in the morning, though he doubted he would ever be on her playlist again.

'Nice welcome from Susanna,' he said.

Laura didn't look round. 'Don't start. What do you expect, Johnny? She's not going to welcome you with open arms. I mean, she had a ringside seat for everything that happened. Plus, she's the only person I can share anything with, so she knows all our guilty secrets.'

'How long's she going to keep this up for?' He pulled a stool out from under the breakfast bar. 'I know she's got me down as the villain, but if *we* can move on, why can't she?'

Laura sighed as she towelled her hands dry, her face softening. 'The kettle's hot . . . do you want a cuppa or something?'

'Please, yeah . . . just a quick one, though. I've got to see a man about a dog.'

She glanced around uncertainly. Johnny had always used that phrase when he'd felt confident about some new development in his career. It was probably the last thing she'd expected to hear from him a couple of days after he'd lost his home. *Their* home. 'What's going on? Have you got a gig?'

Johnny glanced at the floor, fleetingly avoiding eye contact. 'Not exactly, got more chance of winning the lottery. Past my sell-by date. But something . . . It'll pay anyway.'

'OK . . . so?' she persisted. 'Have you got something or not?'

'Yeah, I have.' He nodded. 'But it's early days yet and it's best I keep it under wraps.'

'Something's better than nothing, I suppose.' She handed him a steaming mug. 'I knew you'd get something. It's not like you're not brilliant at what you do. At least you're not just sitting around. I always said that, if life's not coming for you, you have to use your initiative . . . go and get it.'

'I know, I know.'

'Look, what about getting the band back together? Have you thought any more about it?'

'Yes, I have thought about it, and no, I'm not doing it. Those nostalgia tours are for . . .' Johnny couldn't bring himself to say it, so Laura helped him out.

'Losers? Come off it, they're for bands who want to carry on doing what they love, playing to their loyal fans. All the old bands are doing it. It's your job, and you could earn good money. It's not like we don't need it.'

He held a palm up. 'Look, I'm sorry, Laura, I've just' – he swallowed a mouthful of hot, sweet tea – 'had enough of these self-help book clichés today. I don't mean any offence, but Pete's full of stuff like that and—'

She frowned. 'You've been to see Pete? Pete James?'

'Him and Don, yeah.'

'Don! Christ, I hate that fella. He's always given me the creeps.'

'Sometimes you've got to deal with the Devil.'

'Is that the gig? You're going back on the road with Pete?'

Johnny tried not to look evasive. He was being more than economical with the truth here, but he couldn't stand the idea of Laura considering him a loser.

'I went round to see them,' he said.

'And?'

'I heard Pete was putting a band together for a new album. I told him I'm up for it . . .' He trailed off. A bare-faced lie would never get past Laura; she knew all his vulnerabilities and could read him like a book. Instead, he hedged and dodged, hoping she'd drop the subject.

Laura, probably knowing how hard it had been for him to lose Mill Hill, and sensing he'd shut down if she pushed too hard, obliged.

'How did the house handover go?' she asked, her tone sympathetic.

He shrugged again. 'Oh, you know . . .' He took another slurp of tea. 'Fucking awful. But I've got to get straight somehow, haven't I? That's why I sold it lock, stock and barrel. Every picture, every television . . . even the kettle.'

'At least we're in the clear now, no more bailiffs or embarrassing court cases.'

'Yeah. No debt.'

She tried to be philosophical. 'Well, at least it's out of the way. A clean slate.'

He laughed mirthlessly, remembering Mona's almost identical words. He couldn't really argue with any of it, but neither could he express how he felt about it. The full reality of his loss hadn't even started soaking in.

'Yeah, new beginnings and all,' he said. 'Look, at the weekend, do you mind if I come *here* to see Chelsea? My new place is, well . . . I need a bit more time to straighten it out.'

Laura frowned, but after a pause nodded. 'I suppose that's OK. Where are you staying?'

'I've got a little flat down Brick Lane. It's nice, but I need to get it smartened up.'

'You know Chelsea won't ever judge you?'

'I know.' *But you might.* He still hadn't got used to the idea that he was basically squatting in someone else's attic. The mere thought that Chelsea might discover that truth was too awful to contemplate. 'But it would still be better if I could come here. Just till I've knocked it into shape.'

Laura smiled. 'I'm sure I can get Mum out of the way.'

Thank God for that, he thought, feeling a moment of solidarity with Laura.

Their eyes met in a flash of mutual understanding – the first in quite a while. On its own, that almost made the torturous journey up here during rush hour worth it, though he had another reason for popping round.

'Gotta hit the road, anyway,' he said, standing. 'You can always call me.'

Laura shook her head. 'On that crappy old phone. In the twenty-first century, Johnny? Whenever I try you, it's always switched off or you don't answer.'

He shrugged. 'I always call you back. Mind if I use the loo?'

She rolled her eyes. 'Sure.' Then took his used mug to the sink.

He trotted quickly upstairs. Not that he actually needed the loo.

Halting at the top, he wondered if he was doing the right thing here. It had been ridiculously dozy of him to not realise that, this being a weekday morning, Chelsea wouldn't be around. And he couldn't go off now and come back to see her this evening. Laura would detect that he was up to something and ask some harder questions. He didn't like going behind his daughter's back, but he couldn't make any progress in his new job if he didn't sort his camera issue out.

He glanced downstairs to ensure there was no sign of Laura in the hall, then crossed the landing and entered Chelsea's bedroom.

Immediately, he was transfixed by an age-old poster of the band, as they'd been in their Eighties pomp, on the wall over her neatly made bed. As usual, he stood centre stage, powdered and eyelinered, his black hair slicked into a huge Tommy Steele quiff, wearing his trademark leather. The poster was ancient, frayed around the edges, dog-eared at the corners, but to see it taking pride of place in his daughter's bedroom put a lump in his throat. The rest of the room was much as he'd have expected for a fifteen-year-old girl. Posters depicting more modern artists, the likes of Taylor Swift and Harry Styles, hung everywhere. There was a scattering of books and fashion magazines on the floor, make-up on the dresser, the odd soft toy on the bed. The air carried a combined whiff of perfume and hairspray. But there in the middle of it, enshrined almost, these figures from an earlier era, an unknown one where most modern kids were concerned. Particularly the ghost of himself in the middle, who could surely only be present in this place because any feelings held about him far transcended the forgotten songs and outdated imagery.

He shook off the melancholy that threatened to descend and reminded himself to focus on the job in hand.

Hurriedly, he scanned the room, mainly the shelves, and with almost indecent speed, spotted what he'd come for: the Leica M6 camera on Chelsea's bedside table. He'd given it to her a couple of years ago, seemingly as a gift because he knew she was interested in photography, though mainly because things were careering out of control by then, and at least he knew it would be safe with her.

He picked it up, pleased to see that it was in good working order; she'd clearly been putting it to use. The thought gave him a brief pang of guilt, but he told himself it wasn't like he was stealing it. In purely technical terms, the Sony he removed from his jacket pocket wasn't a fair trade. The Sony was the Jaguar XE of the camera world, while the old Leica was the equivalent of a battered old Citroën DS. But that made it perfect for a dinosaur like him.

He placed the Sony on the table, pocketed the Leica and gratefully grabbed a couple of reels of unused film sitting by the camera case.

'Johnny, you OK?' Laura called up from below.

He froze, dreading the sound of her feet ascending the staircase. He crept to the doorway, listening, and then risked peeking out. The top of the staircase was visible, though he couldn't see down into the hall.

'Fine,' he replied, stealthily crossing the landing to the open bathroom, flushing the toilet and swiftly making his way down. She was still in the kitchen, putting things away.

He watched her; her brown hair was pulled off her face in a ponytail and loose strands had fallen around her face. She'd always had an unaffected beauty about her – the hot girl next door. He sighed, thinking what he'd have wanted to do if they'd had the house to themselves before. Little chance of that now, he suspected, though he was tempted to try.

She turned to him with a small smile, 'I know what you're thinking.'

He shrugged. 'Can't blame me, Laura. You're looking good.'

She glanced at him. 'I'm not made of stone, Johnny, but that would just make things worse.'

He knew she was right. It was what had held them together for so long, that and the fact he didn't think he could ever love anyone the way he loved her. He felt the familiar ache, which she must have sensed too.

'We're still a family, Johnny.'

'Yeah. Of sorts. Look, I should go. Tell Chelsea I'll be here at the weekend.'

Laura watched Johnny turn and walk down the passage, and in a voice Johnny hadn't heard for so long, called after him.

'I'll look forward to it.'

All the feelings were still there between them, he knew they were. They'd been too tightly interwoven for so many years – both as husband and wife, as lovers, as best mates. But it was impossible now. Things had changed; life had moved on.

Johnny threw a glance back over his shoulder and pulled on the brass knocker, closing the door. Outside, the October air felt chilly and he huddled into his jacket. Looking up to the grey sky, he felt the weight of the planet on his shoulders.

6

MENTOR

Wednesday

'Dad?' Chelsea looked genuinely startled, which was hardly a surprise. Johnny was probably the last person she'd expected to see waiting for her at the school gates. 'Twice in one day?'

'Erm, yeah . . .' He aimed for nonchalance. 'How was it? Your day?'

'Boring, same as always.' She hovered there warily, her bag slipping from her shoulder, dangling by her side.

Herds of other kids pushed past, shouting, laughing, shoving each other, all the usual horseplay. Thankfully, the fact they were under eighteen meant that his appearance in their midst was no big deal. None of them seemed to recognise him. It would have been a different story twenty years ago, but Chelsea still looked worried by his presence here.

'Why do you want to know?' she asked.

He shrugged. 'A dad can make conversation with his

daughter, can't he? We didn't really get a chance to talk this morning and I thought I'd pop by as I was in the area.'

'You were in the area?' She couldn't conceal her scepticism. Not that she was trying to. 'Since when?'

'Chelsea, cut me a bit of slack for fuck's sake? I just want a chat.'

She considered that for several seconds, then seemed to relax a little and nodded across the road to a café called Artisan Roastery. 'You can buy me a gingerbread latte,' she said.

He smiled, relieved he had a few bob in his pocket at least. 'Yeah . . . all right.'

She walked out through the gate, making some vague hand signal to the silver-grey Volvo parked in the pick-up zone on the other side of the road, which doubtless contained Julie and her mum, Sharon, and then crossed over towards the shop. Johnny followed, halting only to let the Volvo swing out into the traffic and cruise past him, a curious schoolgirl face regarding him from its back seat.

As coffee bars went, this one ached hipster cool: lots of plants, box-crate tables, shelves lined with jars of exotic-looking beans, beanie-hatted customers sipping oat lattes with designer dachshunds at their feet.

'Make sure you get it with cinnamon sprinkled on top,' Chelsea said as they queued at the counter.

Johnny nodded, got them both a drink, and they found a table in a quiet corner, where they sat down and faced each other.

'First of all, I've got to come clean about the fact I nicked your camera this morning,' he said.

Chelsea blew out a cloud of cinnamon froth. '*What?*'

'Well . . . "traded it" is a more accurate term.'

She looked perplexed. 'Dad? I don't have a clue what you're talking about.'

'I've taken your Leica – that old second-hand one I gave you. And in its place, I've left a Sony. Fair exchange, wouldn't you say?'

Chelsea who, for all her tender years, was well-used to the domestic absurdities of living with rock and roll parents, gave him a teenage eye-roll. At least she wasn't angry, he thought.

'Well . . . no,' she finally said. 'Not really. The Sony's probably worth a lot more.'

He spread his palms in a magnanimous gesture. 'Least I could do.'

'How did you afford a brand-new camera, Dad?'

'Oh, you'd be amazed at some of the favours I can call in.'

There it was again, that old rock-star bravado, which had got him precisely nowhere.

'Yeah, you're right. I *would* be amazed. You know, if you wanted your old one back, you only had to ask, Dad.'

He wasn't going to tell her the real reason he needed the old one. 'It was *yours*. I *gave* it to you. And now, well, I've given you a new one . . . a better one.'

'OK, cool.' Chelsea sat back, looking pleased. 'Thanks. I can't wait to try it out.'

He smiled. 'Thought you'd like it.'

Johnny shifted uncomfortably in his seat. It had never really entered his head to give his daughter any kind of present. Not for its own sake. *I'll make it up to her*, he told himself, *as soon as I'm back on my feet.*

'So?' she asked. 'What are we doing this weekend?'

'Well . . . here's the thing. If it's OK with you, I'm going
to pop round and see you at your grandma's this weekend.'

'Oh.'

'The new place isn't quite ready yet.'

'OK, well . . .'

She looked disappointed, but not quite as disappointed
as he'd expected. Chelsea was a streetwise kid in so many
ways. How could she not be after the life she'd led at Mill
Hill, with her mum and dad squabbling over the least little
thing? He suspected she knew that his reluctance to entertain her at his new place this coming weekend was unlikely
to be because the new place 'wasn't quite ready'. But she
was already mature enough to know that it was better not
to ask too many questions.

'How's it going at school, love?'

Chelsea shrugged. 'All right, I suppose.'

Johnny could tell she was holding something back. 'No
one's pushing you around, are they? If they are, I'll . . .'

Chelsea rolled her eyes at him. 'No, Dad, nothing like that.
Well not really . . . everyone knows who you are, though.'

They always do.

'I miss my friends, that's all, from Chase Lodge School.'

Johnny winced. Chelsea had been to one of the best
schools that money could buy near their home in Mill Hill.
Now, to clear their debts, they had been forced to pull her
out, and Chelsea was now attending the local comprehensive in Muswell Hill.

'I'm sorry, darling. I promise it won't be forever. Just
until I'm straight again.'

Chelsea didn't meet his eyes with her own. 'Yeah, you
said before.'

'Julie seems nice.'

'She is. Can we talk about something else?'

'Yeah, course, love.' They sipped their coffee and chatted a little longer. Chelsea moved the subject onto safer territory, towards trivial stuff: pop stars, the idiot boys in her class. Johnny inhaled the normality of it, feeling her words wash over him; steadying him, softening the ruffles on his frayed nerves.

'Julie's parents are going to the Dolomites for Christmas this year. What are we doing, are you coming to Nan's?'

'Eh?' Johnny was brought back from his reverie.

'Christmas?'

'It's a bit early for that. Shouldn't you be focusing on your O levels?'

'O Levels? Dad, you know I'm only fifteen?'

'Well, yeah . . . course. I guess they don't call them that anymore?'

'Not since the Stone Age.'

Reaching to change the subject again, and to get her off the topic of Christmas, he was about to suggest ordering another round of coffees, but then remembered the cost in this place. Only a day had passed since his meeting with Pete and Don, and that few hundred quid was already diminishing at a rate of knots. Besides, Chelsea kept glancing at her phone. He suspected it was less a case of there being more interesting conversations going on there, more a need to keep an eye on the time. This wasn't the latchkey existence he'd known back when he was running round Finsbury Park in drainpipe jeans. A kid was late home from school these days and people got worried, usually with good reason.

'Perhaps we should make a move, eh love?' he said.

Chelsea nodded. And again, she was polite enough not to look relieved.

They left the café, stopping to chat a little longer on the pavement.

'You know I love you, Chelsea. And your mum. Even Nan,' he said, shoving his hands into his jacket pockets because he didn't know what else to do with them.

'Course I do.'

She hugged him and he hugged her back, holding on a little longer than was strictly necessary.

'I'm sorry things are the way they are,' he said. 'But I mean it this time, I'm going to fix everything, OK?'

Though these words were as honest and heartfelt as he could muster, he knew inside that it was a lie. He couldn't fix the one thing in her life that was *really* broken: her parents' marriage.

Chelsea pulled away gently, giving her dad a reassuring smile.

'I'll see you on Saturday, then?' he said.

'Don't forget!' She shouldered her bag.

'I won't . . .' He diverted his gaze along the street to where a bus was approaching. 'Looks like my ride. Oh . . . how're *you* going to get home? Your lift's already gone.'

She waved it away. 'I'll be fine. I'll call Mum and she'll pick me up.'

After saying a final goodbye, and lost in thought, Johnny found himself a seat on the lower deck, installing himself amid a gaggle of everyday Londoners, most looking tired and grumpy after another tough day in the office or the factory or the shop, only a couple stealing puzzled sidelong glances at him as if they couldn't quite believe they were in the presence of rock and roll royalty. Even then, Johnny was too preoccupied to notice. All he could think about was how bewildering it was that each new day felt somehow worse than the one before. Half a week had passed since his home had been repossessed and still, it seemed, he was headed on a downward trajectory.

It was early evening when Johnny got off the bus near Brick Lane, the journey back having passed in a flash, with too much on his mind to let in his paranoia at being spotted.

Another day all but gone. It was nagging at him now that he hadn't exactly used his time wisely since he'd left Pete and Don yesterday morning, but it was a struggle to believe that he genuinely owed those guys anything. If they really thought him capable of doing the job they'd given him, why would they only have paid him five hundred quid up front? If they didn't trust him to play guitar and sing – two things he was actually *good* at – why would they trust him with something he had no experience of? It was all a bit nuts when he thought about it.

As he cut towards Brick Lane through a side alley, he could already smell the spices on the air, the curry and coriander, the tandoori cooking in clay ovens. It was Wednesday evening, after all. The hump of the week was past; the downhill rush to the weekend had begun. Business would be picking up, and indeed, as he approached the end of the alley, he heard the hubbub of that ever-thronging East London artery.

Then he heard something above the usual soundtrack of drinkers and would-be dinners on a big night out.

It stopped him in his tracks.

He glanced right along the narrow passage running behind the nearest row of restaurants. There were bins and bulging rubbish sacks all the way along it. But something else too.

The strains of 'Lonesome Tonight' drifted towards him, the plaintive question of whether someone was sorry they had drifted apart, cutting through the soundtrack of Brick Lane.

It was a solo voice, but the words floated towards him in a harmonious melody.

Johnny shook his head in disbelief. That couldn't be . . . ? Surely not?

He ventured along the entry, passing the open gates to several rear yards. The atmosphere was now richly aromatic, but this was also the functional side of the cuisine miracle, the yards crammed with further sacks of stinky refuse, the kitchen windows smeary with heat, the burly staff who came in and out wearing uniform jeans, white T-shirts and stained aprons, carrying more cartons of disposables, dumping them down unceremoniously.

But the harmonious singing persisted.

'Elvis . . . is that you?' Johnny said under his breath. *Surely fucking not.*

It was so soulful, so gentle on the ear, and yes, so tuneful.

It wasn't perfect, but . . .

He came to the fourth yard on the row, which corresponded with the rear of Graceland itself. It was partly occupied by an old brick washhouse on the right, the door to which stood wide open. Johnny couldn't resist peeking inside.

Zipped neatly into a black Cisco Kid jumpsuit, Ravi

81

stood with his back turned, facing a blank wall as he worked his way through several pages of sheet-music.

'Elvis, mate!' Johnny blurted.

Ravi spun around, startled; his pages cascaded to the floor.

'Sing that again,' Johnny said, entering.

For several seconds, Ravi seemed so surprised and embarrassed that he'd been overheard that he didn't know where to look. His eyes were everywhere except on Johnny. He even fluffed his attempts to pick up the sheet music, dropping it all over the place again.

'Go on, mate, sing it,' Johnny urged him.

'Which part?'

'All of it. Take it from the top.'

The guy grabbed his music up, but then shook his head sadly. 'I can't, you see. Not now you're watching me.'

He still wouldn't look up, and now Johnny had his first inkling of the problem.

'You're saying you can't do it when you've got an audience?'

Ravi nodded despondently.

Johnny pondered that. It wasn't an unusual thing in his experience. Many wannabe artists in the past, particularly singers, had failed to make the grade because they couldn't perform in front of spectators. Even an audience of one put the fear of God into them.

Though that couldn't be the case with Ravi here.

'You were singing in the restaurant,' Johnny pointed out.

'That's different.' Ravi gave a self-conscious laugh. 'The people there come to hear me because I'm bad.'

'But you can see there's nothing to be nervous about?

Everyone loves you. You get a standing ovation every time you sing.'

Ravi shrugged. 'They know me as a laugh, you see.' He shuffled his sheet music, taking pains to get it into the right order. 'A bit of a clown.'

'I wouldn't go that far—'

'Don't get me wrong – they like me for it. The Major says it's what makes me unique.'

Johnny nodded. 'Well, he's not wrong there. But now I understand why he thinks you've got something – because you have.'

He wasn't being 100 per cent truthful. In the age of *The X Factor* and *Britain's Got Talent*, so many people thought they had what it took to get up there and do a Susan Boyle. It was no wonder they were often crushed when faced with a hard dose of reality. In this business it wasn't about having a genuinely good voice, it was about having an *amazing* talent.

Elvis Sharma didn't occupy such a lofty perch, no one around here had realised it, but he *did* have something.

Immediately though, a bolt of frustration went through him.

Did he really have the time to coach someone through the twists and turns of performing live? Just as quickly, a voice in his head asked him what other urgent business he had to attend to. He had a job of sorts, yes, which he hadn't even started yet, but that had never been likely to keep him busy every hour of the day.

'Look, Elvis,' he said. 'I'd like to help you out . . . and maybe I can. Show you some tricks for calming the waters before you go onstage . . . relaxing your vocal cords. Basic stuff.'

Hope visibly surged in Ravi's face, but he fought it away. 'Would you really do that for me, Johnny?'

'I'm not talking nine-till-five. Maybe I can find an hour here and there? What do you think?'

Ravi suddenly seemed too flustered to speak properly. 'You *would*?'

'I can't promise anything but I can definitely put you through your paces. Smooth off any rough edges. Because we've all got a few, you know?'

Ravi nodded vigorously. 'I think I have more than a few.'

Not as many as I thought, Johnny told himself.

'But any help would be good!'

'Johnny!' It was Mona. She sounded as though she was calling from the restaurant. 'Did I just see you coming in?'

'Won't be a sec,' Johnny shouted. He turned back to Ravi. 'I've got to go.'

'I'm so grateful,' Ravi replied, his eyes glistening with emotion, and he grabbed Johnny in a rib-cracking bearhug. 'More grateful than I can say!'

'*Johnny?*'

'Don't be too grateful, mate.' Johnny gently disentangled himself. 'Not yet anyway.'

As he went back out into the yard, he wasn't sure that had been the most sensible promise he'd ever made. Could he teach anyone anything these days? Technically speaking, his credentials were impeccable. But how much of it did he actually have left? He didn't know the answer, but maybe that was part of the reason he'd agreed to give the young wannabe a few pointers. To remind himself he'd once had what it took; and give himself something he could aim for, something connected to the talent that once had propelled him to the top of the charts again and again. He was Johnny Klein, wasn't he?

Yeah, maybe it was time to drag himself out of this ragged hand-to-mouth existence and actually start living again.

7

TAKING CARE OF BUSINESS

Wednesday

'Why are you coming in the back way?' Mona asked, meeting Johnny in the doorway connecting the restaurant's kitchen to the backyard.

He hadn't seen her since yesterday, and he had to cover up a double take, as she was looking particularly attention-grabbing today. Her lips ruby-red, her bobbed hair so black it was gleaming. Snug in tight leather jeans, her tasselled jacket worn over a tight T-shirt, she was the very definition of a rock chick.

He shrugged. 'When I went out this morning, well . . . the word seems to have travelled that I'm here.'

That much was true, at least. No sooner had he stepped out that morning than he'd spotted the front window of the newspaper shop opposite, where a huge poster of him and the band had been stuck up with strips of Sellotape. In that same moment the owner of the Prince of Bengal, the establishment next door, had hurried out into the street, grabbing Johnny by the arms and pumping both his hands. 'Johnny Klein,' he'd beamed. 'Welcome to the East End!'

None of it had bothered Johnny hugely, not when he had so many other troubles, but he wasn't always in the mood for such adulation.

'Uncle Rishi, I'm afraid,' Mona said, leading him in through the busy kitchen. 'He's such a fan, I knew he wouldn't be able to keep his mouth shut for long. To make up for it, he's got something nice lined up for us tonight. Foodwise, I mean.'

Johnny's gut rumbled. He hadn't eaten all day.

They slid into a booth, facing each other, and no sooner had they settled than the Major appeared alongside them, smartly dressed in his maître d' outfit. Next to him stood an equally dapper waiter, carrying a tray of Indian food which they proceeded to serve up, bowl after delicious bowl.

Johnny's mouth watered, but again he was humbled by the hospitality on show.

'You know you don't have to do this . . . feed me so well, I mean,' he said.

'Not a bit of it.' The Major waved the protest aside. 'Mona's friend is my friend.'

'Don't look a gift horse in the mouth, Johnny,' Mona said, spooning herself sizeable portions of curry and rice, and tearing off a generous chunk of Peshwari naan. 'This won't last forever.'

'I was thinking, Johnny,' the Major said. 'Can I call you Johnny? I feel like we know each other now . . . I was thinking, if you like the dish, we can do a one-night-only "Johnny Klein Special". Only if you like it, of course.

Look . . . I'll leave you two now, but please let me know what you think.'

Plenty of other customers were taking their seats in the restaurant, and the Major bustled off to greet them.

'He means well, you know,' Mona said. 'He thinks you're besties now.'

The first couple of mouthfuls Johnny sampled were heaven on a fork. 'As long as he serves up nosh like this, he can be my bestie forever.'

'So, how did your meeting with Pete James go?' She eyed him with interest. 'I haven't seen you since you went over to Chelsea.'

He hesitated. 'Well . . . it was productive.'

'And . . . ?' She waited for more.

'We're working on something.' He continued eating, trying to shut the conversation down.

She looked puzzled by his evasion, possibly smelling a rat. 'Why can't you tell me?'

'Look, can we change the subject, Mona?' he snapped, instantly regretting the words when he saw their effect on her. But at this point, he couldn't bring himself to admit that he was now Pete's (barely) paid snoop, rather than securing the real lifeline he'd been hoping for.

He softened. 'I'm sorry, Mona. It's been a shitty week. When there's something to tell, you'll be the first to know, all right?'

She nodded, but her smile had gone. 'Whatever, Johnny.'

It was a timely intervention indeed when the Major called everyone's attention to the stage, where Ravi was about to cut loose with his nightly repertoire. With minimum preamble, but after another typically fulsome intro from his number one fan, and a quick salute thrown in the direction of Johnny and Mona's table, Ravi went straight into 'Trouble'. The number had been the real Elvis's seminal moment in *King Creole*, a showstopper in movie and music history, and it was being sacrificed and hung out to dry by Elvis Sharma, who, now that he was back in front of an audience, had reverted to the excitable 'bash it out there' caricature that the regulars around here had come to expect.

Mona, for one, was already clapping along.

'I don't suppose you know a London-based journo called Jerry Fox?' Johnny asked her. 'An old Fleet Street hack. Not really part of your scene, but you know the type . . . been doing it too long, no friends and all that?'

Mona raised one of her eyebrows. 'Just about.'

Johnny could tell she was holding back. 'Come on. I've said I'm sorry.'

She relented. 'Everyone knows Jerry Fox. He's a legend. Not always for the right reasons, though.'

'No?'

She picked up some naan, dipped it and nibbled. 'He's just . . . well, he's a bit dodgy. Would sell nude pix of his own wife to get a story. If he still had a wife, that is.'

Johnny mulled this over.

'Any particular reason you want to know?' she wondered. 'Or am I not allowed to ask about that either?'

He ladled himself some more curry, ignoring the barb. 'It's just that his name came up in conversation . . . you know, nothing particularly interesting.'

She gave him a long, level stare. 'This isn't something to do with Pete and Don, is it?'

He didn't return the look. 'Does it matter? I'm just asking if you know the guy.'

'You really don't want to get in with Jerry Fox, Johnny. Not someone as vulnerable as you.'

That nettled him a little. 'Vulnerable?'

'If he'd been doing what he does now back in the Eighties, he'd have hauled you over the tabloid coals. And that's when you were a hotshot. Christ knows what he'd do to you now.'

They locked gazes, challenging each other.

'Where can I get in touch with him?' Johnny broke first.

'Are you seriously not listening to anything I'm saying?' Mona's previous good humour had evaporated completely.

'Mona . . .' he lowered his voice, 'I'm on the fucking basement floor here. No one who matters gives a shit what I'm doing these days.'

'So why do you want to contact Jerry Fox?'

'You've already guessed the answer to that.'

'Don and Pete?' She shook her head. 'They've got you gofering for them in some way?'

Johnny forked a piece of chicken into his mouth. Delicious though it was, he rapidly felt he was losing his taste for it.

'Seriously, Don the wanker?' Mona said. 'This is the job Pete promised you?'

'Work is work and if there's a few quid in it, I'm interested.'

'But what do they want and how much is he paying? Did you even ask?'

'Give me some credit, eh?' That came out louder than he'd intended; he lowered his voice again. He knew she was right, and it was rattling him. He also wasn't used to being on the backfoot with Mona. The dynamics between them had changed and he was struggling to adjust. 'Mona, you and the Major are doing me a favour and I'm grateful, but that's not going to help me get back on my feet, is it?'

Her expression softened; and he saw a glimpse of the fan-girl she could never entirely ditch, the one that let him get away with things.

'Look . . . it's not just the cash.' He laid his fork down. 'It's a way back in. Potentially.'

'Potentially?'

'Potentially is bloody better than nothing.'

She sighed and sat back. 'He works for *Maxi* magazine. It's based in the Reuters news building. It's on Canary Wharf, not too far from our own office. Most nights he goes to a press club called the Hole in the Wall. You know that place? Near Blackfriars Bridge.'

He shook his head. 'Last time I looked, you guys were all on Fleet Street.'

'Jesus, Johnny, those days are long gone. Look . . .' she leaned forward, 'the Hole in the Wall is one of those "press badge only" joints. It's filled with dinosaurs who can't get used to the idea that life's different these days, that brown people live in Britain, that women aren't just there to flash their tits and model lingerie.'

'But *you* don't mind going in?'

'Goes with the journo territory, doesn't it? But I avoid it.'

'Fancy going there tonight? Maybe taking me along as a guest? It'd be helping me get off first base.'

She groaned. 'Johnny, no disrespect, but I hate those people. Besides, they'd eat us both for breakfast.'

'I wouldn't be too sure of that. I've been around myself, you know, and it's not like I'm gonna try to make friends with the geezer.'

She gave him another long stare. 'What are you up to? Do you really need any more trouble at this moment in your life?'

'No, but I *do* need cash. You've said it yourself, these freebies won't last forever.'

She sighed again, shaking her head. Eventually, and reluctantly, she dug into her handbag, taking out what looked like a pile of mail and setting it on the table alongside her, and then producing a small leather wallet, which she pushed towards him. He flipped it open and saw a laminated press card.

'There, I barely get asked for it these days,' she said. 'But you can't hold out on me forever, I'll find out what's going on eventually.'

He looked at the card again. Mona's photo was on it, but he might be able to conceal that. It ought to see him through.

'Some mail for you, by the way.' She pushed the heap of envelopes across.

Johnny arched an eyebrow. 'It came here?'

'Hardly. I swung by Mill Hill earlier today. Told them you'd asked me to. Good job too. We're lucky that Dave What's His Name was there. Him and his missus are off on holiday from tomorrow. Cruising to New Orleans and Mexico, would you believe. Five weeks at sea.'

Johnny picked through the deliveries almost gingerly, mainly seeing bank notices, council headed letters and way too many unopened red bills. They might have paid off their big creditors, but there were still quite a few left. He might as well bin the lot.

'Thanks, just what I need right now.'

He glanced up at Mona, who, presumably out of politeness, was affording him what privacy she could by turning in her seat to watch Elvis. He was halfway through 'Hound Dog', his body shaking like a southern preacher about to bestow another miracle on his flock.

Johnny pushed the pile around in the hope it might magically disappear, but was surprised to spot an actual, honest-to-goodness letter. The white embossed envelope was crisp and clean, while his name and address had been written by an elegant hand, in expensive-looking black ink.

Wiping his orange-stained lips on his pink napkin, he peeled the envelope open. Inside, there was a small handwritten note.

> Hey Johnny,
> It's been a while. Could you give me a call. I don't have a number for you, and it's urgent.
> Jackie

A mobile phone number was written at the bottom, next to a row of three kisses.

Jackie . . .

Johnny's thoughts raced as he chewed the soft skin on the inside of his mouth. He barely noticed the applause erupting around him as Ravi reached the end of his number.

'Wow!' Mona said, sitting down again after standing and clapping. 'He really went for it that time. No one can say he doesn't give it everything.'

Johnny re-read the note again.

'Hello?' Mona said. 'Earth to Johnny?'

Distractedly, he tucked the letter back into its envelope.

Mona looked bemused. 'You just inherited a million quid or something?'

'No . . . I wish. Sorry, Mona . . . gotta make a call.' He nodded towards the bar, at the end of which an old-fashioned Bakelite phone was clipped to the wall. 'Think I can use the bar phone?'

'Suppose so.'

Mona watched curiously as Johnny left the table and made his way across the dining room, weaving between the tables and chairs. What was he up to? In truth, there was a lot about Johnny Klein that she didn't know, but from what she'd seen the last couple of years, he was often his own worst enemy. Now, having lost everything that mattered to him, it was no surprise that he was ready to grab at any straw he could. Which was why this business with Jerry Fox had her worried. Grabbing at that particular straw would be like playing Russian roulette with a loaded gun. Not for the first time, Mona felt the need to protect Johnny from himself.

Johnny had now slotted himself behind the bar and jammed the heavy receiver under his chin. Holding the letter in front of him, he studiously dialled the number.

'Mona, my lovely!' the Major exclaimed, sliding into the booth alongside her. 'How excellent was Ravi? There's nothing better in this world than Elvis in full flow . . . in his full glory.'

Mona smiled. Her uncle's enthusiasm for his protégé was

infectious, but as a serious member of the music press she couldn't get too carried away by someone who, though he threw himself into his act body and soul, was still only a passionate amateur.

'He's certainly on form today, Uncle Rishi,' she agreed.

'I know, I know. It's a thing of beauty . . . to see him TCB-ing it.'

'Eh?'

'TCB, Taking Care of Business.'

'Ah . . . OK.' She smiled, and turned her head to see how Johnny was doing. He was still on the phone, now deep in conversation.

The Major moved in that bit closer, leaning against his niece so that he could whisper.

'Mona, you know me, I hate to push . . . but has Johnny had any luck with that tape I gave him? Apparently, he's going to give Ravi some one-to-one tuition, which is marvellous, but he didn't mention anything about the tape. Do you know whether he's played it for anyone yet? Because we're obviously all impatient to take things to the next stage.'

'I don't know.' Mona took her uncle by his soft hand. 'Look . . . if Johnny's said he'll help Ravi out, then he'll do it, I'm sure. But he has things in his own life to sort out too. If you want my opinion, we should all give him a bit of space.'

'I understand that, I do. But Ravi's very excited. He really thinks things are going to happen. That's why he went for it so hard tonight.'

Way to go, Johnny. She hoped he hadn't made Ravi an empty promise. One of his specialities.

'It's probably best if we don't give Ravi any guarantees at the moment,' she said. 'You know it's a tough business and you only gave it to Johnny yesterday. If he has any luck with the demos, I'm sure you'll be the first to know.'

She looked at her uncle again; he was watching her with the intensity of an eager but worried puppy. 'Look . . . if you can give us some privacy when he gets off the phone,' she glanced towards the bar, 'perhaps I can . . .'

Her words ran out.

The green Bakelite phone was back on its cradle, the cord gently swinging.

But Johnny, it seemed, had gone.

8
NIGHT CREATURES

Wednesday

'Rajesh?' Mona said.

The Graceland barman, a short, pleasant guy with a gleaming bald head, looked around from where he was drawing two pints of Kingfisher. 'Mona?'

'I don't suppose you overheard that conversation Johnny was just having?' She indicated the phone, which was no more than five yards away from where Rajesh usually stood.

At once, he became serious. 'Oh no, Mona . . . I'd never eavesdrop.'

'I'm sure. But you didn't overhear anything by accident?'

'Nope.' He shook his head solemnly.

'Which way did Johnny go?'

She knew that he'd left; she'd just checked upstairs, and his apartment was locked.

'Through the fire exit.' Rajesh indicated the stock-room, the entrance to which was also located behind the bar. The fire-exit door wasn't alarmed, and so the staff routinely used it as a shortcut to the alley at the side of the restaurant.

Mona nodded. 'And you definitely didn't hear who he was talking to, or what the conversation was about?'

Rajesh looked awkward.

'No one's going to get in trouble if you tell me,' Mona added.

He considered. 'I didn't hear anything he said. But he looked a little tense.'

'Yeah, I saw that too.'

'I made a big effort not to listen.'

'Very commendable, Rajesh, but I'm a bit worried that something's going on here that we need to know about. So, there's nothing you can tell me at all . . . ?'

'You can look in that bin.'

She glanced, puzzled, at the swing-top wastebin under the washing-up area.

'He got the phone number from a piece of paper,' Rajesh explained. 'Then threw the paper in there after he'd rung it.'

Mona delved into the bin. It was filled with the usual bar-room detritus, but on top of it all lay a screwed-up ball of paper. When she unfolded it, it was the same letter that Johnny had read at the table, including the name and telephone number.

Someone called Jackie?

She went through into the stockroom. It struck her that this was blatant prying, but what the fuck? It wasn't in her nature to get swept aside, so she whipped out her iPhone and tapped in the number.

Several seconds passed while it rang at the other end.

Then a female voice answered. 'Jackie Phillips.'

Mona rang off, her insides twisting with angry frustration.

Jackie Phillips. *Jackie fucking Phillips . . .*

Jackie Phillips had been a rare kind of creature. One of those who do very well out of the music industry without having any real talent at all. But then film-star looks could get you a long way in most walks of life.

Which might explain why Johnny found himself riding the Northern Line, that finger-licking dinner left unfinished on the table, and all because Jackie had snapped hers.

He'd got to know her a lifetime ago, when she'd been a presenter on MTV. That had been back in the Nineties, after the first wave of Kleinmania had passed, though he and the rest of the band had still been producing high-quality, high-charting records. Their relationship had at first been strictly mates, though with looks like Jackie's it had been difficult for a bloke like him not to have ideas. She was a few years younger than him, but already known for targeting rock stars, most of them at the top of their game; anyone on the slide got dumped, sharpish.

Yeah, that was Jackie. She'd only ever gone for the ones that really counted. She was addicted to the adrenaline of her boyfriends playing the biggest stadiums around the world, watching as they were adored, lauded as inter-galactic gods while casting their towering shadows across those gigantic white stages or floating amid clouds of dry ice. Sure, she had her own gig as TV DJ, presenter, broadcaster, or whatever she could wangle, but she was addicted to the stardust left scattered her way by the men in her life; the charisma that emanated from their well-worn faces, the way their tiny arses squeezed into leather pants so tight that they squeaked with success. And all of them had been associates of Johnny's – or rather, cocaine cohorts, glassy-eyed caricatures of the real people they'd once been, who shared meaningless conversations with him in the dingiest toilets in every corner of planet Earth.

'Johnny!' Jackie hissed, nipping out from a recessed entrance by Highgate tube station, her blonde hair tucked messily under a pulled-up hood. 'Thank God!'

It was mid-evening now and the suburban streets were dark and quiet, drizzle falling on the pavements, so he'd nearly jumped out of his skin when the scruffy figure in a baggy hoodie had darted out and grabbed his arm as he exited the station. It *was* Jackie, though. She was nearly fifty now, but still with those bright blue eyes that shouted 'come and get me'. Maybe there was a touch too much Botox and filler around her lips, but she was still sexy, and she knew it.

'Jackie? What's going on?'

She stared at him wide-eyed, those baby-blues intense under her long black lashes.

'When I said get here quickly, I didn't think you'd be this quick.' She looked past him along the street. 'Which car have you come in?'

That was Jackie all over. Which of his former collection of flash motors might she get to ride around in tonight, her queen to his king? He shrugged. 'Does it matter?'

'Suppose not. The main thing is you're here. Come quick . . .' She nipped ahead, leading him by the wrist.

'What's going on?' he asked again. As far as he knew,

they were still a couple of streets away from her pad. 'You told me on the phone that some guy's been watching your house?'

'He has, and he's there now,' she replied. 'He's been there a couple of hours. This is the third time I've seen him this month. That's why I tried to get hold of you. I couldn't think of anyone else. But you're here now . . . and it's perfect timing, because we can catch him in the act.'

Johnny wasn't so sure about that. 'You got any idea who he is?'

'None at all. But I knew I'd end up with a peeping Tom or stalker at some point.'

'What about the Old Bill? I mean, stalking's a criminal offence these days, isn't it?'

On reaching the corner, they stopped again. 'Come on, Johnny! Thanks for coming, by the way.' She stood up on tiptoes to kiss his cheek. 'You know I don't trust the police.'

Johnny didn't know that. In truth, he didn't even know what she'd been doing with herself all this time; they hadn't seen each other in a while. No doubt she was doing better than he was. She'd presumably had a nice pot of gold over the years, courtesy of her flings with the minted: jewellery, cars and a stunning three-storey townhouse in this nifty part of town. Her wealth had always struck him as being way out of proportion to her talent, though maybe she'd made some good investments over the years. Either way, he'd always carried a soft spot for her. There was much about Jackie not to like, yet he *did* like her, and always had.

Johnny knew Laura would be upset if she knew where he was. Even though they had separated, Laura hated Jackie, blaming her for sticking the knife into their marriage, sucking the last breath out of it. She had heard rumours flying around about Jackie and Johnny over the years, but she'd always tried her best to ignore them – until she couldn't anymore. Laura had called them 'two peas in a pod, both made in the same selfish mould'. Johnny knew it had finally broken the trust between them, even though they'd hung on together for a few more years.

'I've had the cops out twice,' Jackie said. 'Each time there was no one here when they arrived, so they thought I was messing them around. I got a feeling that if I carried on calling them, it'd end up in the papers. I don't trust the police these days. They're either bent or just plain crap.'

Johnny shrugged. 'And what do you think *I* can do?'

'You're a bloke, aren't you?'

He grinned. Jackie hadn't exactly been short of blokes in her life.

'I know what you're thinking,' she said. 'There must be some young stud on the scene, because there always was in the past. Why can't *he* sort it out? Well, there isn't, OK? Look, Johnny, I know I've played around, and I've had plenty guys on the go over the years, but every one of those relationships ended in tears. Except for the one I had with you.'

'I wouldn't have called it a relationship, Jacks.'

'We had something good for the short time it lasted, didn't we?' Her voice was soft . . . tempting.

It had been a very short time, he reminded himself. If memory served, he'd slept with her twice. Course, he'd been married at the time, so he hadn't wanted to take it any further than that. Even now, his feelings about that particular bout of adultery were mixed. Back in the day, there'd been no red-blooded man in England who didn't want to bed Jackie Phillips, but as usual, those two nights had demonstrated yet more weakness on his part. Infidelity had come so easily back then. He hadn't fully realised what he was playing with, or what exactly he stood to lose.

They rounded a corner, and Jackie's house stood on the other side of the road.

It was a Georgian-era semi-detached, set back from the main drag along a short gravel drive, its front garden nestling under a canopy of hundred-year-old maples. It could have come out of a classic Dickens novel, following Oliver Twist as he made his way through the town gates, past the workhouse and into old London Town. There were lights on inside, but no sign of movement on the premises.

Johnny eyed it uneasily. 'What exactly is it you want from me, Jacks?'

'Go into the back garden and have a word with him.' She said this as if it was the most obvious thing in the world. She even pushed something into his hand; when he looked down, he saw that it was a small electric torch. 'Shine this in his face. Chase him off.'

'What if he won't be chased? I mean, what's if he's more of the chasing type?'

'He's not a big bloke. Well, being honest, I've not seen very much of him. Just a faint shape moving round in the bushes. Slim build, I think. Not particularly tall.'

He blew out a sigh.

'Please, Johnny.' She batted those sexy lashes again. 'I'm frightened.'

He nodded, swallowing any further reservations. They crossed the road together and walked up the drive, Jackie diverting to the front door, saying she'd watch from the windows and have her phone in hand should things get nasty.

'Nasty . . . great,' he grunted as he crept along the side of the house. Just how did you handle a situation like this? It was highly likely that any kind of stalker or peeper, once confronted, would run for it. But if he didn't, Johnny wasn't sure what he'd do.

Every bloke liked to think he could look after himself if he needed to, but he'd never been much use in a fight unless he was drunk. Perhaps even then, he hadn't been *that* much use. Klein had seen their fair share of brawls during their early days, when touring the rough bars and clubs, but they'd always had roadies to help.

Led Zeppelin or Motorhead, they weren't.

But Jackie was Jackie, and she'd always woven this kind of spell. Back in the day, she'd taken the babe thing to a whole new level. That hourglass figure squeezed into its regular attire of strappy top, miniskirt and thigh boots, that glorious blonde hair, that mischievous feline beauty. She'd out rock-chicked them all.

He'd only been back in her company five minutes and she'd already got him eating out of her hand.

He pushed open the tall wrought-iron gate at the end of the passage, and just the other side of an expansive patio stood the house's rear garden.

He hesitated before going any further.

They all had sizeable gardens, these houses. This one was perhaps eighty yards long and about fifty wide, but even in mid-evening darkness, it was clear it wasn't so much a garden as a jungle. It was October now, so the vegetation should be thinning out, but the grass and thorns, while slowly turning brown, still stood waist-deep. The leaves on the bushes and trees might have withered as well, but there were enough of them to throw deep, dark shadows the length of the property. An old pear tree stood in the centre with a circular love bench wrapped around it, perfect in the summer but right now, in the darkness and the rain, it was just another blind spot as he scoured the garden. Beyond that, there had to be a hundred hiding places where a prowler could lurk unseen.

Johnny's collar was turned up to shield his unshaven neck and his wet rat-tailed grey hair was now falling around his face. The smell of damp earth was creeping into his nostrils and making him question how in the name of Christ had he ended up here? Had he really done something so wrong that it had brought him to this?

Probably.

To make things worse, the drizzle was obscuring the garden's further reaches even more. Holding his breath, Johnny went forward. He didn't switch the torch on yet. This had been Jackie's parting advice: 'If the torch is on, he'll see you coming from miles off and leg it.'

And what the fuck would be wrong with that?

It struck Johnny that the further he pressed into this jungle, the sooner he'd be in a position where an intruder could be standing right alongside him and he wouldn't notice until it was too late. He glanced over his shoulder and saw Jackie's shapely silhouette in one of the upstairs windows.

She could have been a lot more use out here.

He was now deep in the garden itself, creeping forward, half-enveloped by the murk around him. A few yards further in, kicking through piles of wet, mulchy leaves, the naked fingers of branches clawing him, the lights from the house had receded far to his rear.

'Fuck this for a game of soldiers,' he whispered.

He halted, cocking a nervous ear. It was easy to forget that he was still in the middle of suburban London, but he felt reassured by the hum of traffic, the occasional tooting horn. Glancing left, he spied a squarish outline in the mist.

He halted again. Probably just some old shed. Nothing to get jittery about.

He veered towards it, pushing more rotted vegetation out of his way.

He switched the torch on, its narrow beam of light revealing a lopsided, dilapidated structure with moss and lichen growing all over it. Its sagging door hung open, leaving a gap of several inches. He paused again, listening. Then leaned forward to peek inside, his heart thudding like a bass drum. It was pitch black in there, a fetid stink drifting out. But when he shone his light through the gap, all he saw were interior walls riddled with fungus and a pile of cobweb-covered firewood.

A single piece of the firewood shifted. Johnny froze. Was someone under there?

It didn't seem possible . . .

The firewood flew apart, and a rat the size of a cat bolted out, rocketing between his legs, its tail whiplashing both of them as it vanished into the garden.

'Fuck me sideways!' he exclaimed, one hand on his heart.

How far was he from the end of the garden now? He must have come fifty yards easily, but he could hardly go back and tell Jackie there was no one here if he didn't at

The Game

least make it to the far end. He pressed on, swearing under his breath.

A few yards on, the rear fence emerged into view.

The torchlight played over a straight row of upright planks, all about seven feet tall and covered in ivy. The fence looked ancient. When Johnny touched it, it creaked and rattled. There were gaps across the length of it, old and rotten planks falling into each other. It wouldn't be too hard to pull a couple aside and slip through.

Johnny stood back. Whoever the perv was who'd been coming here, they'd probably never catch him; he'd scarper at the first sign of trouble, so the only real solution was to replace the rear fence.

He set off for the house, again having to negotiate clumps of rotted vegetable matter.

'Jacks!' he called. 'Can you hear me? It's OK. I think I've sussed—'

He only heard the feet coming towards him at the last second.

Johnny spun left, but it was too late.

He managed a half-duck, but a fist in a thick glove slammed into the left side of his face, sending him sprawling, where he lay flat on his back before a boot flew in. It missed his head by inches, but a second followed, and a third, which both connected. Johnny rolled into a foetal position, hands wrapped across his skull. The fourth kick was harder and more accurate, and he grabbed out, catching hold of the foot, pulling his attacker down to the ground, though the bastard was behind him and managed to lock one arm around his neck in a stranglehold. Choking, Johnny reached backward over his head to grab anything he could. All his hand latched

107

onto was a woolly red hat. He yanked it off a thatch of sweaty hair, then grappled for something else, hooking the hair itself. It was long and straggly, so he was able to wrap his fist in it properly.

The blood pounded in Johnny's ears, reverberating through his skull like a bass drum in a sound check, like the slap back, the sound returning from the far wall of the arena. Struggling to breathe, Johnny threw a wild punch over the back of his head, and by sheer luck it landed squarely in his opponent's face.

With a hefty *smack* of fist on bone, the guy's grip was broken and he reeled backwards.

At the same time, there was an echoing *bang* from the rear of the house. Fresh light flooded into the garden as the back door swung open.

'*Johnny!*' Jackie screamed.

Johnny rolled forward, anticipating another attack from behind, but it never came and, when he looked, he saw a pair of black trainers disappear through a gap in the fence. The bastard looked back once, and Johnny caught a blurry glimpse of longish hair, a wispy goatee and moustache, and a curved, beaklike nose. The next thing though, the bloke had gone.

There was a crunching impact of collapsing timber, and then nothing.

Johnny sat up, shaky. He prodded at his left eye-socket. He didn't think much damage had been done, but it fucking hurt . . . He'd just been decked by Jackie Phillips' stalker.

9
WITH A LITTLE HELP FROM MY FRIENDS

Wednesday

'Johnny . . . Jesus, are you OK?'

Jackie took his hand to help him to his feet.

'I think so,' he said, swaying slightly.

'I saw it from the window. He came out of nowhere.'

Johnny nodded. His left eye-socket throbbed and his shoulder felt numb, which was nothing compared to the damage done to his pride. Jackie, who appeared to have changed into a pink tracksuit, held his face between her baby-soft hands. She gazed at him, very concerned.

'Christ, he could've killed you! I honestly had no idea anything like that would happen,' she said. 'I'd never have asked you to do it if I'd known the guy was dangerous.'

'Well, he got the drop on me . . . but he didn't do much damage, so I'm not sure he's *that* dangerous.'

This wasn't just bravado. Johnny meant it. Whoever the geezer had been, he'd launched himself at him in the darkness and the mist, giving himself a clear advantage, but he'd got clouted in the face himself and had legged it when a woman came outside shouting. He wasn't someone the Krays could have made use of, that was certain.

'I'd never have forgiven myself if you'd got hurt,' Jackie said, her voice shaking. 'Come on, let's get you out of the rain.'

She led him across the garden and patio, and through the back door into a bespoke wooden kitchen. Johnny sat at the end of a long pine table, the sort you'd find down Camden Market on a Sunday morning. As well as his aching face and shoulder, he had a tender spot at the back of his head; when he felt it, a small lump had risen.

Jackie opened a cupboard on the kitchen wall.

'You sure you're all right?' She brought out two crystal glasses. 'I seem to remember your old poison was bourbon. Sorry, I've not got any. Scotch do?'

'Anything.'

She filled the two glasses and handed one over. Johnny took it gratefully, then felt gingerly at the back of his head again.

'Let me look at that.'

'I'm fine.'

'No one's fine when they've been kicked in the head. Let me at least have a look.'

Jackie parted his hair, probing the bump with a damp cloth.

'You know, this might be a police job,' Johnny said. 'I know you're worried that one of them might blab to the red tops, but for all that this guy didn't kill me, he's obviously the violent type . . . ouch!'

'Sorry.'

'How long's this been going on?'

'I don't know. Not for sure. But, like I said, I don't want coppers here. That's why I came to you.'

'Call me dim, but what rep have *I* got for catching criminals?'

'It was Don Slater who suggested it.'

Johnny looked around, surprised. '*Don* did?'

'Only sort of.' She crossed the room, dumping the damp rag in the bin and washing her hands. 'You know what a fixer he is. I rang him and asked if he could send someone round, and he told me to call you.'

Thanks, Don. 'No cash in it for him, I suppose.'

'That'll be it.'

She sipped her Scotch. Now, in proper lighting, he could see that time hadn't been quite as good to Jackie as he'd thought. She was still a beautiful woman, her eyes a sparkling blue, her hair hanging in long, well-tended layers, but she wasn't in the first flush of youth anymore. Then again, neither was he. But underneath the snug trackie, there were strong hints that her body, doubtless gym-toned, was still in great shape. He sucked in his stomach.

'He wasn't even particularly polite,' she added. 'Said I should get one of my exes to sort it. Apparently, there are enough of them to form an army.'

For a moment, Johnny thought she was going to cry. She made an effort to resist that but, however briefly, she'd dropped her guard. The facade of strong, independent woman had fallen, exposing someone underneath who was frightened and vulnerable.

For all the scandalous razzamatazz of her early career, Johnny knew that things hadn't worked out brilliantly for Jackie in the long run. OK, she had money and lots of it by the looks of it, but for all the high-profile men she'd had in her life, none of them had loved (or liked) her enough to stick around. Plenty in the industry had said that was the way she preferred it. Jackie Phillips was a free spirit. Some had admired her for that, but others thought it reckless, perhaps foreseeing what Johnny thought he was witnessing now: the life of the party on the outside, but inside, someone lonely, lost and regretful.

On reflection, it wasn't very flattering that, of all her ex-lovers, *he'd* been the one she'd called on to assist with this peeping Tom business only because he was the sole relic from her early life who'd still speak to her. But they had to be realistic. This really wasn't his bag.

'I'm sorry I dragged you into this,' she said. 'If I'd had any idea that it might get out of hand . . .'

'I'm only sorry I wasn't much use.'

'You were very brave.'

'Sometimes being brave isn't enough, as I think I've just demonstrated.'

'Did you get a look at him?'

'Not much.' Johnny held his glass aloft as she topped it up again. 'But you need to get that back fence fixed. That's how he's getting in and out.'

'I'll have to call someone.'

'Soon as possible, I'd say.' She nodded, but still seemed wary of that for some reason. 'Jacks, I'm always happy to help, you know. I'll always have a spot for you—'

'Aww, Johnny . . .'

'—but I'm just not the man for work like this. I mean, with all your money and connections, surely there's someone you can bring in who's more up to it?'

'You mean like a professional bodyguard?'

'I was thinking more like a private investigator. Someone who does this for a living.'

She nodded, uncertain.

'It's just that . . .' she shrugged, 'I guess we single girls, well, we're generally not too keen on having a bloke we've only just met hanging around the place. That's why we tend to go for what we know.'

This set him wondering what she did for a living these days. She'd left MTV in the late Nineties, if he remembered rightly, and done a brief stint fronting *The Scene*, a late-night music-themed chat show on Channel 4. But in recent times she'd been notable more for her absence from the TV. She'd guested once on *The Girlie Show*, and had done a comedy routine with French and Saunders on *Children in Need*, though that had been over a decade ago. More recently, there'd been guest appearances on *The Wright Stuff* and *Loose Women*. What had happened to her career? He mulled over the possibility that her multiple affairs might have landed her in hot water. A lot of the guys she'd bedded over the years had been married, and in some cases, their jilted wives were better connected than Jackie was. She'd never had the cheeky charisma of Paula Yates or the music chops of Jo Whiley. When all you really had were baby doll looks and great boobs, where did you go next?

Jackie changed the subject. 'How's the family? I hear you and Laura finally separated.'

'Yeah.'

'Divorced?'

'Almost.'

She sipped more whisky. 'Nice payday for her, I imagine?'

Only in that she is free of me.

'How they all coping?' she asked.

'OK. Laura's getting on with life. Chelsea's still cross about it.'

'Chelsea? Good God, I haven't seen her since she was . . .' Jackie made a gesture.

'She's fifteen now, would you believe?'

'Fifteen! Christ. Do you get to spend much time with her?'

Johnny wasn't sure how he could answer that question without digging a hole even deeper for himself. 'I've never been much good at that, Jacks. Spent half my life on the road, and now . . . and now I'm at home all the time, I'm still not able to be there for her.'

He hadn't intended to expose the true depths of his despair. That wasn't why he'd come here. But it was out now and there was no taking it back. Jackie regarded him long and hard, before letting it drop.

'Did Pete and Don invite you to the playback for the new album at his record company offices in Soho? They're live-streaming him talking about it with all the music journos. I'm doing a report for Heart FM – getting paid for it too.'

That was the first he had heard of it. He wondered why Mona hadn't mentioned it to him. 'Why don't you come along? There'll be a few old faces there, it'll be a laugh, free champers and all that. I'll be interviewing all of them . . . I can interview you too.'

'How come's *you're* doing it?'

'Yeah, I know . . . I might not seem like a natural fit for that gig, but I'm vintage now, you know, just like you are.' She laughed and winked at him.

Johnny's first thought on hearing this was that it might be a chance for him to hustle a bit of work, actual work, as in playing a guitar. But just as quickly he realised that it would all be about Pete James, and he was unlikely to get a look in if Don Slater had anything to do with it.

His second thought had been that Jackie Phillips, mainly famous, as Lemmy had once told *Kerrang!*, for her 'tits and arse', was not doing as badly as he'd imagined if she was fronting a piece for a major radio station.

So, what did that say about him? No one was asking him to do anything.

And hooking up again with some of his contemporaries from those distant heady days would only make things worse. Who exactly were the 'old faces' who were going to be there? His fellow Eighties stars, Duran Duran? Still rocking and rolling and selling out six nights at London's O2 (he'd seen that gig advertised on the side of a bus earlier today). Tears for Fears . . . as popular as ever. The Whack, for Christ's sake, with all the prospects Pete James had ahead of him.

How could they all still be working while his life had come to this?

Jacks clearly didn't know the straits he was in, or not the full extent of them. The same would presumably apply to everyone else. But how could he get into it with them all, scruffy and unshaved, and pretend that everything was hunky-dory? They'd see through him easily.

'No . . .' he said. 'No, I don't think that's my scene anymore, Jacks.'

'C'mon, Johnny, it'll be fun.'

'Nah, I'm good.'

'OK.' She didn't push it. 'Well . . .' Her voice had become huskier, more seductive. She sashayed over to him. 'I have to make it up to you somehow. To say thank you properly.'

'Come on, Jacks . . .' He backed off. 'We're not doing that, are we?'

She batted those lovely lashes. 'Aren't we?'

Standing on tiptoes, she pecked his cheek again, though this time it lingered, her perfume washing over him, her warmth enfolding him. Johnny almost melted. He'd forgotten the sense of calm that a tender moment could bring, even a stolen moment like this.

They locked gazes from close-up. Her breathing was soft, sweet; Jackie looked at him from under her lashes; he had seen that look before many years earlier. This time though, he noticed her blue eyes had faded, they seemed tired, like a sapphire that had lost its sparkle. He breathed her in for a moment – she was intoxicating, and it was hard to walk away from her, but Johnny knew he had to.

Despite the stirring in his groin, he pulled away.

It wasn't just that starting a new relationship with Jackie seemed like a really bad idea. He and Laura were just getting back on an even keel, and if she heard that he and Jackie were a thing, even if only for a single night, it would put them right back at each other's throats – and Chelsea deserved better than that. Anyway, he could do without the distraction. If he didn't try to get back on his feet now, he never would. As things were, the one job he had was on a timer, and it was rapidly running down.

'Sorry, love . . . I truly am.' He pulled the collar of his

jacket up to his ears as he walked to the back door. 'I'm off.' *God, I must be getting old.*

She watched him with a disappointed half-smile. 'I'm grateful, Johnny.'

'I didn't do anything. Get the lights and the fence fixed.'

'See you, Johnny.' Her voice followed him down the side passage of the house.

On the street, a black cab was trundling by, showing an orange light. He waved, and it pulled up at the kerb.

Maybe my luck's changing? He climbed into the back. He couldn't afford to travel by cab with his reduced coffers, but things were different tonight. The clock in Jackie's kitchen had told him that it was only just after ten, so there was still plenty of time.

'Embankment, mate,' he told the cabbie. 'The Hole in the Wall Club.'

10

THE HOLE IN THE WALL

Wednesday

The mist had cleared by the time Johnny reached the Embankment. A stiff, cold breeze was coming off the river, the clouds overhead racing, a whole host of seagulls swinging about in it, screaming tunelessly, an orchestra of airborne devils warming up their violins. He huddled into his jacket as the cab drove away, unsure if it was the bitter cold that was getting to him or the shock of being attacked earlier. His hands were pale, pudgy, colourless as lard. It struck him that he could probably have been tucked up in a nice warm bed with Jackie now. But then he looked at the press card that he'd already taken from his pocket, his gaze fixing on the photo of Mona, looking young, fresh-faced and beautiful, and he was glad that he hadn't succumbed to temptation. Things were complicated enough.

Three concrete arches now faced him, all located directly underneath Blackfriars Bridge. Back in the day, they'd been used for storing horses and carts, then for selling second-hand car batteries. Now though, they were a trendy wine bar, a Turkish restaurant and the secretive Hole in the Wall Club. The latter lurked behind a green wooden door with a flap at eye level. If you didn't know it was there, you'd never notice it, and that was the way its clientele liked it. That was the way it had been since Fleet Street was the beating heart of the British press. Even now, Johnny saw an on–off stream of men in suits, ties undone, and the odd woman, saunter up to it, knock on the heavy timber, and wait for it to swing open, or not in some cases.

He wondered what his own chances were. It all depended on the card, which if it was checked out properly, would clearly show that he was not the holder. He tried several ways to hold it, wondering which would be the best and yet least suspicious method of covering Mona's picture, before finally opting for the three-fingered cub scout salute.

As he walked towards the door, another bunch of wannabe patrons had got there ahead of him and were waiting. He squashed up to the rear of them as they slowly filtered inside, keeping his head down, flashing his card quickly to a trendy girl in her twenties with a Seventies afro and purple shades. He joined in with the laughter to a crude joke that one of the blokes in front of him had just cracked, trying to blend in, which appeared to do the trick, the girl barely glancing at Mona's pass. They proceeded through the brick foyer and descended a flight of red-carpeted stairs. Johnny glanced back and was disconcerted to see the concierge staring after them intently (at *him* perhaps?) and talking on a mobile phone.

He turned back hurriedly. They rounded a corner, a deep crimson light embracing them. If nothing else, whatever happened now, he was in.

At which point, a heavy hand clamped his shoulder.

From out of an alcove had come an orc from *Lord of the Rings*, except that he wasn't wearing mail and leather, but a monkey suit and bowtie.

'I'm sure you know the drill, sir,' he said meaningfully.

Johnny's heart sank. He shrugged though, implying puzzlement, as if they'd got the wrong guy. But then he saw that several equally ugly bouncers had emerged from the red-tinted gloom to accost the rest of the party.

'Cursory pat-down,' the orc explained.

'Oh, right . . . yeah.' The other new arrivals now stood with arms outspread, while the security team slapped hands up and down their bodies. He spread his own arms, and the orc patted him down, only to straighten up and give him a quizzical stare. 'Something in your pocket, sir?'

Johnny tried a wolfish grin. 'Lots of ladies would love to know that.'

The orc didn't laugh. 'Please remove it, sir.'

'Oh, right, yeah . . .' Johnny felt in his pocket and took out Chelsea's camera.

The orc offered a level palm. 'No cameras in the club, sir. You know that.'

Obviously, Johnny hadn't known that, but there was nothing more likely to reveal his bogus status than displaying ignorance of the house rules. Inconvenient though they were. 'Sorry . . . slipped my mind. Been a long day.'

He handed the camera over. The orc remained grim-faced.

'We'll keep it in the office, sir. You can collect it on your way out.'

Johnny pushed thankfully on, finally entering the club proper.

Inside, it was typical subterranean London. Massive, barrel-vaulted, like it had once been a warehouse undercroft or a forgotten tube station. It was also packed, hot and sweaty. The décor was almost exclusively red: the chairs, the drapes, the well-trodden carpet. In the crimson-hued lighting, there was something vaguely hellish about it. At one time he'd have felt right at home here, but tonight, he was nervous and self-conscious.

He slid over to a space at the bar, deciding that the best tactic was to stand unobtrusively somewhere and observe.

'What can I get you, Johnny?' the red-bearded barman asked.

'Large JD and coke?' Johnny filched some notes from his pocket, only belatedly registering what had just happened.

Shit . . .

Two minutes into being on manoeuvres and his cover was blown.

The barman chatted on while he poured. 'What're you doing here?'

Johnny had to think quickly. 'Just . . . you know, catching up with someone.'

'Anyone in particular?'

'Yeah, as it happens. Jerry Fox. Is he here?'

The barman chuckled. 'He's always here . . .'

Before he could finish, the sharp blast of a whistle pierced the muggy air. All heads turned, just as the back doors at the far end of the club burst open and two policewomen marched purposefully in, halting at the first booth.

The room went very quiet, very quickly.

'Jerry Fox?' one of them asked, in a strident voice.

'As if by magic . . .' the barman muttered, pushing Johnny's drink across the polished counter.

Johnny had only previously seen Fox on TV or in photographs in magazines and newspapers. Even now, he could only see the guy side-on and from an awkward angle, but he probably would have recognised him.

Fox had a squat, heavy build, the sort that never looked good in any kind of suit, least of all the crumpled, sweat-stained two-piecer he was wearing now. He was red-faced, his hair a lank, sandy-grey mop. He seemed startled by the arrival of the female officers rather than alarmed, eyeing them up and down almost appreciatively.

Johnny couldn't help feeling the same. To start with, they wore old-fashioned policewomen's gear instead of those modern, sexless paramilitary outfits, including tight skirts, dark tights and . . . *high heels*? The woman who'd spoken was a tall brunette. The other was blonde, a little shorter and very shapely. Their uniforms literally fitted where they touched. And then he realised what was actually going on . . . just in time for David Rose's classic Fifties anthem, 'The Stripper', to boom from the club's speakers.

Immediately the duo started bumping and grinding, though not before the brunette had grabbed Jerry Fox by his tie and hauled him to his feet, to encouraging roars from the rabble in Fox's booth. They kissed him on both cheeks, turned him around and disentangled him from his jacket, but mainly it was their own clothes they were removing.

'Strippergrams? In the 2020s?' Johnny said.

'It's always 1989 in here,' the barman said with a distant smile. 'That's how they all like it. That lot did the same to me on *my* birthday,' he added with a wry smile. 'Only the girls were dressed as nurses!'

Johnny had to smile. This was a bit more debauched than anything he'd experienced for a while, though there'd been much wilder times back when Klein were in their pomp. So many that he often struggled to remember any of it, but every now and again something would happen, a face would get into his, a smell would strike his nostrils, or he'd arrive somewhere familiar, that would take him straight back to hedonistic times that were his introduction to life, to who he was and who he wanted to be.

It was a pity he didn't have the camera with him at present, though he suspected that snaps of a drunken Jerry Fox in the company of two strippers would hardly be adequate for Pete James's needs. Looking at the company Fox kept, obviously members of his own profession, some of them women, all totally plastered, cheering him on crazily, it was going to need to be something a lot more shocking.

Johnny tried to formulate a strategy.

Fox had exposed shameful shenanigans among the entertainment world's elite for many years now, and in most of those cases drugs were a factor. He'd made his name, and a small fortune, lambasting those who did drugs. If he were to be exposed as a user himself, it would finish him.

That would be the dirt to get on Jerry Fox.

Not that Johnny was comfy with the idea of getting close to illegal substances.

He'd struggled for years to get clean, but one incident in particular, a relatively recent one, had galvanised him. Of all places, it had happened at an NA/AA meeting. Officially, he hadn't touched any real gear for a decade by then, but in all honesty, the battle against addiction was a football match that tilted from end to end. It was feast or famine, binge or bust. He'd been seated in a back room at Hendon Town Hall, listening while a young woman with straggles of unwashed black hair stood before the group and told them she was having a really bad week. Suddenly she'd fallen to the ground, a bundle of bones wrapped in a dark, cape-like coat, the Wicked Witch of the West after she'd been doused in water, shrivelling away before their eyes into wisps of smoke. Even after everything Johnny had seen during the years of his own dependency, he'd been shocked at the sight of her.

She'd writhed on the floor, arms and legs jerking out, kicking and punching at nothing. The rest of the group just sat there, stunned, so Johnny jumped in and gripped her head between his hands. By this time, the woman had almost stopped breathing; her eyes rolled white, her shrunken chest rising and falling shallowly. When he felt for a pulse, it was dangerously low. Her skin had turned an eerie translucent grey, almost blue. He'd knew enough about ODs to know there was only one thing to do in this situation: force air into her lungs, get oxygen into her blood. He'd supported her head with one hand, pinched the soft tip of her nose with the other, leaned down to give her the kiss of life, and almost immediately, literally as they'd locked lips, the woman coughed, and a lungful of stale, alcohol-soaked breath poured into his mouth.

The rancid taste of Scotch mixed with stomach acid hit him like a ton of bricks.

Even now, he shuddered, fighting off a pang of nausea.

Things were pretty crap at present, but he couldn't put into words how glad he was to be out of *that* world, at least. And yet there was always a prowling fear just beneath the surface that if he breezed into the toilets here and heard a whole row of shouty-voiced idiots doing coke in the cubicles, he'd be tempted to knock on a door and demand to join them. That was the trouble with addiction. Once you were an addict, it was for life. Temptation could strike anytime, anywhere.

Of course, the big question now was: did Jerry Fox do drugs?

The strippers, miraculously clothed again, their routine complete, were blowing kisses to every lewd comment. Fox was back with his mates, chugging down a pint of lager and following it with a whisky chaser. He was a pisshead for sure, but everyone knew that. There might be no option but to furtively follow the guy into the toilets later on, hoping for the best.

And then that plan was blown out of the water too.

Johnny tore his eyes from the strippers' curvy legs, glancing back along the club in the direction of Fox and his mates, only to see him gazing back, wiping his long, sweaty hair off his forehead, a smile as long as the Regent's Canal splitting his face as the red-bearded barman whispered in his ear.

'*Johnny Klein!*' Fox shouted raucously, now approaching. '*Johnny fucking Klein!*'

'Fuck,' Johnny whispered under his breath.

Up close, Fox stank of sweat, fags and booze. His face was as red as bacon, his hefty paunch bulging out of the bottom of his shirt. Pure heart attack material.

This wasn't quite in the game plan, but there was no going back now. Johnny smiled. 'How you doing, Jerry?' he asked.

'Fucking rocking, mate. Considering I'm sixty today. Mac, our lovely barman here, tells me we were down for a chinwag tonight . . . ?' Without asking permission, he put a heavy arm across Johnny's shoulders. 'Before you say anything, let me apologise for forgetting . . . I've been like a tit in a trance this last week. Haven't seen a fucking email or text for days . . . these fuckers down here have been keeping me busy, know what I mean . . .'

Johnny was distracted by a tiny bubble of carbon dioxide encased in saliva, which ejected itself from Fox's fat, wet lips, and burst on his cheek. He tried not to flinch but made a mental note to wipe it off as soon as Fox was out of his personal space. He could hardly complain, though . . . in fact, he cheerfully played along as Fox steered him down the length of the club, pushing past other groups of drinkers. This was his way in.

'Come and meet the boys,' Fox shouted in his ear; more spittle speckled Johnny's cheek. 'They're a bunch of old Eighties wankers, but they'll piss their pants meeting you.'

Fox's mates, several of whom were near enough carbon copies of the man himself, rose to their feet to heap Johnny with acclaim, though some of them just seemed to be howling like animals. All were blind drunk.

Jesus.

It was like a stag night in Amsterdam. Stuck with a bunch of dickheads you'd normally try your hardest to avoid.

Fox patted the air to calm them down, then introduced Johnny as if he was his new best mate. Johnny smiled along.

The stink of Jerry Fox's bodily odour seemed to linger far too long after he removed his arm from around Johnny's shoulders.

Fox swivelled to face him. 'Now, Johnny, I know we should, by rights, be working here tonight, but what the fuck, eh?'

The boys laughed and jeered. 'He never does any fucking work! Lazy fat bastard!'

Fox shouted them to order, then turned back to Johnny with an air of forced sobriety.

'However, it is my birthday. Which is a big thing after the life I've led. What do you reckon, eh, Johnny?'

Johnny supposed he agreed with that. There was no guarantee that *he'd* reach sixty.

'So, I am allowed to let my hair down a little,' Fox added.

'What's left of it, you ancient bastard!' one of them laughed.

Fox ignored him. 'On stage over there, Johnny . . .' Johnny looked round, puzzled. He hadn't noticed a stage when he'd first come in here. 'On stage over there, is a guitar and a beautiful old Marshall . . .'

Johnny was now able to see that, about thirty yards to the right, on the other side of a small dancefloor, there was indeed a low, narrow stage. Strips of glitzy material hung down at the back of it, but in the middle, a microphone stood next to a stand on which a guitar was resting, while behind that was a battered old drum kit. As Fox had said, there was an amp too, in the wings to stage left.

'We're all Eighties kids, here,' Fox said. 'And it is my birthday, an' all and everyone knows I like a little jam. So, would you do me the honour, as a special birthday treat, of accompanying me?'

'Accompanying you?'

Fox grinned. 'All right, it's not really accompanying me. I'll work the skins . . . but if you could sing and play that old classic of yours, "I Feel Fine", everyone in here would be chuffed to buggery.'

Johnny laughed. This was a joke, right? It had to be.

Everyone around him though, which was a lot of them as the word had now spread that he was here, spontaneously erupted. *'JOH-NNY . . . JOH-NNY . . . JOH-NNY!'*

Wildly, he tried to fumble his way out of the situation. 'C'mon, fellas . . . I haven't played anything off that album in years. I can't even remember how those songs go.'

It was no use. The crowd thickened, eager hands guiding (if not actually pushing) him towards the stage. Once up there, he had no choice but to grab the guitar and sling its strap over his shoulder. Stomach churning, he looked out at the expectant mob.

How many times had he done this?

A sea of faces. Wavering in the sweaty dimness, blurred by the heat and fug. But all eyes fixed on him like laser beams. A forest of hands raised, either as clenched fists or with fingers jutting up and outward in rock and roll devil horns. The back of his shirt was suddenly soaking. He could feel his heart thump in his carotid artery. Fox then came up alongside him, the arse almost breaking free of his baggy trousers. Ridiculously, he'd stripped his tie off and fastened it around his head like a bandana.

'Ladies and gents,' the journo announced, taking the mic to much hooting and ribaldry. 'My new band . . . The Foxes!'

The room erupted again; it was like some kind of weird dream . . . or nightmare. He could barely speak as Fox

128

replaced the mic on its stand, then pushed it in front of his guest, before sloping to the back of the stage and sliding himself into the drum kit, where he raised the sticks over his head. Johnny gazed at him in disbelief. In return, Fox winked and counted them in.

'One . . . two . . . three . . .'

11

THE VORTEX

Wednesday

Johnny had no idea how it had come to this.

He was supposed to have *sneaked* into the Hole in the Wall Club, and yet in almost no time was being hailed here as the conquering hero. His sole purpose had been to obtain images of Jerry Fox in compromising positions, and not only had he lost any means of doing that, he'.d found himself performing a gig at the bastard's birthday party.

And yet ironically, standing at the front of that stage, drunk on the heat and excitement, a mob of worshippers at his feet, the old song had come back to him note for note, line for line. In fairness to Jerry Fox, he'd proved himself a decent drummer. OK, he had one beat and one fill, but he kept time well enough; Johnny had certainly heard, and played, with worse. The crowd meanwhile sang along, familiar with every word, clapping in perfect synch.

Fleetingly, he pictured Pete and Don's faces, etched with

astonished fury. 'What the actual!' they'd say. 'This wasn't what we meant when we requested a bit of James Bond, a bit of Mata Hari. Johnny Klein? More like Johnny fucking English!'

As the Foxes went into the chorus, the room exploded, almost everyone in the club now joining in, and the adrenaline surged through Johnny's veins, his skin tingling. He swung to glance at Fox and couldn't help smiling. It came naturally, in fact. He hadn't experienced a high like this for years and years. Neither gambling, drugs nor sex had set him buzzing like this. As they went into the final chorus, the crowd took it up for them.

'I feel fine . . . I feel fine . . . I feel fine . . .'

It was so loud and enthusiastic that Johnny could only just hear Fox shouting to him across the stage: 'Johnny . . . I fucking love you, man! Big ending, yeah! Let's do it!'

Instinctively, Johnny shouted back. 'Let's do it!'

It was crazy. Johnny could feel himself bonding with Jerry Fox and strangely, in that moment, he couldn't stop himself, and as long as it didn't get back to Pete then why not? The pair were perfectly in time together as they slowed the tempo down and went into the classic rock band ending of five massive power chords.

The patrons of the Hole in the Wall were ecstatic.

'More . . . more . . . more!' echoed from the farthest corners.

The two musicians linked arms at the front and bowed as one.

'That was the fucking business,' Fox said, mopping away fresh sweat. 'Best night of my life.'

His mob of muckers were still whistling and cheering as

he jumped down and rejoined them to a standing ovation. Johnny stayed up there, dazed, wondering what had just happened. He was exhilarated but at the same time shaken, as though a whirlwind had hit him.

It was an incredible feeling, but that wasn't what he was here for.

The best policy now might be to slink out before anyone noticed, perhaps use a rear door, keep his head down. He'd attended so many screenings or concerts over the years, friends having eagerly invited him along, hoping for a gold-plated endorsement for their new product, but from which he'd had to creep away because he couldn't face telling them that actually he thought it was shite. But that wasn't going to work. Wherever he ran to now, he'd still be obligated to Pete and Don, and he'd seen half a dozen phones filming him while he was singing and playing, so the evidence would be on YouTube forever. In any case, no sooner had he descended from the stage, multiple hands slapping his shoulders, than Jerry Fox called him over again.

'Johnny, mate . . . don't tell me you're even thinking of leaving! Here . . . get your laughing gear round that.' He shoved another double JD and Coke into his hand, which Johnny sank in a single gulp. 'Listen,' Fox said, 'I've got an idea to go for a cheeky Chinese in a little place I know. It's got what you might call a *special* menu. Thought you might want to join us.'

Johnny pondered. His cover was now blown, but that wasn't the end of the world. He was *in* with Fox now. He probably couldn't be better placed to get something on him.

Fox slid his arm around Johnny's shoulders again. 'Come

on, fella . . . I'll stick it on my company card. Then we can do that interview we were meant to do. What do you say?'

Johnny had heard that purring 'come on' tone a thousand times over the years, and a thousand times it had got him into trouble of some sort or other. He already had more than a sneaking suspicion that, whatever this 'special menu' contained, it wasn't going to be food.

'Sounds good,' he said.

'Excellent.' Fox now circled among his drunken buddies, saying his goodbyes, while pulling on his suit jacket and his Barbour coat over the top.

'Aren't the boys coming with us?' Johnny asked.

'Nah. Weeknight, isn't it? They're all wimping out on me. Only me, the birthday boy, gets treated tonight. And you, of course. As my special guest.'

They headed to the exit, Johnny reminding himself over and over that, whatever this turned out to be, it was a means to an end. But it was one thing being in a group of blokes with Jerry Fox, but now being on his own, going to bloody dinner with him, he was meant to be flying under the radar and this felt like a high-risk strategy. Was he really the one in control here? The cold fresh air hit them as they stepped outside. Fox had a bit of a stride on, and Johnny had to rush to keep up before hearing a woman's voice calling after him . . .

'Hey, sir!' The young girl from reception was coming towards him with his camera, the one that the orc had confiscated on his way in.

Johnny's heart skipped a beat. He knew he had to play it cool; he didn't want Jerry to know he had a camera with him at all. 'Thank you, darling.'

Johnny shoved the Leica into his large inside pocket, cursing himself for nearly having forgotten it. That would have been all he needed. Getting the goods on Fox and having no way to photograph it.

He couldn't even get this right.

Fox hadn't noticed; he was too busy trying to order a taxi on his phone. Johnny joined him as an Uber glided up alongside them. 'In you go,' Fox grinned. 'Age before beauty and all that shit.'

They didn't speak much as they drove. Johnny was unsure where they were going. The streets flipped by, blurry and dark. It wasn't like he was unfamiliar with central London, but after the day he'd had, he was close to exhaustion. He'd also sunk two double bourbons, on top of the several large Scotches he'd had at Jackie's place. Not that they were in the cab for very long.

When they got out, Fox steered him across the pavement. 'Best fucking place in town, this, mate.'

At first glance, it was small, looking more like a takeaway than a restaurant, with painfully bright fluorescent tubes overhead, five or six tables and a counter covered in dark brown Formica. There were only two other people in there, a youngish, heavy-set man with long hair, wearing a T-shirt and apron, who stood behind the counter with arms folded, watching them suspiciously, and a much older man who looked like he could have been the other man's father. The latter stood on the customer side of the operation and wore a shiny silver-grey suit and heavy dark-rimmed glasses, though he was pale and sallow. His sunken cheeks reminded Johnny of some of the rock and roll casualties he'd left behind over the years.

The second guy didn't seem particularly friendly either, but he raised no objection as Johnny made a beeline for a table in the corner and plonked himself down. Fox, meanwhile, had a quiet word with him. All Johnny craved right now was the MSG his stomach had been promised. He could sense something was going down and, if he was right, he wanted no part of it; he had stopped taking drugs a long time ago and was far too old to be doing anything like that now.

'Shit,' he muttered.

This was it, then. This was what he needed, if he wanted to find a way to get Fox's nuts in a wringer. The question was, was he up to it?

Fox beckoned him, and he got up and joined him. The Suit with the glasses walked the length of the restaurant and opened a door with a key. Fox went through it first, glancing back once to ensure that Johnny was coming too. The Suit came last, locking the door behind him. They descended a grubby timber staircase and then took a bare brick passage, along which a single light threw weird, distorted shadows.

Johnny couldn't resist plucking at Fox's arm. 'Jerry, if this is what I think it is,' he whispered, 'I don't want it.'

'Relax, you're making me nervous,' Fox chuckled. 'Just a bit of fun. We're having a blowout!'

He sauntered along ahead, clearly knowing where he was going. There was already a pungent, aromatic whiff that Johnny found unmistakable. It took him back years, to a part of his life he'd tried so hard to leave behind. At the end of the corridor hung a red velvet curtain. The Suit pulled it aside, giving a coded knock on the metal door behind it. A slat slid back, a pair of eyes appraised them, and then a series of bolts were withdrawn, and the door swung back. The Suit ushered them through but didn't go in himself.

They now entered what seemed to Johnny the archetypal drug den, a network of rooms and passageways which had obviously been an old warehouse at some point in its past, with more than a hint of Fagin's mythical den than part of the restaurant above. It all seemed respectable at first, even opulent, with luxurious drapes and divans covered in plush cushions, low-key lighting and unidentifiable background music. But behind the facade Johnny knew it was a different world. The customers were nearly all male and of the moneyed sort, clad in Thomas Pink shirts, sporting jewellery and Rolex or Mariner watches. There were women too, but they were clearly working here and had come from every part of the world – most of them trafficked, no doubt.

As the two new arrivals wandered in, it became apparent that many of the men were in a semi-comatose state, and if not slouched or draped over the comfortable furniture, were only able to blunder around because they were propped up by girls. For the same reason, there was very little sex going on. Some of the women were gamely attempting to ride their half-dressed clients, or perform blowjobs, but in most of the open bedrooms Johnny passed, the male customers were enveloped in chemical clouds as they chugged on reefers or pipes, or snorted lines of snow from shelves, sideboards, even their exposed forearms.

Every so often, he spotted a discreet security man, inevitably younger and brawnier than everyone else, hovering in the background, eyes watchful. He'd need to be careful if he intended to get his camera out in here. As for who was actually in charge, that was resolved when an elderly woman, spry and quick, and draped in black understated clothing, came delicately up to them and, without speaking, took Fox by the arm, leading him down a side corridor. Every molecule in Johnny's body was now telling him that this was a bad idea. He knew he was going to succumb. There was no way not to. He'd inhaled God knows how much dope just by breathing the air, and he'd only been here a few minutes.

Somewhere in his inner self he found a vestige of resistance. 'Jerry . . . Jerry, mate.'

Fox glanced back, his ruddy features already a mask of juvenile bliss.

'Not for me, mate,' Johnny stammered. 'I'm done with all this.'

'Nah, nah . . .' Fox grabbed Johnny's shoulder between thumb and forefinger, squeezing it painfully, the way a crab would pinch you. 'I've got something special lined up for us. Come on, Johnny . . . don't let me down. Costing a fucking fortune, this.'

Johnny shuddered. He'd reassured himself constantly in recent years that the worst of all his old habits had been well and truly shoved into the darkest realms of his memory, that dust-shrouded room in the back of his mind that he'd sworn never to open again.

And now, before he knew it, here they were in another kind of room.

It was large, but not airy. The air felt damp and reeked of joss sticks, though there were fouler odours underneath:

sweat, dirty clothes, maybe even vomit. The room was carpeted but empty of any furnishings except for eight bare mattresses, which had been set out in a regular pattern, several of them now occupied.

Johnny's stomach writhed with butterflies. He knew unequivocally that he shouldn't be here. All that work on his recovery, all those promises to Laura and himself . . . they were all about to go up in smoke. As he slumped down onto the nearest mattress, he knew he couldn't prevent it. He'd lost the fight the moment he'd gone through that red velvet curtain.

A young woman wearing a crop top and tight skinny PVC trousers, her blonde hair shaved to flat-topped bristles, piercing green eyes staring out of a clear-skinned face, knelt alongside him. He tried to speak to her, but she shook her head as if for quiet, and then, almost reverentially, presented a pipe to his lips. It was an opium pipe of the old style, covered in glittering black lacquer, with a painted red dragon, a sinuous, worm-like creature, crawling up towards the mouthpiece. As the girl waved a lighter over the small wooden bowl, Johnny glanced across the room and saw Fox on another bed, already lying in a foetal position as he was similarly attended to by another young woman wearing a silk wrap dress, her lush, thick dark hair tumbling down around her shoulders.

The blonde girl gave Johnny a gentle, reassuring smile as he drew the sweet smoke into his lungs and straight away felt a comforting warmth surge through his body. The sense of release deep within him was intense. The red dragon was now a physical being, swirling around his head. He felt a breeze from the beat of its wings, the tip of its tail brushing his forehead each time it swept gracefully past, at which point it popped into a cloud of red smoke.

Fleetingly, he fancied the girl was older than he'd first imagined . . . much, much older, her pale skin more like flaking parchment, her eyes rotted holes, her mouth full of blackened teeth. He would have resisted her, kicked out at this impudent leering hag who'd dared to come near him, but he no longer had strength in his limbs. Besides, she was suddenly young again, this time with perfect skin and hair that was so long and sparkled like a mirror and floated around her head in slow motion while her lips were so intensely red they sparkled. He barely even noticed as she shifted him over onto his side.

Johnny was OK with that, because all his issues were settled.

He was back with the band. With his band of brothers. Not only that, it was the Eighties again, that glorious moment in time when they were soaring in the charts, and yet still discovering each other, and realising how much they needed each other. But . . . no, no.

Something else was happening.

They were seated at a blocky wooden table in the middle of a Japanese dining room, encircled by paper partitions through which diffuse rays of sunlight penetrated. One of these sparkled on the features of drummer, Mike Penfold, who sat directly across from Johnny, but those features were now grotesquely distorted. This went beyond the ravages of time on a sixty-year-old face. The years of heroin, to which he'd been addicted since the age of twenty-four, had also taken their toll, eating away at every cell in his body, transforming the cherubic youth he'd once been into this grizzled horror.

Seated to the left of him was bassist Tim Carson of the asymmetrical fair hair, a brilliant player before they'd even met him, who'd seen the advert for the band in the back of *Sounds* and fitted in perfectly from day one. Sharing the same brand of childish humour as Johnny, he'd been a close and regular drinking partner in the early years; when those two went out together, it would always get messy. He seemed to be unmarked by the passing of the years. He was young again, undamaged, and yet he didn't look happy.

Next in the circle of friendship was Russell Withers, the band member Johnny had been closest to, a bosom buddy from their earliest days at school together. Russell . . . something gnawed at Johnny's mind . . . but though he tried again and again to focus on his friend – the kid he'd sat next to in every boring class, making plans for world domination through rock music, practising their megastar signatures on the backs of school exercise books until their fingers ached – the guy's face remained a blur. He wanted to reach out, to touch those memories, but his brain could only manage a fleshy smudge.

Frustrated, Johnny moved his wavering gaze to keyboard star, Lee Giles, a recovering alcoholic by the time he was thirty, who'd really let the concept of fame go to his head, seeking permanently to live in that upper stratosphere of rock and roll that he'd read about in *Hammer of the Gods*, the unofficial but notorious paperback account of Led Zeppelin's wildest days, a paperback copy of which he carried around everywhere and regarded as a bible when it came to getting as much fun out of life as possible, even if his aggressive methods did piss off everyone around him.

Johnny scowled. He'd always considered Lee responsible

for his own drug problems. Even now, Lee was laughing in that cocky, sneery way he had, which always implied that he didn't give a shit what others thought.

'Bastard,' Johnny snarled.

It had always been Lee egging him on. Or was it the other way around?

One more joint, one more line, one more night out, which would only end about six in the morning, by which time they wouldn't even know where the fuck they were.

'Yeah, isn't it about time you accepted that, once you're an adult, every decision you make is your own?' Laura said from somewhere in the room.

'Aw, come on, Laura . . .'

The figure behind the screen now stepped into view. It wasn't Laura, it was a young chef carrying a large cloche resting on a silver tray. The beams of sunshine struck the polished metal and burst into knives and splinters of blinding light. Dazzled, Johnny squinted, though he could see just enough.

The chef had placed the tray down and now, with a flourish, whipped the cloche away, revealing a dismembered head.

It was a human head, or it had been once. Now it was mangled beyond recognition, the skull smashed, only held together by the lacerated flesh enclosing it, the hair a crimson mop, matted and gluey, the face slashed over and over, the eyes gone, the nose gone, the mouth a yawning, gory crevasse. Johnny felt a lurch of recognition – *it couldn't be?* – as a pair of eyes within the mangled mess swivelled towards him, he wanted to scream, but his mouth wouldn't work . . . he knew that face, those eyes.

141

Karl Jones.

With a thunderclap, his eyes snapped open.

He blinked to get what felt like grit out of them, and then reality swam into view.

He was back in that sordid, smoke-filled room in the drugs den. His breathing came short and hard as his heart raced, while his entire body was so soaked with sweat that his clothes were wringing wet. He'd had bad trips before but none quite as lucid as that one. Previously, they were more of a feeling, a vague sense of impending terror, but this one had been very different, like he'd been in the middle of his own personal horror movie.

He levered himself up to look around, but still had to blink to clear his blurry vision, as though his eyeballs had been smeared with Vaseline. He had no idea what time it was, or how long he'd been curled up here. Not far away, Jerry Fox had already come round. The curvy girl who'd been his companion had stripped off her clothing and now lay flat on her back, naked and giggling, while Fox, like some predatory reptile, crawled up her body, his hair hanging in sodden strands. At first, Johnny had assumed this would be a prelude to sex, but then realised that the self-indulgent bastard was snorting lines of coke off her flat tummy. The girl giggled again, cupping the back of his head with her right hand.

Immediately, though his brain felt like sludge, it struck Johnny that this was likely to be his best chance.

Neither of the twosome had noticed that he'd woken. He glanced around. The door was open and other punters, mostly indistinguishable in the reddish gloom, were coming in and out. Others were sprawled on mattresses while the female sex workers assisted them. There was no such thing as privacy in this place, but equally, no one was paying attention to anyone else.

Johnny reached furtively for his jacket, which lay in a crumpled ball, and extracted the camera from its pocket. He paused, holding his breath. Still, no one was looking. That moment, Fox leaned over and picked up a glass pipe from the side of the bed and held a lighter to it.

Crystal Meth.

It was a hideous image, Fox's bloated ruddy face running with sweat, the lank hair streaked across it, the mouth drooling as he inhaled the treacly substance, the hairy nostrils dabbled with cocaine, the eyes screwed shut, as he inhaled either in pain, pleasure or both. But it was also perfect. Certainly, for Johnny's purposes.

And too good to miss.

Quickly and smoothly, even though he was lying sideways, he lifted the camera to his eye, pointed it and snapped off half a dozen quick shots. Pete James hadn't been exaggerating when he'd described *Road Warriors* as a remarkable record of an amazing world tour, and its creator as a man of genuine talent. Apparently, there was indeed something else Johnny Klein was good at, aside from song-writing and performing.

Just as quickly, just as smoothly, he slid the camera back into his jacket pocket. Then, though it took tremendous effort, he got to his feet.

As he did, the spindly old woman glided towards him. 'You want more?' she asked, her accent indeterminate, her tongue splitting in two even as he watched, two serpent heads whipping and hissing.

Johnny waved her away, fighting the hallucination off.

Pulling his jacket on, he swayed to the doorway and then out into the crowded passage.

He was jostled all the way along it by people he at first thought were wearing Halloween masks, some visages melted as though by acid, some deformed like church gargoyles, others more like straightforward movie monsters, the Mummy, the Wolfman, Frankenstein. He bit down on a scream. When he came to the metal door, it was covered with fluorescent spiders scuttling back and forth. He closed his eyes while a doorman opened it for him, but could still see them, as though they were on the insides of his lids.

He blundered along the bare brick passage and then attempted to scale the timber staircase. The stair treads creaked loudly, *too* loudly. They also seemed impossibly steep. He swayed again, fancying that river water was gushing noisily downward, foaming over his boots. He fought against it as he tried to ascend. Was this the Thames itself? When he looked back, he saw that he was climbing a flight of stairs away from the river, which was flowing in a raging torrent below. But the stairs were rotting and rickety, huge waves smashing against them, rocking the entire structure, threatening to pitch him backwards to his death.

'No!' he growled. What the fuck was in that stuff?

It was just a vision. Just the drug, dredging up nightmares as it slowly vacated his overwhelmed system. When he reached the top, he had to sit down just to get his breath. It *must* be the top because there was a door in front of him. With his heart juddering in his chest, he glanced downward again, wondering if he'd still see the river. Thankfully, all he saw now was a dry stairwell with a weird, distorted light at the bottom. He rose up shakily and pushed at the door. It wouldn't open. He groped around its edges, but there was no handle. Frustrated, he banged on it with the side of his fist. No one answered.

He leaned on it, gasping, sweating. But more and more, he felt that he was back on firmer ground, slowly regaining his equilibrium. Which is why, when he turned to his left, he noticed a second door, one he hadn't seen before. With a single horizontal bar, it looked like a fire exit. He pushed the bar down, and the door clunked open.

When he stepped outside, the sun, which was just rising over the rooftops, stung his eyes so much that he had to shield them with his arm. He saw that he was in a narrow passage, with a nondescript building on his right, a head-high wall on his left. He walked along it, negotiating a row of bins, finally emerging onto a side road he didn't recognise. He walked anyway, gradually steadying himself, his heart rate reducing as the cool, clean air filled his lungs. His clothes were damp, including his jacket, so huddling into it was no protection against the early morning chill, but he kept going, at last turning a corner and finding himself on Sloane Square. He stopped to take his bearings, thankful that he at least knew where he was now, though it was a hike from here to Brick Lane. He shoved his hands into his jeans pockets, but they were empty of cash, which was no surprise.

Last night he'd run through a wodge of his cash, firstly on the tube ride to Highgate, and secondly on his ill-advised purchase of a double JD and Coke in the Hole in the Wall. Johnny had a fleeting memory that it had come to something like thirty quid.

Well, a brisk stroll to the East End wouldn't do him any harm.

He set off walking again. His limbs ached and his feet felt strangely spongy, but he was so keen to get away from that subterranean hellhole that he travelled quickly. Street cleaners and rubbish collectors were the only people around and a handful of early joggers as he made his way across town. Even though it was a cold autumn day, homeless folk were tucked up in recessed doorways, wrapped in sleeping bags or packaged with newspaper and old cardboard.

He could probably have passed for one of them, himself.

After a couple of hours, Johnny walked the last hundred yards down Brick Lane. The leather on his cowboy boots was sodden and his socks squelched with every tired step.

Johnny stopped for a moment opposite Graceland and glanced up. Elvis was looking down over his manor but even he seemed to have lost his shine, this morning lacking his usual charisma and the glint in his eye had disappeared.

'I know how you feel man . . . believe me.'

Mona had given him a key for the back door of the restaurant. The stainless steel door led into the dark empty kitchen, and squeaked far too loudly on its hinges as it swung open. The kitchen felt strange, empty of staff and the chaos of service; the eerie silence was almost deafening.

Johnny pressed the button on the coffee machine that sat on the side counter and grabbed a small white cup, placing it on the metal tray below. The machine coughed and spluttered into life before spitting out the revolting dregs of last night's coffee beans.

He looked at it for a moment, then with a 'fuck it', chucked it down his neck.

The door at the end of the kitchen led into the hallway where a flight of stairs went up to Johnny's room. Each stair creaked under the pressure of his leaden legs as he slowly made his way up to the top landing; it seemed so much further than he remembered, and by the time he reached his room he could feel his heart pounding in his neck, and felt like he had just climbed Mont Blanc.

As he fell back against the thin pillow on his bed, he allowed himself a tiny sliver of a smile. Because, if nothing else – he patted the camera in his pocket – he had a way out of this now.

He'd got the goods on Jerry Fox.

12

DEAD TO THE WORLD

Thursday

Johnny, please . . . can you call me as soon as you get
this. It's serious.

He'd barely kicked off his cowboy boots earlier that day
before crawling under the duvet; now he clambered out of
the Victorian bath, its clawed feet gripping at the floorboards
as if keeping Johnny's anxiety company.

He stood naked in front of the mirror; his once toned
pop-star body sagged loosely and was aching and sore. He
sat on the toilet, his head in his hands, the smell of his piss
assaulting his nostrils – he was dehydrated and could feel
it in his kidneys. But more than that he could feel the crawl
of addiction scattering across his scalp as the gear left his
body and the craving nibbled around his consciousness.

So much for chasing the dragon. Today the dragon was
squeezing his nuts.

You're a fucking idiot, JK.

Johnny pulled the chain on the high cistern and moved into the bedroom. Exhausted, he slumped on the end of the bed and gulped down a glass of water that had been there since he'd arrived. Straight away, in the half-light of his room, he caught sight of his Motorola. He picked it up, flicked up the cover, and saw the voicemail notification. He dialled 222, put the phone to his ear and listened as Laura's voice came through.

Hello Johnny, it's Laura . . . can you call me as soon as you get this. *Press one to save, two to delete, three to skip to next message.*

Johnny pressed the number three key.

Johnny, where are you, it's me again . . . look, I need to talk to you . . . *Press one to save, two to delete . . .*

And so it went on, the last message from Laura shortly before four in the morning. Hard experience had taught him that no one called at that hour unless it was serious.

He wasn't sure he was up to a call with her yet, so he lay back on the bed for a while, watching a sharp beam of sunshine light up his room. He'd had a couple of hours' sleep at most but the street outside was coming to life. He got up and walked over to the window, threw it open, scattering the pigeons on the ledge, and poked his head out of Elvis's tinted shades. The sky was filled with pinks and purples and it looked like a fire was raging over the city.

Red sky in the morning, shepherd's warning . . .

Johnny breathed in and filled his lungs with the new day, no matter what it held in store.

Laura hadn't told him what the problem was. Would she be calling about Chelsea's schooling? It was the only thing she ever wanted to talk to him about and the one subject they could manage without the old resentments being churned up.

Nervous, his skin turning dry and pimply, he picked up the receiver and called her back. There was no response, so he hung up. He sat there, shivering. Then dug into his bag, extricating his one dry change of clothes. As he did, the phone rang again. He snatched it up.

'Johnny?'

'Laura, I—'

'Where the hell have you been?'

'I, well—'

'Never mind. I need to see you.' She sounded upset.

'OK, well—'

'*Now*, Johnny.'

'OK, fine . . .'

'I'm in town.'

'Whereabouts?'

'I'm doing some shopping. Give me an hour, and I'll be at The Bar.'

He nodded. The Bar was still one of the hippest bars in London, located on Hanover Street in the West End. It had been a favourite of theirs in their younger days. He also felt slightly relieved. Laura wouldn't be out shopping if this was something life-threatening.

'You *are* going to be there, Johnny? I really need to talk to you.'

'Yes, but can't you give me a clue first?'

'No, because I don't want to give you an excuse not to turn up.'

'Laura, come on—'

'You're Mr Unreliable, Johnny. And that's a reputation you've made for yourself.'

'At least tell me that Chelsea's OK?'

'Yes, Chelsea's OK. This is nothing to do with her.'

'Thank God.'

'One hour, Johnny.'

'I'll be there.'

She cut the call, and he finished getting dressed. Hanover Street was only about half an hour away, but at present he was burning through what little cash he had left just travelling around London. Could he make it on foot? Probably, but he was literally getting worn out by all of this.

And then another thought struck him, equally important. He grabbed the phone again and called BT, seeking a telephone number for *Maxi* magazine. He scribbled the digits down with a stub of pencil from the side pocket of his bag, and then called it.

A chirpy voice answered. 'Maxi Mag, how can I help?'

'Ray Caldwell, please.'

'Can I ask who's calling?'

'It's Johnny Klein.'

'He's not taking calls today.' She sounded less chirpy now. So he went for it.

'Oh really? He's expecting me, I'm an old mate . . . Johnny Klein, you know, from Klein, the band.'

He thought he could hear the girl's synapses crackling.

'Oh, yeah! I know you, my mum loved your band, she's got all your old singles in a plastic case, I think she even got

151

you to sign her tour T-shirt when you were playing at the Hammersmith Odeon. She said you wrote across her tits in marker pen.' The girl giggled.

'Oh yeah, I think I might even remember her,' he lied.

'Really! Oh, I must tell her! She'll wet herself!' The girl was beyond chirpy now and positively fluttering.

Thank God for middle-aged mums.

'Ray's not taking calls, but I'll see if he'll make an exception for you.'

'Thanks, darling. Tell your mum hello, won't you?'

The girl giggled again. It wasn't strictly true that he and Caldwell were friends, though they were certainly acquaintances. Johnny had first got to know him when he was big news and Caldwell no more than a rookie photo-journalist working for The Buzz, a scandalous weekly column in *The Sun* that broke a thousand hearts, ruined a thousand marriages, and ended a thousand celebrity careers, and which many of the wider public reviled, even though they all read it avidly, though they'd never admit to it.

Caldwell came on the line. 'Johnny Klein?' He sounded understandably wary.

'How you doing, mate?' Johnny replied.

'Good . . . it *is* actually you?'

'Why would anyone impersonate me, Ray?'

'Good point . . .' Though he still seemed sceptical. 'How can I help you?'

'I've got a reel of film you might like.'

'Yeah?'

'I want to bring it round and see what you make of it.'

Caldwell's interest was now pricked. 'We talking scoop territory here, Johnny?'

Johnny smiled at that. 'I think we can say so, yeah.'

Caldwell didn't immediately respond. He had a well-honed suspicious nature, and it was years since they'd spoken.

'Gonna need to press you, Ray,' Johnny said. 'I'm a busy man and there are other fish in the sea.'

Johnny was now certain he'd bite. The guy must have heard on the grapevine that Johnny was on his uppers, so maybe the washed-up former star was looking to earn some dosh by selling a few trade secrets? He was sure that would prove irresistible.

And he was right.

'Can you bring it into the office?' Caldwell said. 'This afternoon, say . . . threeish?'

'I'll be there,' Johnny replied, hanging up.

Time was not on his side now, so he pulled his jacket on, even though it was still so damp that he felt it through his black Levi's and Alice Cooper T-shirt. But it was his only jacket, so there was no choice. He yanked the door open, and almost jumped with fright.

Mona was on the other side. She too stood wide-eyed with surprise.

'Johnny! Thank God you're back.'

He retreated into the room impatiently. He didn't need this now, but he already regretted the abrupt disappearing act he'd done the previous evening.

'What are you doing here?' he asked.

She glanced around curiously, and he guessed she'd over-heard him on the phone, and wondered if he had someone else up here. Another woman maybe.

'Just looking in on my way to work to see that you're OK.' She seemed satisfied that the flat was otherwise empty.

'I rang Uncle Rishi last night when he was locking up, and he told me you hadn't come back.'

'Yeah, well . . . I had stuff to do. And believe it or not' – he indicated the door – 'I've stuff to do now.'

'You're going out again?'

He shrugged. 'It's called getting back on my feet. And that's a good thing, isn't it? You don't want me to leech off you guys forever, do you?'

She frowned. 'What happened to your eye?'

'My eye?' He went into the bathroom and looked in the mirror. His left eye-socket was still tender, but now he saw that it was swollen as well, and visibly bruised. 'Shit.' He'd almost forgotten about his run-in with Jackie's stalker.

'You're going to have a right shiner there,' Mona said, when he went back into the bedroom.

'Must been when I . . .'

She eyed him with an intense scrutiny.

'When I walked into that door.'

'You walked into a door?'

'Last night. Coming in. There are no lights out back, you know. It was pitch-dark.'

She gave him a long, level stare. 'Johnny, what's the fuck's going on?'

He sidled past her to the door and pointedly opened it. 'Nothing. Everything is fine.'

'So, where are you going now?'

'Laura left me a message. She needs to see me. Says it's urgent.'

'And are you going to fess up to her that you were on the phone to Jackie Phillips last night?'

154

Johnny sighed. He'd been worried that this would come up, but it also annoyed him. Mona had proved herself a true friend thus far. But she wasn't his keeper, for fuck's sake. 'You know, Mona, you and your family have been kind to me. Kinder than I deserve. But some of this stuff . . . it really isn't any of your business.'

She locked eyes with him. 'There's something you're not telling me. Something important.'

'Look, stop worrying. I'm already running late. I'll try and catch you later, yeah?' He stepped out onto the landing, again with purpose. Living under her uncle's roof was screwing up their beautiful friendship. 'Maybe we can have dinner? You know, pick up where we left off last night?'

She followed him out. 'I'll find out. I'm a journalist.'

He closed the door with an exaggerated smile, locked it and thudded away downstairs.

'Have fun, Johnny.'

Mona watched Johnny run down the stairs from the top of the banister. From down below, she heard a mumble of voices as he exchanged words with the cleaning staff while making his way through the restaurant. Though she knew it was absurd to feel that Johnny owed her an explanation, she had to fight the urge to stamp her foot in frustration.

She felt frustrated with herself too, for acting like a suspicious girlfriend. They had already established that the two of them would never be an item, and she was absolutely *fine* with that. It would be madness to get involved with someone like Johnny. She'd been in the music business long enough to know that men like him were trouble. Big trouble.

So why was she fluttering around him like some kind of anxious butterfly? Johnny was a danger to himself, she told herself, and that was why he needed someone to look out for him. Someone who wasn't trying to get into bed with an Eighties legend and brag about it to her mates on a WhatsApp group.

They were mates, that's all.

Nothing more.

However, this was the first time ever he'd told her to mind her own business. On reflection, she couldn't blame him. His life was his own, even though there wasn't much of it left.

But something *was* happening and it was time Mona found out what it was. First Pete and Don and some mysterious goings on with a camera, which Johnny didn't think she knew about, but she had eyes as well as ears, for fuck's sake. Then a call to Jackie Phillips, followed by a disappearing act and a black eye.

What the hell was Johnny Klein doing this time?

Johnny stopped short outside the front of the restaurant, surveying the line of delivery mopeds used by the Major's small fleet of delivery riders, each one with the obligatory emblazoned hotbox behind the seat. They looked pretty low-fi, but they were probably ideal for nipping around central London. He glanced back through the window. Inside, the staff were preparing the restaurant for lunchtime, hoovering and laying the tables. There was no sign yet of the Major, or Ravi, while Mona was still upstairs. Hopefully, she'd stay up there a few minutes longer.

He went back in.

'All right, Johnny?' Aamir said. He was the Major's head waiter, a handsome bloke with a head of neat, chalk-grey hair. He wasn't in his uniform but was getting the restaurant ready for service, making minute adjustments to napkins and cutlery.

'All right, Aamir . . .'

Johnny felt guilty about what he was going to say next, even though it wouldn't strictly be a lie. On his arrival here, Mona had suggested that he might earn some extra cash by making home deliveries. At the time, he'd almost thrown up. But now, well . . .

'I was thinking . . .'

'Yeah?'

Johnny mentioned the Major's offer, but explained that before he could seriously consider it, he needed to see if he was able to ride one of the mopeds around the neighbourhood without looking like an idiot or worse, killing someone.

'Can I take one for a spin?'

Aamir chewed his cheek, weighing up the likelihood that their celebrity guest, this one-time rock god, was in need of spare cash. Or maybe he just thought Johnny was better with a guitar in his hands than a delivery bike.

'Are you sure that's a good idea?' Aamir said doubtfully.

Johnny shrugged. 'Thought I might have a go now. The morning rush being over and all.'

'Well . . . OK then, if you're sure the Major was all right with it. The delivery staff arrive in an hour or so for their shift.' Aamir turned towards the bar and snapped his fingers. 'Rajesh, a helmet for Mr Klein, if you please.'

Rajesh showed Johnny outside to the bike in question, and handed the helmet over. Johnny thanked him and put it on. He only hoped that Mona wouldn't come downstairs right this moment. Ordinarily, he'd trust her to keep quiet regarding his private business, but she'd looked pretty peeved up there, and might consider putting a spanner in the works.

He mounted the bike and put his feet on the pedals. The bike wobbled from side to side as he tried desperately to keep it straight, the huge hotbox on the back that was brightly painted with the restaurant's logo making it feel unstable. But with a little determination he was soon up and running, leaving Graceland and Elvis's giant sparkling portrait shrinking behind him.

As he nipped through the streets of the East End, his balance had returned. He could feel the sides of his mouth pull up against the lining of the helmet in a broad smile as he sped through the traffic; he felt like he was able to breathe for the first time in weeks. The crash helmet was covering his face; he had no worries about being recognised, no worries about being pointed at or a cab driver asking him where he had been for the past decade or if he was still making records . . . none of that bullshit.

Johnny hadn't ridden a bike for years; the last time was when he was back in LA, when he and Russell Jones, the bass player in the band, had taken a couple of old Harleys into the desert. In their tasselled leather biker jackets, aviator shades and gas tanks that were painted in beautiful stars and stripes, they were living the dream as the sun's heatwave rippled on Highway 66 in front of them.

Now he sped west along Quaker Street, and it struck him again that his relationship with Mona was getting complicated. Did he fancy her? Who wouldn't? But he cared for her too. Johnny hailed from an era when close platonic relationships between blokes and birds were quite unusual. He knew himself well enough, too, to realise that he wasn't happy at the shift in the balance of their friendship, and it was making him tetchy with her. But they were mates, and right now he needed her more as a friend than anything else, but he knew she'd find out what was going on eventually. He didn't want her to know because he knew what she would say.

You're a guitar player, not Remington Steele.

'Mona, you're right,' he said to himself as he swung on to Appold Street. 'And I really hope this bollocks isn't the end of our beautiful friendship.'

He made it to Hanover Street in half an hour, which was good going, as the traffic in the West End was by then building towards its usual midday chaos. He then wasted five minutes searching for an empty bike bay. So, he was only a couple of minutes short of the full hour when he entered The Bar, huffing, puffing and shiny with sweat, and spotted Laura sitting in a quiet corner, a cup of coffee and a piece of cake on the table in front of her.

He smiled as he slid himself into the facing seat. 'So? What's so—'

'I'm pregnant,' she told him quietly and without any preamble. Her face was expressionless.

Johnny's mouth dropped open.

'Yes,' she said. 'You heard me right.'

'You're joking . . . how? I mean . . . ?'

'Well, it's a miracle!' she said. 'An immaculate conception.

It was that night that you came back to Mum's and stayed over.'

Johnny shook his head. 'Not that night after Chelsea was upset?'

'When else?'

For a second Johnny thought he was going to pass out, his heart was thumping so hard.

One night a while ago, they'd gone for a drink together after the school had called Laura in because Chelsea had been struggling to settle in. Pulling her out of her private school in North London and sending her to the local comprehensive, it was hardly surprising that she'd found the adjustment hard with everything else that was going on. He and Laura had been separated for months by then; their mutual loneliness had become close to unbearable. Later on, he'd seen Laura home. Both her mother and Chelsea were in bed by then, so she'd invited him in for a nightcap and one thing had led to another. But even so . . .

'Laura, that was weeks ago,' he said. 'How come you didn't find out sooner?'

She rolled her eyes. 'Johnny, I'm a forty-something woman. Perimenopausal! My periods are all over the place . . .'

He still couldn't quite believe it. Like he didn't have enough problems.

'I knew coming back with you that night was a mistake.'

His words stung Laura and he could see her disappointment in him. He knew allowing his selfishness to surface was a mistake, but he couldn't help it.

That attitude was everything she'd left him for, everything she hated. Johnny had thought the world revolved around him for most of their life together. Never taking responsibility.

She shook her head. 'This is just so typical of you.'

Johnny's mouth had dried up.

'I know it's my fault,' she continued, shaking her head. 'I came off the pill when we separated, I didn't want another relationship. Christ, I can't believe it! I'm too old for this, Johnny. What a mess!'

Laura's eyes filled with tears and her bottom lip started to quiver.

Johnny felt ashamed then, and told himself to get a grip on the situation. 'Hey, come on, don't blame yourself.' He stroked her hand and she didn't try to stop him.

This moment was so different from when Laura had found out she was expecting Chelsea. They had tried for years to have a child but it just never worked out. Laura always blamed his alcohol and drug abuse and said his sperm couldn't swim straight because they were pissed and rolling around inside his balls, and like him didn't have a clue where they were going anyway.

'Well,' she said. 'You don't need to worry, I'll take care of it, as per usual.'

'What do you mean, I don't need to worry?'

She turned away, sipping more coffee. 'I've booked into a clinic. I'm having a termination.'

A chill passed through him. 'An abortion.'

She nodded.

'Well . . . If that's what you think is best. It's *your* body.'

Anger flashed across her face. 'And it's *your* child.'

'And yours.'

'Tell me about it. How do you think I feel, having to

play God with a potential life? The one that's growing inside me as we speak?'

Johnny felt useless. An all too familiar feeling. 'I . . . I just . . . I don't know what you want me to say,' he stammered.

She placed her coffee down. 'Don't say anything. It won't make any difference anyway.'

He nodded. The silence stretched out between them.

'I don't *want* this,' she suddenly said, 'but you've made me feel this way. If it was left up to you, we wouldn't have had Chelsea in the first place.'

'That's not fair. This is different – look at us now.'

But Laura had the bit between her teeth and wouldn't let go; years of pent-up resentment came spilling out. 'You know it's true. "I'm not ready for it" is all you ever said when we were trying.'

'Well I was wrong. We've been over this a thousand times. Look, I'm sure it will be all right . . . if you had another kid.'

'Says *you*.' Her eyes stabbed accusation. 'Who'd barely be involved and leave everything to me as usual.'

'I'd try to be, if you'd let me.'

She shook her head. 'You say that now, but we both know the truth.'

He did. Johnny had never been good at commitment. Even Laura's quest to get pregnant with Chelsea had made him scared, convinced it would leave him feeling old, force him to give up his dreams too early. Laura disentangled her hand from his grasp.

'I would have spoken to you first, just to see what you thought. But you didn't get back to me last night. I barely slept a wink. So, when I got up this morning, it was all decided.'

'Look, if you think this is for the best . . .'

Laura sighed, all the fight seemingly gone. She reached out and touched his grizzled cheek. 'It takes two to tango. Look, it was stupid of me to let that night happen. It's not like you forced me. So, I'm accepting my fault in this too.' She sat back. 'That's why I've made the decision I have.'

Her eyes threatened to fill with tears again and her lips trembled, but she straightened herself.

'What happened to your eye, by the way?'

'Oh . . . bumped into a door.'

'You sure it wasn't a window frame? While you were jumping out of some married woman's bedroom?' He smiled weakly, and they locked eyes for a moment. Johnny felt his heart ache for them both. How the fuck had they ended up here?

'When's it happening?'

'Monday morning. Ten o'clock. I've made an appointment.'

'I'll come with you.'

'Christ, no!' She snapped that so sharply that he flinched. Again, she made an effort to soften. 'Look . . . I know you didn't look for this.' Her tears reappeared. 'I just wish you'd been around last night . . . in my hour of need. What the hell were you doing at four in the morning, or dare I not ask?'

No, you daren't.

'I don't know.' He made a hapless, helpless gesture. 'I was dead to the world.'

'Story of your life?'

'Laura . . . look, let me come with you to the clinic. You

shouldn't have to face something like this alone, I'll come and get you at Susanna's, we'll go there together.'

'God, Johnny . . .' Her shoulders began heaving and a sob escaped.

He scrambled around the table, slipped in next to her and wrapped her in his arms. 'I'll definitely come with you. I'll meet you there at two.'

She nodded. 'I'm so scared though, and worried . . . what will I tell Chelsea?'

'We'll figure something out, love, don't worry.'

He glanced about him, suddenly anxious in case some arsehole had spotted them and decided to take a photo of this miserable moment.

'Look let's get out of here, I'll put you in a cab.'

'OK,' she sniffed. 'I'll pay on the way out.'

Johnny felt the air rush out of him as they left. After all that emotion he couldn't even afford to pick up the tab. How were they ever going to figure any of this out?

13

LIVING THE LIE

Thursday

After putting Laura in a black cab, he'd found himself shell-shocked on a bench in Hanover Square. The only people he'd thought anywhere near him were a bunch of rough sleepers who were gathered near the modern sculpture in the centre. They were dishevelled, and smelling of booze and weed even from here. They were paying him no attention whatsoever but had been talking to a bloke who clearly wasn't one of their number. He was about Johnny's age, his clothes were clean, and he had soft but lined features, his pure white hair cut very short.

The man looked over his shoulder and saw Johnny; there was a flash of recognition on his face which broadened into a wide smile, as the man turned and headed towards him.

'Graham?' Johnny said as he came close.

'Yeah, it's me,' the man's face crinkled warmly. 'I thought it was you, Johnny!'

It was Graham Dwell, one-time frontman for a rival Eighties outfit, The Peril, who'd famously given it all up to become a Church of England priest, and who in his last interview with the *NME*, had said that the homeless of London were now his audience, 'if they'll have me'.

Graham shook his hand. 'So, what brings you to a park bench this Thursday morning?'

You have no idea.

'This 'n that.' Johnny rose to his feet and shook hands, immediately noticing the clerical collar under Graham's jumper. He glanced again at the group of rowdy drinkers. 'You're still ministering to the flock then?'

'That's what I do these days. So . . . how are you, man? You look . . .'

'Like I could be one of them?'

'Well . . .' Graham cocked his head to one side. 'You've always trodden a bit of a fine line.'

'Don't I know it.' Johnny slumped back onto the bench.

Graham's smile had faded a little. 'Working on anything exciting?'

Johnny thought about the job he had lined up for that afternoon, the sudden turn his life had taken. Then he remembered the previous night, felt the call of another hit lurking just under the surface of his self-control. He'd been an idiot and he knew it now, but there was no guarantee yet that he wouldn't get lured back in, having already given in to weakness once again. The most truthful thing he could say in that regard was: 'A little bit of this and that.'

'Got time for a chat?' Graham asked, his face open and honest.

How long have you got?

Tempting as it was to spill his heart out to an old music industry friend who had God on his side, he was just about holding it together this morning and could do without opening the floodgates.

He hesitated before saying, 'Not right now, Graham, mate.'

'Why don't you come and see me another time, then? I'm only a short stroll away, Bridle Lane, the Church of St Lawrence the Martyr. All comers welcome, Johnny. I'm there most days . . . if you ever need to talk . . .'

'Maybe I'll take you up on that some time.'

They shook hands again and Graham walked back to the desperate collection of street drinkers and homeless people. Johnny mulled running into Graham here of all places and wondered if the universe was trying to tell him something. He filed away the name of the church for future reference.

He looked around and overhead. The wash of grey cloud had broken apart, revealing blue sky, rays of midday sunshine poking through. He crossed the road and glanced through a shop window. A clock on the wall told him that it was approaching one. He was due to see Ray Caldwell at three. He had two hours to kill, and as luck would have it Hanover Square was only a short walk from the offices of Polydex Records, where Pete James was having his album playback event. The one Jackie had told him about.

Johnny started walking. He headed around the square rather than through it. The last thing he needed was to get embroiled in a fracas with Graham's flock, even though it looked as though Graham was doing a bang-up job of sorting it out. But his bike was just around the corner.

On first hearing about the album event, he'd resisted the thought of going there. Like Jackie had said, faces from his past would be swarming the event, but Laura's news made him want to fill his head with something else – anything else, in fact. Anyway, his confidence might have taken a knock and he might be skint, but he did have one thing that was still worth something.

A bit of front.

Johnny pulled the bike up close to the Polydex offices. How many times had he been in and out of places like this? Snorted charlie off their glass-topped tables and peeled a grape with his feet up on the company boss's desk. He eyed the entrance to the building on Brewer Street, and the ragtag of workers and music journos who were entering, while also noting the discreet drop-offs of small men with big hair from a small queue of Bentleys and limos. How many did he know?

As he sat on the bike and watched them go in, Johnny wondered how *he* was going to blag his way through the entrance. Would his face alone do it? His name, maybe? Would Jackie vouch for him? Perhaps, but how would she even know he was here?

With all these concerns bouncing around, he didn't notice that someone he knew was approaching along the pavement. Not until it was too late.

It was Stevie Lewis, lead singer of Chow, another band from the Eighties. A bunch of Brummies whose electronic drum synth had never dated – certainly not in Europe, and Germany in particular; they'd made an absolute fortune over there playing stadiums last summer on a reunion tour.

Johnny locked eyes with Lewis, who was making a beeline towards him. This guy had once been the smoothest customer in the business, his flaxen hair slicked into a huge Tommy Steele quiff, his preferred stage-wear a frill-fronted white shirt under a stylish silk evening jacket. These days, he was strictly a jumper and jeans man, his hair a greying mop, just like Johnny's. Unlike Johnny, though, he still had a spare, rangy physique, and a rock chick in tow, blonde and bountiful, and at least ten years his junior. Johnny was about to remove his helmet and greet another old mucker, but there was something about Lewis's approach, something that made him stop.

'Shit's not happening here for another half-hour or so,' Lewis said, making no attempt to introduce himself. 'And I could murder a curry before I go in. You got anything spare in the hotbox?' He nodded at the box on the bike used for keeping the deliveries lukewarm.

Johnny was struck dumb.

Lewis shook his head. 'No can do? Look . . . let's not fuck about. I'll give you one-fifty for everything.'

Behind Lewis, Johnny was briefly distracted by the sight of Jackie, looking incredible in a glimmering white, figure-hugging Gucci trouser suit, her hair in a French wave, dazzling all around her with that thousand-watt smile. She hadn't seen through his disguise either. In fact, she hadn't seen him at all, as she was too busy with the camera crew at her heels like a bunch of eager lapdogs.

'Come on, mate, what d'you say?' Lewis persisted. 'I'm gagging, here.'

This was close to being the most bizarre moment in Johnny's life. The last time he'd been face to face with Stevie

Lewis was after *Top of the Pops* in 1989 in the BBC bar. At that moment, they were both sitting pretty at the apex of the charts, clinking glasses as they dominated the Top 10. Even though Johnny's chin strap didn't cover his face, Lewis clearly didn't recognise him, though up close, he too had changed. There were lines around his eyes and mouth, his nose was red, his cheeks had sunk.

'You do understand English?' Lewis said.

Johnny shrugged his shoulder and shook his head, flipping open the hotbox, to show that it was empty.

'No worries, mate. Here, take this.' Lewis handed over a fiver.

Johnny wasn't sure which to be more humiliated by: that this had happened at all, or that he accepted the money. Meanwhile, Lewis sauntered off toward the entrance, the dolly bird wiggling after him in her tight, polka-dot minidress, her six-inchers clacking on the pavement. As they went inside, joining a general mob of new arrivals. Johnny waited a moment or two, then took his helmet off, stashed it in the empty hotbox, and went over there himself. He knew he was taking a chance. He wasn't on any guest list, but past fame and friendship had to count for something.

'How you doing, Marv?' he asked, strolling nonchalantly up.

The security man, who, close in, was older than he looked, grinned. 'Very good, thank you, Mr Klein. Nice to see you again.'

Pete James and The Whack had been with Polydex for their entire careers, but Klein had made a couple of albums with the label too, before a dispute had seen them go their separate ways. It had been long enough for them to become part of the Polydex 'family', at least until it all went tits up. Marv didn't bother checking his list, assuming that Johnny's name would be there, and stepped aside.

Johnny entered the building and was filtered through to a large atrium that was humming with chatter. The majority of people appeared to be music press. Stevie Lewis and his latest squeeze were on the other side of the room, which was a relief. Johnny didn't want to have to explain why, five minutes ago, he'd been delivering fast food.

He scanned the room, hoping that Mona wasn't here. Relieved not to see her, he was approached by two Polydex PR girls, wearing the usual rock chick uniform of tattoos, All Saints and DMs. They welcomed him chirpily, even if they didn't recognise him.

Wrong generation, that's all . . .

He was offered a drink from a tray laden with brandy and champagne cocktails, the other with fruit juice. Johnny opted for the juice, and allowed himself to be ushered further into the room, which was a gleaming modernist design, with a glass roof and cool white walls.

Most of the guests were milling together and chatting. Straight away, he recognised Paul Young, Chris Watson and Mel C, while Pete James, looking dapper in a neatly tailored Armani suit, was near the bar, in deep discussion with two younger blokes who had 'Polydex exec' written all over them. Pete caught sight of Johnny, a brief look of irritation crossing his face, before he continued with his conversation.

Johnny moved around. He might have felt self-conscious about his scruffy appearance, especially given that everyone else here was in their casual best, but he was too busy looking for Jackie. It was a surprise that she didn't seem to be here.

That said, it was starting to worry Johnny that no one else appeared to want to chat. Had they really all forgotten him? At the far end of the reception area, a door stood open, a corridor tilting downward to what he guessed would be the auditorium. Jackie must already be down there. She'd have made sure to get herself the best seat in the house.

'Well, if it isn't rock god himself,' a familiar voice said.

Johnny spun around to find two *very* familiar faces behind him. Two old muckers of his who he hadn't seen in ages yet who suddenly brought back a thousand shiver-inducing memories.

'Mat?' he stammered. 'What're . . .?'

'What're *we* doing here, Johnny? Same thing as you, I suppose. They're bringing out the dead.'

Johnny shook his head, emotions tumbling. They were older now, leaner, a lot more wrinkly, their hair cut sensibly short, their dress Paul Smith smart-casual. But there was no mistaking Russell's older and dourer replacement on rhythm guitar, Mat Cookson, not to mention the one guy Johnny had never fallen out with all the time they were big; the bassist, Tim Carson.

Tim give him a boyish grin. 'Great to see you, man.'

Johnny finally found his voice, 'Yeah, likewise, it really *is* great to see you guys.'

The rush of genuine joy at suddenly finding them in the midst of this scrum of strangers who either didn't know who he was or didn't care, gave him such a rush that he couldn't put it into words.

Instead, he wrapped his arms around them, the trio slapping backs and pumping hands.

'How you doing, mate?' another voice said, also coming over, this one leather-jacketed, his famous blond mop-top now run to sandy white and shorn to bristles. It was Lee Giles.

'Lee, mate!' Johnny grabbed his hand too. Any deep-down bitterness he'd harboured about Lee's excesses proving a bad influence on the band was forgotten through the pleasure of seeing him again. Johnny scanned the room for the one other member of the band still living. 'No Mike?'

'Nah.' Lee shook his head. 'Mike's on the other side of the pond . . . Aspen, Colorado. Rehab again. Flashest place you've ever seen. Mountain retreat.'

Must be great to still have that kind of cash.

'So . . . better go and press some flesh, that's what we're here for?' Mat said, businesslike. That had never changed about him, a true hustler.

Lee pulled a face. 'Suppose we should.'

The duo moved away, leaving Johnny with Tim.

'So, how you doing *really*?' Tim asked, his expression switching from pleasant surprise to genuine concern.

Johnny shrugged, unsure how much he knew. 'Not bad, you know.'

'Working on anything good?'

'A bit of this and that.'

Tim nodded. 'I hear you. Secret project.'

'Something like that. How about you?'

Tim shrugged. 'The bars are doing all right. You know me and Fiona opened another one?'

'No, I didn't.' Johnny had some vague memory that Tim had poured a load of cash into a smart members club in

Brighton, and that it had paid him huge dividends ever since. 'Anywhere nice?'

'Miami.'

'Oh . . . wow.'

Oh, fuck.

'I miss it, though, the band . . . the scene. I mean, I *really* miss it, Johnny.' Tim looked wistful. 'Mat's doing session work and earning a packet, and Lee's still threatening to write his memoirs, trying to get his shit together to bore the world with it. But I think they miss it too.'

'I'd get back into the game if I could.' Johnny replied. 'Least, I'd give it a try . . .'

Tim cocked his head. 'A reunion? A tour, you mean?'

'Maybe?'

Tim blew out a long breath. 'Never even thought you'd be up for that.'

'What're you two still nattering about?' Lee said, rejoining them.

Mat drifted over again, too. 'Just been down to the audio room. Jackie's there.'

Johnny nodded. 'Thought she would be.'

'Saw her in Dover Street the other week,' Tim said. 'She still looks good, I'll say that for her.'

Lee gave Johnny a mischievous sidelong glance. 'I heard she's footloose and fancy free again.'

Johnny raised two palms. 'Don't look at me.'

Lee frowned. 'You're not really as fucked up as they're all saying, are you?'

'What? Me? I'll be OK.'

Now Tim looked curious too. 'This isn't why you want us back together? You actually serious about that?'

Johnny shrugged again. 'Couldn't hurt to see if we can still hack it, could it?'

Tim pulled a face. 'I don't know, Johnny. It'd have to be a better reason than us all being bored. First of all, I'm not bored. Second, I doubt I've got the energy these days. Look at the fucking state of me.'

'You're in better shape than me.'

'No disrespect, pal . . .' Lee said, 'but that wouldn't be hard.'

Charming.

Johnny's band moved off with the rest of the crowd.

His bubble burst, Johnny exchanged his fruit juice for a brandy cocktail from a passing tray, and necked it before grabbing another and pushing himself further into the fray. However, before he'd gone halfway down the auditorium corridor, he was intercepted by Don Slater, looking uncharacteristically dapper in a sharp-cut suit, even if it did bulge a little here and there.

'Haven't you got some other stuff to be doing?' Slater asked quietly, under the guise of shaking Johnny's hand. 'Time's running out on our little agreement.'

Johnny snorted. 'Perhaps if you'd paid me a decent whack, I could speed up.'

Slater looked serious. 'Just don't fuck us about. For all our sakes . . . but especially yours.'

Feeling increasingly rattled, Johnny followed the others down to the lower ground floor. It was a fairly typical recording studio set-up, with its sound-proofed live room and its control booths, but there was a small auditorium too, accessible through a door on the left, fitted with seating for about a hundred and a small central stage, on which

Pete and Lennie Rice, his long-standing producer, were both now waiting behind mics. Most guests had already taken their seats, including the rest of Klein's band members. This left Johnny with the backrow which suited him just fine.

As he'd expected, Jackie was down at the front, deep in conversation with Glen Matlock on one side of her, and Mick Jones on the other. As he stood there, Jackie happened to glance around. They fleetingly locked gazes, but she afforded him no more than a brief smile.

He knew why. There might be a better offer here in this room.

Keep your options open, Jacks.

When they finally got going with the music itself, Johnny was impressed. It was very much Pete's new style, muscular hard rock fused with a solid, Gothic undertone, but he didn't get very far into it before someone came down the stairs behind him and crouched at his shoulder. It was one of the young execs Pete had been chatting to when Johnny had first arrived. His hair was dyed blond and he sported a full hipster beard.

'Can we have a chat?' he said.

'Yeah, why not.'

He followed the bloke through the recording studio next door and then all the way up the corridor to the atrium on the ground floor, where he swung around.

'You haven't been invited,' he said curtly.

Seriously?

'Mate,' Johnny said with more than a hint of weariness. 'I've probably more right to be in here than you have.'

'Oh, really?' The young exec, who couldn't have been a

day over twenty-five, gave a sarcastic smile. Then called
out: 'Marvin!'

The security guy strode in.

'Don't worry, Marv, I'm going,' Johnny said.

'Good to see you again, Mr Klein,' Marv replied.

'Thanks, mate. Catch you later.'

Johnny tried to shake it off as he stepped out into the
cool autumn air, but it wasn't easy; he knew he should have
stayed away. He inhaled the stale Soho air and headed
towards the bike, retrieving his helmet stored in the hotbox.
As he glanced inside, he saw something he hadn't noticed
before, a baseball cap with 'Graceland' emblazoned across
it in rhinestones. He took it out and examined it – no
marketing costs spared by the Major. He was just about to
mount the bike when he glanced back over the road at the
Polydex building . . . and froze.

A familiar-looking guy was loitering outside the building.
Almost immediately, he knew why.

The bloke was early twenties, lean built but tall, with a
scruffy head of mouse-brown hair, a wispy moustache and
a goatee beard. Even then it might not have struck Johnny
immediately that this was the same bloke from Jackie's back
garden, had he not been wearing a woolly cap very similar
to the one that Johnny had yanked off his head.

He remained astride the bike, still helmeted, watching
covertly as the fella, though he was more of a kid really,
came towards him. Only when they were very close, the
bloke not realising it was him, did Johnny become certain.
Something to do with the livid purple bruise across the
bridge of the bastard's nose. Johnny hadn't realised it at
the time, but he'd landed a good one after all. In daylight,

there was nothing frightening about this customer at all. But the business with Jackie had bugged him the other night and now was bugging him again.

This little shit was undoubtedly stalking her. He wasn't just a peeping Tom who got off trying to spy on her in the altogether. He'd now come to her place of work. So, what came next? An attack on Jackie herself?

Johnny dismounted, took the helmet off, stowed it in the hotbox, grabbed the Graceland baseball cap, shoving it on his head, before locking the hotbox and heading after the bloke on foot.

The kid was now about fifty yards ahead and unaware he was being followed.

This time, for once, Johnny was happy to remain anonymous.

14

PAST DAMAGE

Thursday

'Laura Hall?' Mona asked.

Laura, who'd just arrived at her mother's front door in Muswell Hill, and was in the process of unlocking it, looked around. Immediately, Mona saw a woman who was attractive and well-groomed in a Burberry mac, but underneath her sheen, Mona thought she looked tired and stressed. The last time she'd probably laid eyes on Johnny's ex had been years ago, arriving at Mill Hill to interview Johnny. She'd looked beautiful and relaxed and in control, heading out in her car for the TV studios as Mona had arrived. She seemed less confident now, more vulnerable.

'Sorry,' Laura said. 'Do I recognise you?'

Mona offered her business card. 'Mona Mistry. *Classic Rock* magazine.'

Laura's expression hardened. 'This'll be about Johnny

then?' She backed towards the front door. 'Sorry, darling . . . he's not my problem anymore.'

'Anything I ask you will be strictly off the record.'

'Then why ask me?' Laura pushed the door open.

'It's not about the fact he's just had his house taken off him,' Mona said quickly. 'That's not news. Besides, I get all that from the horse's mouth. I mean from Johnny himself. I'm currently his landlady.'

Laura turned back, scepticism written all over her, to the point where she almost looked amused. 'You're his *landlady*? What do you take me for?'

Mona shrugged, feeling a little self-conscious. 'Looks can be deceptive.'

'I bet they're not too deceptive in your case.' Laura moved to shut the door on Mona.

'Laura . . .' Mona pleaded. 'I've got to speak to you,' she pleaded. 'I'm worried that Johnny's got himself into something.'

'That's his usual situation. He normally falls in shit and comes up smelling of roses.'

'Not this time, I'm serious. I think he needs help.'

Laura gave a wry smile. 'And let me guess . . . does that help involve me and him getting back together? And he didn't send you to give me this message . . . honestly?'

'He doesn't even know I'm here. He'd probably go nuts if he found out.'

Laura gave her a long stare. Then sighed. 'Just so long as you know that I haven't got very long. I'm busy even if you aren't.'

Laura went inside, but left the door open behind her. Mona stepped over the threshold and ventured inside the house.

This certainly wasn't the chilled, supercool Laura Hall of daytime TV sofas, though it was easy to picture the press being all over her since her break with Johnny. Not to mention the glee the gutter press had shown, at her expense mostly, when the not infrequent stories broke about his habitual infidelities. Maybe it had been wishful thinking on Mona's part, hoping she'd find a sympathetic ear here.

She went inside. There was no turning back now.

He'd seen it a dozen times on films and TV, but Johnny had never realised how difficult tailing someone through London was in real life. Full concentration was required at all times in order to keep him within sight.

However, once they'd rounded the corner onto Oxford Street, Johnny was warier. If his target suddenly hailed a cab, and there were plenty cruising past, there'd be nothing he could do and he would lose track of Jackie's stalker.

Johnny crossed the road and followed him from the opposite side of the street, occasionally losing sight of him and having to alter his pace to keep up discreetly. The next problem though, came at the junction with Davies Street, where, completely without warning, the bastard veered left, vanishing into Bond Street underground station.

'Shit!' Johnny increased his stride, glancing left to right for a break in the traffic.

One came quickly, but now he knew that he was in trouble as the bloke disappeared from view into the crowded station.

He broke into a run, the entrance to the tube station still seeming miles ahead of him. 'Sodding, bloody shit!'

Grateful again that he had Mona's Oyster card in his pocket, Johnny nipped in across the busy concourse and quickly tapped through the barriers.

Which way had his target gone?

He hovered uncertainly, before taking a gamble that Jackie's stalker was heading towards Highgate, where she lived. That could mean either the Central or the Elizabeth to connect with the Northern Line. Taking a chance on the Central Line, he hurried down, taking the escalator two treads at a time.

As he came out onto the westbound platform, he glanced at the overhead monitor. The next train wasn't due for two minutes. The guy should still be here.

But though Johnny stared down the arcing length of the platform, conscious that he was breathing hard, his face beaded with sweat, he saw no one he recognised.

So, what the fuck now, Johnny?

Suddenly the kid appeared from behind, halting at his shoulder. Less than a foot away.

Johnny went rigid. Felt his breath catch. The kid also gazed along the platform.

Has he sussed me?

Johnny risked a sidelong glance.

The kid still stared along the platform, seemingly lost in thought. Johnny held his ground, pivoting slightly away, trying to look nonchalant though his heart thundered in his chest. The kid strolled forward a short distance, never once glancing at Johnny.

With a low groan and a soft, warm breeze, the next train approached.

Johnny steadied himself. The chase was still on.

*

In truth, Laura didn't know what to make of this unexpected guest. On one hand, the girl who called herself Mona was cute and pretty, typical groupie material, and dressed with rock chick confidence. It would be just like Johnny to send a message through someone like this, even someone he was shagging. But then, on the other hand, whoever this Mona Mistry was, there was something honest about her.

'How do you take your coffee?' Laura asked, brusque and businesslike as she took her mac off, hung it over the back of a chair, and flipped the kettle on.

'Erm, black . . . please. No sugar.' Mona came warily into the kitchen. She glanced around, as if to ensure they were alone.

'Don't worry,' Laura said. Her plans to have lunch in town had been kiboshed after her meeting with Johnny; she had lost her appetite and started to feel unwell, so opted to come home early. She'd recovered a little since then, and her mum and Chelsea had gone to the flicks without her. At least, this meant they had the house to themselves now. 'There's no one else here.'

'I want to make it quite clear, Ms Hall—'

'I'm still Mrs Klein. How long for, I can't say. Sit down, by the way, you're making me nervous.'

Mona sat at the breakfast bar. 'I want to make it clear that Johnny and I are not an item.'

Laura snorted. 'I bet that wasn't *his* decision.'

'Actually, it was . . . or *is*.' The girl shrugged, awkwardly. 'Lots of people must find him hard to resist.'

'What about you?'

The girl didn't answer immediately. 'I was very young when Johnny was a star.'

'Weren't we all.'

'That's not what's going on. I'm more of a friend.' The visitor nodded her thanks as a steaming mug was set in front of her.

'That's interesting, I wasn't sure he knew the meaning of the word where women are concerned.' Laura leaned against the sink to sip from her own mug. 'He doesn't normally need a come-on. So, what're you trying to tell me, he's turned over a new leaf for real?'

The girl shrugged. 'I don't know. I don't even know where he is. Even for Johnny, he's being a bit hard to pin down.'

'You do surprise me.' Laura sniffed. She still wasn't sure she was buying all this, but she decided to play along. 'OK, Mona . . . you and him aren't sleeping together. I won't pretend that last part of it isn't hard to believe, you being a hot babe, an' all. But I've got to take you at face value. So what did you come here for?'

'I came to ask about Jackie Phillips.'

It was a gut-punch to Laura. Just the sound of that name was enough to make her blood boil. 'Jackie Phillips? That snake?'

'There's obviously no love lost?' Mona ventured.

'Seeing as she was the first high-profile person the paparazzi caught Johnny shagging while we were married, then no there isn't.'

'This was quite some time ago, though?'

'It might as well have been yesterday as far as I'm concerned.'

'Did she break your marriage up?'

'Why should I tell you any of this?'

'I promise you it's off the record.'

Laura sighed. 'I never got over the betrayal, and it ate away at us.' She sipped at her own coffee. 'The first unspoken rule of the rock n roll wife. One, don't ask questions if you don't like the answers. Two, what happens on tour stays on tour, all those old clichés are true, unfortunately. This was different.'

'In what way?'

'There's another rule that says don't shit on your own doorstep.' Laura felt shivers of rage pass through her. 'I wish I could tell you the answer was simple. But let me assure you of something, Mona Whoever You Are . . . Jackie Phillips is a conniving little bitch. And a slapper of the first order. You know that his wasn't the first celebrity knob she'd been caught riding on?'

'Yeah.' Mona nodded. 'She's got – or had – a bit of a reputation.'

'Reputation? She went through rock stars like most of us go through hot dinners. And that doesn't take into account all the wannabees she jumped in the sack with. Young lads trying to get on in the industry, who thought she was going to help them.'

'I know . . .' Funny thing was, Mona did know a bit. When she'd first started out, there had been a big story in the papers about Jackie, and one that she'd covered briefly in her first sub-editor job for the music press. It involved an up-and-coming star who'd fallen foul of the tabloids after getting tangled up with her. Mona tried to remember his name.

'Not that there was much she could get out of *them*,' Laura continued. 'Apart from two or three orgasms more than the one and a half she probably managed to crank out of drug-addled idiots like Johnny. But it was mainly VIP dicks that she notched on her bedpost.'

'Yeah . . .'

'So, if you've come here to talk to me about Jackie Phillips, Mona . . . it had better be with news that she's been tarred and feathered and run out of town by an army of angry wives and girlfriends, because right at this moment, nothing less would cheer me up.'

Johnny hopped into the next carriage of the Central Line train, positioning himself so that he could see through the door-windows where the carriages joined and keep an eye on his target. They were now heading towards the centre of town. The crowds thickened dramatically when they stopped at Oxford Circus, more and more people piling on board. The two windows continually moved out of line with each other as the train jolted onward, which made it impossible to keep his eyes on the bloke.

As they pulled into Tottenham Court Road, the platform was chocka and as the doors hissed open, Johnny had to push hard to get out. He hadn't seen his target get off, but he'd assumed that he would, and he wasn't wrong in that at least.

There was another nerve-racking moment when the kid came straight towards him, shouldering roughly past as he sought to make progress through the mob. Again, he didn't seem to notice that Johnny was someone who'd been shadowing him since Brewer Street.

The kid wore a persistent snarl, seeming irritated that he was sharing the same planet with everyone else.

He'd just entered an intersection of passageways when a whole mob of yammering students came trundling in from the left, completely swamping him, causing him to lose sight of his quarry. Frantic, but keeping it as polite as possible so as not to draw attention to himself, Johnny fought and struggled his way through them. But the bloke had vanished.

Quivering as he hovered there, Johnny scanned the various avenues that he might have taken. It had to be the Northern Line. It *had* to. Hastily, he threaded through the students, following his instinct. The crowd extended down onto the escalator. There was barely room to pass by on the left. When he got to the bottom, he made a beeline for the northbound platform, where a train was just pulling in. Johnny ran the last thirty yards, ducking and sidestepping his fellow travellers with an agility that surprised him. He slid out onto the platform, where a quick glance at the nearest indicator showed that the idling train was bound for High Barnet, which meant that it would stop at Highgate.

He had to force his way into the closest compartment just as the doors slid closed behind him. Torturous moments followed, Johnny standing shoulder to shoulder and front to back with chattering, laughing tourists. He was so squashed by them that he couldn't even reach out to the handrail when they rounded bends, simply swaying back and forth, trusting to his fellow passengers to keep him upright. As least it meant that no one was taking any notice of him in his Graceland cap, and the anonymity of the tube meant that no one looked up and recognised him, but he had no idea where peeping Tom had got to.

He'd only know for certain about that when he finally got to Highgate.

*

'Even with Johnny's bad behaviour, I had a fairly good idea it was Jackie who did the seducing,' Laura said, though not with the same intensity of feeling as before. Hurt lingered there, evidently, but she seemed mostly to have a grip on it. 'Don't get me wrong, Mona. Johnny was always like a dog with two dicks, but I doubt that Jackie played hard to get. Even then, though . . .' she hesitated. 'I don't think he saw her more than a couple of times. Once the story broke, she disappeared from his life.'

'Well, now she's reappeared,' Mona replied.

Laura thought about that. She didn't seem hugely moved. 'This is the trouble you think he's in?'

'All I know is that Jackie is in contact with Johnny again, and I don't think it's a good decision on his part.'

'It certainly wouldn't be, if he had any cash left in the bank for that gold-digging cow to stick her nose into.'

Mona shook her head. 'I think it might be more serious than that.' She described Johnny's sudden departure from Graceland the previous night, and how he hadn't reappeared until early this morning, sporting a black eye.

'I saw that so-called black eye, myself,' Laura replied. 'Didn't look too serious.'

'No, but he'd been duffed up.'

'Darling, people are queuing up to do that.'

Mona stared at her. 'Seriously?'

Laura sighed. 'Probably not, no. But he told me he banged it on a door.'

'You didn't believe that?'

Laura was noncommittal as she sipped more coffee. 'How do you know he actually went to see Jackie? Did you follow him or something?'

Mona explained how she'd found the scribbled number in the bin and traced it to Jackie Phillips' home address. She took it from her jacket pocket and offered it as proof.

Laura looked amused again. 'Maybe Jackie's seeing someone already, and three was a crowd.'

Mona had considered that possibility too. If you were going to shack up with someone like Jackie Phillips it would always pay to be sure that some jilted boyfriend or even husband wasn't going to turn up halfway through.

'It could be that,' she said. 'But I know a few people in the business . . . I've been asking around, and they all seem fairly certain that Jackie's on her own at present.'

Laura placed her empty mug on the draining board. 'You seem to be very interested, considering you say you're not involved with Johnny.'

'Look, the truth is that he's already hanging out with some slimeball types.'

'I know he's been to see Pete James and Don Slater.'

'I'm talking worse people than that.'

'Mona, you are aware that Johnny's an adult, and perfectly capable of lying on beds that he's made for himself.'

Mona wondered how cruelly you had to mistreat the supposed love of your life for them to think that, whatever bad thing was coming for you, it was no more than you deserved.

'You want to know about Jackie Phillips?' Laura said. 'Try contacting some *real* wreckage that she left behind. Is the name Ben Randall familiar to you?'

Bingo, Mona thought. 'An actor . . . singer?'

'Both. Good-looking fella, or he was.'

Mona now remembered him. A tall, well-built guy.

Very dark hair and intense looks. This was the story she'd worked on as she was starting out. Ben Randall had started on stage, appearing in hit productions like *Miss Saigon* and *Phantom of the Opera*, before moving into film and TV, where his brooding macho presence had secured him straight acting roles, often as villains or tough guys. She remembered that he'd seemed like a nice bloke.

Ben Randall's was not a face she'd seen on screen any time recently.

'The poor sap was going steady with Jackie for quite a few years,' Laura explained. 'Apparently, he was besotted with her. This was post-Johnny, of course, but there were plenty other fish . . . certainly where Jackie was concerned, and eventually it got to be too much for him. He had some kind of nervous breakdown.'

'Poor guy . . .'

Laura arched an eyebrow. 'Or lucky guy, depending on your point of view. But you want to find out everything you need to know about Jackie Phillips, every evil thing she's done in her life, or will do in the future, go to the person she hurt most in all the world.'

'I thought I had.'

Laura chuckled bitterly. 'No way, darling. Not even close.'

By the time the Northern Line train pulled into Highgate station, the crowd that had filled it had been reduced to a handful. Johnny felt exhausted; his untrained body hadn't done this much exercise in ages.

He hesitated briefly before stepping out.

Only three other people got off the train, and the kid was one of them. Still blinded to the presence of everyone else by vanity, he strode towards the exit, enabling Johnny to tail him again at a distance of fifty yards or so. Outside on the street, it almost seemed inevitable where they were going, though in truth, Johnny couldn't believe it.

We're heading towards Jackie's place? Why the fuck does that not surprise me?

But what the hell was this kid up to?

But when they came onto Jackie's road, Johnny halting at the corner to watch, he saw the bloke had crossed over to the side where Jackie's house was, and had now walked straight past it.

And then turned into the next property along.

He's her next-door fucking neighbour?

Johnny was thunderstruck. So much so that he came out and walked slowly and disbelievingly along the road himself. It explained the easy access the bastard had had to her garden through the rickety fence at the rear. The fact that he was in the habit of suddenly disappearing when the cops arrived.

Johnny stayed on his own side of the road as he walked, but he eyed the house as he did. It was the same size as Jackie's, a three-floor townhouse, though not as well maintained. At a guess, it had probably been divided into flats.

Johnny strode on, mulling things over.

If the little bastard lived here, that made things easier. All Johnny needed to do was contact Jackie and let her know what was what. As for Johnny himself, well . . . he could now get on with his day.

'Oh, bollocks,' he shut his eyes tightly.

The appointment with Caldwell! It had been scheduled for three, over at the Reuters news building. Johnny had no way of telling the time – he didn't even own a watch or have his Motorola with him, damn his stupid arse – but it had to be well past two.

Weary though he was, he hammered back along the street. It didn't matter if the kid saw him now. In fact, nothing really mattered . . . except making that appointment.

There's only five fucking grand riding on it.

15

RIGHT ACROSS TOWN

Thursday

The sky was dark and overbearing, and Johnny felt a strange pressure pushing down on top of his head as he raced towards the end of Jackie's road. It had started to rain, and despite the fact he was running down Pete's five hundred quid at a rate of knots, he knew there was no other way he could get across London without getting back on the tube again, a prospect he couldn't face. He pulled up the collar of his jacket as a black cab stopped just up ahead of him and a woman got out. Johnny ran across the road and before she closed the door to the cab, he was at the driver's window.

'Take me to Canary Wharf, the Reuters building . . .'

The driver nodded and Johnny got in. His head was feeling like it was about to explode; all he wanted to do was sit in silence and stare out of the window like everyone else was allowed to, to try and get a grip over what had just happened, but he wasn't like anyone else.

The driver's intercom crackled to life. 'It is, innit?'

Johnny didn't respond. *Bollocks.*

'I saw you back in the day. Wembley arena, great show it was, I was there with my missus; first date.' There was no avoiding the cabbie, whose eyes met his own in the rear-view mirror. 'I'll tell you what, lot of water has passed under the bridge since then, Johnny-boy. I had your mate in here the other day, what's his name – it'll come to me, Lee something.'

'Lee Giles, our keyboard player.' Johnny replied, blankly.

'Yeah that's him. He's doing all right for himself, ain't he – nice bit of Armani he was wearing.'

Lee Giles had kicked the hard stuff and ended up marrying the heir to a giant clothing brand in the early Nineties; the brand went public and they had made millions. Lee had made all the *right* choices in life.

'Yeah, I dropped him at his gaff in Holland Park. Tell you what, you don't get many of them in a pound! Anyway, he gave me a twenty-quid tip, lovely job!'

The driver prattled on for the journey; Johnny nodded and smiled robotically, adding the odd oh and ah where he thought it was needed, but the cabbie didn't seem to care.

It gave Johnny time to mull over what had gone on that morning. If Jackie's stalker was living next door, was she walking past him every day and not realising it? Hopefully he'd done enough for her to talk to the police, but he couldn't understand why she didn't want to. She couldn't expect him to solve the problem, he could barely work out what day of the week it was.

By the time the driver had finished his speech on how well Lee Giles had done for himself, and how he'd once had that

Liam Gallagher in his cab, and how Joan Collins had once tipped him a oner after he dropped her at the Savoy, the journey across town had come to an end and they had reached Canada Square. Johnny jumped in over the cabbie's cockney growl, cutting him off.

'Just on this corner please, pal.'

The cab pulled to a stop and he jumped out. 'That'll be thirty quid please, Johnny.'

Johnny delved into his pockets and pulled out a crumpled twenty-pound note, a used tissue and an old guitar pick with his face printed on the front. He'd had them made for his last arena tour to throw out to the crowd.

The cab driver could see Johnny starting to get flustered as he re-checked his pockets, looking for the extra tenner.

'Johnny, I take cards if that helps,' he said, with the tone of a man who'd seen it all before.

'Nah, I haven't got one. Bank cancelled it.'

The driver looked at Johnny, reading his embarrassment.

'I read about your split in *The Sun*,' he said. 'My best mate split up with his missus and ended up with fuck all. Living back at home with his mum now, in his old bedroom.'

Johnny shrugged. 'Things could have been a lot worse for him, believe me.'

'Look, I tell you what,' said the cabbie after a pause. 'Gimme that guitar pick and we'll call it evens, how's that?'

Johnny felt humbled, and a twinge of guilt for not showing more interest in the bloke, who was clearly salt of the earth. He smiled and handed over the plectrum.

The driver threw him a wink. 'My missus will love that. Mind how you go, my old son.'

Then, he put his toe on the gas and left Johnny outside the looming Reuters press building.

It was another of those faceless concrete offices that had sprung up all over the top end of the Isle of Dogs since Johnny had been a lad. When he entered the sterile glass and steel reception area, he was booked in by a sweet middle-aged woman who recognised him straight away, and nonchalantly spoke to him as if she spoke to the rich and famous every day. Which she probably did.

'Johnny . . . are you here for an interview? Who are you seeing?'

'Ray Caldwell please,' he replied.

'Sixth floor, Johnny.' She pointed towards the lifts.

The doors slid open, and Johnny found himself stepping out onto the sixth floor, and into the realm of Ray Caldwell.

16

THE NEWS OF THE SCREWS

Thursday

During the short ride up in the lift, Johnny thought hard about what he was about to do. He had never sold a story to the press about anyone, and had never dealt directly with anyone in the press, always relying on a record company PR go-between. He'd always thought of them as the enemy that you held at arm's length like a firework you knew would explode but you just didn't know when.

The lift doors opened and Johnny was face to face with Ray Caldwell, the editor of *Maxi* magazine.

'Johnny Klein . . . Johnny fucking Klein,' Caldwell said. 'Now there's a face I know well.'

They shook hands, Johnny reminding himself he was being pragmatic. If *Maxi* didn't do it, someone else would.

In so many ways, Caldwell was just right for this kind of work. He even resembled a vulture. At one time, newspaper editors were one of a kind, all shirtsleeves, braces, thick glasses, half-smoked cigs and unruly iron-grey hair, but Caldwell preferred jeans and a T-shirt – Johnny was sure this was the same T-shirt he'd worn back in the Eighties – and was short and skinny in stature, his hairless skull shrivelled with age, his nose curved and beaklike, his eyes two hard black points that gleamed with permanent, unhealthy curiosity.

'Come into my lair.' He led Johnny through a network of corridors and offices, only a few of which looked to be manned.

They entered an empty photographic studio, where Caldwell closed the door behind them and then rubbed his hands. 'So . . . there's some film you want me to look at?'

Straight to business, Johnny noted. It would have been nice to have been offered a coffee or tea first, but probably for the best that he hadn't been.

Johnny handed over the roll of film in question. 'Can you still develop glossies here?'

Caldwell chuckled. 'You bet your boots we can. Gonna be worth my while though, is it? I mean . . .' his eyes twinkled darkly. 'Better not just be your fucking holiday snaps.'

'Let's just say . . .' Johnny mused. 'Let's just say it's someone doing something they really shouldn't. Only took 'em last night.'

Caldwell smirked. 'Good enough.'

He crossed the room, opened the door with a red bulb over the top, and ushered Johnny through into what had once been a darkroom. There was hardly space for the pair of them in there together; it was a ten-by-ten box, though it still felt empty. Johnny was sure there ought to be more equipment on show.

Caldwell chattered on, 'I haven't used this room for a long while now. Stroke of luck we have any fluid left. But I forgot how much I used to love it . . . got me out of the office for a bit, plus brought a little artwork into the day, know what I mean? Developing pictures. David Bailey and all that. Fucking digitalisation.'

He hit a switch, the main light going off, the red safelight activating, throwing a lurid crimson glow across the blank walls. He got to it quickly, working first with the enlarger, projecting a bright beam through the negatives on the base. Johnny stood back, waiting patiently, listening with interest as his host reminisced about the good old days.

'Tell you, the world was fucking ours back then. If you didn't have a front-page story come deadline, you made one up . . . no bother.'

Johnny stood transfixed and watched the magic happen as Caldwell moved the pictures around in the development fluid, then lifted them out one by one with a pair of plastic tongs, clipping them to a horizontal wire stretched across the room just above their heads.

'I know you fancied yourself a snapper back in the day,' Caldwell said. 'But I'm surprised you haven't gone digital yet. I mean, fuck's sake, a bloke with your dosh. Thought you'd be well up on your tech. Check out *The Gadget Show*, mate. Best thing on telly. They're always wanking over the latest bits of digital kit.'

Johnny shrugged. 'Nah, I prefer it old school.'

Caldwell nodded. 'Know what you mean, my old son. Tell you what, times have changed, though. I mean, here we are, cooped up in my little sanctuary, chewing the fat about better days . . . days when I used to tear you apart in the centre pages of this fucking rag. I was only able to do that, though, because your generation were proper rock stars. There was nothing you lot weren't getting up to. Shagging, snorting, all-night boozing, drugs, police busts, and some of the birds you lot knocked about with. These days it's all yoga and smoothies and therapists.' He whistled. 'Hey, do you remember the time you were up in court for doing coke in the Queen's private loo at Buckingham Palace? What was it . . . oh yeah, you were giving out some prizes in the back garden and ended up being escorted out in front of all the nippers.' Caldwell hooted. 'Mother of God, we were rolling up in here. Fucking rolling up. I can still see the headline now: *Johnny de-Kleined*. Fucking brilliant.'

Johnny smiled; he could still laugh at that himself. It had been a favourite anecdote of his for years.

But Caldwell had more.

'I must have waited outside your gaff for about a week before I got that picture of you putting the rubbish out in your dressing gown. Do you remember?' Caldwell chortled again. 'Your gown flapped open and you could see your tackle . . . not being funny, mate, but I made a fortune off that shot. You didn't look great, though. Bag of shit, really.'

Johnny's smile faded. Of all the candid shots taken of him over the years by so many different photographers, many of them chronicling some of his truly worst moments, this was the one he'd hated the most. At the time, he'd wanted to sue the magazine, but was told in no uncertain terms by his record company that he needed them. That he wouldn't get the press necessary for his next album if he turned against them. It was shit, but that's how it worked, everyone had to play the game.

In the long run, that had probably been true. But he still wished he'd sued them.

'Good job you had enough pixels to cover my dick,' Johnny grunted. 'Otherwise, it would've been really embarrassing.'

Caldwell shrugged. 'Nothing to be ashamed of there, lad.' He chuckled to himself. 'Course, in Germany they printed the untouched version.'

'I never saw that.'

'You win some, you lose some.' Caldwell shrugged, no apology in his voice. He did what he did, and had no shame about it. They were all in the game. 'C'est la vie, Johnny . . . C'est la fucking vie.'

Caldwell switched on the main light. 'OK, JK, let's have a look at your smudges.'

He spread the newly developed glossies on a giant light table. Johnny stood close, though not too close. He was dismayed to see that the first couple were too grainy and blurry to show anything of interest. The light in that seedy cellar had been awful after all, but then the camera appeared to have adjusted itself, because the next two were clear as day, both portraying a person in such a state of deterioration that he looked more like an animal than a man. It was Jerry Fox, rearing over the voluptuous form of a prone naked woman, lines of coke still visible on her flat belly, his nostrils also caked with the stuff, his eyes screwed shut as he sucked on a pipe.

Johnny tensed but felt a deep thrill of satisfaction as he watched Caldwell's puzzlement turn slowly to cold, simmering anger. The editor glanced at his guest sidelong but didn't say anything.

'Yep . . . Jerry Fox, your number one reporter,' he said,

trying to sound nonchalant. 'You know, that journalist who's made his entire career exposing junkie celebs?'

Caldwell looked down at the picture again, the glow from the light table bouncing off his bald head. Without speaking, he took a small, round eyeglass from a drawer.

'That won't change anything,' Johnny said. 'It's him, your chief reporter. I guarantee it.'

Caldwell's face had now turned blood-red, but still he kept his cool. 'So, you gave up the music business to turn into a fucking little creep, did you?' he said.

'No, being a creep would be doing it for a living. I'm only doing it once.'

Caldwell reddened even more. 'Get off your high horse, Klein.' He jammed a finger down on the print. 'You think this fucking clown's never been caught with his strides down before?'

'Not just his strides though, is it? He's lucky he didn't OD.'

'And what the fuck were *you* doing there? You telling me *you* didn't partake?'

'I'm not the one in the pictures, am I?' Johnny felt that scratch of addiction crawl across his scalp, and he pushed it away.

'This some kind of belated revenge, Johnny? Or are you just desperate for a few quid?' His anger transformed into a hard, bitter grin. 'Yeah, that's right . . . we're well aware how much of a no-mark you've turned into. We *know* how skint you are.'

'I'm not here for the money . . .'

'Good, because you won't be getting a fucking penny, you sad, washed-up bastard.' Caldwell's pent-up rage was at last breaking through. 'If only *you* were making the news, eh, Klein? If only the Great British public gave a shit about *you* these days. I mean, it wasn't even worth our while paying for the tip-off that you're now living upstairs in the *Bengal Palace*, or whatever the fuck it's called. Who'd be surprised by that after the way you blew your career?'

'Here's the deal, Ray—'

'There'll be no deal, loser!'

Johnny held his ground. 'You're planning on running an exposé on Pete James next week . . .'

'What?' Caldwell looked genuinely startled. '*That's* what this is about? You're now doing the dirty jobs for Don weirdo Slater? That fucking Seventies relic? And there was me, thinking you'd finally shown some nous off your own bat. You're even more pathetic than I thought.'

'Pete's an old mate . . .'

'Pete's no one's mate. Least of all yours. How do you think he's still going strong if he doesn't take advantage of useful idiots like you?'

'If you let the story on Pete slide . . . forget it altogether, you get these.' Johnny grabbed the negatives of the Jerry Fox pictures and held them up. 'You don't, and I'll make sure every newspaper in this country gets to see them. The whole country will know what a bunch of hypocrites you bastards are. And that includes you, Ray. You're the fucking gaffer here. It'll all come from you, they'll say.'

Caldwell eyed Johnny. 'You're really serious about this, aren't you?'

'You and your paper will be left with zero credibility, nothing, nada, zilch.'

'You know . . .' Caldwell barked with laughter. 'Looking at you, it's like looking at a Russian platoon sent to the front line with no bullets to fire.'

'However it looks, we are where we are.'

'You seriously think no one in this business knows what Jerry Fox is like? There's not a man in this building that hasn't partied with him at one point or another. Not a man, or woman. He can't do a number on himself if he fucking wanted to. You won't get a soul to touch those smudges, I promise you. You're wasting your fucking time. And if you seriously think you're gonna ruin *Maxi's* credibility, I've got news for you, my son . . . we lost that years ago. We've got none. The only reason we sell millions of copies each weekend is because we haven't got any credibility. You want credibility, go buy *The Times*. Now fuck off.'

Johnny felt the ground slipping underneath his feet.

'You deaf as well as thick?' Caldwell asked. He pointed at the darkroom door. 'Go.'

Johnny shoved the negatives into his pocket, then headed out of the studio, his tail well and truly between his Levi's, feeling like a little boy lost in a man's world. He opened the door and sloped out into the photographic studio, a sense of abject failure fast filtering through him. His humiliation was suddenly so intense that he felt an urge to run.

But run where? To who?

Pete and Don? Like that would get him anywhere.

'Klein . . . wait up!'

Johnny halted uncertainly. Glancing back over his shoulder, he could still see through the door to the dark-room, where Caldwell was leaning down over the prints, the eyeglass jammed to his left eyeball as he examined them up close.

'Get your arse in here!' the journalist shouted. Warily, Johnny edged towards the entrance. 'Get in here!' Caldwell shouted again. 'Get the fuck in! And close that fucking door!'

Puzzled, Johnny complied. Had it all been a game of brinkmanship? Had Caldwell blinked first?

'Come on, Ray, it's not going to cost you much,' he said. 'Letting that Pete James story slip.'

'Shut up, I wanna show you something,' Caldwell muttered, still examining the glossies.

Caldwell glanced round at him, but all his anger had vanished. In fact, he'd paled, his skin almost ashen. He offered Johnny the eyeglass. Confused, Johnny took it and leaned down, his magnified gaze following Caldwell's stubby index finger.

It singled out the top right corner of the photographic image, in particular two figures who'd clearly been in the background all along, but who, in his own drugged-up state at the time, Johnny hadn't noticed. One of them was middle-aged and wore a suit without a tie, the shirt underneath open at the collar. He was shaven-headed and lean-faced, with a small moustache. This other guy was younger by a couple of decades at least, wearing a black beanie hat and low-slung Adidas joggers. Though taller by several inches, he looked genuinely frightened. He was offering two empty palms as a sign of peace.

He looked again at the shaven-headed figure with the tash, squinting through the eyeglass.

'Fuck,' he breathed.

'Yeah, that's right,' Caldwell said in a voice of grim satisfaction. 'You haven't been completely buried alive in that crumbling white elephant of yours up in Mill Hill?'

'Karl Jones,' Johnny said.

'Correct.'

Johnny thought back to the newspaper article. 'I haven't seen him in the flesh for years,' Johnny muttered. 'I wouldn't have recognised him, but . . .'

'You *know* the evil fucker?'

Johnny nodded. 'We're from the same manor.'

'Hah!' Caldwell sounded delighted. 'Then you're in even bigger trouble than I thought.' He leaned against the light table. 'You can't show these pictures to anyone, Johnny, old son. You wouldn't even be advised to show them to Slater and James, because they're just about stupid enough to try and get something out of it.'

Johnny's mind raced. 'Eh? Known gangster seen in brothel? In drugs den? Is that going to surprise anyone? Is it going to worry Karl Jones? Everyone already knows what he's like.'

Caldwell arched an eyebrow. 'So, you'd publish them? Well . . . don't fucking stop there. Why not put them online. Let the whole world see for free.'

'I'll do what I want with them, Ray. Unless, like I say, you ditch that Pete James story.'

The journalist now seemed genuinely surprised. 'Are you fucking stupid? Look at that picture again. Tell me what you see. You know who that kid is?'

From Johnny's blank expression, the answer was evident.

'It's a good thing you came to me, Johnny, old son. Because I'm just about to save you from making the biggest mistake in your life.'

'Who is it?' Johnny asked tightly.

'You've seriously not heard of Sean Rogers?'

Johnny shook his head.

'Rogers was briefly a big noise down in South London. Independent record producer, working with up-and-coming Grime artists. But about a year and a half ago, he got busted for dealing. Did eight months in Pentonville. Probably only been out a couple. Whether he'd have got his legit career back on track, who knows, but there wasn't much chance of that after this morning . . . when they fished him out of the Thames. Both arms and legs broken, skull cracked.'

Johnny shuddered at the horror of that, but Caldwell hadn't finished.

'You know the form, son. He either owed someone something he couldn't pay, or he'd proved too talkative before he got banged up . . . maybe to get himself a sweeter sentence. Didn't help much in the long run though, did it? And now look who he was with the very night this happened. Captured for posterity.'

'Shit,' Johnny breathed.

'Like I say . . . you can't show these images to anyone. Or sell them. Except to me.'

Johnny shook his head. 'No chance. *You* can't use them either. Not if you don't want Jones and his crew on your case.'

'You can leave me to worry about that.'

Johnny shook his head. 'If they're worth something to you, then they're worth something to us.'

'You haven't got the contacts I have.' Caldwell offered an open hand for the negatives.

Johnny shook bis head and backed away. 'You seriously think Jones is going to offer you money for these?'

'He won't pay *you*, I can tell you that. Not someone with your zero status.'

'Pete and Don have got dosh . . .'

'Pete's a poncey pop star who thinks he's a hard man. Don thinks he's part of Jones's world, but he's playing at it. Me though . . . I'm in it up to my elbows. So, here's *my* deal, Johnny. You get five hundred, cash in hand, and you leave those negatives here. Not only that, we never talk about this again. I didn't get them from you.'

'No . . .' Johnny backed to the door. 'No way.'

'All right, I'll tell you what. Two grand, and that's it. Absolute final offer. I'll throw the Pete James story in as well, it's a load of bollocks anyway. Can't say fairer than that, can I?'

Johnny's thoughts were tumbling. On one hand that seemed reasonable, Johnny thought. And on top of everything else, like Caldwell said, he'd get some cash out of it. He didn't need to declare that to Pete or Don. They were being stingy bastards with him, anyway.

Are you fucking serious? You're going to hand these pictures over to a guy like this . . . knowing what you now know? For what'd be nothing more than pocket money?

Something clicked in Johnny's head. 'Forget it. If it was anyone else, I'd take the two grand, and I'm having these too.' Johnny quickly reached past him, whipping the glossies off the light table, and snatched the ones still suspended from the drying wire. He hurried out into the studio. 'The stakes are too high, mate. C'est la fucking vie.' He said over his shoulder. 'Sorry, Ray.'

'You fucking will be.'

Johnny glanced back before leaving and saw Caldwell reaching for his mobile phone. 'If you're calling who I think you're calling, remind him that *we're* the ones holding the stuff.'

'I'm sure that'll scare him shitless.'

'Hey, Ray . . . this is just business, nothing personal.'

Caldwell didn't look up from his phone. 'You've been watching too many gangster movies, Johnny-boy. It's *always* fucking personal.'

17

OVERSTEPPING THE MARK

Thursday

Johnny came out from under the Reuters building canopy into a furious rainstorm. He crammed the photographs and the negatives into an inside pocket as he stumbled, wet to the skin, across the plaza. When he finally made it onto a road, he didn't even notice the vehicle bearing towards him through the downpour. Only at the last second did he see the glare of its headlights, hear the protracted screech of its brakes.

'Johnny!' Ravi said, leaning out from the driver's window. 'What are you doing here, are you all right?'

Johnny nodded dumbly, climbing in through the front passenger door, not thinking to apologise for the droplets shaking themselves loose from his wringing-wet jacket.

'I've just been to Billingsgate to pick up some fresh lobsters for the Major,' Ravi said cheerfully, pointing his thumb towards the back of the van.

The old fish market sat in the shadow of One Canada Square, the iconic skyscraper of London's Docklands. Johnny thought of the boxes in the back filled with lobsters, their black pincers trussed up with rubber bands, destined for the cooking pot at Graceland. At least they were having a worse day than he was.

'What are you doing here, Johnny? Was that the Reuter's Building you were coming out of? Were you in there for some kind of publicity thing for a new project? Must be really exciting, being in the newspapers all the time.'

He chattered on as they swept along West India Avenue through curtains of rain, finally connecting with a slower-moving logjam of traffic on Westferry Road.

'One thing that the Major was saying,' Ravi said, adopting a slightly more serious tone, 'is . . . well, is that these singing lessons you offered me . . . well . . . he feels that we should get these out of the way as soon as possible. So that I'll be ready to go into the studio at the first opportunity.'

'You're probably right, Ravi, mate,' Johnny muttered.

'Do you think we could maybe start this afternoon?'

'Hmm?'

Ravi smiled bashfully. 'I'm going to try my hand at some new songs. I've never tackled "In the Ghetto", for example, or "A Little Less Conversation". And we have the backing tracks for both, so . . . why not? I thought striking while the iron was hot was the best route?'

Give it a rest, Ravi . . . Johnny zoned out. He was back in that meeting with Ray Caldwell, trying to work out where it left them now.

Caldwell had called the Pete James story nothing but bollocks anyway. And in a way this chimed with what Pete himself had said; his main worry was that it might distract from the launch of the new single, there'd been no mention of anything as drastic as ruining his reputation. The question at this stage was how would Caldwell regard the story now that all these other potential bombs were attached? He wasn't the sort who'd normally respond to blackmail. He'd made that abundantly clear, but he couldn't be absolutely certain the threat of Karl Jones would dissuade them from running the Jerry Fox pictures.

Certainly, if Johnny himself was in Ray Caldwell's shoes, he'd write that Pete James story off. Not just because it was bollocks but because it wasn't worth the risk.

'What do you reckon, Johnny?'

Johnny tuned back in. 'Erm . . . I don't really know about today, Ravi.'

Caldwell had bragged that he was part of Karl Jones's dodgy world. *I'm in it up to my elbows*. The very notion that he might have something to hang over Jones's head had spurred him to offer two grand there and then . . . even to kick the Pete James scoop.

What did that mean?

'Look, I'd like to help you out, Ravi . . . I really would. But I've got other shit going on, you know.'

Ravi couldn't hide his disappointment.

'I didn't mean that to sound the way it probably did, I'm not saying "never".' Johnny said. 'Don't worry, we'll get stuck in soon. I promise. But I'm going to need a little space for a couple of days or so.'

'Of course, yes.' Ravi nodded soberly, clearly trying to be grown-up. Most likely, that was the same thing that Mona had told him, probably more than once.

It was then that he remembered the delivery bike – he'd left the fucking thing in Soho.

Ravi dropped Johnny off in front of Graceland before heading to the restaurant's garage round the back. Johnny went in through the front door, to find the place heaving.

'Johnny, Johnny!' the Major shouted, crossing the dining area. 'This is wonderful, look, you're all over the news!'

Johnny saw that the Major was carrying a scrolled-up newspaper, which he rapidly unfurled and passed to Johnny. It was that day's issue of the *Standard*, and about five pages in was a grainy reproduction of a screen grab, presumably courtesy of one of the crowd in the Hole in the Wall the previous night. On it, Johnny stood tall at the front of the stage, guitar in one hand, saluting the rapturous audience with the other. Jerry Fox was visible behind him, still on the drumkit. The headline read:

80s heartthrob rises to occasion!

Johnny's heart sank.

The Major beamed at him. 'A comeback! I thought you were retired. This is the best news. Maybe you can entertain my guests . . . while you're here, I mean.'

Yes, this is just dandy. Precisely what you need at this moment.

'I just knew you were cooking something up.' The Major clapped his hands with joy. 'But now you're on the comeback trail, you can do a special performance here. Just imagine if I can announce that you'll be performing with Elvis. Our regulars would go bananas!'

'OK . . . obviously not at this particular moment.'

'Oh, no, obviously,' the Major said, in apparent sincere agreement. 'But soon? I can have some posters made and we can put them up in the windows. Some flyers maybe, which we can give out on Brick Lane . . .'

Johnny nodded, yearning to get away. 'As soon as we can manage it, yeah?'

'Absolutely, as soon as . . .' The Major clapped again.

Johnny all but staggered up the stairs, still holding on to the crumpled copy of the *Standard*. The smell enveloping him as he ascended was the usual concoction of rich, sweet spices. What had once been mouth-watering felt suddenly heady, clingy, overpowering. It was a relief to let himself into the flat, close the door and open the window, fresh air floating in through Elvis's gigantic eye. He leaned out, poking his head through the eyehole.

Down below, though rendered dimmer by the gauze, Brick Lane was its usual chaos. Shouting revellers streamed back and forth. On the other side of the road, a drunken vagrant was pissing against a wall.

He used to wonder how you could ever finish up like that. Broken, destitute. A member of the living dead, with no one to give a damn if you lived or died.

He *used* to wonder that. He didn't anymore.

He drifted back across the room to the bed, where he shucked off his jacket, then stood on the back heel of his right cowboy boot so that he could kick it off. After doing the same with the left, he plonked himself down. It was so tempting now to simply lay his aching, fifty-seven-year-old bones flat, close his eyes and go to sleep. But not yet.

Instead, he remained seated as picked up his Motorola from the bedside table, took a card from its drawer, and tapped in the number.

Don Slater answered on the fourth ring. 'Aye?'

'Don . . . it's Johnny.'

A brief silence followed. 'We were wondering when you were going to call.' Slater wasn't inclined to be the friendliest guy on the block anyway, but today he was even sourer than usual. 'We were wondering if that was five hundred quid badly spent. You want the truth, Johnny . . . we still are. What the fuck have you done?'

'Look . . . I've got the crap on Jerry Fox.'

'Your new best mate, you mean? Or is he just your drummer? We're a bit confused.'

'OK, you've seen the *Standard*.'

'The *Standard*? You're saying it's in there too?'

'Look I can explain, it got a bit out of hand . . . Don, I got what you wanted, a very compromising picture of Jerry Fox.'

'Don't fucking worry about it?' came a brash Yorkshire voice from somewhere in the background. Pete, presumably. 'Give that here!' There was a kerfuffle as the phone was handed over, and then it was Pete's mouth to the device. 'Johnny, you really are one stupid bastard.'

'Pete, mate—'

'Don't mate me! All I wanted is for you to get some dirt on Jerry Fox, nothing else. Tell me what's complicated about that. I'll tell you what: nothing. The next thing I see, you and him are all over YouTube, playing a gig together.'

'It was just a fuck-about in the press club,' Johnny protested.

'YouTube, Johnny. And now, it's all over the red tops too.'

Johnny was rattled. 'All I could use to get near him was who I am, which is why you asked me, and that's why he wanted me on stage with him. Gave me a chance to get close enough to him afterwards to get some pics.'

Pete didn't immediately respond. 'What kind of pics are we talking?'

'Good 'uns. Though you wouldn't know that from Ray Caldwell's reaction.'

'Ray Caldwell? At *Maxi*?'

'That's who you wanted me to take them to, isn't it?'

'I didn't want you to take them to anyone, you silly bollocks! It's up to Don to decide what to do with them!' Pete shouted. 'Jesus, Johnny . . . you know the kind of pressure I'm under, trying to get this new mix finished for the album before I go away? I've still gotta do the artwork and I've got PR coming out of my fucking ears . . . and now, on top of that, I've got this problem to worry about.'

Slater's voice cut in again. 'Let *me* talk to him. Why get a dog if you have to bark yourself.' With much disgruntled muttering he took the phone, Pete still shouting in the background. 'What's happened that we don't know about?'

Johnny gave it to him scene by scene. How he'd blagged his way into the Hole in the Wall Club, how his presence had been revealed to Jerry Fox before he could do anything about it, how he'd been invited to play alongside him, and how afterwards, Fox had taken him to a drugs den, where he'd managed to get shots of the guy pursuing seriously questionable activities.

'The guy's a total dope factory,' Johnny concluded. 'I don't know how he's even alive.'

'And then you went and took them to Fox's boss your-self?'

'I thought that's what you wanted.'

'Tell him he's a fucking idiot!' Pete's voice sounded from the near distance.

'What did Caldwell say?' Slater asked.

Johnny hesitated. This was a big moment. It had all gone so badly pear-shaped thus far that he didn't dare mention the Karl Jones situation.

'Just talked a load of shite,' Johnny said. 'Came the big "I am", you know. No one blackmails me and all that trash.'

Yeah, he offered me a kind of carrot and stick deal, the carrot being two grand and a none-too convincing guarantee that he'd bin the Pete story, the stick – most likely a very big one – the possibility that, if I didn't hand the pictures over, Karl Jones might come looking for them himself.

He had to admit it: the pictures were fucking useless. And if he wanted his money, Don and Pete were going to demand that he go out there and get something else, which would be next to impossible with Jerry Fox now on his guard.

'But you've still got the pictures and the negs?' Slater replied. 'Hold on to them.'

'I will.'

'Keep them somewhere safe. What's this number you've called us from?'

Johnny yawned. 'My phone.'

'Right. This is the number we'll call you back on when we're ready to receive. You got all that?'

'Yeah, sure.'

'I mean it, Johnny. Don't fuck this up.'

If it wasn't for the remote chance that Pete had made some vague promise to try and shoehorn him back into the music biz, Johnny might have let rip, telling them that *they* were the fuck-ups. They should have coughed up for a proper private dick, instead of hiring some cut-price jackass who couldn't even afford a black cab.

Before he could reply, Slater cut the call.

Weary to his bones, Johnny dragged himself to his feet and swayed into the bathroom, where he squirted what felt like a pint of urine into the toilet bowl.

He returned to the bedroom and opened up the copy of the *Standard* again. Johnny didn't recognise himself straight away; there was something different about his face that the camera on someone's phone had captured. The pixels had caught a look that hadn't been there for years, a look that could only come from the high of performing. He hadn't seen that smile for as long as he could remember; it belonged to a younger man. A man who lived in a world where no grass was greener on the other side, no road led to anywhere more exciting than where he was going. It was the look of perfect ease.

It disappeared as the decades went past and he became more dependent on booze and drugs, and it definitely hadn't been the face that had just looked back at itself in his bathroom mirror.

Johnny hated the feeling. It was like bumping into a twin who had been blessed with luck, who had won the lottery in his early twenties and was still living his best life. That was the person who was staring out at him from this grainy picture. It filled him with a sense of doom; his veins tingled with anxiety. Johnny closed his eyes, blocking out his surroundings, trying to calm himself, but that night with Jerry Fox was still hitting him like a ton of bricks in continual flashbacks. The more he tried to put it to the back of his memory, the more it would raise its ugly head. Johnny knew there was only one way to forget about it; it used to be his answer to everything, simple, just do it again, but he had been down that road before and he knew that he would need to put every ounce of his being into making sure he didn't slip again.

Why bother, you're fucked anyway?

He dropped full length onto the bed, his head burying itself in the pillow. The street noise from outside gradually faded. A police car siren passed by below, but Johnny didn't stir. In fact, its echoing wail pushed him deeper and deeper into the void. All the way back to Italy, where he was being driven towards the Megadome Palace in Rome in the back of a cop car.

The rest of the guys, of course, were in the minibus following.

It was the beginning of the end for Klein. Johnny's individual fame had massively outgrown the rest of them. The hysteria reached fever pitch when *he* walked onto the stage. It was *his* autograph the fans screamed for. It was during that trip to Italy that he'd first begun toying with the idea of a solo career. But what would happen to them if he broke up the band? They might argue that they didn't need it anymore. That they had their wives and kids. But Johnny knew better. Klein was still the main thing in their lives, their only real earner. Without it, without *him*, where would they be?

The slick cobblestones under the police car's tyres caused the vehicle to shift and swerve as it raced down the Apian Way. Laura was seated next to him. She'd flown out for the weekend to see the show, but now he looked past her and out of the car window as it careered from one side of the ancient highway to the other, feeling ever more unstable.

Instead of cypress trees lining the Appian way, he saw tall wooden crosses bearing the tortured bodies of crucified naked men, groaning and twitching, arms outstretched, wrists nailed, fresh blood creeping down the timber uprights. *It's not real*, he told himself. Just the after-effects of a bad trip. And yet it looked *terribly* real. So real that he didn't want Laura to see. He tried to tell her not to peep from the window but couldn't get the words out. Then, the car hit a bump in the road and fishtailed out of control, spinning across the cobbles . . . Johnny grabbed his wife.

'Not again!' he screamed.

Laura didn't seem frightened or even alarmed, looping her arms around his shoulders gently, whispering into his ear: 'Darling, it's all right . . .'

Johnny's eyes snapped open as it hit him where he actually was.

A female form was snuggled alongside him on the narrow bed, lying at his back, her sensual contours melded into his, one arm hooked over his chest.

'Mona,' he muttered. 'What . . . are you . . . ?'

'You OK, babe?' she breathed into his ear. 'You were shaking, trying to speak . . . like something had really scared you. You had me worried. I haven't seen you like that before.'

Johnny realised that his pillow was damp, most likely with tears, as he rolled to face her.

'Just . . . I was . . .' He tried to explain that he'd been having a dream, but she wouldn't let him, instead enveloping his mouth with hers. Softly at first, tenderly, then with steadily more urgency, her tongue twisted between his lips.

It came as a shock to him, but not an unpleasant one, that she was completely naked.

BLAM . . . BLAM . . . BLAM . . .

Three thunderous impacts landed, so loud they were like gunfire.

This time Johnny's eyes really did snap open.

He sat upright on the bed, too fuddled to think straight, though it was clear that he was alone, the room otherwise empty.

BLAM . . . BLAM . . . BLAM . . .

A knocking on the door. It didn't sound as loud now, but it couldn't have failed to wake him.

Slowly, achily, he got to his feet and opened it.

Mona was standing there. The real Mona, not the naked fantasy from his dreams, though clad as ever in her rock chick uniform – denim jacket over short cotton dress, cowboy boots.

'Did I wake you up?'

He nodded dully, scratching at the thick grey nest of his hair. 'Half and half.'

'Jeez, Johnny . . .' Her beautiful eyes widened. 'You look totally done in.'

'Erm, yeah . . . feels like I've been here, there and every-where today.'

'I'll give you a bit of time to get sorted.' She backed towards the top of the stairs.

'It's OK.' He stood aside so that she could come in.

'You . . . hungry?' she asked, standing by the window. She seemed wary, as if talking to someone who wasn't quite there.

Not for food.

'Dunno,' he replied, unable to get a grip on himself, and only now remembering that his clothes were still crumpled and damp, which probably explained the pillow as well. 'Could probably do with a bath first. Though I had one this morning. Then I had another on the Isle of Dogs.'

She frowned. 'You've been to the Isle of Dogs?'

Johnny eyed her as he slumped back onto the bed. There she was again, snooping. He felt irritated.

'Just, you know . . .' he shrugged. 'Don't worry about it, Mona.'

'I'm worried about *you*.'

'Yeah, you said that this morning.'

'How did it go with Laura?' She watched him carefully.

'Laura?'

'You had to rush off last night. There was something urgent.'

'It was nothing. Just some cash I owed her.'

'Johnny, you haven't got any cash.'

He gave a long, frustrated sigh. 'Mona, come on . . .'

'OK, OK. I shouldn't snoop, but you know, a problem shared and all that.'

He shook his head. 'That has to be the dumbest thing anyone ever said.'

She frowned. 'Excuse me?'

'A problem shared is a problem halved.' He scrubbed his hand through his hair again.

And now suddenly it all came pouring out, and there

was no way he could stop it. How this so-called refuge he'd been provided with was more like a punishment room, where his every move was monitored, where constant, ridiculous demands were made of him.

'It's an excuse for being nosy,' he said flatly, 'pretending to give a shit when all you really want is to get all the sordid details about someone's private life. Isn't that what you're paid for? Isn't that why you're here at all?'

Mona now stood rigid, gazing at him with horror. Then lurched for the door.

Johnny jumped up. 'Mona, wait . . .'

She ignored him, hauling the door open and going out onto the landing.

He followed, already riddled with regret. 'Mona, I didn't mean it.'

She spun to face him, eyes glistening with tears. 'Why say it then?'

'It's just . . . look, things are getting on top of me a little.'

'I don't want to point this out, Johnny, but they'd be much worse if it wasn't for me.'

'Yeah, look, you're right, I know, but . . .' He stumbled to the banister, wondering for half a sec if he was going to pitch himself over it into the gloom below. 'But that doesn't give you the right to keep tabs on me day and night, I'm fine.'

'You're not. And it's not like we haven't got a vested interest.' She tapped his shoulder to get him to look round at her. 'If you're in trouble, Johnny – I mean *real* trouble – I don't want you bringing it here to my uncle's restaurant.'

'Yeah, OK.' He nodded. 'Fair enough.'

'Maybe, but you still told me to mind my own business.

Quite rudely, if I may say so.' It was said in a tone he'd never heard her use before.

'Mona, come on. Look . . . we were supposed to be having dinner together tonight.'

'Oh, don't let me get in the way of another free meal.'

'Mona . . .' He reached out, but she backed away.

'Get the hell away from me, Johnny Klein. You may think I'm just another fan going doe-eyed at your every move, but right now I'm the only friend in the world you've got who doesn't want something in return. And you've got the nerve to call me a nosy bitch!'

She pushed past him and descended the staircase.

'I didn't say that.'

'You didn't need to. And by the way, where's my uncle's delivery bike?'

'Ah well, about that . . .'

'Fuck off, Johnny.'

And with that she was gone, vanished into the lower floors of the restaurant.

He knew he had to go after her, and quickly. It wasn't true that he hadn't directed that brief tirade at *her*. He clearly had. But he hadn't meant it. Taking drugs with Jerry Fox had fucked everything up, let in all sorts of shit he'd been trying to keep at bay. Mona might well be the only thing between him and a life on the street. If he'd genuinely upset her, he might be the next junkie on Brick Lane pissing up a wall.

He lumbered back into the room, lugged his boots on and thudded down the stairs in pursuit.

As he hurried out through the back of the restaurant and down the cluttered yard towards the washhouse, he could hear Ravi crooning away to himself. As before, when the guy didn't have an audience, it was much smoother and more tuneful. But there was no time for that now.

Johnny ventured into the alley, where he heard Mona before he saw her. She'd come out of the yard and walked about twenty yards, then stopped. She was facing the wall, crying softly.

'Shit,' he said under his breath, and advanced towards her. 'Mona . . . you must know I wasn't talking about you up there. Not *you* specifically.'

Her shoulders shuddered, and she dug a tissue from the pocket in her denim jacket, sniffling into it. Johnny was about to speak again, perhaps try for a more fulsome, more heartfelt apology, but this time he was distracted by something else.

The sun had sunk behind the surrounding buildings, a blue-grey dusk having filled the narrow backstreet, but not so much that it didn't conceal a figure walking down it towards them. It was male and wearing a long coat, but it was also a good hundred yards off, and yet of such stature that it seemed to fill the alley from side to side.

This guy had to be the size of a bear. In addition, he was coming on at pace, as if now that he'd seen them, he'd speeded up.

An ugly seed planted itself in the back of Johnny's mind – were these Karl Jones's heavies?

'Caldwell, you fucker,' he said under his breath. 'You didn't?' Hurriedly, he put a hand on Mona's shoulder. 'Listen, love . . . we need to go back inside, OK?'

She shrugged him loose. 'Leave me alone, Johnny.' She sniffled again. 'You've really messed up today. I thought we were at least friends.'

'We are friends. For that reason . . .' His eyes strayed again to the approaching figure, which was now close enough to see that it had a thick black beard, that its open coat was of black leather, that it wore a black sweater and jeans underneath, and light glinted off steel toe-capped boots. 'For that reason, I want you to come back inside straight away.' He tugged her arm urgently.

The advancing shape was now less than fifty yards off and heading straight for them. An animal grin split the hefty bush that covered the lower half of the guy's face.

'Johnny!' She glanced round, mascara still streaking her cheeks. And then she froze. She was staring behind them.

He turned. Two more massive figures had entered the alley. They too wore long, heavy overcoats; both were built like brick shithouses. One of them had dark hair scraped back in a ponytail, while the other, who was younger but with eerily similar features, wore his in a razored-off flat-top. These two were both close enough for him to see their faces properly. To call them Neanderthal would have been unfair to that prehistoric race.

'We've got to get indoors right now,' Johnny said, steering her towards the open gate to the Graceland rear yard, only for a pair of immense toe-capped boots to come clomping up as Beard broke into a run.

'Johnny!' Mona screamed.

'Quickly!' Johnny shouted, his own voice turning shrill, but he already knew that they weren't going to make it, not least because the other two would get to the gate first.

He halted, wrapping Mona in his arms, spinning her around, not sure which direction the greatest danger threatened from. Though he discovered that half a second later, when a mighty fist – literally a bone knuckleduster, though there were gold sovereigns on it to add metal – slammed into his face. Mona screamed again, staggering away as Johnny fell.

He rolled in the dirt, his skull ringing.

'You bastards!' Johnny heard Mona yell. 'He hasn't got any money. Neither of us have.'

'Out the way, darling,' one of them replied. 'It's not *you* we're after.'

Johnny glanced up. It was Biker. In a single motion, he'd snatched hold of Mona and flung her aside like a doll, so that she hit the wall, gasping in pain as she slid down it. Biker and Flat-top now converged on him along with Beard.

'Fellas, wait . . .' Johnny raised a desperate hand.

'Seems you've got something we need,' Beard laughed, swinging in with a steel-tipped boot. It dug into Johnny's left kidney like a fiery javelin, the pain filling his entire body.

'That not so?' Flat-top aimed a kick of his own, this one connecting with his victim's right temple. Johnny had never realised until this moment that you really *could* see stars.

'Look,' he blubbered through a mouth filled with blood, 'I haven't . . . I haven't . . .'

'Let me guess . . . you haven't got it with you?' Beard hauled him to his feet by the collar of his T-shirt. 'So boring when they say that. Especially for them.'

He headbutted Johnny on the bridge of his nose.

Johnny slumped down into a jellified heap. Biker's left boot flew in again, from behind. Like a sledgehammer, it struck Johnny between the shoulders. Flat-top swung his boot too.

'First we're going to rip the clothes off you,' Beard said. 'Every stitch. Just to see for ourselves. And if what you're saying's true, we're going to take you to it, wherever it is, and you starkers and all, and then you're going to give it to us.'

Johnny could only grunt in response, before a knee crashed into the side of his head, keeling him all the way over.

'All right, boys,' Beard said with a chuckle. 'Strip the—'

Only for a different voice to intervene.

'*FUCK YOU, MOTHERFUCKERS!*' it yowled.

Johnny glanced up again, groggily, to see that four of the Graceland kitchen staff had emerged from the restaurant's rear gate wielding blades, a baseball bat, and any other weapon they could lay their hands on. At their forefront stood Ravi, complete with rock-solid quiff, wraparound shades and rhinestone jumpsuit. He was only short, but right now he looked mighty and ready for anything with an Elvis Presley kung fu kick.

Like everything that had happened over the last week, it was a surreal scene, and it was the last thing Johnny remembered before darkness engulfed him.

18

BROTHER FROM
ANOTHER MOTHER

Russell Withers and Johnny had been friends since their first day at secondary school, when they'd found themselves side by side at identical wooden desks, both of which had been engraved over the years with the names and logos of pop stars and rock bands of every era, from Cliff Richard to the Beatles.

It had surely been fated, because they were the last two boys standing when the new class had first piled in. They weren't similar at all. Johnny was shy, backwards in coming forwards and hadn't really found his personality yet, whereas Russell was outgoing, loud and funny. He had a cheeky way about him, the Artful Dodger, a class clown that everybody loved, but no one believed he would end up with much in life.

If there was one thing they did have in common, though, it was the guitar.

Both had had lessons, and both could play. It helped them form a bond quickly, and it wasn't long after they'd first met when they'd started hooking up at weekends, playing along to Russell's older brother Vince's record collection: Bowie, T. Rex and the Stones, and later on, the New York Dolls, the Velvet Underground. If Russell's brother bought the record, Russell and Johnny would learn it. Like most kids of their age, their chord changes were a little slow and their voices lacked depth, but what was missing in terms of maturity, they made up for with enthusiasm. Russell's adoring mum, Carol, would press her ear up at the bedroom door, a small smile would creep across her lips as the boys sang at the top of their teenage voices, but it would be a little longer before she was invited to listen to them play.

That came a few weeks later in Carol's living room, the lads with their backs to the three-bar electric fire, Russell's mum on the red velvet sofa, hugging her mug of tea. It was their first ever live performance, and as they bashed out their own versions of 'Honky Tonk Women' and the Faces' 'Stay with Me', Carol smiled softly all the way through, keeping the beat with her foot, and probably doubting if either of the boys knew what they were singing about, but that wasn't the point.

Russell and Johnny hit those strings so hard and with so much passion it surprised Carol. After the living room show, she'd hugged them as if they were both her sons.

'Congratulations, boys . . . that was well worth the wait. Now, go over and show Johnny's mum and dad. I'm sure they'll love it,' she urged gently in her warm, Irish brogue.

Johnny's face fell, and Carol realised that she'd put her foot in it.

'Ah Johnny, it was just an idea. You boys are welcome to become rock stars here in my house, and maybe one day we'll be putting a blue plaque on the wall outside.'

The problem was that Johnny's mum and dad had spent most of his young life shouting at each other. Johnny, even at the tenderest age, hearing every 'shit', 'fuck' and 'bitch' that erupted from their North London mouths. The walls in their small council house in Crouch End were paper thin, and he'd routinely disappear under his blankets, torch in hand, seeking escape. On Christmas Day 1972, he woke up to find a badly wrapped small Spanish guitar at the end of his bed. His disappointment in not getting the toys he'd asked for that year evaporated as the usual morning arguments broke out, and he soon discovered that the sound of the guitar was perfect for drowning out the abuse. The louder and more aggressively his parents rowed, the heavier he'd hit those strings. It was no wonder that he'd quickly grown away from his own family and much closer to Russell's.

The lads became more like brothers than friends by the time they'd finished school as sixteen-year-olds. Johnny's parents had divorced, so his own home was quieter, but his mum had begun taking it out on the gin and had retreated into herself, so it was easier for everyone if Johnny moved into Russell's house full-time.

There were moments in their lives when small things happened that changed everything, that put everything they knew into order; a straight line that sorted out the confusion, the questions, the whys and the wherefores, and even sometimes gave them the answers.

One of those was December 1976.

Russell's brother suddenly stopped buying pub rock records by the likes of Dr Feelgood and Eddie and the Hot Rods and started collecting Pink Floyd. That might have been OK for him, but not so much for the other two, whose musical lives were built around Vince's record collection. Playing along to the protracted, dreamy poetics of deep prog was near enough impossible, so it could all have ended there. But then, one Tuesday night, when Johnny and Russell were eating their tea – Bird's crispy pancakes, mash and tinned peas – something happened on the television, on the *Today* show in fact, when strait-laced presenter Bill Grundy introduced a young band who would change everything.

Johnny, Russell and Carol watched as the Sex Pistols tore their way through seven minutes of early evening telly, shocking the nation with their obscene language and 'fuck you' attitude, their anarchic performance underpinned by anger and antipathy. But what hit Johnny and Russell most was the effect it had on Carol, who was both stunned and disgusted at the same time. Carol had always been a cool kind of mum, open-minded about most things, but this hit her like a ton of bricks, driving an immediate wedge between her generation and the boys', which was the way it should be – and they loved it.

Over the next few weeks, the two budding punks sought out everything and anything on the Sex Pistols, the Damned, the Clash, the Buzzcocks. It had been one of those thunder-clap moments when everything falls into place. Punk rock was *their* thing, and they were determined to enjoy every second of it, ripping up their T-shirts and putting them back together with safety pins, cropping each other's hair and even spattering their guitars with paint, wearing eyeliner, daubing a huge 'PU' on Johnny's instrument, and a matching NK on Russell's, which made sense only when they stood side by side. But above everything else, it was the music. It was fast, exciting, it had no shame, it answered to nobody, and you didn't have to be the best musician in the world to play it.

They were sixteen when they caught the bus into London to see their first gig, Johnny Thunders and the Heartbreakers, both now in their regulation black jeans, cap sleeve T-shirts and eye make-up. The queue for the Roxy that first night straggled all the way down Neal Street, the air buzzing. The Heartbreakers were from New York, but a spearhead act for the punk movement, and this was their London debut. As such, every punk in town had to be there, including Russell and Johnny, who, if anyone asked, had never been anything else.

Arriving late, they'd been forced to stand at the back of the queue, but then something else happened. Another of those moments came along, those seminal incidents in life.

A white Rolls-Royce pulled up at the kerb right alongside them. The longest they'd ever seen. It went on forever, glimmering all over with reflected neon. It was the sort of motor you expect royalty, either of the British or Hollywood variety, to be ferried around in.

Even as they stood there, mesmerised, the tinted electric window *whirred* quietly downward and Johnny and Russell leaned forward to peer at an interior that *gleamed*: rich white leather, shiny orange teak, a bar sitting open in the central console. And lounging in the back seat like a god, clad in a long white fur coat and black sunglasses, wielding a Queen Anne glass filled with champers in one hand, and a black ebony cane in the other, was Keith Moon, the Who's very own wild man of rock.

The boys stood open-mouthed as the window slid up again and the car cruised forward, but that one, brief moment surely had to have been divine intervention. Whatever Keith Moon had, they wanted, and punk would help them get it.

Over the next few weeks, they worked feverishly, practising hard, writing songs of their own, and, crucially, recruiting drummer Mike Penfold and bassist Tim Carson by putting small ads into the back of *Melody Maker*, *Sounds*, the *NME* and of course into the obligatory paper-shop window. After that, they spent six months playing to an imaginary audience in Carol's garage and then to half-filled pubs, usually in support of bands that were going nowhere. But they knew they were good. Their songs were catchy, with clever lyrics and uplifting, anthemic choruses. But most of all, they looked amazing: four young kids who had grown out of their acne and greasy skins, and now attacked their instruments like fully fledged pop stars. It wasn't long before word was getting round that they might be the next big thing, and with almost indecent speed, it seemed, even though in truth it had only come after months of hard, focused rehearsal and sleepless nights. And then they were offered a recording contract with EMI.

That was all they'd needed. A two-album deal with an option on the second would give them more than a fair crack of the whip, and easily enough time to prove themselves.

But their first three releases crept in around the bottom of the Top 40, not enough to get them on to *Top of the Pops* and certainly not enough to keep EMI from losing interest. They were different and new, and they already possessed what would soon be recognisable as the elegant yet flamboyant Eighties style, but something just wasn't clicking.

Then another of those game-changing moments came along, the ultimate one, after which life would *never* be the same.

Three days after the release of their fourth single, they were playing a small club in Stoke. It was the last stop on the tour. They hadn't had a chart position yet and knew the sales figures were tanking. That gig itself was hard work. Again, the venue was only half-full, and when the promoter had tried to make it look respectable by filling out the empty spaces with tables and chairs, it had looked worse.

When it was over, tired and sweaty, and to the accompaniment of half-hearted applause, they trooped back into the small dressing room, where the first thing Johnny did was open a bottle of Jack Daniels and flick its plastic top at the wall. 'Won't be fucking needing that.'

The rest of the boys nodded. Instead of closing out the tour on a high, they were all hacked off. Where had it gone wrong? What the fuck had happened?

No one needed to be asked if they wanted a drink. They were going to drink that bottle of Jack dry. Even Russell had a couple of swigs. Up until then, he hadn't drunk all the tour. He'd used his share of the advance to buy himself a state-of-the-art, ember-red Ford Mustang, and had followed the band's transit from gig to gig, rather than ridden with them. He'd always been into cars, and his pride in this American beauty easily surpassed his yearning for a drop of booze.

Until that night.

It was well after midnight when they stumbled from the stage door to find that a freezing fog had risen. Tour manager Derek Potts, who was also their driver, roadie, sound tech and therapist, jumped in the van and started the cold engine. While the aged rust-bucket choked into life, stinking of fuel and exhaust, Johnny stood close by, weary and drunk, thinking how cold, grimy and rank it was going to be in there. He glanced back towards Russell, who was busy signing a couple of autographs, but was also twirling the keys to his Mustang.

Without a second thought, Johnny sloped over towards him. 'Riding with Russ,' he told the others. 'Can't do another trip in that shit-wagon.'

'Jump in,' Russell replied.

The four-litre engine bellowed to life, smoke pumping from the exhaust as they roared out of the parking bay. Johnny offered the bottle to Russell.

'Thanks, mate, but no. Already had more than I should, and it's a long drive.'

'Suit yourself.'

Johnny swilled the rest of it down, while Russell swung a fast right onto the main road, then a left at the junction, rocketing along the frosty dual carriageway with all cylinders blowing.

Johnny reclined in his seat. The adrenaline from the gig as ebbing, and the Jack had put him into a pessimistic mood.

'What you gonna do *if* EMI drop us?' he asked.

'You mean *when* they drop us?' Russell replied.

'You reckon?'

'Don't kid yourself. We're making no dosh for them. What's the point keeping us?'

Johnny looked out of the window into the gloom.

'It's Mum who I'm going to hate telling,' Russell added.

'She was the only one who ever believed in us.' Johnny wound the window down, at the same time pulling two fags from his jacket pocket. He poked both between his lips before lighting them. But the wind blasting through the window was too strong. As the flame caught, the cig on the left slipped loose, spun glowing across the interior and landed between Russell's legs. Russell gave a squawk as its fiery tip seared through the fabric of his trousers.

'Shit, Johnny . . . fuck! Get it out . . . get it fucking out!' He scrabbled at his crotch with his own hand, shouting again as he smelled burning velvet. 'Fuck! Oh, shit . . .'

Johnny's response was sluggish, the drink and depression slowing his reaction, but finally he leaned across and put his hand between Russell's legs for the lit fag. Russell looked down; it must have been only for a split second, but a split second that was enough to take his eye off the road, and one that seemed to last forever; like a slow motion moment where Johnny's brain took in way more information than it could process; a camera shooting a thousand frames a second instead of just twenty-four. Johnny and Russell looked at each other in the exact moment they hit the central barrier, they both knew what was coming.

The Mustang, which was doing nearly eighty, took

off like a graceful bird, arcing silently through the air. Then the car slammed nose-down into the tarmac. The impact was like a train wreck. In those few final seconds, Johnny would always swear that Russell turned to him and smiled.

19

HOSPITAL

All Johnny knew for certain was that he lay on a wheeled trolley, and that someone was pushing it fast down a sterile corridor. A succession of fluorescent lights passed by overhead, dazzling him through the sticky red gauze that covered his eyes. He was paralysed with agony. Couldn't move, speak, moan or scream.

'Everything'll be fine,' a soothing voice said. 'The meds'll kick in, then the pain will go away.'

But everything wasn't fine. Somehow, Johnny knew that. Where was Russell? Had he made it? He tried to call out, only to find that an oxygen mask had been placed over his mouth. Instead of trying to attract attention, he focused on staying conscious. He had some vague memory of a paramedic demanding that of him, as he lay on the tarmac, covered in blood and petrol, the huge hunk of burning, twisted wreckage only a matter of yards away.

Johnny knew all this was his fault, offering up the Jack Daniels, passing the lit cigarette to Russell. He'd started to feel himself being pulled on to a stretcher and pushed into an ambulance, it was all a blur after that.

Something Carol used to say to him and Russell when they were kids crossed his mind. 'Look after each other . . . and life will look after you.'

Carol and Russell had looked after him, but he hadn't looked after Russell, and now he was fifty feet away, lying flat on his back . . . a blackened carcass. His best mate. His brother.

'Stay with me . . . come on, mate, stay with me.' Had that been what they'd said?

But then there was another voice, 'I know you can hear me, Klein. I'm putting something in your pocket. It's a number, and you'd better fucking ring it . . . or we'll be back.'

He was confused, and too preoccupied trying to make sense of the pain running like a single icy vein through his entire body to focus on what was being said. Stay awake. That was the key. If you were conscious, you couldn't die. The trolley halted as it collided with something, and Johnny's red-tinted gaze fixed on the light source directly overhead. It was searingly bright, a blob of phosphorous reacting to the air, and yet he could gaze right into it, beautiful golden sparks cascading around him.

Ladeeez and gentlemen, the biggest band in the world . . . KLEEEIIIN!

As the sparks descended from above, dry ice rose from below, thick white billows on every side of him, like cushions, pillows, fleecy blankets.

'Least we gave him a good send-off,' Lee said from the

other side of the room, his legs straddled across the armchair.

'Closed casket, obviously. Jesus, Johnny, you don't know how lucky you were to get thrown clear. Everyone's asking about you. No one was surprised you were there.'

What the fuck, Lee? Johnny still couldn't get the words out.

'That said, there's *some* good news today.'

'Good news?'

'It's a bit shitty, though. Not the sort of thing you want to shout about.'

Good news that's shitty?

'We're Number One, mate.'

'Number . . . *One?*' He croaked the words out, finding his voice at last.

'The new record. It's gone to Number One. It's all the publicity over the crash. I mean, no one wanted it that way, obviously. But it made the front pages everywhere.'

'But . . . Russ . . .' Even in his banged-up state, horror and dismay washed over Johnny in a tsunami of emotion. 'But . . . Russell . . . *burned.*'

'I know, mate, but hey . . . I guess there really is no such thing as bad publicity.'

Johnny heard a scream pierce the scene, then realised it was coming from him.

'Johnny, Johnny!' someone said urgently, leaning down, wrapping him in an embrace.

'Lee, don't . . . just, fucking don't . . .'

'Lee's not here, Johnny, it's me.' He blinked, only now realising that it wasn't Lee Giles.

It was Mona.

*

241

Friday

'Russ . . . Russell,' Johnny stammered, trying to sit up, though physically he was all but immobilised by stiffness and pain. 'It . . . it was Russell . . .'

'Johnny, it's me,' Mona said, lowering him gently back onto the pillow.

'Yeah, but . . .' Pain gripped him again, all around his back, his chest, his neck . . . Jesus, his head was swimming, his mouth so dry that his tongue felt like a leftover raisin on Boxing Day. 'Russell . . . he died.'

Mona gave him a concerned smile as she tucked him back under the blanket. 'That was years ago, Johnny. Back in the Eighties.'

'Everything we've got . . . everything. Because Russell died . . . and it was my fault.'

'What're you talking about?'

'I've . . .' But now his memories were surging thick and fast. Who he was, why he was here, why he felt as though he'd been shoved feet first through an industrial mangle. 'I've . . . fucked everything up, haven't I?'

Mona straightened up next to the bed. 'Johnny, you're not making sense.'

He knew that and willed his brain to focus. 'Mona, what happened . . . exactly?'

'You got the hell beaten out of you, that's what.'

'Shit . . . yeah.' Now he remembered the storm of blows, the explosive impact of each one. No wonder even breathing hurt his ribs. 'But . . . well, I obviously survived. Unless you're an angel?'

'Your nosy angel. Yes, Johnny, you survived. Mainly thanks to the staff at the Royal London Hospital.'

'Yeah?' Johnny looked past her, seeing that he was on a standard ward, beds to left and right of him and opposite. Directly facing him, an elderly patient in his pyjamas sat up, his family around him.

One of them, a woman in her fifties with permed, beige hair, threw a quick glance in Johnny's direction, probably not the first. The unpleasant reality of the situation now hit home like another hard punch. The Royal London Hospital. Not a private hospital then. Of course not. Private healthcare, so essential for rock stars prone to drinking and drugging themselves to destruction, had been one of the first casualties of being skint.

'How long have I been here?' he asked.

'We got attacked on Thursday afternoon,' Mona said. 'It's now Friday teatime.'

'Friday teatime? Christ, I can't lie around like this, I've got . . .'

He tried to sit upright, but pain and disorientation overwhelmed him. He reached cautiously to the side of his head, finding thick padding held in place by a strip of bandage.

'You can't go anywhere at the moment, Johnny,' she admonished him. 'You were unconscious for ages, and then you were sedated. You need to give your body time to recover.'

'Has Laura seen me?'

'Laura doesn't know.' Mona seemed uneasy about revealing that, but Johnny was relieved. With Laura's current predicament, the last thing she needed was more bad news about her ex.

'It's best if we don't tell her,' he said. 'Not yet.'

'If that's what you want.'

'This is no good, though, Mona. I can't stay in here. It won't be long before the paparazzi find out.'

She shook her head. 'Johnny, it's probably not safe for you out there.'

'What do you mean?'

'Come on, that wasn't just an ordinary mugging.'

He tried to think it through, but it was difficult. One side of his head felt as though an iron spike was being hammered into it. 'I don't remember much, if I'm honest.'

All he had was dim and broken: the dirty floor of the alley, flying boots.

In response to this, Mona started to sniffle. He glanced at her in surprise.

She dug a tissue from her bag and put it to her nose. 'I honestly thought they were going to kill you. They just kept kicking and kicking. It was only when Ravi and the kitchen staff came out that they backed off. Before that, though, one of them leaned down, said something to you and put a piece of paper in your pocket.'

I know you can hear me, Klein . . .

'What's going on, Johnny?' she asked tearfully.

It's a number, and you'd better fucking ring it . . . or we'll be back.

'Please tell me . . .'

Johnny could only shake his head. Cold shivers passed through him.

'Mr Johnny Klein?' a voice broke in, a bit too loudly for Johnny's liking.

Johnny winced; if there was any doubt among his fellow

patients that he'd once been a legend of the stage, it had gone now.

'Mr Klein?' the doctor said again, approaching. A nurse in scrubs hurried at his heels.

Mona stepped away from the bed.

'So . . . you're back with us.' It was a statement rather than a question.

Johnny nodded weakly. 'Look, just call me Johnny and close the curtains, for fuck's sake.'

The doctor looked unimpressed.

'He used to be famous,' Mona explained. 'He thinks everyone's talking about him.'

The doctor's expression didn't change, but he nodded to the nurse, who obediently drew the plastic curtain around Johnny's bed.

The doctor gave his clipboard to the nurse, leaned down and shone a pen-sized torch into Johnny's eyes. 'Full pupil constriction,' he said, partly to himself, but also to the nurse, who was hurriedly scribbling notes. 'Good response. Any headaches, nausea, any uncontrolled shivering?'

Johnny had all those symptoms. He didn't just feel like shite, he felt like shite that had been trodden in. More than once. But he had to get out of this goldfish bowl.

'I feel OK,' he said weakly. 'Fighting fit.' The doctor looked dubious, so Johnny plucked at the collar of his NHS gown. 'I'll feel a lot better once I've got this off and my own clothes on . . . and once I'm back in my own bed. See . . . look.'

He levered himself up and tried to swing his legs to the floor, wincing as a pain that was far worse than anything he could remember from the previous night lit up his groin like a thousand fireworks exploding in unison. He glanced down in disbelief at the long, plastic tube of a catheter emerging from underneath his hospital gown. He rolled back onto the bed in agony, realising the catheter line was coming from his penis and into a bag hanging on the side of his bed.

The doctor shook his head. 'Look, you're going to be with us for a few days so we can keep an eye on you. You suffered a severe concussion yesterday, and we don't take that lightly.'

Johnny shook his head. 'I'll stay till tomorrow, but then I'm outta here.'

The doctor seemed impervious to whether this was a promise, a warning, a threat or standard patient fantasy. 'We'll see how you are in the morning.' He added something to the notes. 'Until then, lie back in bed and relax. Let nature take its course.'

'Fine,' Johnny grunted, watching with alarm as a stream of urine coursed down the length of the tube. 'And get rid of this bloody thing!'

Johnny probably slept more that night than he realised, though it didn't feel like it at the time.

The nurses brought his meds promptly on the hour, but his head and ribs pounded with pain, and he spent what seemed like endless hours adrift in his own tortured thoughts, staring dully at a ceiling patterned with subdued lighting, cocooned in his plastic curtain sarcophagus, listening all the while to strangers cough, fart and snore.

In periods of fitful sleep, he fancied that Laura was sitting alongside him, holding his hand. He wondered why they were in the hospital together. Surely, it was because of Chelsea? Hadn't she just been born? She had, yes. And he'd only just made it in time to see her suck in that first breath, having dashed all the way from a tour in Italy.

But it had been worth it. The most wonderful thing he'd ever witnessed: his own little baby squalling, covered in blood and mucus, but wriggling about gamely in the midwife's arms.

'Welcome to this world, little one,' he remembered saying.

Yeah. Thankfully you've no clue yet what a bag of shit it's going to turn out to be.

Johnny's eyes snapped open.

Laura wasn't there, of course.

Neither was Chelsea, either at fifteen years or fifteen seconds. He was alone in that empty, lonely space inside the plastic curtain, the steady bleep of a monitor, the pain in his bruised and battered body, and the interminable deathly stillness of the hospital night.

Saturday

As morning light filtered into the ward, Johnny was already dressed, albeit grimacing with pain as he tried to pull on his cowboy boots. The rest of the ward had come alive beyond the curtain, the day staff chatting cheerfully, trying to rouse the torpid patients, the smell of hospital food more like an old fart than breakfast.

He half-jumped as Mona yanked the curtain back. She looked shocked.

'You're obviously feeling better?' she observed.

Johnny shook his head as he searched through the pockets of his jacket. 'Doesn't matter. I've got to get out of here.'

'Of course it matters. Have you even been discharged?'

'They've said I can go,' he lied. 'Look . . . one of those gorillas put something in my jacket pocket. Mona. Now it's gone.'

'You mean this?'

He saw that she was holding up a scrap of paper. '*You* took it?' he said.

'I wanted to keep it safe,' she replied defensively.

He held out a hand, and somewhat reluctantly, she placed it in his palm. A phone number had been scribbled there.

It's a number, and you'd better fucking ring it . . . or we'll be back.

He shook his head. 'Bollocks.'

'What's bollocks is you not telling me what's going on,' Mona said.

'Mona . . .' he pocketed the number, 'why should I? This is *my* life, yeah? If I've got into a mess, then it's *my* mess.'

Her eyes blazed. 'What if these thugs come back for Round Two at Graceland? Johnny, we're a restaurant, not a fight club.'

'You think I want this?'

'Nobody wants trouble, but some of us seem to attract it more than others. And I don't want my uncle's pride and joy, the restaurant he's put his whole life into, becoming famous for all the wrong reasons.'

Johnny checked in the bedside cabinet just to ensure that no more of his belongings had been stashed there. What else could he say to her? It wasn't as though this was none of her business. She'd been roughed up too. Couldn't she see he didn't want her dragged into all this?

'Do you owe these guys money?' she asked. 'Is that what this is?'

'It's best if you don't know.'

'Well, that's bloody marvellous,' she replied. 'The kind of logic that says it's better not to see the bus coming that runs you over. You know . . . like it doesn't really matter that you might have had a chance to get out of the fucking way—'

He swung to face her. 'If you must know . . .' He paused. Quite a few others on the ward had noticed their raised voices and were watching and earwigging with interest.

'If you must know,' he said more quietly, 'it's to do with . . . well, you know, I've got things going on. Let's just say they're not proving straightforward.'

'Jesus, Johnny, it's not as if I hadn't worked that out already.'

'Look, I appreciate you got hurt,' he said, 'and I know you were scared, but all that was accidental. You were in the wrong place at the wrong time, and that's it. Period.'

'You patronising git.'

'You know, you're right about one thing, Mona.' His own frustration was at last boiling over. 'I *do* need to move out of Graceland. I've not got a clue where I'm going to go, but I can't stay there.'

'I spent the whole of Thursday night sleeping on a chair out in the corridor,' she hissed. 'That's when I wasn't shuffling out to the coffee machine in the foyer just to keep myself awake in case there was some news.'

'Mona, I just want to get back on my feet. And I can't do that while I'm your uncle's performing monkey.'

She gaped in disbelief. 'Johnny, how can you say that?'

'And I can't work miracles where Ravi's concerned, either. He's a nice guy, but he's a pub singer. That's the best he'll ever be, and the sooner he realises that, the better for everyone – including him. You should've told him already. *You're* in the music press. You shouldn't have strung him along.'

Her eyes had hardened. 'Don't even bother coming back to Graceland,' she spat, 'seeing as you hate us all so much. Not ever.'

She turned on her Doc Martens, walking stiffly down the ward, only to swing back, search in her handbag, pull something out and throw it at him. It bounced off his chest and landed on the bed.

It was his Motorola. Johnny picked it up.

'In case Chelsea was trying to call you,' she said through her tears. 'After all, you're the only dad she's got.'

'Mona, I . . .'

But she was striding out of sight. In his efforts to follow, Johnny almost toppled. Valuable seconds passed as the blood pressure in his head took several moments to settle itself, then he stumbled on. She was on the landing below when he finally caught up.

'Mona, wait . . . look, you're well within your rights to chuck me out, I am a wanker. But there's some stuff I need to collect first.'

There wasn't much: a single change of clothes, a few paltry toiletries, but also the small matter of some creased photographs and their negatives.

'When you call round, make sure I'm out,' she said angrily. 'I thought you were a good bloke, but you're just like all the other arrogant shits in this business.'

'If only I was still in the business,' he muttered, unable to meet her gaze.

'Enough with the self-pity. It's bloody boring.'

20

ROCK BOTTOM

Saturday

Mona spent the rest of that Saturday in her Shoreditch flat, trying to catch up with some of the work she'd neglected during the week, but mostly she was sulking.

It wasn't the first time she and Johnny had been at loggerheads. They might have settled into an uneasy friendship, but Johnny was still his own man and hated the idea that anyone might have tabs on him. She could just imagine what it might have been like to be his wife.

Well, you're not his wife, are you?

She huffed over her laptop. He'd been so rude. Not just to her, but about Uncle Rishi, about the free board at Graceland, the dinners he was eating for free, the endless supply of drinks from the bar, though he hadn't taken advantage of that offer in the way that he could have.

'Johnny,' she said to herself, sitting back from her desk, 'you're such a fuck-up.'

Johnny Klein had left the normal world behind when he was still a teenager. He'd gone from man to myth before he was even an adult, progressing all the way to middle age with no responsibility, having everything done for him. Now the world he'd been spat back into was a dark, hostile place.

No wonder he was confused. But it was no excuse for being a dick.

She was already regretting telling him not to go back to Graceland in his current state. Where else could he go?

She contemplated calling him on his Motorola and telling him that she hadn't meant it, but resisted.

'Not backing off yet,' she muttered to herself. 'You deserve some pain, mister.'

But by early evening her resolve had wavered and she set off down to Brick Lane. It was a Saturday, so the restaurant was heaving with punters. They hadn't seen Johnny, they told her, through the busy service.

Ravi was working through his second and final set of the evening, treating the audience to his less-than-tuneful version of 'In the Ghetto'. Johnny's accusation that she was stringing him along still bothered her, mostly because she knew it was true. Mona wished that she had been straighter with Ravi – but at present he was on his knees, weeping and sweating as he pleaded for the life of the nipper who would grow up a criminal and die without ever knowing love. She hung around at the bar, and when her mobile pinged, she grabbed it from her pocket, hoping it would be from Johnny.

It wasn't. It was Ted Travis, a fellow staff writer from *Classic Rock*.

Thirty years her senior, and generally regarded as the office sage, Ted had partied in his lifetime with everyone from Iggy Pop to Bruce Springsteen, from Tina Turner to Julie Andrews.

His text read:

Call me. Any time's good.

Mona ducked out the back door and called him.

'Mona, babes,' Travis said. 'How's it hanging?'

'Wild and free,' she replied. 'You got something for me?'

'I have indeed. You asked me about Ben Randall?'

'Yeah . . . ?'

'Well, I've asked around, and he's another burnt-out relic these days.'

'Really? He can't be older than forty.'

'He's forty-five, practically middle-aged! Anyway, it's a right sob story . . . wanna hear it?'

'Hit me.'

'Well, you know he had the world at his feet? Was in *Phantom* and *Les Mis* in the West End. Did a stint in *The Music Man* on Broadway. Always on telly playing cops, SAS guys. Tipped as a future Bond . . . then he just disappeared?'

'He's not dead, is he?' she asked.

'No, but his career is. You know he shacked up for a while with Jackie Phillips?'

'Yes, I do know, I'd forgotten but someone reminded me. Let me guess . . . sucked him dry and left the shell?'

'That's right. Drove him to drink, apparently. But in the end, he dumped her, met someone else, got married.'

Now that Ted mentioned this, Mona remembered. 'Wasn't it that Sasha Jakeman?'

'Yeah, gorgeous actress. Started in the soaps, but way too hot for that. Had Hollywood written all over her from the start.'

'And . . . ?'

'And they split up. Very acrimoniously, about two years ago. The story is, he was still drinking . . . think he always had a booze issue. Anyway, Sasha wasn't up for that. She whizzed him out and his whole life fell apart. She's LA-based now, while he's a bummed out alcoholic and lives in obscurity in a council flat in Edmonton. Place called Daffodil Court.'

'Interesting. Another showbiz casualty.'

'Yeah, that's it. I can text you Randall's actual address if you like, but I warn you, it's a bit dodge around there.'

There was something else that was nagging at Mona, something she knew she should remember.

'Ted, did Jackie ever have money problems? When I first worked on that story about Randall, I recall there were rumours she was skint?'

'Well, that's the funny thing.' Ted said. 'I heard that *The Sun* was about to run a story that Jackie was about go bankrupt. She stood to lose her house, her cars, the lot, and the bank were about to foreclose.'

'And?'

'And nothing. The story seemed to go away, and shortly after that Jackie was flashing it about like it was going out of fashion, turns up with Meg Mathews and Kate Moss in St Tropez for someone's £200k fortieth birthday party. Business as usual.'

'Interesting. Thanks, mate.'

'OK, catch you on Monday, babes.'

'Yeah, cheers.'

Something felt off, but she couldn't line up the pieces, so what did she do now? She didn't know Daffodil Court, but she knew Edmonton had its rough patches, some estates where you had to watch yourself. She wasn't going over there unless she had to, but it couldn't hurt to have the info.

She glanced at the clock and saw how late it was, then glanced at restaurant's front window which was streaked with rain. If nothing else, she needed to get Johnny back here. He wasn't thinking straight and was still suffering from the after effects of the blow to his head. They should never have argued in his current state. She needed to get Johnny back before he vanished into those dark London streets forever.

It was several hours now since he'd checked out of the hospital, hours he'd spent on the streets of Whitechapel, watching the noisy procession of life go past without him. He'd ripped his head bandage off to avoid attracting attention, but soon wondered why he'd bothered, as he seemed to be invisible to most folk anyway. Anonymity was something he'd craved before, but now he'd found it, he wasn't sure he liked it. He was regretting checking himself out of the London Royal. He could have got free food there, a free bed, and even free drugs with no strings.

Where he was going now, he didn't know. He had nothing. No Mona, no flat, no free curry, and by late afternoon the October sky was turning darkest grey, while the air was much damper and colder. He'd blundered on, regardless, huddled in his old khaki jacket. Maybe it was concussion, but he felt detached from the world, his thoughts unable to penetrate the fog, or to work out what he should do next. And he was caught up in his own self-pity.

He could have called Laura, but how would he explain to Chelsea that he was homeless? Jackie might understand, but even though she might let him stay the night, what would happen the morning after? Jackie being Jackie, she'd have no long-term room in it for a penniless ex-lay. He could call Mona and apologise, but what would be the point? He'd let her down again in a heartbeat.

Johnny felt like he was in his own bubble and couldn't burst it, as if the world was happening around him but he couldn't join in. He wasn't sure that, if he spoke to anyone, they would even hear him.

Night-time had fallen properly when he drifted into Smithfield, the temperature having plunged so sharply that he knew his old army fatigue jacket would be useless. He pulled a small canvas hood out of the back of his collar, a fashion accessory that had become a survival necessity.

A small van with an open rear door sat at the next corner and a lady emerged, handing out Styrofoam cups of tea to the rough-sleepers. Ironically, Johnny had raised money for charities doing exactly this back in the day, claiming he was giving 'something back' but in reality using it as just another PR vehicle. Johnny trudged towards it.

The woman had a kind face, which drew him in. There was something about her that reminded him of Russell's mum, Carol.

'Hello, love,' she said, smiling at him encouragingly. 'Here you go, it's warm and wet.'

It took him a moment to comprehend the cup of tea she held in front of him, but eventually he accepted it without comment, scarcely bothered whether she recognised him or not.

Course she doesn't, you look like a tramp.

Nearby, several other ragged shapes stood hugging their cuppas while another of the charity workers chatted to them. Johnny would have loved to join them, to feel a bit of human kindness, but he knew he had to keep his head down if he didn't want to attract unwanted attention. Alongside the van lay a pile of cardboard and blankets that had been donated.

He helped himself to one blanket and one sheet of cardboard. It reminded him of a nightmare he used to have when he first started out: that somehow or other, almost overnight, everything would be stripped away from him, his fame, his fortune, his dignity, and he'd be left at rock bottom.

'No nightmare now,' he mumbled, stumbling from the van and the fire, an injured animal seeking somewhere private to lick its wounds.

It was raining by now, only slightly, so he took the first alcove he found, nothing more than a cubby hole in a wall of black bricks. He used the dim light from his phone to check there was nothing dangerous in there like used needles, then laid his cardboard down, slumped on top of it and drew the blanket over his head. Immediately, a stench of bleach engulfed him. The blanket had clearly been soaked in the stuff.

That was when the Motorola rang, bouncing around in his pocket, its too-cheery ringtone piercing the night air. Dazed, Johnny dug it out. Mona's name came up on the screen. She'd obviously put her number in there before giving it to him.

He didn't answer it. He was nothing anymore, no use to anyone. A tattered effigy of a man, a dummy, smoke and straw. No one as vivacious and full of life as Mona was should be running around after a past-its-sell-by-date waster like him.

The mobile beeped.

He looked down and saw that she'd sent a text.

Johnny, come back to Graceland. I know we argued, but it's your home right now. M xxx

Johnny slipped the phone away. It was nice to know that *someone* cared about him enough to forgive his behaviour, but he didn't think he could stand, let alone walk back to Brick Lane.

Within moments, Johnny was asleep, curled up under the bleached blanket. There was no dream, no pleasant escape from his situation, just darkness, a world akin to death.

Johnny had no idea of time, he didn't know if he had been asleep for five minutes or an hour, but what he did know was that someone was lying on top of his back and his neck was being squashed in the crook of a man's elbow, and a blade was up against the corner of his eye. It was impossible for him to move.

He tried to fight back – but he could hardly breathe, and a stench of booze and stale body odour smothered him.

'Give me that fucking phone or I'll cut off your oxygen supply,' his assailant snarled.

Johnny gargled that he couldn't breathe anyway. The chokehold relaxed by an inch or so.

'Take it,' Johnny gasped, holding the phone out, waggling it. 'It's worthless.'

The man snatched it, releasing Johnny and letting him drop down onto his arse, but then simply stood there, turning the device over in his hands. 'What are you? A dealer?' He spoke with a cockney accent.

'Do I look like one?' Johnny glanced weakly up. It was another rough sleeper; that was evident from the unwashed smell of him, not to mention the reek of booze. He too was wearing khaki, but in his case trousers as well as an old combat jacket, the jacket displaying a pair of winged-dagger insignia on its shoulders. He was tall and lean, with long, matted hair and a grizzled, wiry beard and moustache. He looked as though he'd been out here for a while, but for all that, there was something lithe and energised about him. He still wielded the blade, a lock-knife, but seeing that Johnny was broken, he now closed it one-handed and slid it out of sight, fiddling about with the phone again.

His eyes flitted back to his victim. 'What else you got?'

'Millions,' Johnny replied groggily. 'What do you fucking think? Look where I'm sleeping.'

'Watch your fucking lip, mate. I've killed more men than you've . . . wait a sec!' The guy dropped to a squat. He eyed Johnny more closely. 'You're not . . . you're *him*, aren't you? I remember you.' Suddenly he looked uneasy, glancing back along the wet, deserted street. 'This a game or sumfink? A TV show? You looking to find out how the other half live?'

Johnny knuckled his aching brow. 'I wish.'

'I *am* right, though? You're Johnny Klein?'

'Pleased to meet you.'

'Fuck me. We used to listen to your mob all the time. They were always playing you on Forces Radio. What the fuck happened, man?'

'Shit happens, doesn't it? To everyone.'

'Yeah, does.' The guy pondered. 'Duran Duran, wasn't it?'

'Yeah,' Johnny replied.

'Knew it. But how the fuck'd you end up out here?'

Johnny gazed to the night sky. It was jet black. Not even a star to be seen. 'It's a long story, mate. Seriously . . . too long, too boring. How about you?'

'Usual thing. Got fucked up overseas. Came back home, struggling to deal with it, pissed up every day. Wife finally chucked me out.'

'Aren't there people . . . you know, help for ex-squaddies?'

The guy gave a crooked grin, exposing alternating black and brown teeth. 'Gotta *want* to be looked after, haven't you? All I ever wanted, all I want now, is a fucking drink.' On which note, he slid a vodka bottle from his pocket. It was filled with clear fluid, but when he unscrewed the cap, the smell gave it away. It was no kind of vodka Johnny was familiar with. It smelled more like paraffin.

'You'll die out here, Johnny,' the veteran said matter-of-factly. 'Fucking guarantee it. You're too soft for the streets, they'll eat you for breakfast out here.'

Johnny scrubbed a hand through his hair. The wound on his scalp still open and leaking blood, still hurting. Part of him wished this lunatic had actually killed him.

'How long you been out here?' Johnny finally asked.

'Dunno . . . five years.'

'Five years!'

'Ish. Who's fucking counting?'

'What's your name?'

The veteran smirked. Up close, what Johnny had thought were black teeth were actually holes. 'Why's that matter? You're on your own. That's why *you* won't make it.'

'Yeah, you've already said that.'

'Only being honest with you, pal. Could've opened you like a can of beer. Might have done if I hadn't recognised you.' He looked at the Motorola again and prodded at it. When the tiny LED screen came to life, he looked it over.

'Who's Mona?' he asked.

'Someone who cares about me more than I deserve,' Johnny replied.

The veteran offered him his phone back. 'You'd better ring her. She'll be worried.'

Johnny put it back in his pocket. 'Five years is a long time on the street.' Then he found himself asking a genuine question. 'How do you survive? Seriously? I mean . . . five years?'

The veteran shrugged. 'Make the street frightened of you. Do it to them before they do it to you.'

'Didn't you have enough of that in the army?'

'You see, Johnny, it's a hard life on the street, but there's something to be said for sleeping under the stars, no one to answer to, no one to provide for. Living each day an hour at a time, no bills, no invoices. No one caring if I live or die.'

He looked at Johnny, all the aggression gone, showing a glimpse of the bloke he used to be: husband, friend, war hero . . .

'Listen, I'd go home to this Mona while you can. Before it's too late. Because, believe me, Johnny, "too late" comes quick out here.'

'I'm gonna try and get some shut eye and I'll think about going back in the morning.'

The veteran got to his feet. 'Don't know what's happened to make you think you belong out here.' He lumbered away. 'And first light, when you've had a kip, get your fucking arse gone.'

21

SMASHING PUMPKINS

Sunday

The early-morning bus ride to Brick Lane, thanks again to
Mona's Oyster card, was tough. It was only a mile and a
half from Smithfield, but he couldn't have faced even that
on foot. Now though, every bump in the road kicked him
in the arse, every sleeping policeman rattled his cranium,
his muddled and exhausted brain jarring about between
the walls of his skull. Even when he got off the bus, and
even though it was still only six in the morning, an ambulance went flying by with inches to spare, its siren blaring
at mega volume, setting off his tinnitus, a long-term
by-product of his habit of always standing too close to his
giant Marshall stack.

He trudged along the street towards Graceland.

On Brick Lane, the streetcleaners had already been
through, but traffic was humming, staff were about and
preparations underway for the day's business, despite it

being a Sunday. But none of that explained the huge crowd of people who seemed to have gathered outside Graceland. Johnny halted.

'What the fuck?' he muttered.

There weren't just people milling confusedly around, there were police cars in attendance too, their blue lights swirling. Johnny walked forward. When he realised that he was hearing consternation in the voices of many of those gathered there, he started running.

'Bollocks . . . bollocks . . . *BOLLOCKS!*'

He'd just seen the restaurant's huge front windows, or what remained of them, which was little more than shards of glass in splintered frames. He thrust his way through, stumbling to a halt again as he came in sight of the front door, which had been smashed open. Its beautiful carved woodwork depicting Ganesha, the elephant-headed god, had been defaced with spatters and slashes of bright red paint.

Johnny pressed forward to enter, only for a uniformed copper in the doorway to hold up a palm.

'Sorry, sir,' the cop said sombrely. 'Family and staff only, at present.'

'I am . . .' Johnny stumbled over his words. 'I live here.'

The cop's eyes narrowed as he scrutinised the guy in front of him, clearly thinking that under the bruises and dirt, he recognised someone. 'You live here?' He seemed doubtful, his gaze flicking to the clot of congealed blood just visible in the matted mess of Johnny's hair. 'Do I recognise you from somewhere? You don't know anything about this, do you?'

'No. Look, I don't even know what's happened, I live here and . . . and I really need to know what's going on.

These are my friends.' Johnny felt his stomach clench, and had to fight the urge to retch, anxiety gripping his entire body.

The cop considered this before stepping aside. 'Better not lose my job over this, mate.'

Johnny couldn't have cared less whether he did or not.

Johnny pushed on in, feet crunching and slithering on broken glass.

A scene of utter devastation met his eyes. More red paint had been splashed over the whole interior, particularly across the huge mural depicting rural Indian life. Some of the richly upholstered seats had been slashed open, their stuffing yanked out. Ornaments had been smashed, tables and chairs flung at the walls and the bar until they too were broken and useless.

He started. 'What the actual . . . ?'

'A gift from those people . . . from those friends of yours.'

It was Mona who spoke, her voice thick with tears. She was seated in one of the velvet booths, arms looped around her uncle, whose hanging head was clamped in both hands, his eyes glazed.

'Mona . . . my *friends*?'

'You know who I mean.' Her eyes, though red with tears, were hard, her tone accusatory. 'Whoever they are . . . whatever they are. They came back here in the early hours of this morning. And look what they've done. They've destroyed everything.'

Johnny could only shake his head. He still couldn't take it in. 'It was definitely the same guys?'

'I think so.' She wiped her eyes with her fingertips. 'I wasn't here. But Ravi . . .' Her voice broke.

'*Ravi!*' A spear of alarm pierced Johnny clean through. The cop had mentioned that this wasn't just vandalism. Then there'd been the ambulance. 'Did . . . fuck, Ravi get hurt?'

Fresh tears rolled down Mona's cheeks. 'He'd come in early to get some practice in. Said you'd given him a really useful tip.'

'I did?' Johnny couldn't remember, though his thoughts were scrambling in his mind. 'But . . . Ravi . . . is he all right?'

'He was in the wash house out back. You know he used to like to rehearse in there on his own. And he heard them wrecking the place. We think he ran in, and from what I hear, they were glad to see him.' Her tears were streaming now, her voice racked. 'I guess they don't like it when people stand up to them.'

Movement through the open kitchen door caught Johnny's attention. He spied figures clad in hazmat suits moving around. 'How bad is it?'

'Johnny, they gave him a real beating . . . they found him unconscious.'

'I know he'll survive,' the Major interrupted, shaking his head vehemently. 'I know my cousin.'

'Mr Klein!' someone called. 'Mr Klein?'

Johnny swung round. 'That's me.'

A woman in her late thirties advanced to meet him. She'd just divested herself of a hazmat suit, and wore a smart trouser suit underneath. She was good-looking and wore her hair in long cornrows; she was brusque and no nonsense and held up a warrant card.

'Detective Sergeant Thomas, Lorna. Can we have a word?'

Johnny caught Mona's eye as he walked away with the detective. It was fixed on him intently.

They found a quiet corner, where DS Thomas turned to face him. 'I understand you might have a line on who these attackers were?'

Johnny shrugged. 'I . . . I honestly don't.'

'But they *did* come to see you on Thursday night? At least, that's what I'm told.'

Johnny's mouth had dried again. Natural instinct told him to be economical with the truth. For one thing, if he told them about Karl Jones in the drugs den, he'd have to admit that he'd been in there too; his self-preservation tightened around his conscience.

'Me and Mona,' he said, stumbling a little as he tried to think this through. 'Mona . . . that's the owner's niece, we got attacked in the alley out back on Thursday evening. I don't know what the reason for that was. Ravi and some other members of staff chased the bastards off . . . but they must've come back.'

DS Thomas regarded him doubtfully. 'None of these assailants were known to you personally?'

'Absolutely not.'

'And none of them gave any indication why they wanted to beat you up?'

'Well . . . I was in hospital from Thursday night to Saturday morning. I don't remember it much.'

DS Thomas pursed her lips. 'In that case, it's a good job Miss Mistry was able to give us descriptions. But presumably you'd remember if one of them had spoken to you? Perhaps put something in your pocket?'

Johnny shrugged again. Mona must have told them, but he had no right to feel betrayed by that, or even grassed on. She was loyal first and foremost to her uncle, and why not? He was a far more positive influence in her life than Johnny had ever been.

'I was out of it, it's all just a blur.'

'Look, Mr Klein,' the detective sighed. 'I know this is a big shock and that's everyone's very upset, but I need to be straight with you.' Her gaze bored into him. 'The East End now isn't the East End of old,' she said. 'I know, because I grew up in it during the Seventies, when being black or Asian brought a brick through your window. Incidents of violence and intimidation like this are never as straightforward as they seem. And I'm absolutely certain that neither you, Miss Mistry nor Mr Mistry's restaurant were attacked at random.'

'How should I know?' Johnny asked.

'Aren't you famous?'

'Once, yeah.'

'Sometimes the world of showbiz and crime like to get into bed together, I'm sure you know that. Trust me, I've seen everything. Everyone is a suspect right now. '

'Hey. I've never done underworld shit.'

'How do I know you're telling the truth?'

'If someone's told you different, *they're* lying.'

This much, at least, Johnny was being truthful about. He'd never sought out the company of villains. He knew others who'd considered it groovy to hang out with gangsters, but not him. He'd had too much of that as a lad.

'I don't know anything that might help you,' Johnny said tightly.

She nodded, her watchful eyes never leaving his face. 'I'd still like you to give us a statement about the assault the other night?'

'Sure.'

'Don't leave anything out, Mr Klein.' She then produced a contact card and, without asking his permission, slid it into one of his jacket pockets. 'Here's where you can get me, should your memory miraculously recover.'

She moved away, leaving Johnny with his insides churning. It didn't take long for Mona to come over and join him. 'What did she say?' she asked quietly.

He gave it some thought. 'Well, it's early days. They haven't made much headway . . .'

'For God's sake, Johnny! Stop dodging. Not now. And before you even think about lying to me, think about this . . .' She pointed across the room to where the Major sat slumped with head in hands; he couldn't have looked less like a military man. 'Uncle Rishi's not as youthful as he may seem. This place is insured, but it'll be ages before everything's back up and running. That's assuming these bastards don't come again. He's in his mid-seventies, so I'm not sure he'll be able to get through this.'

Johnny was in turmoil as he stared at the broken relic of the man who'd unconditionally given him a roof over his head. He knew it was an underworld tactic to terrorise the friends and family of an enemy, and they could all be in danger. But again, he needed some hope in his life, even an unrealistic one, that getting back with Laura and Chelsea was a possibility, and that could never be if all this got out.

At the end of the day, someone had been assaulted and a couple of windows broken. Ravi was young, he'd bounce back. It was no more than happened in towns all over Britain every Friday night.

'Level with me,' Mona said. 'Is this something to do with Jackie Phillips?'

'*Jackie?*' Even Johnny was startled by that.

'Has that cold bitch got herself into something she can't get out of? Is that why you went scuttling over there the other night, and came back with a black eye?'

'No . . . Look, I promise you, that's not what's going on here.' As before, it was nice to be able to tell her something true. 'Look, Mona . . . all I can say is . . .' he groaned, 'when I was a kid, there was this other kid. A bad kid. He grew up to be a bad man. A couple of times when I was with the band, he tried to get in on it, you know . . . tried to get himself a cut of the action.' This part of it was true; even as a young man, his modus oprandi had been to put the screws on any contacts where he thought he could milk them for his own ends. He'd tried it on Johnny.

'Back then, I was able to brush him off, we had minders and A&R men to keep the big bad wolves away. But . . .' Johnny couldn't tell Mona anything about the photos, not yet. 'He still wants in . . . still thinks there are riches to be shared. He still wants to get his own back.'

She eyed him suspiciously. 'That's all it is?'

'That's all is pretty bad, this guy's bad news.'

'And you know for a fact that he's the one who sent those thugs?'

'I don't *know* it. Not for a fact.'

'What about that number they gave you?'

'I, erm . . .' he turned sheepish. 'Look, I lost it.'

'You lost it?' For half a second she was aghast, then scornful. Here it was again, he realised: Johnny the dopey git, Johnny the fuck-up.

'Mona!' he protested. 'I spent last night sleeping under the arches. I had a knife against my eyeball at one point. Some psycho ex-para who reckoned he'd have killed me if he hadn't liked Duran Duran so much.'

'Duran Duran?'

'Don't even ask. I'm sorry if it meant I didn't manage to keep track of a scrap of paper smaller than a fucking bus ticket.'

'All right.' She backed off a little. 'Did you tell DS Thomas this?'

'What would be the point? I can't prove any of it. All they could do is have a word, and that'd put me even more in the sights of people none of us want to know. But look . . .' He adopted a more conciliatory tone. 'Ultimately, I'm the reason they came here . . . I can't deny that. So now I'm going to find a way to fix this. I am one hundred per cent going to find a way, Mona. I promise you.'

Mona shook her head. 'What makes you think you can fix this' – she cast her eyes around, taking in the devastation – 'when you can't even hang on to a piece of paper?'

She walked back to her uncle, looking broken.

Even Mona was losing faith in him now, unsurprisingly. Her uncle's pride and joy reduced to this bombed-out shell.

Somewhere amid the mess, a phone began to ring. Aamir, who'd been seated morosely in a corner, got up and lumbered through the wreckage to answer. Johnny himself went partway up the stairs, sat down, dug out the Motorola, which thankfully that nutty ex-para had voluntarily returned, and filched out the fragment of paper, which he'd lied to Mona about having lost. He gazed long and hard at the number scribbled there . . .

Sod it, eh? What's a few grand between mates?

He tapped it in.

The call was answered quickly.

'Yeah? Who's this?' The voice spoke in gruff cockney.

Johnny swallowed hard before replying. 'I think you know?'

The voice chuckled. 'J fucking K himself. Suppose I'm honoured.'

'I don't know who *you* are, but I've got some pictures your man wants.'

'Yeah, I'll bet you have.' Johnny could picture the smile on the lips at the other end. 'How's your 'ead?'

'You want the truth, I've been hit harder by my missus.' Another chuckle, though not quite so amused this time. 'But I don't give a shit about myself,' Johnny added. 'And neither does anyone else. If it was just me, none of this would matter. But you've hurt innocent people, and that's well out of order.'

'Your little kung fu fighting Elvis needed a lesson, mate.'

Johnny could feel the blood beating through his veins, the pressure rising, and knew he had to get off the phone before he said something he'd regret. The Mistrys weren't his only loved ones.

'I've got those pics,' he said. 'And the negatives. They're all yours, so long as that puts an end to all this.'

Before the other guy could speak, a wild pandemonium broke out downstairs, a shouting and wailing. Even as he stared downward, the figure of Mona came staggering into the foot of the stairwell. Their eyes met; hers were awash with tears again.

'That was the hospital,' she half-sobbed and half-screamed. 'It's Ravi . . . Johnny, he's dead . . . *Ravi's dead!*'

Johnny sat there frozen. His breathing turned shallow as his scalp prickled and his heart raced. If his mouth had been dry before, now it was a desert. The staircase itself seemed to be spinning.

Suddenly, Johnny felt sharper than he had for weeks, months, possibly years, like a shard of ice. 'I'll tell you what, pal,' he replied slowly, 'why don't you go and fuck yourself. And your fucking boss too.' He rang off.

In one devastating moment, *everything* had changed.

22
BABY

Ravi's assault was now murder, so a forensics tent and a whole rack of arc-lights had been set up out back of Graceland. Several forensic technicians were still moving about out there as Johnny tried to sleep in the early hours of the following morning. Now he could hear boards being hammered into place, covering the broken windows. The Major's crying seemed to rattle what was left of the building once or twice every hour. A patrol car blocked their section of Brick Lane to other traffic, its blue light swirling around Johnny's attic room as he lay taut and sweat-soaked on his bed.

Of course, it wasn't just the police presence that kept him awake.

It was also the total horror of everything that his life had become.

Ravi was dead because of *him*. And because of *him*, the crime would not be solved. The culprits were hardened gangsters who knew what they were doing, but the only person who could finger them was never going to say anything. It seemed that the assault had triggered a deadly bleed in Ravi's brain, and by the time he made it to hospital, it was already too late despite desperate efforts to save him.

'I can't . . . I can't, Ravi, mate,' Johnny muttered as he drifted in and out of consciousness. 'What good would it do? Wouldn't bring you back . . . would fuck up my life, and Laura and Chelsea's, maybe Mona's too.'

Needless to say, at no stage did Ravi's ghost appear in the corner, not even clad in his ripped-up, bloodstained Elvis costume, to say that it was OK, that he understood, that they all had stuff to get on with, even if he didn't.

If that wasn't torture enough, the dawn of Monday morning was approaching, and so was Laura's appointment at the clinic. Johnny knew he had to stay strong for her, not pass on his own problems, his own terrible feelings of guilt that were overwhelming him.

He dragged himself out of bed, stood in front of the washbasin in the tiny en suite, shaved, washed his face and dragged a broken-toothed comb through his hair. Nothing he did made him look even vaguely human. It haunted him when he thought about the perfect specimen he'd once been, the slick, handsome, imperious figure who'd cowed tens of thousands simply with his presence on stage. He'd soon learned to don that guise, to put on that mesmerising persona, in a matter of twenty minutes. Just him, his dressing room mirror and a box of make-up. Yet now, he'd been at it half an hour and he still resembled a sack of shit.

He pulled his khaki jacket on, and then rooted the photographic evidence out of the drawer, cramming it all into one of his pockets. The way the forensics team were going at it downstairs, it wouldn't be long before they came upstairs. He felt as though he was deliberately batting for the wrong team. But it was the corner he'd been backed into; it wasn't through choice.

He stumbled downstairs and headed for the exit. A couple of detectives glanced his way. Maybe they were wondering why he was squatting in an attic off Brick Lane.

'Morning,' he said, walking out.

They didn't return the greeting.

South of the river, in Battersea, just past the high rises at Nine Elms and behind the new American Embassy, was a clinic specialising discreetly in the unwanted reproductive results of the rich and famous. The sign above the front door was a nondescript whiteboard with the name *St Mary's* stencilled in simple silver lettering. The entrance itself was partly concealed by a beautiful giant oak, which carpeted the pavement surrounding it with golden leaves.

When Johnny arrived, he was on edge. It struck him that he'd never experienced life like this before; he'd spent his time in his superstar bubble, away from the unpleasant reality of life's messy problems. At least it was peaceful and quiet. He headed straight to the glass front doors, hands deep in his jeans pockets.

The clinic's sterile, impersonal aura hit him as soon as the automatic doors slid open. Inside, there was a small reception area, five or six chairs, each one set a respectful distance from the next. A young woman occupied the desk, her heavy-framed glasses just about clinging to the bridge of her tiny, freckled nose as she banged on her keyboard.

Before Johnny could approach her, a voice called across the lobby.

'Dad . . . *Dad!*'

He turned to see Chelsea running over from a vending machine. She all but threw herself onto him. Johnny was too surprised to think straight, firstly because Chelsea was even here, but also, because Laura hadn't wanted her to know about any of this.

'Chelsea . . . what's going on?'

'What do you think's going on?' His daughter broke away from him, her eyes filled with hurt. 'You weren't there for Mum, so I had to come with her.'

Johnny was bewildered. 'I wasn't there . . . ?'

'I wouldn't even have known about this if you'd done what you'd said you were going to do!'

At first, Chelsea had seemed massively glad to see him, but now, suddenly, she was angry. Really angry. And then his memory assaulted him. He'd promised he'd meet Laura this morning at her mother's house, so she wouldn't have to make the journey on her own.

'Oh, Christ,' he groaned.

Despite what happened last night, it wasn't as if he couldn't have kept his promise. He'd risen at the crack of dawn anyway.

'Where was Grandma?' he asked.

'Where were *you?*' Chelsea demanded.

'I . . .' Yet again, he couldn't give an answer that would make sense to her. She didn't know about his life at

Graceland, let alone the terrible thing that had happened there.

'Grandma doesn't know anything about this either,' Chelsea said. 'About . . . the baby, I mean. I only know because Mum was in a right state this morning, I made her tell me.'

'Has your mum gone in?' he asked lamely.

'They took her in as soon as we arrived – ten minutes ago.'

'I'm so sorry, Chelsea—'

'What's the point saying sorry to me?' Chelsea's eyes shone with tears. 'You know, Mum would do anything for you. But you always do things like this. Not just to her, but to me too.'

Johnny's mouth dried. He'd tried to avoid grown-up conversations with Chelsea, but clearly, she'd been picking stuff up anyway, and she was right about this.

He glanced at the receptionist, who was purposefully buried in her computer.

'Chelsea, listen . . . sit down a minute.'

She glowered at him. 'I don't want to sit down.'

'There are things you don't know—'

'I don't care about any of that. It's just the same load of excuses, isn't it? You only ever turn up when it suits *you*. When there's something *you* want. Mum's not your therapist, you know. Someone you only ever see when you need your back rubbed—'

'Chelsea, I love your mum very much . . .'

'Why don't you show it then?'

Johnny felt himself shrivel inside. He wasn't so self-absorbed that he didn't know that he and Laura had had a one-sided relationship. Even when they were happily married, the line between Laura being his wife and his PA had blurred. It was a sobering thought that his daughter had observed all this. His little girl, Chelsea, the only one he'd ever been able to rely on for unconditional love, and yet deep down *she'd* been wounded by his behaviour too.

'What were you thinking, Dad?' she said through tears. 'That if you couldn't do this thing today, if it got a bit inconvenient, I'd just step in? Yeah, Chelsea can do it. Doesn't matter if she has to miss another day at school, if she has to help her mum mend her broken heart . . .'

'Chelsea, come on,' he stammered. 'You must know I'd never—'

He reached for her, but she pulled back, glaring at him as if he was a stranger. 'You didn't even turn up on Saturday at Nan's. Do you know what it's been like, being your daughter?' she hissed. 'Not growing up as a regular person but always as Johnny Klein's kid? I wish I had a quid for every time I heard people saying nasty things . . . people who didn't even know me. "Who does she think she is? Little princess. Spoilt little bitch. It's all right for that one, isn't it. Gets everything she fucking wants!" But it was a long way from being all right for me, Dad. Not that I had a dad. Instead of that, I had a poster Sellotaped to my bedroom wall . . . I used to imagine that person tucking me in at night. I looked up at it while Mum read me bedtime stories, wishing you were there to share them.'

'OK . . . I get it—'

'No, Dad, let me finish. I felt lonely, frustrated – all the things a kid shouldn't. And I felt that all the time. That's what it was like, being your daughter.'

The two of them stared at each other. Chelsea flushed, visibly quivering, Johnny helpless, struck dumb.

At that moment, Laura appeared from one of the inner hallways, white-faced and shaking, assisted by a young male nurse. At first, she regarded Johnny and Chelsea as if they were people she didn't know, with dark, bruise-coloured rings under her eyes.

'I . . . I couldn't do it,' she said in a faltering voice. 'I couldn't . . .'

The nurse stepped back as all three of them held each other. For a few fleeting seconds, they were a family again.

'Don't worry, Mum,' Chelsea said soothingly. 'Don't worry. It'll be all right, I promise. I'll help you . . . like I said.'

Johnny rested his chin on his wife's shoulder and added: 'It'll all be OK. As long as you're sure that's what you want?'

'What did you say?' Laura said sharply. She pulled away from him, her voice brittle. '*If* I'm sure? You mean because you hope there's a chance I'm not?'

'Laura, wait . . .' He raised his hands. 'I didn't mean . . .'

'Am I sure, Johnny? Don't you think this has been tearing me apart for the last couple of weeks and days, the closer it got? I've been to the ends of the earth, trying to work out the best way forward. How often have *you* thought about it?'

Johnny again tried to protest, but her eyes were flashing fire. Even Chelsea, so often a moderating presence when they'd fallen out, clung to her mother and stared at him bleakly, as if there was too much truth being told for her to intervene.

'Let me guess, Johnny!' Laura said. 'Not even once. Let's leave it to Laura, eh? It's nothing to do with me, it's not my problem. Well, guess what, Johnny. You're right about that at least, it *won't* be anything to do with you.'

'Laura, I honestly didn't mean . . .' He was almost tempted to put his pleading face on, the one he'd used so many times over the years. But that was an old and tired trick, and Laura and Chelsea were worth more than that.

'You want to know the real reason I couldn't have this baby?' Laura was still so angry that she had to take a breath to steady herself. 'It was you, Johnny . . . *you*.'

'Laura—'

'It was always the same. The only reason I ever did anything was *you*. Will Johnny be OK with this? Will Johnny be happy? Will he be able to cope? Well, not this time. This time I'm doing it for *me* . . . and for Chelsea. And for the first time, I don't care what you think.'

Johnny was still reeling when Laura turned to her daughter. 'Let's go, darling. Let's get out of this bloody awful place.'

'I'll . . . get us a cab,' Johnny stuttered.

'No, you won't!' Laura cut across him, less angry now but still speaking with assured venom. 'You won't do anything. This is *my* baby. I don't want *you* having anything to do with it.'

Johnny stood there as his ex-wife and daughter, virtually propping each other up, walked slowly through the sliding doors. He couldn't pretend that he hadn't hoped the problem would just go away, and that Laura would have the termination, if only to remove another impending problem.

It wasn't like it wouldn't be a serious one. Him, penniless, living above Graceland, relying on the Major to feed him, and now responsible for Ravi's death, and soon due to be a dad again. And yet, somehow, things had gotten even worse. He glanced at the receptionist, who wouldn't meet his gaze. Then he stumbled outside in pursuit.

They were already by the kerbside, climbing into the back of a black cab.

Breaking into a shambling run, he reached the car as it pulled away.

Chelsea watched him desolately through its fogged-up window.

'Chelsea, just . . . call me at least!' He pressed his hand against the glass. '. . . please, Chels—'

An agonising half-second passed, the cab hovering, Laura not even looking round. Then, Chelsea's window powered down an inch. She grabbed his hand with her own for a fleeting second.

Then they were gone, the cab pulling from the kerb, the outline of his family visible in its rear window, neither of them looking back. Despair gripped at Johnny's heart so deep that he didn't notice when another car, a gleaming black Mercedes E-Class, pulled up by his side. Not until someone got out of it and strolled along the pavement towards him.

Someone wearing a heavy leather coat, with pony-tailed hair and a mean grin.

Johnny backed away, only to sense a second presence, this one at his rear. He spun round, to see another ogre-like face from the alley that night. This one under a razored-off flat-top.

Before he could duck away, a voice sounded from the car, the rear door to which had now opened.

'Quit fucking around, Johnny,' the voice said. 'And get in.'

23

THE BROTHERS

Monday

'If you bastards have come to beat the shit out of me again,' Johnny said. 'You'd be doing me a favour.'

'Get in the car, Johnny,' the voice repeated.

Johnny glanced at Flat-top, who indicated the Merc's open rear door.

With no option, Johnny bent down and folded himself into the back seat, the door slamming behind him. Karl Jones, the bloke he hadn't seen for so many years, sat at the far end. There was no mistaking the neighbourhood thug of their youth. He might be much older now, shaven-headed, his features narrow and vulture-like, but his eyes were still a pair of cold, grey bullets. He wore a suit these days, Savile Row's finest, and sported a neatly trimmed grey moustache. Everything about him said 'crook'.

'You know that bloke your gorillas beat up has died?' Johnny said, cutting to the chase.

His blood simmered. His hands trembling, the adrenaline building as fight or flight kicked in.

'Which,' Jones replied, looking dead ahead, 'should make it clear how serious this business is.'

His two henchmen had now climbed in, Flat-top behind the wheel, Biker in the front passenger seat. Without a word, they started driving.

'First of all, Johnny,' Jones said, without emotion, 'don't mistake me for someone who gives a flying fuck about your little singing waiter. He wasn't supposed to die, but that's the way it goes sometimes. Collateral damage.'

Johnny didn't reply. He was now wondering where they were driving to. It was like that moment he'd seen in so many crime dramas, when someone gets driven to the docks dressed in a bespoke concrete suit.

'Secondly,' Jones said, 'don't think that just because the filth are involved, that'll put the skids under us. It won't.'

'Where we going?' Johnny asked tightly.

'Just a little excursion.' Jones made a casual gesture.

'I'd prefer to get out right here,' Johnny said.

'Still got your sense of humour,' Jones replied. 'Which is impressive, given where we picked you up. So, who's losing the baby today? Some other gormless old tart getting off on shagging yesterday's man?'

'Don't take this the wrong way, Karl,' Johnny replied. 'But fuck off.'

'I can see you're upset, And I can respect that. Family matters are painful, aren't they?'

'If you go anywhere near my family . . .' Johnny blurted.

'You may not believe this, Johnny-boy, but I don't want to hurt anyone. Least of all you and yours. Would you believe I was a fan? I remember the day I bought your first album. There was a record shop on Upper Street in Islington. Went in there with my brother, all Billy Big Bollocks, waited for the girl behind the counter to turn away like she always did . . . then I leaned over the counter and grabbed a copy.'

'So that's why the record never made it to Number One.'

Jones snickered. 'Possibly, yeah. Never thought about it that way. Been keeping my eyes on you over the years, Johnny Boy. You know I've always been interested in your progress in life.

'I'm flattered.'

'Now, what I *have* been thinking is, are you in a position to give us what we want, Johnny-boy? As in *now*, at this moment?'

As it happened, Johnny *was* able to give them what they wanted. And a few days ago, he might have handed over every negative and photo he had in his pocket without hesitation. But now he knew that, once they had the evidence connecting Jones to Sean Rogers' murder, they'd feel free to dispense with him. He *knew* that Jones had been one of the last people to see Rogers alive. He knew it was Jones's men who had beaten Ravi. Which meant that he, Johnny Klein, could finger Karl Jones for two murders. Why not kill him too?

Take a gamble.

'I've obviously not got it with me now,' he said.

'I have no doubt that's true,' Jones said. 'So, wherever you've stashed it, or whoever's looking after it for you . . . you're going to have to go and get it.'

Johnny sat stiffly. 'You'll have to give me time.'

Jones's eyes didn't leave the road. 'You wouldn't be playing games with me, Johnny?'

'Course not. I'm not that stupid.'

Yes, you are.

'I mean, the only reason your legs, hips and spine still work is old times' sake.' The mobster glanced round, his voice silky smooth but his face hard as stone. 'You know the Taylor brothers, by the way?'

Johnny glanced at Ponytail and Flat-top. 'Where's your other caveman today?'

'We're a busy outfit, Johnny, plenty of work to keep us all busy. They're just champing at the bit to have another go,' Jones added.

'I'm not messing you around, Karl,' Johnny said quickly. 'I don't even want that fucking photo. I took it by accident.'

'There you go then. Makes sense all around. Because, let me assure you, as long as you hang on to that stuff, the human cost is going to keep going up. That was your ex-missus I saw getting in a cab back there, wasn't it? Don't bother denying it. Not sure what to read into that. Was it *your* dick that got her up the duff? Or was it some new dick? Who can tell, eh? Women, they're here, there and everywhere. Can't do fucking right by them.'

'Karl,' Johnny fought to keep the wheedle out of his voice, 'leave Laura out of it. Come on, mate.'

'It's all in *your* power, Johnny. Get us what we want, none of you ever see us again. On the other hand . . .' he sighed, 'let me down . . . and old times' sake will just be a few meaningless words.' He paused to let that hit home, then clapped his hands loudly, making Johnny jump.

'Anyway . . . seeing as how you said you needed a bit of time, I'll give you a couple of days. After that, anything can happen. Time to say *au revoir*.'

Johnny looked round, surprised. They must have crossed the river at Lambeth Bridge, because they were now heading up Whitehall.

'One final thought, Johnny,' Jones said, as they circled past Trafalgar Square. 'Murder charges are water off a duck's back to the likes of me. I've got mates everywhere, you see. So talk to the filth – because I'm sure that's what you're thinking – and I'll know about it.'

He said nothing else, never even looked at his passenger, as they pulled up outside Scotland Yard on Victoria Embankment.

Jones gave Johnny a mocking smile and pointed to the entrance to the headquarters of the Metropolitan Police. 'Friends everywhere, Johnny. Have a good day, and don't forget our little arrangement, will you.'

Biker climbed from the front passenger seat and opened his door for him.

'I seen videos of you when you were a singer,' the longer-haired Taylor brother said. 'You looked a right fucking ponce.'

Johnny held his gaze. 'I was a fashion icon, mate.'

They locked gazes for several seconds, and Johnny thought the guy was going to take a swing – but then he simply grinned again, before climbing into the car with a chuckle.

Johnny watched as the car drove away, feeling like he'd been punched in the stomach. He felt dazed as he headed towards St Martin's Lane, skirting the edge of Soho. He feet seemed to move of their own accord as they pulled him towards Bridle Lane.

It was only when he reached the front porch of St Lawrence the Martyr, a Victorian red-brick church sandwiched between the scruffy back entrances to two retail blocks, that he registered where he was.

He felt equally surprised as he took in the figure of Graham Dwell, wearing his parka again, standing on the church steps, saying his goodbyes to two homeless men.

'Johnny?' Graham said, approaching. 'Didn't expect we'd be seeing each other quite this soon.'

'Me neither,' Johnny admitted.

'Anyway,' Graham smiled, 'what can I do for *you*?'

'Can we go inside?' Johnny asked. 'I always feel a bit exposed on the street.'

Graham smiled. 'Not yet acclimatised to normal life, eh?'

'I'll be honest, Gray . . . I'm not sure I want to be. Not yet.'

'That's what this is about?'

'No. This is a bit more serious.'

Graham patted his shoulder. 'Whatever it is, let's see if we can help you fix it.'

They went into the church together, Johnny thinking that only the Big Guy himself could fix this.

Yeah, and you're well up in His favour, aren't you.

24

HEAVEN AND HELL

Monday

Mona was glad to be away from Graceland as she headed north on the Overground that afternoon. It was still crawling with detectives, not to say the heartbroken relatives and friends which only served to ram home the senseless events and how helpless she felt.

At least, that was what she told herself.

In truth, she'd had enough of Johnny's evasive tactics. That meant Mona was going to have to sniff around herself, and the one lead she had was that troublesome cow, Jackie Phillips. In turn, this meant speaking to the last person Jackie was known to have dumped on: her former boyfriend, Ben Randall.

She glanced at her phone and the screen grab she'd saved. It depicted Randall in one of his most successful TV shows, *Squad Zero*. He'd played an SAS officer tracking a terrorist cell in Eastern Europe, and had looked every inch the part:

a mop of black hair, laser-blue eyes, square jaw. But Randall was no angel himself. After Jackie, he'd taken to drink, let himself go, and in due course, midway through his time with the actress Sasha Jakeman – the whole edifice had tumbled down.

All the same, it wasn't going to be easy.

Mona hadn't been able to contact Randall. He had no known working telephone number or email address and seemed to lack any presence on social media. At least Ted had come through, getting her his home address, but it wasn't going to be fun going up there alone. She'd dressed down for the occasion, wearing jeans, trainers and an old Wrangler jacket over a Ramones T-shirt, and carrying a vintage Seventies crocheted shoulder-bag. She'd also toned down her make-up. Mona knew she could turn heads, but the trick today was *not* to get noticed.

They'd just passed Seven Sisters. Edmonton Green was four more stops along, and then there was no turning back.

The interior of the church was quiet and shadow-filled, but Johnny's eyes soon adjusted. He saw medieval artwork on the walls, a beautifully carved pulpit. It was dim now rather than dark, but a silky kind of dimness, cool and serene.

'Sit down.' Graham showed him into a pew.

Johnny looked around again. Behind the altar towered an arched stained-glass window. It depicted Christ on the cross, hanging there in agony, his head bristling with thorns, the Virgin Mary gazing up at him. Johnny's eyes tracked up it and then to the high vaulted ceiling, which was painted eggshell blue and was speckled with golden stars.

He hadn't been inside a church for decades, always having considered himself an atheist, looking at religion as something other people needed, and the cause of too many arguments and wars. His own religion had been rock and roll, but that felt like a tired old line these days. It might not have caused any wars, but it had certainly been trouble.

Graham returned. He'd taken his parka off, revealing the dark shirt and clerical collar underneath. 'So . . . what's going on?' Graham put a warm hand on his shoulder. 'I can help, Johnny – let me in.'

Johnny shook his head slowly, 'I don't think you can, I don't think anyone can.'

'Try me,' the priest replied, taking a pew facing Johnny.

Trying to maintain the crumbling facade of his wreck of a life suddenly felt like too much. Besides, this was Graham Dwell, someone who'd been there himself, who'd done it, got the Vivienne Westwood T-shirt.

'I'm barely a few quid away from joining your congregation for real.'

Graham regarded him long and hard. 'Well, you always did have the knack of flushing money away like toilet paper. Maybe you're not working, Johnny, but you must be getting royalties here and there? Even I get those.'

Johnny shook his head. 'Not as many as the average punter might think. And most of them go straight out again.'

Graham considered. 'To Laura? I read about your split in the paper.'

Johnny shrugged. 'Laura's the one I owe the biggest debt of all.'

'At least you know that, Johnny.'

Johnny sighed. 'There are some debts you can never take

care of no matter how much cash you slosh in. Sorry, Graham, mate . . . hitting you with all this when we've only just hooked up in God knows how long . . . what is it, twenty years?'

'I asked,' Graham said. 'You're only being honest, I thought you'd end up coming to see me.'

'You want the truth, it's been agony. But you probably deal with that every day, so . . . I'm not going to bore you with it now.'

'There's no question that the folk I deal with have it rough. But everything's relative, Johnny. Just because you once had it all, that doesn't make your troubles any less real. In some ways it may feel worse, because you're not used to this life.'

Johnny eyed him. 'You don't think I deserve it?'

Graham smiled. 'Deserve's got nothing to do with it, Johnny.'

Johnny was puzzled. 'You don't think the Guvnor up there is punishing me for my sins, of which there are many?'

'That's nonsense,' Graham replied. 'Life is hard, and bad luck, or bad choices, we're all susceptible to those. No one is perfect, Johnny, not even me.'

'I thought you were religious.'

'I believe in Jesus,' Graham confirmed. 'But he came to Earth to save sinners, not condemn them. You're going through a difficult time, Johnny. But see it as a lesson rather than a penalty. And don't forget, you're a man of talents. God-given ones. If anyone can find a way out of this, you can.'

Johnny was about to reply that he was clean now, off the junk completely. But then he remembered his night with

Jerry Fox, felt the call of another hit lurking just under the surface. He'd been an idiot and he knew it now, but there was no guarantee that he wouldn't get lured back in, having already given in to weakness once again. 'I'm fighting my demons as hard as I can, Graham. But you know what the *hardest* thing is? It isn't going detox or cold turkey. It's pretending to the rest of the world that I'm still the guy I was. I know that sounds bloody stupid. I mean, you gave all that up years ago, and you're happy?'

'I did it voluntarily. It wasn't snatched away from me.'

Johnny mulled that over. 'I walk around London even now and people recognise me. They want selfies, they shout lyrics across the street. I went to a club the other night as a punter, and they got me up on stage to perform.'

'Is that so terrible? Sounds like things could be an awful lot worse.'

'Why did you do it?' Johnny wanted to know. 'I mean, give it all up?'

Graham put his head to one side. 'You want to know the truth? I lost my bottle.'

'Stage fright?'

'Yep. Started getting the heebie-jeebies bad before going onstage. In the end, it was making me ill, self-medicating through drink and drugs.'

Johnny raised his eyebrows at this. He'd heard of artists who were crippled with stage fright, of residencies being cancelled at short notice and Wembley gigs that were pulled at the last moment due to 'damaged vocal cords'. He'd never had that problem; the opposite, in fact, couldn't get him off the bloody stage.

'There was no Road to Damascus moment, or anything

like that. Remember, The Peril never hit the heights that you guys did. Then the Nineties came along. Britpop, Oasis . . . Blur. We were yesterday's men. You guys were versatile enough, but we weren't, and I'd had enough. Our time was up.'

'Jesus Christ . . .'

Graham laughed. 'I always knew it wasn't forever. I never expected as much from it as you did. You know why? Because I wasn't as good as you. I had enough to see me through. More than enough, really. And I'd always been a Christian deep down. I suppose I just thought it was time to give something back other than prayers of gratitude.'

Johnny decided there was no point asking whether it made Graham happier than fame and fortune had. Because what was good for Graham wasn't necessarily good for him. Even the thought of spiritual enlightenment was a turn-off where Johnny was concerned, if the price for it was boredom. Maybe in *his* case, it really would take a Road to Damascus moment.

Johnny leaned forward, staring up at the vivid image of the crucifixion. 'Something you said to me just now . . . how God doesn't punish us on Earth for our sins? Do you believe that?'

Graham frowned. 'No one on Earth knows the mind of God. According to scripture, we'll all be judged together on the final day.'

'Someone's died, you see . . . A friend of mine . . . I should have been a better friend. He's died because of things I did . . . or rather, things I didn't do.'

Graham didn't look shocked. 'Such as?'

'Put it this way. I got myself in trouble. I mean *bad* trouble. This friend tried to help, and he shouldn't have.

Because he put himself in the firing line. And he died when it should have been me.'

Graham frowned. 'Actions have consequences, Johnny. Lots of men and women have died in history doing heroic things. Acting to save others or suffering martyrdom for good causes. If these people, your friend included, died by the hand of another, that's not the will of God, that's the will of the person who did the killing.'

Johnny nodded, but the emotional pain of this business was creasing him inside. He sat back wearily. 'Everything's gone, Graham. I've lost every single thing that ever mattered to me. But this one came right out of the blue. I never even saw it. Elvis got—'

'Elvis?'

'That was his nickname. He got topped when it should've been me.'

Graham regarded Johnny with kind eyes. 'Johnny, from what you've told me, your life's at its lowest ebb. All sorts of different things are going wrong. Is it possible that's because you're making bad judgements?'

'I suppose . . .'

'You make a bad call on one front and a bad call on another. Different things go wrong. But they *are* connected. It's not God, Johnny, it's you.'

Johnny hung his head. It hurt to hear this, though he'd known it all along.

'Can you at least tell me what happened this morning?' Graham asked.

Johnny sighed and puffed out his cheeks. If he couldn't open up to this guy, he couldn't open up to anyone.

*

Daffodil Court didn't look as bad as Ted had made it sound. But appearances could be deceptive. Mona crossed the road towards it; not only was this place high up the league tables when it came to street robbery and burglary, it was also a hotspot for dealing.

The estate itself comprised row after row of medium-rise flats, no doubt all with underpasses and subterranean parking areas, meaning there'd be a labyrinth below ground as well as on top. Walking in, it seemed quiet – it was only mid-afternoon – but already she was spotting gang tags on the walls and footways. A park bench was occupied by a large group of teenagers who gave off a whiff of menace, eyeing her suspiciously as she passed by.

Elsewhere most of the residents were going about their everyday business, but there didn't seem to be any signposts, leaving her to roam at random, scanning the square-shouldered structures, ascending and descending flights of steps, wandering along concrete gantries.

In one lobby she encountered an old man walking with a limp.

'Excuse me,' she said as they passed. He looked round, startled. 'This isn't Primrose House, is it?'

The old man relaxed. 'Primrose?' He pointed through the nearest window, indicating a residential block taller by several storeys than many of the others, but also on the far side of most of them. It was hundreds of yards away.

'Quickest way's to go down again and across the car park.' He indicated a doorway on the other side of the lobby. There was no actual door on it, and no light on the other side, though Mona sensed a flight of concrete steps descending. 'Go straight over,' he added. 'Don't dawdle.'

'I won't, don't worry.'

He stumped away with his awkward seesawing gait.

Mona approached the doorless aperture and peeked down. She'd been right about the steps. They dropped a couple of flights, with a switchback in the middle. There appeared to be light below, but it was very faint.

'Great,' she muttered.

But she descended all the same. She was a reporter, wasn't she? She'd never live with herself if she didn't at least have a look.

Once Johnny started to tell Graham about what had happened, it was like opening the floodgates, and it all came tumbling out. Not just the day at the clinic, but his years of infidelity, letting Chelsea down, not just recently but ever since she'd been born. Ravi. Mona.

The lot.

It was easy to see why Graham's lost sheep followed their shepherd so willingly; he listened with patience until Johnny was spent.

'So you can see, I fucked up . . .' Johnny looked up at Jesus and Mary. 'Oh . . . sorry.'

'Don't be – you won't shock him; he's heard everything. Look, you and I have both messed up at some point, that's why we are where we are. Johnny, the way we grew up wasn't easy, it seemed like it was at the time, but what it did for us as people, as human beings . . . now that's another question.'

Johnny nodded, his head bowed.

'I can see you're distraught about all this, Johnny. But it's all about you, isn't it?'

Johnny looked up at him.

'Laura was in a bad state,' Graham said. 'You made it worse, not just by failing to recognise that she didn't really want to have a termination but by failing to be there when she had the final chance to make a decision.'

'I didn't fail to turn up . . . I was . . . late.'

'Being late is no use. In fact, that underlines it. It was important that you were on time. But there are other examples too. I mean, you've come here today to speak to me . . . about *yourself.*'

Johnny stiffened with unease. 'You said we could talk.'

'And that's what we're doing. But counselling doesn't just mean holding someone's hand. Your friend, Elvis, he died . . . and your take is it's all about *you.* Does he have a family?'

'Yeah.'

'And how are they dealing with it?'

'Struggling.'

'Course they are.' Graham leaned towards him. 'I'll lay you ten to one, though, that they're upset because they're thinking about Elvis, not about themselves. They're not saying, "Look, God, *I've* lost a friend. How could you punish *me* like that?"'

Johnny closed his eyes. 'I didn't intend it to come over that way.'

'People who are selfish usually don't. They don't even see it.' Graham smiled. 'But it's a curable disease. Look, Johnny, the way we lived back in the day – and I was just as bad as you in that regard – it was all about greed, excess. We lived purely for the pleasure we could extract from each minute. I mean, sometimes we wrote good songs and played cool shows, but that was a small return for what we got out of it. The real cost was the damage it did to us as individuals. We lived in a world of temptation, and we're still paying the price.'

What Graham said rang so many bells. Johnny spoke softly:

'Remember that German tour we were on together, and that night after we did that *Musikladen* TV show, be honest, you were up for it as much as my band, and we were bad.'

Graham smiled at the memory. 'I was no angel, you're right, and I'm still not now. We still have long lines of people who'll never forgive us for the way we treated them.'

'I've never have moved on, have I? Still stuck in 1984.'

Graham smiled sadly. 'The irony is that Johnny Klein the supernova . . . that wasn't really you. It was a facade you created. You aren't really a god and you never were. But it's the real you who's paying for it.'

Johnny shook his head. 'It's not just me paying for it.'

Graham was right: he had only thought about himself for years. Laura, Mona, Pete, the Major, Jackie, even fucking Don Slater had all tried to help him since he moved out of his mansion, but he'd either messed it up for them, or held it against them.

'And you know,' Graham added, 'understanding all this . . . that's only the start of the battle, not the finish. Sorry if this isn't what you wanted to hear. You've come here and that's a good thing. But you don't get a free pass from God. You've got to fix stuff yourself.'

Johnny nodded vigorously. 'I want to.'

'Somehow you need to change your direction.'

'The problem is that I've run out of other directions,' Johnny said. 'I'm at rock bottom.'

'In that case, there's only one: up.'

Johnny tried to smile. That was the first thing Graham had said that sounded like a platitude. 'I'll be honest, Gray, I can't stop thinking what it would be like to stand on Chelsea bridge, feel the warmth of the beautiful bright lights on the water, as I jump into the abyss, into the freedom of the dark water . . . I ask myself why I'm still here, why have I got through when so many of my friends didn't.'

'I don't believe you're the suicidal type, and for you that would be the most selfish act of all. Because there are still people who care about you, and all you'd do is leave a mess that would haunt them for the rest of their days.'

'I hear you . . . I'm talking about myself again. But *I* am the problem. *I'm* the mess, Graham. It's *my* ego that ran wild. Anyone who showed *me* their heart got it broken. With me gone, their lives would only improve.'

'Plus, you personally wouldn't have to worry about any of this anymore?' Graham gave him his frankest stare yet. 'Johnny, you asked me why I jacked it in. Well . . . I was a bit economical with the truth. I told you I thought our star was waning, that the stage fright got to me, but there was something else too.

'At the end of the Eighties, we were still smashing it, but deep down I knew I was coked out, burned out, wasted. Then, in the summer of 1990, I was surfing in Cornwall. I was drunk and stoned and high all at once, had been caning it for days. It was early evening, the sun was coming down and the whole coast seemed to be on fire, I was probably tripping a bit. I got on my board and paddled out to the wave break, then, before I knew it, I got caught in a riptide and the current dragged me out. I just got taken further and further out. So, I let the board go and tried to swim back in. But all that did was wear me out. After a few minutes I could hardly see land, then I started going under because I was too tired to stay afloat. And you know what? I accepted my fate. All I could think was: "Fair enough, the Almighty's been pretty cheesed off with me for quite a while, and now he's called in the debt. It's my time." And this voice in my ear said: "Actually, it *isn't* your time. *I'll* tell you when it's your time. So, get your backside in gear, get yourself out of this and fix things."'

Graham paused, mouth twisted in deliberation.

'Whose voice was that, Johnny?' he asked. 'An angel? God? My inner self?' He shrugged. 'I don't know. But the message got home, because suddenly all I could think about was making things right with people. I realised I did *not* want to die, because at that stage I didn't even know who I really was. Anyway, I got back to the surface, but I was way out at sea. So, I offered God a deal: Pluck me out of this, and I'll fix everything I've done wrong, and more. And, well . . . the next thing I knew, I was being lifted aboard a lifeboat.'

'It's no surprise you pulled things together after that,' Johnny said.

Graham shrugged. 'I think you've probably had similar experiences yourself. It's time you recognised them for what they are.'

'Warnings?'

'No. Second chances.' Graham smiled encouragingly. 'Time to get back out there, Johnny, but not on some obsessive quest to conquer the world again. This time, just conquer your ego. Look at the people around you and think what you can do for them, rather than what they can do for you. And when you've made a mess of things, clean it up.'

Johnny cracked a wry grin. 'Gonna be hard, breaking the habit of a lifetime.'

'One step at a time, JK.'

'Might be impossible.'

'No, what you did before was impossible.' Graham squeezed his shoulder. 'Kid from a broken home to mega-stardom. Compared to that, this'll be a walk in the park.'

At the bottom of the steps, Mona entered a spacious under-croft, which the old man had said used to be a car park, though the couple of cars she saw were shells on bricks. There were a few scattered boxes, and lots of rubbish sacks piled around a few large wheelie bins.

All pretty normal.

Shouldering her bag, she headed in the direction he had told her to.

Halfway along the next stretch, ragged figures stood around what looked like a brazier with a fire in it. Other people slumped against the surrounding pillars, wound up in sleeping bags.

'Shit,' she muttered under her breath.

She supposed she could pass them by if she hugged the right-hand wall, but they might still notice her. Who would help down here if she got into trouble? She took her phone from her bag and was dumbstruck to see that she had no bars.

'You dozy mare,' she muttered. 'You're underground.'

None of the ragged group had looked her way yet, so she ventured forward, moving quickly as she hugged the wall. Darting a glance in their direction, she could see that they still hadn't noticed her, so she picked up her pace.

As she hurried through the car park she passed a succession of broken-down doors, the dank unlit chambers behind them containing age-old machinery, cisterns and furnaces, all swamped in dust and cobwebs.

Mona bore to the left, her breathing slowed, her heartbeat steadying.

She continued to where she could see the passage beyond, leading to open space. The sky was visible overhead, but she was now surrounded by wrecked cars, dozens of them jammed together and piled on top of each other.

Mona glanced forward. A shadowy man advanced towards her. He was large and imposing. He wore a shabby overcoat over a denim shirt and a pair of chinos. In one hand, he carried a sports bag, the tops of two milk cartons poking through its open zipper.

He dumped the bag as she approached, and Mona had to fight the urge to run – the man was built like a battleship and she wouldn't stand a chance if he went for her.

Then his face came into view, and Mona suddenly realised who he was.

'Are you lost, love?' His voice was rich and deep, best suited to treading the boards at the National Theatre rather than a rundown estate in North East London.

'Not exactly. I'm Mona Mistry,' she said. '*Classic Rock* magazine.'

He arched an eyebrow. His face had once been handsome, clean-cut, but now was middle-aged and saggy. 'In that case, you must be looking for me. I'm—'

'I know who you are,' she said. 'You're Ben Randall.'

'Well, you must be keen, to track me down here,' Ben Randall said, opening the door to number 48. 'What story are you working on? Another "where are they now" feature?'

Mona glanced back along the passage with its daubings of graffiti, its flickery overhead bulbs and scattered scraps of wastepaper. 'In a way.'

'Well, at least I'm good for something. Call me Ben.' He stood aside and showed her into his home.

Mona didn't feel fully safe until he'd closed the door behind them and double-locked it. 'I'm glad you came along when you did.'

Randall stripped off his coat and dumped his sports bag. 'It's not as bad as it seems out there; there's good people on this estate who look out for each other.'

'That's good to know.'

He led her through into his small lounge. 'It suits me here in a way, it's easy to disappear, but no point pretending I'm living here by choice. Sit down. I'll put the kettle on.'

She glanced around as he stepped through a sliding door into a small kitchenette. She'd passed an adjoining bathroom and bedroom, but the lounge was roughly the size of what she'd imagine a prison cell to be like. It had a single small window looking out at the upright corner of a concrete wall, a vista of austere tower blocks visible beyond it. Inside, it was tidy enough, if cluttered, the shelving piled with books, potted plants trailing greenery everywhere, a magazine rack crammed to overflowing, and too many mismatched cushions on the sofa and single armchair. In the kitchenette, she heard water running and a switch being thrown.

'If you don't mind me saying, Mr Randall,' she called, taking a seat, 'you're very trusting.'

His voice carried out to her. 'So are you. I could be a serial killer!'

'You're Ben Randall. But you don't know me from Adam,' she said. 'You haven't even asked to see my press card. I could be lying that I'm a journalist.'

Randall stuck his head out. 'You could. But in my experience, I'm not sure that would be much worse than it being true. How do you take your tea?'

'Milk please. No sugar. I should stick my hand up and admit that I'm not actually here to ask questions about what happened to you.'

He'd shifted out of sight again. 'That story has been done to death anyway, darling, hasn't it?'

'What I don't understand is, surely there's still a career out there for you? You were great – my aunty took me to see you in *Chicago*, your performance was electric.'

Randall reappeared, this time leaning in the doorframe. 'Miss Mistry, the life of a professional performer is only viable so long as that person can perform.'

'Erm . . .' She hadn't wanted to intrude on his problems, though perhaps it had been inevitable. Either way, he didn't seem angry. 'Well . . . your struggles with alcohol are well documented.'

'In which case, why am I not drunk *now*? It's early evening, after all. Surely, I should be well on the way? I'll

tell you, Mona . . . because I'm dry . . . off the wagon . . .
sober.' He watched her reaction with interest. 'I've been
attending AA meetings for months, 271 days so far; it's
working for me, but it's one day at a time, and I need to
be stronger. For now, Daffodil Court suits me – while I
work on myself, I think that's the current parlance?'

Mona was impressed. 'I . . . look, I didn't come here to
speak to you about this. But you had a remarkable talent,
a great career . . . I hope you get back on your feet soon.'

He considered that. 'The alcoholism was only a symptom
of the thing that brought me down. The final nail in the
coffin, I mean, I've always liked a drink, but habits like
that can get a lot worse if something else is sucking your
life away, and you'll do anything you can to compensate.
I'm sorry, this must sound like a whole load of psycho-
babble?' He smiled. 'I imagine you've seen more than a few
big names come and go, burned out before their time by
excess and indulgence, and always blaming something
else . . . or *someone* else maybe? Of course, excuses like
that will cut no ice with ordinary people. You know, those
everyday folk who struggle weekly to pay their mortgages
and their shopping bills.'

He vanished again, only to reappear quickly, carrying
two steaming mugs and a plate of digestives. Mona thanked
him, taking the mug offered, and a single biscuit. Randall
settled down into the facing armchair, his own mug cradled
to his chest.

'As I said, Ben . . . I'm not here to write a story about
you at all. I'm not here to write any kind of story.'

He arched an eyebrow. 'You came a long way to make
a social call.'

'It's not that either. I need your help with something.' She eyed him steadily.

Ben Randall still had a tough, steely exterior. But he was very much an actor. On the shelves in the corner of her eye, she could see works of poetry, the collected plays of Shakespeare. It must have been a big comedown for him, in this concrete box, buried in this grey sink-estate. Though only twenty-five minutes on the underground to Theatreland, it might as well have been a million miles.

'The truth is,' she said, 'it's a friend of mine that needs help. And from what you've already said . . .' Opting to seize the bull by the horns, she set her tea on a side table and straightened up properly. 'I think I've come to just the right person.'

25
PREY

Monday

'Graceland Restaurant.'

'Aamir, it's Johnny,' Johnny said, standing at the bottom end of Carnaby Street.

'All right, Johnny?' Aamir replied.

Was there a hint of coolness there? Maybe the word had now got out that Johnny was the one who'd brought those thugs to Graceland.

'I'm just calling to see . . . well, how are things over there?' Johnny asked.

'Pretty terrible, if I'm honest.'

'Coppers still all over the place?'

'Yep. I don't think we'll be free of the police for quite a few days yet.'

Johnny didn't think he was going to get arrested today, but that DS from yesterday was no mug. 'Has Mona been around?'

'Not this morning. There was a message for *you*, though. Someone rang the restaurant earlier. A Miss Phillips. She said could you get in touch as soon as possible.'

'OK . . . thanks, Aamir.'

Before ringing Jackie, Johnny thought a little more about Graham's words of advice. Stop being a self-indulgent prick, do the right thing. But, with Karl Jones breathing down his neck, Graceland still a wreck and the Met sniffing around his bedroom, the thought of spending the rest of today and, who knew, maybe tonight, in the safe and cosy environment of Jackie's luxury townhouse was very tempting.

He made the call.

'Jackie . . . it's Johnny.'

'Johnny! Thank God. Look . . . that guy's been around here again. I saw him sneaking across the garden last night. The new security light was triggered.'

Johnny's heart sank a bit; getting tangled up in the weeds at the bottom of Jackie's garden wasn't in his game plan.

'Are you in town?' He fancied he could hear traffic sounds behind her.

'I'm shopping,' she replied. 'Harvey Nicks.'

She might have fallen from the peak of her success, but she never let small matters like money get in the way.

'I'm in Soho,' he replied. 'If I head over there, we can share a cab back to yours?'

She sounded pleased. 'Can't think of anyone else I'd rather share a ride with.'

'You hungry?' Jackie said as she let them both in through the grand front door and led them through to the kitchen.

'Yeah, as it happens.'

She tossed a couple of menus towards him, one Thai, the other Italian.

'First though,' he said, 'we need to talk about this peeping Tom of yours.'

'Yeah?'

'I followed him home the other day.'

She visibly turned pale. 'I'm sorry?'

'I saw him. He was at Polydex, checking you out.'

'You . . .' Her mouth dropped open. 'You sure it was the same guy?'

'I'd put my house on it, if I still had one.'

'OK, tell me.'

'Jackie, he lives next door.' Johnny pointed to the side of the house in question.

She paled even more. 'Good Christ almighty!'

He stepped forward, taking her shivering form in his arms. 'Listen, I don't think it's as bad as all that. He's a little prick. Probably isn't going to do anything. But now we know who he is, we can call the cops.'

She nodded. 'Yes, yes, you're right. I was given a police number . . .' She scuttled to a drawer, opened it, rooted through a pile of bric-a-brac, and came out with a small contact card. Dragging a chair to the kitchen table, she plonked herself down and got on her mobile.

Johnny watched from the other side of the kitchen.

'Hello . . . hello?' Jackie said. 'Is that . . . erm, Detective Collins? It's Jackie Phillips. You know, Dunmoor Close, Highgate. Yes . . . yes . . . that's right, the woman who thinks she's got a stalker.' She arched an ironic eyebrow at Johnny. 'I've got a friend here who not only saw this guy, he had a bit of a run-in with him . . .'

Johnny tensed, hoping to God she wouldn't mention that he'd thrown punches, not when he was already on the police radar.

'No, no,' Jackie said reassuringly. 'No one got hurt, but . . . later on, he spotted the guy again, and the guy lives in the house next door to me. Number 17 . . . No, I've never even spoken to him. I don't know his name or anything . . . But can't you just knock on his door? . . . OK . . . I see.' She broke away, covering the device with her hand. 'You staying here tonight, Johnny?' She pitched it as a question, but it felt like an invitation.

'Sure,' he replied coolly. 'If that's what you want.'

'Yes, I'll have company here all night,' she told the cop. 'So, I should be OK till tomorrow . . . Yeah, absolutely . . . so, ten tomorrow? . . . I'm sure that'll be fine.' She glanced at Johnny again. 'They'll get some details from us first. Then they're going next door.'

Johnny nodded.

'That'd be perfect,' she said into the phone. 'Thanks so much.'

She cut the call, her shoulders sagging with relief. 'That was Detective Inspector Collins. 'He's in charge of this case.' She glanced out into the garden. 'That fucking little creep. How seedy can you get? Bet I'm online now, walking around in my bra and knickers. Maybe less.'

'If that'd happened, I think we'd know about it,' Johnny said.

After they'd eaten, they sat in facing armchairs in Jackie's sumptuous lounge, each cupping a treble malt. Jackie curled like a kitten in a pair of baggy pink silk pyjamas. Her ability to look alluring came naturally to her. When he'd met her outside Harrods, she'd looked dazzling in a red Joseph trouser suit with a white silk blouse that hid little, her hair a tumble of glorious blonde layers. Every guy passing had cast jealous glances at him.

'Anyway,' Johnny said, trying to focus. 'By this time tomorrow, it'll all be over.'

She nodded thoughtfully. 'I've been a nervous wreck, I don't mind admitting. Even before the security light came on last night, I . . . I knew he was out there. Like I'd developed an extra sense.' Her eyes glistened. 'They say all prey animals have that.'

'You're not a prey animal.'

'You think not?'

'I know not.'

'I hear what people say. "Jackie Phillips, hard-faced bitch, brass neck, fucking cow."' Her bottom lip quivered. 'But, when . . . when you're on your own . . . night after night, and you know . . . you know someone's out there who wants to hurt you . . .' Her face crumpled, and the tears welled up.

'Hey . . .' He put his drink down, crossed the room, and inserted himself into the big armchair alongside her, wrapping her in his arms. 'He won't be out there much longer.'

'What if they can't prove anything?'

'They'll still give him a scare.'

'You think so?'

'I've seen him, remember. They'll scare him all right.'

She leaned her head against him. 'Thanks for coming round.' She reached up and touched his cheek. 'I don't deserve you, Johnny. I ruined your marriage.'

'Water under the bridge.'

It pained him to think that, but maybe Graham had been right about needing to get real with his life. Perhaps Laura was gone permanently, and if so, he owed it to both her and Chelsea to pack it in with the hopeful hovering around, and just become a friend. Besides, with a drop-dead woman like this in his arms, there might be compensations.

She brushed her lips against his and the next thing, they were kissing.

They'd enjoyed each other in the past, but those snatched moments had been rushed, flashes of illicit passion. In both their cases, though, the desire to revisit old times had always burned away in the background. They rose from the armchair and ascended the staircase hand in hand. Upstairs, they slipped out of their clothes and climbed under the sheets without speaking. Moments of rapture followed, the hot, dark room spinning, Johnny finding the answer to a question they had each asked themselves for decades: what would it be like if they were free to be together.

It was good.

Several hours later, Jackie lay tangled round him sleeping deeply, one arm across his chest, her head buried in the crook of his neck.

Johnny stared at the dapples of streetlight on the ceiling, a warmth seeping through him. The silk sheet covering the duvet smelled sweetly of perfume, while the lamp on the bedside table bathed them in a dim, mellow glow.

Maybe they'd been destined to come together?

It was a snowy December day in Newcastle back in the

Nineties when Johnny had first met her. Jackie was the new blonde, wide-eyed presenter who was sending television producers into a frenzy with her fresh, seductive way of presenting. She was the new kid on the block, and everyone wanted to be interviewed by her.

It was only her second show when she came face to face with Johnny Klein, and it rapidly became clear that they were two of a kind: flirtatious and competitive, the innuendos flowing freely, almost like tennis. The chemistry had been there from the start. The second the interview was over, Johnny was dragged on stage to perform their latest hit, during the course of which he couldn't take his eyes off Jackie. Every move he made, every pose he threw was like a peacock flashing its iridescent tail in a blatant game of 'come and get me'. Jackie had never taken her eyes off him either.

He'd given her an access-all-areas pass for that night's gig at City Hall, but though he'd spent most of the show scanning the wings and the photographers' pit, she hadn't showed. That just made his desire for her even stronger.

Johnny hadn't realised how much he had missed the feel of a woman beside him, that human connection. He hated to admit it to himself, but he'd been lonely.

Maybe *this* was the new leaf he should now turn? Perhaps *this* was how it was meant to have been? Who could say, but the future suddenly didn't look anything like as bleak.

Outside, a stiffening breeze rustled the maples, rattling the windowpane. The old Georgian house creaked overhead. Johnny closed his eyes in search of sleep. But just as he was about to doze off again, he heard a creak, which seemed to be coming from the floorboards above him.

His eyes flew open. Though Jackie was still fast asleep beside him, Johnny felt wide awake and unable to settle.

He disentangled himself from Jackie's legs and threw his own over the side of the bed, pulling on his boxers that were strewn on the bedroom floor along with the rest of his clothes.

He padded out into the hallway, along towards the kitchen, his stomach rumbling. He opened Jackie's Smeg fridge, disappointed to find only milk, celery and bio-yogurt. His thoughts strayed back to the bedroom. That creak he'd heard overhead. Then his gaze alighted on something else.

Johnny stared at the rack of shelves next to the kitchen window. Mostly they contained plants, but there were one or two cookbooks there too. And a paperback. Something about the name on the spine pulled him closer to inspect it.

He reached out to the stack of shelves and picked it up. It was old and well-thumbed.

It was volume six in the *Detective Inspector Collins Mysteries*.

The very same name that Jackie had called the detective she had phoned earlier.

Johnny headed back to the bedroom and looked at her for a moment. She was still sleeping, her black lashes were so long they almost brushed her cheeks and her tanned legs stretched across the bed like a golden cat.

Maybe the detective's name was just a coincidence? Johnny really wanted to believe that right now.

A light sprinkle of dust fell from one of the spotlights located over the bed. Another sprinkle followed, and another, accompanied by a creak from somewhere overhead. Johnny looked up.

We are not alone.

26

SOMEBODY UP THERE
DOESN'T LIKE ME

Tuesday

Johnny stayed where he was, listening and watching. Another creak sounded, closer. Someone was definitely moving around up there. Slowly, Johnny tracked the tell-tale sounds backwards onto the landing. When they finally fell silent, he was standing beneath a trapdoor to the loft, a metal pole resting up against the wall underneath it.

Surprised at how cool-headed he was being, but nervous too, Johnny fitted one end of the pole into the slot on the trap door, and gently released the catch. The trap swung down on its hinge, a loft ladder unfolding to the landing floor, followed by a hasty thudding as footsteps moved away again across the ceiling. He scrambled up in pursuit and, as his head poked through the opening, caught the slightest glimpse of a man closing a wooden door at the end of the loft connecting with the adjoining house. His heart raced as he hoisted his half-naked frame up between the rafters. When his eyes had attuned to the dimness, he noticed how the insulation had been pulled up in places between the joists, and how the fixtures for the spotlights had been supplemented with webcams. Black cables snaked to the door in the wall, which at second glance was made out of several aged and misaligned planks. It was more like the entry to a mousehole than the door to another house.

Tom's been doing a lot of peeping.

Breathing hard, and head bent to one side to account for the eaves, he scooted across. The makeshift door had no lock, just a piece of rope to pull it open, and through the chinks between the planks, he now spotted the shape of someone on the other side. By the sounds of it, they were fumbling with a bolt, trying to shove it into place. Johnny threw himself forward, slamming his shoulder into the door. It flew back sufficiently for him to stick one arm through, grabbing first a hunk of sweatshirt and then a handful of hair. Hanging on for all his worth, Johnny yanked his arm back once, twice, three times, each time banging his opponent's head into the woodwork.

Whimpers of pain sounded. It was definitely that bloke he'd followed from Soho. Johnny threw himself at the door again, and it swung inward, the bloke hurtling backwards.

They were now in the loft above the next-door house. It was mainly plasterboard, but with a small area of plank for storage. At present, it was more like a UFC fighting ring, both combatants on their knees as they faced each other. Johnny had the advantage.

He made no attempt to block when Johnny threw the best right hook of his life. It landed square on the man's

319

chin, catapulting him backwards. Johnny scrambled forward over the flimsy flooring, landing on top of him, but the lad had come round sufficiently to fight back a little.

'You little toerag, how long have you been filming Jackie?' he said through a glanced jaw.

The kid looked dazed, his left temple cut and bleeding.

'Get off me!' the bloke gargled. 'You stupid or what? She knows all about it, it was her idea.'

'What??'

They rolled over, bouncing off the decking onto the plasterwork of the ceiling below. Both the kid's hands had latched onto Johnny's throat, squeezing, claw-like fingers digging into his Adam's apple. Johnny's eyes bulged, mist clouding his cornea.

'Fuck,' it was a strangled gasp.

But then, with what felt like frame-by-frame slow motion, they both suddenly lurched downward as the ceiling gave way. Tangled together, they went through it as one, the whole mass of plaster and paper bursting explosively downward, the pair turning over together in mid-air as they fell through a fog of white dust. When they hit the carpeted floor, it was with bone-shaking force. Johnny thrust himself back to his feet, wafting at the dust. However, the lad didn't move. He dropped back to a crouch, seeing that his opponent was out cold, blood trickling from one side of his mouth. When he put an ear to the kid's lips, he was still breathing.

Johnny got back up and looked around, noticing that there was no bedroom furniture here, but gradually realising that a huge clutter of glossy photographs covered all four of its walls.

He approached the nearest, eyes popping. Each image – and the majority appeared to be screen-grab printouts – depicted Jackie in bed in her own room, but in various compromising positions with different men. Johnny pivoted to get a better view of the room. Not a single inch of space was left, pictures overlapping pictures in thick wads. On a desk in the corner stood a laptop and two monitors. There, on the left-hand screen, in freeze-frame, was a crystal-clear image, a close-up, of Johnny himself and Jackie clamped together in the throes of sex.

What the hell had been going on here?

Reeling, Johnny had to drag a chair from under the desk and slump down on it.

His heart trip-hammered in shock. Struggling to stay focused, he pulled open a couple of drawers, yanking everything out. When he grabbed a dog-eared leather note-book, he flipped through it and saw that it contained lists of handwritten names, some of them household names – TV presenters, actors, musicians – all with mobile numbers, and with cash amounts scribbled alongside, more than one in some cases, often with dates attached.

It was her idea.

Jackie.

'You could sleep through anything,' Johnny said, as Jackie slowly emerged from sleep, stretching her limbs out languidly.

Even then it was a few seconds before Jackie sat up and rubbed her eyes. 'What time is it?' she asked, puzzled to see that it was still pitch-dark outside.

Johnny shrugged; his hair was covered in dust and his arms and face in grazes. 'Dunno, early hours. I've lost track.'

He was now seated in a chair and fully dressed, wearing his khaki jacket. One by one, he tossed his haul of photographic images onto the quilt.

She stared at him, confused, then down at the photos, and her face froze. Slowly, almost gingerly, she picked a couple up to look at them more closely.

'You should know that when the police get here, it won't be DI Collins,' Johnny said. 'I mean . . . seeing as he doesn't exist. It'll be DS Thomas, a detective I've got to know a bit recently.'

That wasn't strictly true. He hadn't called the police, or been in contact with DS Thomas. But it was certainly an option.

'Johnny . . .' Jackie, whose face was suddenly taut with panic, raised a hand. 'Listen, you don't understand.'

'Try me.'

Jackie closed her eyes and shook her head. 'I wanted you, Johnny, so much. I've always wanted you.'

'Then what's going on with Peeping Tom upstairs, who are all these blokes?'

Jackie took a deep breath, her voice shaking as she spoke. 'His name is Kyle Green. If you must know, I caught him filming me through my window, taking pictures of me naked. He's an IT expert, lives in the flat next door. I could have reported him there and then, but—'

'Why didn't you?'

'He begged me not to, said he'd do anything for me if I didn't.'

'So you had a better idea, put him to good use? Is that where all these other blokes come in?'

Jackie's eyes filled up with tears. 'You have no idea what it's been like for me, Johnny. To be on the cover of every lads' mag in the country, only to be dumped for the newer, younger version of me when I get a few crows' feet; to try and stay in work, to pay my bills, keep this house, it's been hell . . . and it turns out rock stars can also be mean, Johnny. Most of the blokes I was with left me with their dirty underwear, heartbreak and a bigger overdraft every time. I just wanted what was my due.'

'By getting Tom up there to take a few dirty pictures and then screw them for some cash?'

'I was desperate, almost bankrupt.' Her tears were flowing freely now, her face a mask of anguish.

'And I was one of your suckers?'

'No! Well . . . at the beginning maybe . . . but that first night you were here I realised . . . how good it was between us.' Jackie took a step towards Johnny. 'I told him, I didn't want that with you, but it was too late, I couldn't stop him.' Jackie reached out to him, tearfully. 'You have to believe me, Johnny.'

He took a step back. 'I went out of my way to help you, Jackie, and I expected nothing for it in return.'

'Oh no, Johnny.' She gave a tight smile, and there was a flash of that tough chick who could always look after herself. She shook her head. 'No . . . you came here for sex.'

'I came here as a *friend*,' he snapped, his heart still aching. 'And you punish me like this?'

'It's not about punishment.' She swung her feet to the carpet, holding the quilt over her nakedness. 'I mean, it's all right for you . . . but I need *money*, OK? I need cash so that I can continue my life . . . *this* life.'

Johnny shook his head. 'Look at me, Jacks, I've lost the house at Mill Hill . . . I've lost everything! I'm squatting in an attic for fuck's sake! I understand more than anyone what's it's like to be on the floor.'

'I know that, Johnny, but there's no way I was going under. You've been getting away it for years before it fell apart for you. You slept with anyone you wanted and no one thought any the less of you. But I did it, and I was a whore, a slag. I said it was OK for you, and it is, you'll bounce back.'

'Jacks, I feel for you,' Johnny said, finding himself meaning it. 'But I've got problems of my own . . . and I'll tell you something: what you're doing here is *not* going to be one of them.'

'You're not really going to shop me to the police, are you?' she asked, her lips trembling.

Johnny looked at her, sitting there covered only by a duvet. God, she was still bloody gorgeous. 'The moment any one of those pictures or films goes live, Jackie . . . Until then you get a pass. But, Jacks . . .' He shook his head. 'That's enough of this shit. I've got everything I need in here.' He held up the notebook, full of names, dates and amounts. 'It's amazing how many famous faces are hanging on that wall next door. And who might be willing to talk if they knew they weren't the only ones.'

Jackie stood, letting the quilt rustle down. 'You may not believe me, but they got what they deserved. Every one of them came here looking for sex . . . that's all fellas ever want from me, Johnny, even you. Am I so wicked to want to get something out of it?'

Johnny went to the door. 'Who knows.' He pocketed the leather notebook.

He walked out onto the landing. She followed him, naked. 'Johnny, wait . . . Johnny!' Almost pleading. '*Johnny!*'

He turned at the top of the stairs.

'We're still friends, aren't we?' she asked. 'Johnny, I *need* a friend.' She seemed desperate, but how could he ever trust her again?

'I'm not sure, Jacks. Anyway, put your dressing gown on and check Peeping Tom's all right.'

Jackie frowned. 'What are you talking about?'

'You think he wouldn't try to stop me?'

Jackie looked alarmed. 'What've you done to him?'

'What was it you said about people getting what they deserve?'

She ran to the foot of the loft ladder. 'Kyle?' she shouted, panicked.

'Call an ambulance, Jackie.'

Jackie gazed at him in horror. 'Johnny, this is . . .'

'Serious? I know.' He headed for the stairs. 'Pity you didn't think about that before.'

27

ONE BLOW TOO MANY

Tuesday

Soft muzak drifted from the speakers sunk into the tiled ceiling of the Mother & Baby department, chart songs from the noughties, mainly designed for the late twenty-something woman as she moved around the spaceship-white shop, keen to choose the perfect pram, walker or baby bouncer.

Laura felt her age as she roamed the aisles. Other shoppers couldn't work out if it was middle-aged Laura who was the mum, or Chelsea, in her school uniform. Either way, the Klein family was growing. Now the initial shock had faded, Laura was trying to put positive vibes on the situation. She'd stopped questioning herself about the rights and wrongs of going ahead with this, while the morning sickness that had plagued her pregnancy with Chelsea was absent.

She'd applied heavier make-up than usual that morning,

not so much to make herself look younger, more to hide the bags under her eyes. She wasn't sleeping well; her hormones were taking their time settling into their new routine. A long mac and over-sized jumper hid the first signs of her baby bump. Chelsea was captivated by the thought of a baby brother, as she'd grown up believing herself a permanent only child.

As they strolled together, Chelsea grabbed up a beautiful miniature cardigan.

'What do you think? Can I get this for him?'

'Of course,' Laura smiled. 'Put it in the basket.'

'No, I'll take it to the till now. I want to get it, otherwise you'll end up paying. This is *my* present.'

After the heavy scene with Johnny yesterday, she'd never expected to see Chelsea this happy. It was as if they'd finally become a team. For the first time in years, her daughter wasn't constantly asking about her dad. She stood and watched as Chelsea beavered away.

A feeling that they were going to make this work, that they might even be happy, seeped pleasantly through her. Almost on cue, there was an abrupt music change.

The song that came over the loudspeakers now was 'Let's All Love' by Klein, the very last single the band had released before they'd split. The original had been a jaunty ballad, while this version was softer, gentler, apparently being performed by a young woman with a beautiful, angelic voice. If Laura recalled correctly, Johnny had written this one alone, even though he'd been a mess, his body ravaged by alcohol, his brain all-but-fried after one too many drugs binges. Despite that, what a lovely tune he'd created.

Laura was surprised to find herself thinking about Johnny and smiling at the same time; it must be all those excess endorphins coursing through her body. She let her thoughts drift back to the good times with her ex: the wild excitement of the gigs, the glamorous holidays, the mountains of presents; so much fun and enjoyment generally, all of which she'd forgotten during the chaos that followed.

Then the song ended.

More abruptly than Laura remembered, the soft guitar hitting a chord that seemed out of place, a note that started to feedback, as if the guitarist had walked over to his Marshall stack and was shaking his axe right in front of the fifteen-inch speaker.

Laura put a hand to the side of her head. The feedback was actually deafening, burrowing into her middle ear. What the hell was going on? And why was no one else reacting to it?

Shuddering involuntarily, she tottered where she stood, then reached out towards a plump grandmotherly type close by, who only now seemed to notice that she was having problems. And promptly screamed. It was a piercing, top-of-the-lungs scream, and it sliced through the shop like cheese-wire. It brought Chelsea running back into the aisle, where she was confronted by an appalling sight. Laura sitting on the cold vinyl floor, having flopped down like some kind of doll, a pool of claret-coloured blood spreading out between her legs, soaking through her elegant white coat.

Chelsea dropped her bag as she dashed forward. '*Mum* . . . *Mum* . . . *MUM!*' The screams spread from shopper to shopper, almost drowning her out. 'Call an ambulance, please!' she wailed, wrapping Laura in a fiercely protective embrace. '*Someone, call an ambulance, my mum needs help* . . .'

Johnny lay on his Graceland bed even though it was nearly midday. He was fully clothed, his crumpled cowboy boots crowning each bedpost. He stared without seeing at his Motorola, mostly through the bottom of his near-empty bottle of Jack, as it buzzed with a voicemail notification. He was pissed, his tongue dry, his throat sour. He hadn't been in this state for months . . . when he could literally taste his own breath, the acid burning through his guts as he belched out putrid gas. The phone rang again.

'Fuck . . . go away,' he groaned.

It felt wrong not to answer, especially when someone was trying hard to get in touch with him, but it would only be Jackie making excuses for herself again. He'd walked all the way home from Highgate in the middle of the night. Turning over the business with Jackie, the guilt about Ravi still gnawed away at him, tortuously.

When he'd reached Graceland, he'd dragged a bottle of Jack from under his bed and steadily worked his way through it. Which he was now regretting.

Johnny's knees creaked as he hauled himself to his feet, lumbered into the bathroom and gazed at the grotesque face in the smeary mirror. 'Fucking idiot. Why didn't you see that coming? Why?'

Back in the room, the mobile buzzed again. It sounded louder, digging into him. Johnny sloped back in, inclined down onto the bed, and wearily picked the device up.

And saw that the caller was Chelsea.

He sobered in a second, slamming the phone to his ear.

'Dad, where the fuck have you been?' she wept. 'I've been trying to get hold of you.'

'Chelsea . . . slow down, what's happened?'

She told him as much as she was able to, through inconsolable sobbing.

'Where's Mum now?' he finally stuttered.

'We're here at home, she has to rest. Dad, it was so horrible.'

'I'm coming over.'

The taxi ride to Muswell Hill took forever. Johnny had gambled that he'd have enough cash for it. Along with all the other crap, he'd scraped a few twenties out of the bedroom drawer belonging to that bastard Kyle Whatever His Fucking Name Was. He reckoned that had been the least those two lowlifes owed him, but most of that had gone on the taxi ride back to Brick Lane in the wee small hours. Unfortunately, the traffic on the Holloway Road was now crammed and crawling. Johnny kept one eye on the clock as it ate up his funds.

The cabbie kept eyeing him through the rear-view mirror. He clearly knew who Johnny was, but the passenger both looked and smelled so bad that his interest was more like a morbid horror. Yesterday's national treasure could be today's primate at the London Zoo.

Johnny began pulling the cotton lining out of his empty pockets in his quest for change.

'This'll do fine,' he said, even though they were well short of their destination.

'You sure, mate? You got another mile to go.'

'Yeah, this'll do.'

The driver didn't pull over but watched Johnny through his mirror. 'Relax, mate. I've turned the clock off. I owe you one. Met my missus at one of your gigs. Going on forty years ago now. She was stood on the chair in front of me. She's only five foot and a fag butt, but heart of gold, you know. Put your money away, son, this one's on me.'

Johnny wasn't sure where he would have been without the kindness of London cab drivers this week. Since he'd been jolted back into the real world, he'd taken a lot of flak, but he'd also been humbled by the simple generosity of ordinary people. He sat back as they drove down the side of Queen's Wood.

'Thanks, mate, I appreciate it.'

Susanna's house looked quiet as Johnny waved the cab away. He wanted to go straight in but anticipated turmoil on the other side of that front door. He blew into his palm to check that his breath didn't still reek of booze, then rang the bell. Within seconds, the old pine door with its blue-stained glassed window was flung open, and Chelsea was wrapped around him, sobbing.

'Dad, it was awful . . . right in the middle of the shop.'

'All right, baby girl. It's over now . . . it's over.' He led her inside, closing the door behind them.

'I can't believe the way it happened . . . and now we've lost the baby.'

'There are some things we have no control over, Chels. No matter how much we want something.'

'I know that, but poor Mum.'

'Look . . . where is she? Is Nan with her?'

'No, I think it was too much for Nan. But Mum's upstairs in her room. She told me to send you up.'

Johnny gave Chelsea the type of warm fatherly smile that he'd forgotten he was capable of, and handed her a clean tissue from a box on the sideboard, so she could wipe her eyes. 'Put the kettle on while I'm up there, yeah? Could murder a coffee.'

Chelsea nodded bravely as Johnny turned away and climbed the stairs. Laura's bedroom was at the far end of the landing. The door stood ajar, but he knocked on it anyway, very softly.

'Johnny, is that you?'

Her voice was soft, tender, a tone he hadn't heard from her in many years. When he went in, she was lying on the bed in a dressing gown, her pillow still damp with tears. Johnny knelt beside her and kissed her on the head. 'Baby, I'm so sorry.'

A fresh tear rolled down Laura's face. '*I'm* the one who's sorry, Johnny. I'm sorry about all of this.'

He stroked her hair. 'You've nothing to be sorry about.'

But Laura was shaking her head. 'I'm worried that, well . . .' She struggled just to get the words out. 'I'm worried that I only did it to get at you. Not for the baby's sake, just to cause problems for you.'

'I'm sure that wasn't it.' He stroked her hair again. 'Look . . . it took us all by surprise. It was a big shock. But . . . I don't know, maybe this wasn't meant to be for us?'

She pondered that, and he wondered if she was about to explode at him again.

'You're right, Johnny,' she finally said. 'It was for the best. Look at me, holed up at my mother's at my age, a teenage daughter to look after. And our situation—'

'I'll tell you who you are,' he said, still trying to soothe her, but also speaking the truth as he saw it. 'You're someone who's deserved better from life. You didn't deserve the way I treated you . . . we were a partnership, yet it was only ever *my* life that counted. I treated you like my PA, sometimes, not my wife, or my soul mate.'

She shook her head again. 'I'm to blame too. I knew who you were when we first met; I should never have tried to change you, but I should have drawn my red lines a bit stronger. You were a kid living out a fantasy and I . . . well, I should have lived my life for me, and not you.'

Pain shot across her face. She squinted, her mouth tightening.

'You OK?' he asked. 'Can I get you something?'

'No, I'm fine. Just help me up. I need to sit up properly.'

Johnny put one arm under Laura's waist as she hooked an elbow around his neck.

'One, two three,' he whispered, then lifted her up into a comfier position.

For half a moment, their faces were inches apart. They stared into each other's eyes and the years slipped away and they were companions and lovers again. He took her in an embrace and they stayed like that for a few minutes.

I will be a better friend to you and Chelsea. I promise.

This time, he meant it. The moment was broken by Chelsea, who'd been earwigging by the door, bursting in and throwing her arms around them both, all three holding each other tightly.

It was Johnny who pulled away first. 'Your mum needs to rest, Chelsea, so I'd better go.'

Laura looked at him and smiled. 'Whatever it is, get yourself sorted out first. You smell like a brewery.'

He nodded and hugged them both again. 'Look after your mum, Chelsea. I'll call you both later.'

'Is everything all right, Dad?' Chelsea asked, sensing his mood.

Not really.

'Everything's fine,' he assured her, wishing he felt re-assured himself. 'Everything's fine.'

28

LAST BAR BEFORE
THE CRESCENDO

Tuesday

Johnny could almost have rubbed his eyes in astonishment. For all the things that had happened over the last few days, finding that the Graceland moped was still parked up outside Polydex offices felt like a victory. He opened the hotbox, retrieved his helmet and pointed the bike towards Brick Lane.

At least he'd got the Major his bike back.

The damp autumn wind was gusting as he sped through the backstreets, and as he turned the bike into Brick Lane, he could already smell the tandoori ovens firing up, could scent that familiar concert of spices, the pungent curry cumin and turmeric, the mouth-watering odour of naan breads rising in bubbles.

It would have been wonderful if it had been that normal in reality. But of course, it wasn't.

Brick Lane was a quiet shadow of its usual self, as if someone had pulled out its plug and left it hanging, as if its heart had been disconnected. In the middle of it stood Graceland, the biggest restaurant on the street, the centre of the community. But even the giant Elvis mural had somehow lost its sparkle. As Johnny approached, he noticed that the road in front had been cleared of crime-scene tape, and that the police car that had been stationed there was absent. But now there was something he hadn't seen before. He pulled the bike up, stunned.

Someone had used red spray paint to leave a message on the black hoardings covering the window.

CLOCK'S TICKING

'Fuck,' he breathed.

'Johnny!' Mona called to him from the open front doorway.

He parked the bike in the stand outside the restaurant and pointed at the graffiti. 'What the hell's this?'

Are you kidding, mate? You know full well what this is.

'Happened sometime in the middle of the night,' she said, 'while you were . . . "out".'

He ignored that. 'What've the police said? In fact, where are they?'

'Still some at the back, but they've mostly finished. From lunchtime today, we can use the inside again.'

She led him indoors, back into that carnage of broken glass and splintered woodwork. A few members of staff were at work with dustpans and brushes, the small shafts of silver light poking through the boards on the windows lighting up the floating dust. The Major sat disconsolately in one of the booths, staring at nothing.

Mona went straight in for the kill. 'Had a nice night with Jackie, did you?'

Johnny was still feeling groggy but kept his voice low. 'What?'

'Jackie Phillips left a message for you at the restaurant. I know you've seen her.'

'And?'

'Oh, Johnny . . . while all this was happening too.' She sounded so disappointed in him.

'Mona—'

'Yes, I know. It's your life. And on this occasion, you're actually right.' She let that hang for a moment. 'You see, Johnny, I've been worried that whatever shit you've got into with that woman was the same shit that left Ravi dead. But it seems it wasn't.'

'Mona, listen—'

'Guess where I spent the evening?'

'You're gonna need to give me a clue.'

'Ben Randall's apartment.'

'Ben Randall?'

'Singer?' she said. 'TV actor? I was with him for a few hours.'

Johnny wondered why that name seemed more than a little familiar, then remembered Jackie's secret notebook. One name on her list had been struck through, with no cash payment. Ben Randall.

'You've probably heard that he was happily married to that soap queen who flitted off to California, soon be Hollywood's next big thing. Then it all fell apart.'

'Yeah, but . . . wasn't he just a drunk?'

'Will you listen to me. His marriage was going well. The

drinking was nothing they couldn't cope with. And then, out of the blue, he heard from an ex-girlfriend. Guess who?'

Johnny sighed. 'So, Randall ended up in bed with Jackie again, and that's what finished his marriage to Sasha? Why are you telling me this?'

'Jackie got him up to her house in Highgate because she said she was having problems with a stalker.'

A prickle flickered across Johnny's scalp.

'Seems that a video had been shot from somewhere high up in Jackie's bedroom, which had caught the whole thing.' Mona said. 'Apparently, she was completely open about the fact that she'd been left high and dry by all the men in her life and was now pig-sick of it. Johnny . . . she was doing the rounds of all her ex-fellas, getting what she felt she was entitled to, by blackmail if necessary. Randall told me that she wanted regular cash payments – significant chunks, by the way – in return for which the video of them shagging would never reach his wife.'

'Yeah?' he whispered.

'Randall said he wasn't doing it. Came clean to his wife himself. She threw him out and they split up, but at least he wasn't out of pocket. Turns out he couldn't handle it, and his career's now on its arse. But he won a moral victory, I guess. Listen . . . Johnny?'

Johnny decided to let Mona believe that he knew nothing about all this, that it was her discovery alone. Like Laura, Mona had Jackie's card marked already.

'Go on.'

'This is what Jackie does, Johnny. She's not twenty-seven anymore but those Botox injections don't come cheap, nor that designer wardrobe, and the tabloids aren't interested in her now. That's the *real* Jackie Phillips that you've hooked up with.'

Mona had no idea what it was to be famous from the inside; sure, she'd seen a lot of stars fall, but was the Jerry Fox business really any different to what Jackie was doing? Maybe they were more alike than even Laura had thought.

He thought about Graham Dwell too, and what he'd said. *You've got to fix stuff yourself . . .*

'Look Mona, well done for rumbling her, and I appreciate you looking out for me, I really do, but none of this has anything to do with Ravi, does it?'

Her body sagged and she shook her head as she sat down alongside her uncle. 'Maybe not, and it doesn't get us any closer to why someone would have wanted to do this to us.' She looked at Johnny pointedly. 'Why?'

What a tangled web.

'Hey, Major,' Johnny said.

The old guy nodded, attempting a smile. He looked haggard, his sparse white curls all over the place. 'Hello, Johnny . . . They say Ravi's body will be returned to us soon. Then, we can . . .' he swallowed hard, 'make plans.'

Mona clasped one of his hands and held it tightly.

'I'm sorry, Johnny,' she said, though whatever she was about to tell him, she didn't sound particularly sorry. 'But you're going to need to find somewhere else to live. Uncle Rishi's selling up.'

'No!' Johnny blurted, genuinely shocked. 'I mean . . . no, don't sell. Rishi, this is Graceland, this is *you*. You've made the place your own . . . the people want you here, you can't go.'

The Major smiled sadly.

'The insurance will just about cover the damages,' Mona explained. 'But there won't be much left for anything else. Plus, look at the state of the place. Uncle Rishi can't be doing with all this at his time of life.'

'On top of that, it's obvious that someone wants me out,' the Major added despondently. 'I don't know why. But, that message at the front . . . the clock's ticking. They've even put a time limit on it. Whoever those guys were who attacked you two the other night, they clearly don't want me here, either.'

'And Uncle Rishi doesn't need that worry,' Mona said, staring at Johnny hard. 'Not at his age.'

'I'm so sorry, Johnny,' the Major said. 'I gave you a home and now I have to take it back. I'm going back to India.' His eyes were red, and they welled up with tears again.

'Come on . . .' Johnny said. 'Look, there has to be a way. *This* is your home, Brick Lane.'

Mona spoke softly but surely. 'We've been over it twenty times. He's made his mind up.'

'It doesn't mean anything without Ravi,' the Major said.

Johnny ran his fingers through his hair. He wanted to grab it, yank it out. 'There's only one person who's responsible for all this, and one person who can fix it.'

The Major, lost in his own thoughts, didn't react, but Mona's gaze seemed to penetrate to the back of Johnny's skull.

The Major took him in a fatherly embrace. 'We need to sort out the details for Ravi's funeral, when they release him to us. In the meantime, you're welcome to stay here as long as you want. Thank you for everything you've done.'

'Yeah, thanks, Johnny,' Mona said, her face like a stone.

When Johnny got upstairs, he closed the bedroom door before lurching across the room and snatching the bottle of Jack still lying next to the bed.

He had already drained it dry.

He paced the room, his guilt-ridden anxiety slowly building into a stomach-churning crescendo. Stumbling into the bathroom, he threw up the whole of the previous night's takeaway into the toilet, before staggering backwards, still retching and sweating like a pig. He grabbed a towel to wipe his mouth, but before he knew it, was screaming at the top of his lungs into it, only the wadded dirty cloth deadening the guttural cry.

Back in the bedroom, he slumped again on to the bed, checked the JD bottle one last time, just to ensure there wasn't a speck of amber liquid that he'd missed, then stuck his hand into the dark copper bowl on the bedside table, dug through the pile of past-its-sell-by potpourri, and pulled out a keyring. A couple of keys were still attached, alongside a small silver guitar with Johnny's signature down the middle, and a white electronic fob.

He squeezed them in his clenched fist, before lying back, his head on the pillow. Then he took up his phone and placed a call. It seemed like an age before someone picked up at the other end.

'Yeah?' The voice was vaguely recognisable.

'It's Klein,' Johnny said.

The voice chuckled. 'You didn't forget about us after all.'

'Tell your boss I want a meet. I've got what he wants.'

'He'll be pleased.'

'But I'm only handing it to *him*. No one else.'

'That right?'

'Yeah, that's right. This thing's caused a lot of shit. I'm not wasting time with ape men. I want to *know* it's over.'

'Where and when?' the voice asked.

'Tonight . . .' Johnny stared at the keys. 'My place up in Mill Hill. Number 271. You can't miss it. Big white house behind the electric gates. I'll be there at nine.'

The call was cut at the other end.

Johnny lay stiff and cold.

One way or the other, this was it.

29

MILL HILL

Tuesday

Mona I'm sorry. The last thing I wanted was to bring heartbreak to you and your uncle. You've been kinder to me in a short time than I've ever been to anyone else in my whole life. I'm going to be a better friend to you, so, I'm sorting this thing out tonight. By tomorrow morning this problem won't be yours anymore. I promise.

BTW, I'm just borrowing the bike one more time. JK.

Johnny sent the texts, then rode on along Archway Road. Half an hour later, he was at Mill Hill.

The big house that had once been home shone under the glare of the garden spotlights. It was even more ostentatious than Johnny remembered, with its tall chimneys, its antique stone statues along the gravel drive, and the front door made out of the finest mahogany, the brass knocker fashioned into a thunderbolt.

How was this my house? Who the fuck did I think I was?

Overhead, only a sliver of moon remained in the sky, the type that some showgirl in a glittery basque and fishnet tights would ride downward onto the stage.

Johnny had the irresistible feeling that he was home, though his head told him otherwise. He didn't need to imagine the familiar warmth of his La-Z-Boy control chair, or the way its soft leather had moulded to his butt. He could feel it. But it wasn't his anymore, and never would be again.

He hit the fob. With a groaning of cogs, the electronic gates swung inwards. Johnny steered his bike through onto the drive, hiding it behind a hydrangea bush. He checked his phone again. It was bang on 8.30 p.m. Heart thudding, he set off up to the house.

When he put his key into the door and pushed it ajar, he was again struck by the aura of home.

It was the smell of everything he valued. Birthdays, Christmases, family life, though he never appreciated it properly until it was gone. Now it was as though someone had gone through his personal photo stream and given it back to him with only the good memories left and all the bad stuff taken out.

The repeating bleep of the alarm pierced his ears. He moved to the wall-mounted keypad, and hit the buttons.

1 – 2 – 0 – 8 . . . But the alarm kept bleeping.

Bollocks! You can't have changed the number yet! He tried again, with the same outcome. 'Shit!'

If the alarm kicked in here, the cops would be all over the shop. The repeated blurt of sound now switched to a higher pitch, and ran faster.

'Bollocks, bollocks . . . it was Chelsea's birthday, come on! 1208!'

The fuck it was, bozo! We thought she was coming on the twelfth, but it was the thirteenth. She came late, a few minutes after midnight . . .

He bashed the new number in: 1-3-0-8.

The alarm instantly fell silent.

Shaking with relief, Johnny fumbled for a light switch, then glanced along the hall. It was exactly as he'd left it, only the remnants of the glass artwork had been swept up. He walked into the living room; the old pizza boxes had been thrown away, and the giant television and speaker stacks remained in place, his La-Z-Boy control centre still in situ. He couldn't resist sitting down, taking his old command seat again.

He checked the time: 8.45 p.m.

He took the remote and pointed it at the TV. The giant screen flashed to life, the picture split into several sections, each one the viewpoint of a different CCTV camera located somewhere around the premises, one trained on the front gate, which still stood open.

Johnny checked the time again. Bang on nine.

With a sinister punctuality, a large black Mercedes E-Class pulled up at the front, then cruised through onto the drive.

Johnny had known this moment was coming from the instant that bastard Ray Caldwell developed those pictures and toppled the whole stack of cards.

His mind filled with the events of the last few days: from closing the door to this place, leaving everything behind, to the fateful job Don and Pete had given him, to the drugs den, the peeping Tom at Jackie's house, and then the death of Ravi and the violent destruction of Graceland.

All that chaos, and for what?

So many times now, Johnny had asked himself how his life had come to this: washed up, fucked up and deep in a pile of shit.

Graham's voice rang in his cranium. *Still all about you, Johnny?*

He watched as Karl Jones, now wearing a heavy overcoat, climbed from the Merc's back seat. The Taylor brothers, still in their customary dark clothing and black leather, emerged from the car and they walked with Jones towards the entrance to the house.

Johnny stood up, moved to the intercom panel as they approached and hit a button. With any luck, they'd now be so focused on the house that they wouldn't notice the electronic gate at the foot of the drive swinging silently closed.

'Klein!' Jones called from the hallway.

Johnny went to the living room doorway.

They turned as one when they sensed his presence.

'So . . . this is the rock-star lifestyle, is it?' Jones looked round. 'This is the golden cage? Is it true you've got an indoor swimming pool here? A thirty-footer?'

'Back of the house,' Johnny said.

Jones gazed past him. 'And what's that?' He pushed through into the living room, the brothers following. 'A telly or your own private cinema?'

346

Johnny followed them. 'Karl . . . I've got the stuff you want. The negs, the roll of film, everything. But before I hand it over, I need your word that this is done and dusted.'

Jones's eyes roved over the huge, compartmentalised TV screen. He shook his head. 'Real lap of luxury stuff, this, isn't it?'

'Karl . . . promise me that Laura and Chelsea will never hear from you, and that you'll leave Graceland alone.'

'I'm not one for promises, Johnny-boy, we're not fucking kids, are we?' Jones said. 'Boys.' In perfect unison, the Taylor brothers produced baseball bats from under their leather coats. Jones turned to Johnny. 'Why don't you sit down and watch the show?'

Johnny sat back in his seat as the two hoodlums left the room, then switched his attention to the TV screen, where Flat-top headed into the kitchen, his brother bombing up the stairs two at a time.

'Happy watching, Johnny-boy!'

Jones's voice was a whipcrack. The big squarish handgun he'd just pulled from his suit glinted. His mouth crooked into a nasty half-smile.

Back on the screen, the Taylors commenced swinging their bats in every direction, Flat-top hammering the kitchen worktops, his brother working the master bedroom, bombarding its beautiful mirrored furniture, its side tables, cabinets and lamps.

'I thought we had a deal,' Johnny said, as fear gripped his stomach.

'Nah.' Jones smiled. 'The agreement was you give me what I want. Nothing else. You see the real problem here, Johnny, is the grief you caused me. If you'd just handed the stuff over after that first phone call, none of this would've been necessary.'

Already, there was nothing left of the kitchen. The bedroom was a smoking wreck. The two brothers now moved into the bathrooms, one upstairs, one down.

'You've made your fucking point,' Johnny's voice was a strangled whisper.

'You haven't even given me the stuff yet.'

Johnny shoved his hand into his pocket, pulling out a wad of negatives and film. 'There, it's yours, for fuck's sake!'

'You see?' Jones slotted his pistol back into his armpit holster. 'Piece of piss, wasn't it?' He leafed through the various items. 'Why didn't you do this at the start, instead of trying to play Billy Big Bollocks? To show my gratitude, I'm going to speed things along.'

He walked to the two stacks of speakers, inserted himself behind, and pushed both of them over. The leads in the back flapped around like electric eels but stayed connected as the Marshalls crashed to the floor, more dust and splinters flying.

Johnny recoiled as the video machine switched itself on. The CCTV feeds vanished, and a 1988 version of Johnny Klein came onscreen, singing that year's Christmas No. 1, fake snow swirling in the *Top of the Pops* studio.

'Look at that fucking barnet!' Jones laughed, before pulling his pistol again, taking two-handed aim at the screen and firing, the device dying as a trio of massive holes was blasted through it. Delighted, he pivoted, shooting at other fixtures in the room, including the intercom panel, which popped in a shower of sparks, and the webcam on the ceiling.

'I doubt you'll be taking your security footage to the cops anytime soon.'

'Yeah, but it's not mine, is it?'

The gangster threw him a hooded glance. 'What?'

'I don't *own* this place anymore. Didn't you realise that? None of this stuff belongs to me. Why do you think I'm living over a fucking restaurant?'

Jones's smirk stiffened. 'That pretty little Indian bird? You're not shagging her?'

'She's just a mate. My landlady.'

The gangster's cheek twitched. He bared his teeth. 'You . . . you fucking twat. You brought us here deliberately.'

Jones scanned the upper reaches of the room. The red eye of a camera lens occupied a high corner. He hurried to the door and saw the same in the hall.

'Where do these security feeds upload to?'

'No idea. The local nick?'

'*Boys!*' Jones roared. 'Get down here!'

Heavy footfalls descended the staircase.

'We're getting out,' he snarled, when they came in. He pointed at Johnny. 'Bring him.'

Johnny tried to resist, but Biker hooked the shoulder of his jacket and hustled him out into the hall and through the front door.

'Don't make this harder than it needs to be, Johnny,' Jones said. 'Or what we did to this house—'

'Fucking gate's closed,' Flat-top interrupted.

They stopped and stared. The heavy wrought-iron gates were closed, Jones's Merc trapped on the inside.

'Where's the control?' Jones looked at Johnny.

'In smithereens – you shot it,' Johnny said.

The gangster clenched his teeth. 'Back inside.' They retreated indoors, closing the front door. 'There must be some other way out?'

'Tradesmen's entrance at the back,' Johnny said. 'Through the pool area.'

As they blundered back through the empty house and banged through a pair of glass doors, the pile carpet turned into marble tiles. Ahead, the swimming pool lay like a sheet of smooth blue glass. Low-key lights glimmered underneath.

'We'll get that footage, don't worry,' Jones said. 'I've told you, I know people everywhere.'

Johnny said nothing as he was bundled past the deep end.

Then suddenly he pitched his whole body sideways, wedging his right shoulder under his burly captor's armpit, ensuring the pair of them went over the edge together.

His pony-tailed captor's arms windmilled and he screeched like a child as he crashed through the surface. Johnny went too, plunging deeper, but he was a good swimmer, and he quickly swerved away from his struggling captor, before circling back and levering himself upright on Biker's shoulders, forcing him under.

At the side of the pool, Flat-top shouted and stumbled, barging into Jones, sending him tottering as he tried to draw his shooter. Johnny surfaced just as Jones fell shouting onto the poolside, his weapon skittering away. As Flat-top scissor-jumped into the water, Johnny thrashed towards the ladder on the other side.

'Klein!' he heard Jones scream as he hauled himself out. '*Klein!*'

He glanced back across the pool to where Jones had retrieved his weapon and now pointed it. Johnny looked straight down its barrel as Jones squeezed the trigger.

Then the lights went and they were suddenly plunged into darkness.

Thank you, God.

'What the fuck?' Jones hissed.

Johnny dropped to a crouch, unsure what was happening but grateful for the reprieve. The pool lights had gone out too, but when he glanced at the skylights overhead, there was a faint glow from the nearby streetlamps. Not a street power cut then, just the house. But that glow meant Jones would spot him in seconds.

Johnny spun around and moved quickly through the open doorway behind him, where he halted. Commotion still reigned in the pool area, though it sounded as though Flat-top was dragging his brother up onto the side.

'Fucking ponce . . .' he burbled. 'Fucking kill him . . .'

Johnny ran on into the gym. The tiles gave way to polished wood, so his wet cowboy boots clomped. He flopped onto his buttocks, yanking the boots off, crawling on hands and knees. When he came to a row of hanging ropes, he squatted, holding his breath.

Biker's hulking form was vaguely visible, his rubber motorbike boots squeaking on the woodwork. Johnny screwed his eyes shut and groped for anything he could find in the blackness, his fingers closing on the bar of a dumbbell. It wasn't a huge one, a twenty-pounder, but it would do.

'I know you're in here, ponce.'

Jones could only be a couple of feet away.

Johnny swung the dumbbell up and down, striking a massive blow on Biker's left foot, the bones and meat audibly crunching. He gave a prolonged, agonised howl as he staggered away, toppling and falling.

Fresh adrenaline pumping, Johnny jumped up and legged it for the blot of darkness where the fire exit waited. He crashed into the door, depressed the bar and it opened. Hurrying through to the garage door, he saw that one of the corridor windows was open. He felt around its trim. It had been forced. He pressed on, working his way to the right-hand wall, where the property's main fuse box was located. When he got there, he saw that its front had been opened and that every breaker in the house had been thrown.

Someone had turned the power off.

Karl Jones was getting out. He had what he'd come for and Johnny Klein would get what was coming to him, one way or another.

As he and Flat-top blundered back through the darkened mansion, he patted the breast pocket inside his cashmere coat, just to ensure that the films and negatives were all still there.

They entered the hall; his sidekick hung back. 'Dunno where my brother is,' he muttered.

'He can look after himself,' Jones said. The front door swam into view. 'If this power's off, that means the gates are out.'

But no sooner had they descended the front steps to the drive, at the bottom end of which the electric gates had indeed opened, than they saw a different vehicle parked across the opening. Jones's eyes narrowed at the sight of the Graceland logo on its flank.

Neither noticed the slight figure come up behind them and swing the Victorian pine kitchen stool. It struck Jones's cranium with a clatter, dropping him to his knees.

'That's for killing my friend, you bastard!' Mona spat. 'And for ruining my uncle's business.'

Flat-top roared as he swung his bat. Mona ducked out of his way. He swung it again, and again. She kept retreating. Then she tripped, landing on her backside.

'Bitch!' The other Taylor brother towered over her, only to have the bat yanked out of his grasp from behind. He spun furiously.

Johnny had never been so up for a fight in his life than the moment he saw Mona go down.

He tried to kick Flat-top in the gonads but missed, and a hard right hand caught the side of his face. He tottered. Another stinging blow followed, and another.

'Johnny!' Mona screamed, trying to get up.

Johnny flailed with the bat. More impacts landed on him, but he managed to get in a few shots which counted.

Jones had wobbled to his feet, bulky and stumbling, levelling the firearm into the darkness, pumping the trigger. Once, twice, thrice, three blinding flashes.

Startled, Flat-top looked round, letting go of Johnny as he swayed towards the prone shape of his brother.

'No!' Flat-top fell to his knees besides the fallen shape. His voice fractured, became shrill. '*NO!*'

Jones lurched sideways, grabbing Mona by one arm and ramming the hot muzzle of his Glock 17 into her neck. 'Me and you are leaving, now.'

Rigid, Mona let him steer her to the door and out onto the drive. But now it wasn't just the Graceland delivery van blocking the bottom of the drive but three police cars, and a row of coppers aiming their guns at Jones.

Jones's mouth dropped open, especially when ten bright cherry-red dots alighted on his chest.

'*Drop the firearm,*' came a curt female voice amplified through a loudhailer. It took him a moment to recognise Detective Sergeant Lorna Thomas. '*Karl Jones . . . you are under arrest!*'

There was a moment of silence and then a cry stabbed the air. The last thing Johnny saw was Flat-top lifting an antique Chinese vase, which had somehow survived the destruction, and hurling it towards his head. It twisted and turned as it came. Johnny recognised its intricate drawings, the cracked porcelain glaze, the beautiful Chinese girl in her gold and scarlet robe, the dragon with its green and yellow scales, its mouth widening as it came closer, its bottom jaw dislocating, the maw stretching open, swallowing Johnny's head.

Helpless, he sank into a vortex, into a spinning black hole, which pulled him steadily down, a thick, acrid stench overwhelming his sense of smell, further and further down.

Until a warm white light enveloped him.

Johnny was back in his dressing room, staring into the mirror. The face looking back wasn't old or tired or world-weary. This face was in its prime, twenty-five years old, perfect skin, bright eyes. He smiled to himself, bowled over at how good he looked.

'Five minutes Mr Klein,' someone said outside.

Johnny walked to his gold-top Gibson, threw it over his shoulder, plugged it into a small Marshall practice amp, checked its tuning. Several power chords later, he went out. One step at a time, down the white passageway. Halfway along, Russell leaned against the wall.

'Mate!' Johnny threw his arms around him.

His best mate looked amazing: smiling, happy, perfect.

'What gig is this?' Johnny asked.

'Don't worry, JK, just follow me.'

Guitars swung low, they strutted onstage side by side. Thousands of voices commenced screaming. Johnny approached the mic. Everyone was there: Mike on drums, Tim on bass, Lee on keyboards, and Russell back on rhythm. But as they hit the first chord, he felt a surge of panic. He couldn't remember the words.

Russell leaned to his ear. 'Johnny, man, don't worry. We've got a special guest.'

And out from the wings, emerging through a translucent cloud of dry ice, rhinestones sparkling, silver-tipped cowboy boots rattling, Ravi Sharma took centre-stage.

With a wink in Johnny's direction, he started to sing, but now with a voice like an angel, every note, every vibrato, every warble pure Presley. It was mesmerising. The band didn't even need to play, it was just him, singing like a rock god. As he reached his crescendo, his voice became all-consuming. But now Johnny could smell that burning acrid stench again.

He could taste something horrible too. It was tangy, coppery? Blood maybe?

He cried out.

Somewhere above Elvis's divine vocal, he heard three deafening cracks.

It was no bass drum, that was for sure . . .

30

ELVIS HAS LEFT THE BUILDING

Silence had descended over Brick Lane on the morning of Ravi's funeral.

One of London's liveliest cultural melting pots, a part of town usually buzzing, had come to a solemn standstill. You could even hear the breathing of the hundreds of people lining the roadside, even though almost everyone in the neighbourhood was present, staff from every restaurant, the flower sellers from Columbia Road, the road sweepers and of course masses of regulars, Graceland's faithful customers whom Ravi had so often serenaded over their masala and raita.

Even some of the new trendy businesses that seemed to be taking over the entire East End were closed out of respect for a man whom everyone had loved, one of the district's many characters, as famous locally as the pearly king and queen who'd be wheeled out for a photo op at the drop of a pearly hat, or the bowler-hatted old fella in his nineties who'd cooked his chestnuts on the corner forever, the one everyone called Charlie even though that wasn't his name.

The mere sight of Ravi strutting along the street in his Elvis regalia, the silver toe taps on his white cowboy boots rattling with each step, had attracted shouts and greetings and high-fives every few yards, the guy often throwing in a moonwalk or a Presley karate move in gratitude. It was true that he'd secretly wanted a bigger stage than Brick Lane, but all the time he'd been here he was like a kid in his own private sweet shop. His love for life was infectious, he was the cheeriest of men, a guy whose smile brightened everyone's day.

Little wonder they all stood humbled and tight-lipped that cold but clear November morning. The day had started out misty, but much of that was now clearing, a shade of pink colouring the clouds as they drifted over the Shard. The mood was changing too, hints of subdued chatter signalling an air of growing expectation. And then, almost as one, in a single choreographed move, everyone's head turned – it was like a huge Mexican wave running right to left along the street – to see what was coming around the distant corner.

A lone moped rider rode slowly into view, dressed in the full 1973 *Aloha from Hawaii* American Eagle jumpsuit, white cowboy boots, black wig and gold-rimmed sunglasses. He rode alone, proceeding in cool and stately fashion down the centre of the street. Almost immediately, a giant white hearse appeared behind him. It was crammed with multi-coloured garlands, Ravi's open-top casket lying among them behind its huge glass windows, the words *More Than I Can Say* spelled out in white carnations, a Leo Sayer song title the Major would always use to tell Elvis how much he loved him.

Slowly and softly at first, they started clapping, worrying that maybe it was disrespectful, but very quickly it rose to a crescendo of applause, though not loud enough to drown out the hum of low-key engines as an entire flock of delivery bikes cruised into view and started honking their horns and flashing their lights. The bikes were decorated with garlands, dozens and dozens of them, each one representing a different establishment on Brick Lane. Briefly, it was a scene of chaos, and what had started out as the sombre commemoration of a fine man on a cold autumn morning now warmed the cockles of everyone's heart. But it wasn't over yet.

A flatbed truck outfitted in new, brightly coloured paint-work, rounded the bend, and at least thirty Elvises, all in the familiar white jumpsuits, wigs and glasses, rode in the back of it. Right in their midst, adorned in Ravi's gold lamé Elvis suit, gold shirt and black bootlace tie, stood Johnny Klein. As the hearse and delivery bikes came to a stop outside Graceland, the truck rolled into position behind them and Johnny turned to his cohort of Elvis impersonators and clicked his fingers in a slow count to four. In perfect harmony, in perfect key, in perfect tempo, thirty acapella voices rose on the air, Johnny's among them, delivering a clear and beautiful version of Elvis's 'Peace in the Valley'.

This was the cue for Mona and the Major to emerge from Graceland's newly restored front door. Three weeks had passed since the attack on the restaurant, and the insurance money hadn't come through yet, but lots of groups, including other local businesses, had chipped in, creating a healthy 'friend in need fund', and though the restaurant wasn't open for business yet, the front had been fully repaired, with new windows and signage, and a new exquisitely carved entrance door, while the interior had been cleared of wreckage and graffiti.

Mona stood with her arm around her uncle's shoulders. A tear ran down her cheek, but she broke into a grateful smile when she caught Johnny's eye.

When the song ended, Johnny climbed down from the back of the truck and joined the pallbearers, the eight men then proceeding into the restaurant with Ravi's casket on their shoulders.

Johnny hadn't been sure how he'd be received. Rumours had abounded locally about his involvement, and the cuts and bruises on his face attested to the grand finale at Mill Hill. But the weight of Ravi's coffin on his shoulders only added to Johnny's sense of culpability.

'The only person really at fault when someone gets unlawfully killed, Mr Klein, is the person who did the killing,' Detective Sergeant Thomas had said, after she'd finished questioning him. 'In my job, I meet people all the time who feel guilty about things they shouldn't. I'm not saying you didn't make mistakes here, but you're no murderer . . . so don't beat yourself up about that.'

Johnny now found himself unsteady on his feet, the multiple faces around him moving in and out of focus as his vision glazed with tears.

'Easy, Johnny,' came Graham Dwell's reassuring voice from behind, a gentle hand on his shoulder. 'One step at a time.'

Johnny nodded and fell into step with the other bearers as they entered the restaurant.

And took Elvis Mistry home.

*

Considering that Graceland hadn't yet had its full refurb, and food service had yet to resume, its interior looked close to magnificent. All the tables were dressed with flowers. Flower garlands crisscrossed the ceiling, and there on stage, right in the middle, stood a four-by-four-foot picture of Elvis Mistry in full flow.

Ravi's casket was placed carefully onto its trestles close to the front of the stage, directly below his portrait, so people could file past and pay their last respects. The Major slotted a demo tape into the machine, the same one he'd hoped Johnny would work miracles with, and pressed 'play'. It was that familiar tuneless dirge; nothing had changed, but today that didn't matter, and Johnny would have given anything to hear Ravi sing one more time.

The atmosphere was more composed inside. Friends and family chatted amongst themselves, sharing stories as they queued to pay their respects.

Johnny stood back, watching quietly. It was the first time he'd been close to the little singer since he'd passed. The morticians had done a good job. He looked radiant in his Elvis outfit and showed no trace of the beating that had claimed his life. He could have been asleep.

'Thanks for what you did out there,' Mona said quietly, having come up without Johnny noticing.

He shrugged. 'I'm just glad it went down OK.'

'It went down perfectly.'

'Course, that's only the start of it. You going to be all right for the rest of today?'

He nodded. 'I owe it to Ravi. I should have done more while he was alive.'

'Well . . . we all thought he'd have a lot more time.' She smiled. 'That reminds me. I had a message from DS Thomas.'

Johnny stiffened. 'Yeah?'

'There are no further actions for either of us, we're in the clear.'

He sagged with relief. 'Thank God.'

Perhaps inevitably, complications had followed the police investigation at Mill Hill. Both Karl Jones and Taylor had now been remanded in custody charged with sundry serious offences, from murder to grievous bodily harm, and according to DS Thomas, 'Flat-top' Taylor was 'singing like the proverbial canary' after being immobilised by three shots from armed officers at the Mill Hill house.

'I still don't know how you knew I'd gone up to the house,' Johnny said.

'I told you,' Mona replied quietly. 'I realised from that text you sent that you were going to do something drastic. When I went up to your room to stop you, you'd already gone, but I could see you'd taken the keys from the bowl as all the potpourri was everywhere. It only occurred to me when I was halfway over there to leave a message for DS Thomas and tell her what I thought was going on. I still think we were lucky that, when she got there, she had all her mates with her. 'I had no clue you were going to try and take those guys out,' she added.

'Strictly speaking, I wasn't. I kind of made it up as I went along.'

'I'm just glad it wasn't you who did the shooting.'

'Me too,' he agreed. 'Thomas wouldn't have been able to lose *that* in the paperwork.'

'What's going to happen to Karl Jones now?'

'He's going to find it hard to wriggle out of this one,' Johnny said with more confidence than he felt.

'Listen, I'm going to circulate a bit,' she said. 'There are a few people here I need to speak to.'

He nodded, assuring her again that he'd be OK. However, as Mona moved away, he was feeling like a spare part among Ravi's mourners. But he didn't have to wait long before there was a tap on his shoulder. He turned and found that Graham had come quietly into the room behind him and stood there now, though first having dispensed with his black shirt and clerical collar, and replaced it with a Zeppelin T-shirt and a tasselled leather biker jacket. 'We're all set up,' he said.

Johnny expelled a long breath and turned back to the room. Mona caught his look of concern and came over. 'I'm just thinking,' he said, 'shouldn't I attend the cremation ceremony too?'

She shook her head. 'That's just for close family, Johnny.'

'Some of the staff are going.'

'Johnny, you've got a different responsibility this afternoon. The Major thought it was the best idea he'd ever heard. So, get to it, yeah?'

'All set?' Graham asked.

Johnny nodded and followed him up the stairs, entering his flat, which had now become an impromptu dressing room. 'Ravi would have loved this,' he said.

Lee Giles and Tim Carson simply smiled. Mat Cookson, who'd replaced Russell, gave him the high five. Johnny stripped off his Elvis costume, replacing it with clean casuals – skinny jeans over his cowboy boots and a baggy black velvet shirt, nothing too flashy or glitzy today, then went out onto the landing and followed the rest of the band up the final flight of narrow back stairs, through the metal door that was normally kept chained shut, and onto Graceland's roof, where Lionel, Ray and Alex, the handful of former road-crew they'd been able to round up, were finishing off the sound checks.

The Major hadn't known whether he could face the task of rebuilding everything he'd lost, particularly after Ravi's death. So with a little help from Graham – who was an expert, it seemed, at gentle persuasion – Johnny had gathered the guys together for one last gig. Only Mike Penfold had been unavailable; he was currently Stateside, once again in rehab, but seeing as Graham had played drums too back in the day, he was happy to step in.

Thankfully, the weather had held . . . something of a miracle for November, the sky staying clear and blue, the sun a cold jewel soon low in the western sky. The rooftop itself buzzed with energy. There were Marshall stacks set up everywhere, amid a whole range of lighting, guitars and microphones on stands and a huge drumkit, all the instruments set along the roof's parapet in a horizontal line so that the crowd already ramming the street below would get the best view possible. As final checks were made, the guys hung back, not wishing to cause a distraction while Ravi's cortège, now accompanied only by his closest loved ones, proceeded away along the street. An aisle had been cleared using sawhorses and tape and the crowd remained impeccably silent as the sombre vehicles passed them by.

Johnny turned to the others. Cool, confident smiles greeted his own. Smiles that he'd seen so many times before. Smiles that said: 'Here we go . . . let's get it on.'

He held his breath, steadying his racing heart. It felt just like yesterday; once again, they were reliving those last treasured moments of sanity behind the curtain, before the screaming and pandemonium took over.

Johnny glanced back to the end of the street as Ravi's hearse, still moving in slow, stately fashion, turned out of sight. Hearing the rising hubbub below, he glanced again at the others. Unspoken signals passed between them, and as one, they advanced to the parapet.

Roars of delight rose upward, echoing in the tall, narrow street.

Johnny was briefly stumped by the thousands of expectant faces and by the rousing chorus of chants: 'Joh-nee, Johnee, Joh-nee!'

For once, he didn't care who they were shouting for. Today wasn't about him or the band.

He raised his hands and the crowd fell quiet again.

He moved closer to the mic, and it started to gently feedback, a sweet, high-pitched sound that faded out as quickly as it had faded in.

'This place means so much to me . . . Graceland. It's not only the best restaurant in London, it's also owned by some of the kindest people you could ever meet, a community of the best people that I never even knew existed.'

The crowd cheered again. Suddenly, he was aware of the news choppers passing by overhead, of the camera drones, of the movie cameras on the opposite roofs, and less obtrusively, on this one too.

But that was all good if it meant more publicity for the Major and his business.

'And Graceland will be back,' he shouted.

More cheers. Wild and delirious this time.

Half of those people down there wouldn't even know what Graceland was, or why the gig was being held here, but they would by the time today was over.

'But listen, folks . . . I'm not going to talk much more. Ravi wasn't a great one for chit-chat either. He believed in letting the music do the talking. I'm going to say goodbye, Elvis, in the only way I know how.'

Johnny stepped back and slung his guitar over his shoulder as Graham tapped out a four count on his sticks and the opening chords to 'Jailhouse Rock' began to vibrate every last brick down the lane.

EPILOGUE

Johnny found himself on Cheyne Walk again. This time he was buzzed quietly through the gates, and was now being ushered in to see Pete by Don Slater.

The last time he was here, he'd come as a beggar, someone who could be pushed around, because he had no choice, and no pride. Things weren't that way now. Johnny was still in no position to hard-bargain with anyone, but this time he was more sure of his ground.

Slater pointed him along the marbled corridor. 'Pete's in the piano room. You'd better go through.'

Pete, looking absurd in a blue velvet dressing gown and slippers, didn't bother standing up when Johnny went into the room. He barely looked up.

'So, you're back at last?' he said.

Johnny could sense Pete's displeasure already. Even though he had just arrived, it was like he was the last person left at a party and the host wanted him to leave.

'You know he ran that story yesterday?' Pete said in a waspish tone.

Johnny stood sheepishly. 'Jerry Fox?'

'Yeah. Just in time to coincide with the release?'

'Well, that was his plan all along, wasn't it?'

'Yeah, it was,' Pete snapped, glaring at him.

Johnny didn't say what he was thinking, which was that Pete's big secret – namely that his ex-wife of several years ago had gone on record about his umpteen affairs during their marriage and regular drinking binges that wrecked their home – wasn't perhaps the news splash Jerry Fox and Ray Caldwell had expected it to be. He'd certainly heard worse.

'Pete . . .' Johnny struggled to speak over his sense of disbelief. 'You don't understand the shit I've been through, all because I tried to stop that story coming out.'

Pete got up and walked to the door. 'What about the unbelievable shit I'm now going through because you didn't do your job properly?'

'How's the record doing, anyway?' Johnny asked.

Pete left the room, but as he went, shouted back over his shoulder, 'Selling fucking bucket loads.'

'Well, it would be, wouldn't it?' Johnny replied, half to himself. 'The shit may be unbelievable, but it still doesn't stick to people like you.'

Don, who'd just come in, chuckled.

Johnny turned to face him. 'I went out on a limb to get that evidence. I nearly died in the process, and a couple of people actually *did* die.'

'Aye, so you said.' Don seemed less bothered than Pete.

'That story has helped sales, I don't see what the fuss is about.'

Don shrugged. 'It's his ego. He hasn't had it put in its place, like you have. I'll be honest, I never thought the Jerry Fox story was such a big deal. It was easy to put a counter-press release out with Pete saying how he hated the person he'd once been and all that. How he's a changed man these days, stone-cold sober and the like. Besides, you know what they say, Johnny . . . any publicity's good fucking publicity, yeah?'

'Wait a min . . .' Johnny stiffened. 'You saying you weren't that bothered about getting the story stopped?'

'Not really. But Pete wanted me to make it go away, and that's what he pays me for.'

'I don't fucking believe this. All that shit because—'

'Wait up, Johnny-boy. I didn't know the underworld was going to get involved. You can't hang *that* on me.'

'But what did you send me out there for? Just to keep Pete happy? About time he fucking grew up, isn't it?'

Slater shook his head. 'Better be careful there, big man. He's still your mate. I know he doesn't act like it, but he is. It was Pete who wanted to throw something your way, not me. No offence, but you're a fucking washed-up pop star, Johnny, not James Bond.'

'So was the promise to help me get back into the music game also a load of bollocks?'

Slater mused. 'No . . . I hear that Brick Lane gig was something special.'

'We were a bit rusty.'

'Not what I heard. It's all over the TV.' Slater crossed the room to a side table.

'It was a one-off,' Johnny replied. 'The others have got different lives now.'

'Well, we don't want you to leave completely empty-handed, do we?' Slater took something off the table. It was a small box engraved with an ivory pattern. Johnny watched him. He wasn't going to get the cash, because he hadn't earned it, even though he'd put everything on the line. But right now, any kind of payment would be good.

'I can't take a cheque, Don,' he said. 'I'm . . .' He still hadn't got used to the word.

'Bankrupt?' Slater said, showing no such qualms.

'Yeah.'

'Don't worry. I'm not gonna give you a cheque. Come with me.'

He strode out of the room, Johnny tagging behind, puzzled. They left the house through a side door and took a paved path to a small parking area at the rear.

Slater stopped, hands on hips. 'There she is.'

Johnny scowled. 'What am I looking at?'

'Pete wanted you to have his first car. It was always going to be a risk giving you cash, Johnny. You being an ex-addict and all. We didn't want to be responsible for getting you back on the gear.'

Johnny stared at the beaten-up red Porsche 911. Dents marred nearly every panel, rust showing around the wheel hubs, while the paintwork was so tarnished that it looked as if it had been left in a barn somewhere, or been badly crackle-glazed at a DIY craft day. It was a mess.

'It's fully fuelled, taxed, insured and serviced.' Slater handed over the box. 'Here are the keys.'

Johnny's thoughts started racing. How much would it be worth in its current bedraggled state? Not much in itself, but rock-star memorabilia usually commanded big bucks.

'There's a *but*, naturally,' Slater added. 'You can't sell her.

It still belongs to Pete. But if nothing else, she'll get you around . . .'

'You know,' Johnny said slowly, 'when something looks like shit, smells like shit . . . well, you know the rest . . .'

Slater reached for the box. 'You don't want the car then?'

Johnny snatched it away. A fucking battered old Porsche that he didn't even own. 'No, I'll take the car.' Johnny started down the steps. 'Tell Pete he's an ungrateful bastard.'

'I tell him things like that all the time.'

'Tell him I don't want his help getting back into the biz, either. I've already moved on.'

'He'll be impressed you're standing on your own two feet again.'

Johnny glanced back. 'Fuck you, Don. Anyway, I'm going; taking my daughter and her mum for a curry.'

'Nice. See you soon, Johnny.'

'I wouldn't count on it.'

Johnny climbed inside the battered vehicle, which smelled like old leather and cigarettes, inserted the key into the ignition and turned it.

Sometimes you win, sometimes you lose, it's all a spin of the wheel. The only way you can be sure not to lose in this life, is not to play the game at all.

The three-litre engine chugged noisily to life. Exhaust roaring, Johnny swerved out of the parking area and onto the road, then down to the Embankment.

He pulled a hard left and pointed the Porsche towards Brick Lane. The bent and rusty number plate on his back bumper was just about legible. It read:

ST4R 1

ACKNOWLEDGEMENTS

Huge thank yous go out to Kate Bradley and all her team at HarperCollins, for making *The Game* possible and for breathing life into Johnny Klein! Issy Lloyd at Insanity Management for taking care of business, Steve Dagger whose belief is always appreciated and of course Ajda Vucicevic at HarperCollins to whom I am so grateful, 'You Rock'.

JOHNNY KLEIN WILL RETURN IN 2024.

Sunning himself in the south of France, Johnny has started to believe that his life is finally on the up. But the arrival of a face from his past drags him back down to earth with a harsh dose of cold reality.

Johnny Klein once again finds himself walking the tightrope between redemption and despair. When his daughter is in danger of getting consumed by the sins of Johnny's own past, and a dark secret threatens to engulf people he holds dear, light at the end of the tunnel feels further away than ever . . .

Pre-order your copy now in bookshops and online.